K.D. Richards is a native of the Washington, DC, area, who now lives outside Toronto with her husband and two sons. You can find her at kdrichardsbooks.com

Jennifer D. Bokal penned her first book at age eight. An early lover of the written word, she decided to follow her passion and become a full-time writer. From then on, she didn't look back. She earned a master of arts in creative writing from Wilkes University and became a member of Romance Writers of America and International Thriller Writers. She has authored several short stories, novellas and poems. Winner of the Sexy Scribbler in 2015, Jennifer is also the author of the ancient-world historical series the Champions of Rome and the Mills & Boon series Rocky Mountain Justice. Happily married to her own alpha male for more than twenty years, she enjoys writing stories that explore the wonders of love. Jen and her manly husband live in upstate New York with their three beautiful daughters, two very spoiled dogs and a kitten that aspires to one day become a Chihuahua.

D0237357

CHRISTMAS DATA BREACH

K.D. RICHARDS

A COLTON INTERNAL AFFAIR

JENNIFER D. BOKAL

MILLS & BOON

First Published in Great Britain 2021
by Mills & Boon, an imprint of HarperCollins*Publishers* Ltd
1 London Bridge Street, London, SE1 9GF

www.harpercollins.co.uk

HarperCollins*Publishers*
1st Floor, Watermarque Building,
Ringsend Road, Dublin 4, Ireland

Christmas Data Breach © 2021 Kia Dennis
A Colton Internal Affair © 2021 Harlequin Books S.A.

Special thanks and acknowledgement are given to Jennifer D. Bokal for her contribution to *The Coltons of Grave Gulch* series.

ISBN: 978-0-263-28355-6

0921

MIX
Paper from
responsible sources
FSC™ C007454

This book is produced from independently certified FSC™ paper to ensure responsible forest management.

For more information visit: www.harpercollins.co.uk/green

Printed and Bound in Spain using 100% Renewable Electricity at CPI Blackprint (Barcelona)

CHRISTMAS
DATA BREACH

K.D. RICHARDS

To Daphne Dennis.
Thank you for everything.

Chapter One

Mya Rochon had a bounce in her step as she strolled the short distance back to her laboratory. She sipped her gingerbread latte, enjoying the Christmas lights draping the topiaries in the office complex. The starry Sunday night wasn't the reason for her upbeat mood, however. She'd spent the last several weeks subjecting the final part of her cancer treatment to rigorous testing, and at every turn it had responded as she'd hoped. After years of study and research, it finally looked like she'd successfully developed a treatment for glioblastoma brain cancer.

The building that housed her laboratory sat at the back of the office complex and was smaller than the other office buildings. Dr. Timothy Ott's office took up the first floor. TriGen Labs, which she helmed, occupied the second floor.

She headed around the building to the side entrance. There was no security guard on duty on weekends and tenants could exit from the lobby door on the weekend, but there was no entry from that door. She swiped her building identification, which doubled as a keycard, over the security panel by the door and headed down the hall to the elevators.

A man's deep baritone voice from just around the corner in front of her had her pausing. Tenants had twenty-four-hour access to the building, but she couldn't remember Dr. Ott ever coming in on a Sunday night. Nor did the voice she heard sound at all like the tenor of the kindly sixty-three-year-old dentist she knew. No, the tone of this man's voice was chilling.

A shiver snaked down her spine. There was no doubt in her mind that he was dangerous.

Definitely not Dr. Ott.

Curiosity demanded she peek around the wall, but fear rooted her to the spot. She chucked the nearly empty coffee cup and listened.

"I've looked all over for her. Her car is in the lot, but she's not here."

Mya glanced back at the door through which she'd entered. Entry from the outside was granted electronically, but the door was opened from the inside by a metal bar that clanked loudly when pushed. She doubted she could make it out the door and away from the building without being heard.

"I've already started a fire in the lab. I need to get out of here before this place goes up in flames."

Heavy footsteps moved away from where she stood. She waited until she couldn't hear them any longer, then bolted for the door to the stairwell, the laptop in her over-size messenger bag bouncing against her hip.

There were years of work in that lab, not just hers, but her mentor's life's work too. She couldn't just let it all go up in flames.

The lab took up most of the second floor, but she'd carved out space for a reception area and offices for herself and her assistant. On the second-floor landing, she dialed 911, ignoring the dispatcher's order to get out of the building immediately. She tucked the phone into her pocket and charged forward.

Mya burst out of the stairwell into the office's small reception area. Nothing there seemed out of place, so she kept moving toward the lab and offices.

She heard the crackle of flames as she approached her office door. The man had set the fire in her trash can. Fire leaped from the bin and climbed the inexpensive cloth blinds she'd installed to brighten up the sterile office.

Her phone clattered to the floor as she grabbed the fire extinguisher from the wall outside her office and sprayed. The flames died just as a thunderous boom shook the floor. She ran back to the door of her office. Fire had shattered the glass separating her lab from the interior hallway. Shards littered the tiled floor.

No way would her fire extinguisher stand up against this much larger inferno. Fire raced along the tabletops and up the walls. The square ceiling tiles curled as they melted, falling from the ceiling. Smoke filled the hall quickly. She tucked her mouth and nose into the crook of her elbow and stepped away, coughing. There was nothing she could do to save the lab and she had to get out now.

Mya turned and hurried back down the stairs.

Outside, she could hear the distant blare of fire engines. She looked back at the lab where she'd worked eighty-hour weeks for the last decade.

She watched as the inferno moved in a cruel dance on the other side of the second-floor windows. Devouring her life's work.

Chapter Two

Smoke billowed from the shattered windows of the research lab. Several firefighters battled the fire from the ground with a hose hooked up to a nearby hydrant. Two more ventilated the roof, sending smoke billowing from holes made by their axes. Red-and-blue lights reflected off the sides of the gray brick office building nearby. The oversize candy cane decorating the small grassy area at the front of the building lay broken in the firefighter's rush to put out the blaze.

"Go through it one more time for me?"

Mya studied Detective Padma Kamal. Although they shared similar medium-toned brown skin, the detective was nearly a foot shorter than Mya's five eleven and more pear-shaped than curvy. Her brown tailored suit, green silk blouse and half-inch heels marked her as a woman in charge. Despite her size, or maybe because of it, the gun at her hip stuck out like a fly on a wedding cake.

Mya sighed. "I've already told all this to the first police officer who arrived. And the second."

Detective Kamal speared her with a gaze. "I realize it's been a difficult night for you, Miss Rochon, but if you could just bear with us for a little while longer."

"I stepped out to get coffee from the coffee shop a

few blocks away. I entered the building through the side door and I heard a man talking in the front lobby." She hated the shakiness in her voice.

"And what time was this?" Detective Kamal asked without looking up from her notepad.

"About six thirty. Maybe a little later."

Shouting from one of the firefighters carried over the din to where the women stood at the far end of the lab's parking lot.

Mya watched a firefighter direct water at the second floor from a hose mounted on top of a firetruck.

"And do you normally work that late on a Sunday?" Detective Kamal asked, drawing Mya's attention.

"It's not unusual for me to be here until ten or later. I like the solitude."

Mya didn't miss the pitying look that flashed across Detective Kamal's face. It resembled the look her friends gave her when she explained she wasn't interested in dating right now. She ignored it.

"Anybody else working with you tonight?"

"No. We're a small privately funded lab. There are only three of us. Me, my assistant, Brian Leeds, and the receptionist, Rebecca Conway."

"Okay, what happened?" Detective Kamal waved her hand in a "continue" motion with her hand without looking up from her notebook.

"You can't enter from the front entrance on the weekends, so I entered through the side door using my pass card," Mya said, pulling a stray coil of hair from under the strap of the purse she wore slung across her body.

Detective Kamal made the hurry motion with her hand again.

Mya's lips twisted in irritation. "As I told the other police officers, I heard a man's voice in the lobby up ahead."

"Did you see this man?"

Mya shook her head. "No. He was around the corner." But she suspected she'd recognize the sinister voice if she ever heard it again.

"And he never mentioned who he was looking for?" The detective stopped writing and peered over the tops of her glasses. "Never mentioned your name specifically?"

"No. But I was the only one here. My car is the only one still in the lot." Was. Now there were more than a half dozen police cruisers, two fire trucks and a dark green sedan Mya could only assume belonged to Detective Kamal.

"Okay, what happened next?"

"He said he'd started a fire in my lab. I couldn't just let all the work I'd been doing for the last ten years go up in a blaze. I slipped into the stairwell and ran upstairs to put the fire out."

"You weren't concerned about this man hearing you or getting trapped in a burning building?" Detective Kamal's tone dripped with incredulity.

"All I could think about was saving my lab." It sounded foolhardy when she heard it out loud, knowing what could have happened, but it was the truth. "Anyway, he said he was leaving. I heard him walk away."

Detective Kamal exhaled heavily. "So you went upstairs to your lab and what?"

"The lab and my adjacent office were on fire. I called 911 from my cell and reported the fire, then I grabbed the extinguisher from the maintenance closet. I think that's when I dropped my phone." A wave of anxiety at being without her phone, the twenty-first-century version of being caught naked in public, flowed through her.

"You told the first officer on scene that you put out the fire in your office."

"I did. The fire in my office was in the trash can and hadn't moved beyond."

"What did you do then?"

"Something exploded in the lab, so I got out of there."

"Better late than never," Detective Kamal muttered. "Did you see anyone when you exited the building?"

"No." Mya ran her hands up and down her arms. The temperature had dropped since she'd gone for coffee and despite the heat emanating from the nearby burning building, she was freezing.

"Tell me again what kind of research you do here?" Detective Kamal waved toward the burning building.

Mya's gaze followed the detective's. Orange flames danced in the windows of what had been her lab. "Cancer research."

The fire was undoubtedly a setback. Thank goodness she'd instituted a failsafe system to protect her research. Her mentor, Irwin Ross, had been fanatical about protecting his research, to the point where he'd had a panic room–like safe built in his home. She wasn't as paranoid as Irwin, but certain of his eccentricities had rubbed off. She kept her work on a private server in her home. And she always kept her laptop on her, a habit that had paid off in spades tonight.

She ran her hand over her shoulder bag, reassuring herself that at least the formula was safe and sound.

"Okay. I think that's enough for now," Detective Kamal said, closing her notebook.

"Can I get my car now?" Mya asked, eyeing the chaos between her and her ten-year-old Volvo.

"Sorry." The detective shook her head. "It will be a while before you can get your car. Stay here. I'll send someone to drive you home."

Another jolt of irritation flowed through Mya. This night had been awful, and all she wanted now was to take herself home, have a nice hot bath and sleep. None of that seemed to matter to Detective Kamal though, who strode away into the throng of uniforms unconcerned with Mya's distress.

Thank goodness she'd had her house and car keys on her. As she waited for her ride home she chewed her bottom lip, considering whether it was unprofessional to ask Brian to ferry her back to the building tomorrow to pick up her car. They had a collegial relationship, but she didn't know much about either of her coworker's lives outside of the lab.

"Ma'am."

Mya jumped, spinning around.

A sandy-haired police officer stood in the shadows behind her. His shoulders hunched forward and she could barely make out the blue of his eyes under the rim of his uniform's cap. "Didn't mean to scare you," the officer said with a southern twang. "I'm supposed to take you home?"

The officer gestured to a police cruiser just outside of the metal gates that surrounded the parking lot.

"Right. Thank you." She followed him to the cruiser and slid into the back seat. "My address is 875 East Randolph Drive."

The officer nodded but said nothing, for which Mya was glad. She was in no mood for chitchat, and she didn't want to rehash the evening for the umpteenth time. It was bad enough her brain wouldn't stop replaying every detail from the time she returned from the coffee shop until the first fire truck arrived.

Who would destroy her lab? The medical research industry could be cutthroat, she knew. The stakes were high. Billions of dollars were spent each year on research and attempts to develop medications and therapies to treat everything from heart disease to foot fungus. And most failed, but that was just the cost of business. She couldn't imagine anyone she knew setting fire to her lab. More than that, only a handful of people knew her research had finally borne fruit, and she trusted each of them implicitly.

None of this made any sense.

She exhaled heavily, pushed the images of fire out of her mind and focused instead on how good it would feel to slip her sore bones between the Egyptian cotton sheets she'd splurged on last month.

Mya glanced at the car's dashboard clock, noting that it had been nearly ten minutes since they'd left the lab. Her townhouse was a five-minute drive from the lab, one of the primary reasons she'd bought the place over less expensive and larger options. The view outside the window confirmed her suspicion.

"Excuse me. I think you've missed my street. If you just turn around here, I can direct you back—" she said, leaning forward between the two front seats.

"Shut up and sit back." The cop spat without looking at her.

"Excuse me. I... This isn't the way to my house."

The cop's eyes met hers in the rearview mirror. "I

said shut up and sit back!" he barked, the southern twang gone, replaced by a deep baritone.

Fear stole her breath.

It was the same voice she'd heard in the lobby of her building; the man who set her lab on fire.

Not a cop. Or, maybe, a dirty one.

Why hadn't she demanded to see identification? She knew better than to get into a car with a man she didn't know, even one in a uniform. But the destruction of her lab, the fire—her defenses had been down and now it was too late.

Think!

She reached for the door handle and pulled. Unsurprisingly, the door didn't open. It was probably best since they were going forty miles an hour. Not fast enough to attract attention, but more than enough to cause serious damage if she tried to jump from the car.

She had to get herself out of this somehow.

They'd turned off the main road and onto a rural one, the headlights of the police cruiser the only light cutting through the darkness. The occasional house interrupted the woods that lined both sides of the two-lane highway.

"Who are you? Where are you taking me?"

"I told you to shut up." Venom dripped from the man's words.

Would Detective Kamal worry when whoever she sent to take Mya home reported she was missing? Or would the harried detective assume she'd found her own way home? The difference meant there could already be people looking for her, not that she could be sure they'd find her before… She wasn't sure before what, but she knew she didn't want to find out.

Without warning, the man swerved onto the side of

the road and put the car in Park. He flashed the head-lights twice.

Mya glimpsed a dark-paneled van parked a few feet ahead in the car's headlights. No one emerged from the van, but panic threatened to overwhelm her. The only reason to flash the headlights was to let a partner know you were there.

Leaving the headlights off, the man exited the car.

Mya fought with the door handle on the back passenger side door until the shadow of the man rounded the front of the car and loomed at the door. She slid to the other side of the back seat as he wrenched the door open.

"Get out."

She had no idea what the man had planned for her, but the danger she was in couldn't have been clearer.

"Out!"

Malice creased the hard lines of the man's face. He was big and could yank her from the car like a rag doll if he chose to. If she had any chance of getting away, she'd have to get out and fight.

Mya slid sideways along the back seat to the door the man held open. At the edge of the seat, she turned, throwing her feet out of the door. She didn't aim for the ground though, instead jerking them upward and toward her captor.

His face registered surprise, but his reflexes were quick. He jumped backward and the kick to the groin glanced off him. The blow still sent him doubling over. His breath skirted her cheek as she pitched forward past him and out of the car.

Her laptop bag banged against her hip as she raced down the embankment toward the relative safety of the trees. As she reached the tree line, a crack split the air.

Bark flew off the tree closest to her, cutting a slash across her cheek. She kept running. The foliage gave her some cover, but instinct screamed that putting as much distance between herself and the man after her was her only chance of survival.

Mya plowed deeper into the woods. Her heart pounded, more from fear than exertion, but she pressed on, willing her legs to move faster.

She slowed to get through a thick area of brush. Thankfully, her eyes had adjusted to the darkness of the woods, or she'd have missed the steep drop-off on the other side of the thicket in time. She reached out, grabbing hold of a low tree branch to slow her momentum. The dirt under her boots shifted, rolled forward and toppled over the side of the drop-off. Her right knee slammed into a rock, but she held on to the branch, praying it wouldn't give way. Teeth clenched, she breathed through the searing pain.

Dampness from the rain showers the day before seeped through her slacks. The air was a mix of pine, the several species that lived in these trees and death. An animal had recently expired nearby.

The pain in her knee subsided, but her pulse was roaring in her ears. Was the man still after her? She scooted behind the tree, moving to the balls of her feet in case she needed to make a run for it again, and listened.

Crickets chirped. An owl hooted. A screech sounded somewhere in the distance, and she tried not to think about what kind of animal made the sound. She wasn't a woodsy kind of girl, preferring to keep her outdoor time to her back garden and laps around the park near the house.

She looked down at her leg as she listened. Mud-covered, with patches of blood seeping through her gray slacks at the knee. Her pink silk blouse was torn in several places, nothing but an expensive rag now. Thankfully, she'd thought twice about wearing the ballet flats she'd originally put on this morning, exchanging them for a sturdy pair of flat leather boots that appeared to be holding up.

The chilly night was moving toward frigid.

She couldn't stay out here forever, but she had no way of knowing whether her kidnapper was waiting for her to reappear alongside the road. Hunched over and listening for human sounds, she began moving again, parallel to the road but back toward the major road.

And then what?

She had no way of knowing whether the man who kidnapped her was a dirty police officer or whether he'd just dressed like one to get her to get in the car with him. Either way, she couldn't trust the police right now.

And could she go home? She'd given her abductor her address when she thought he was a police officer. It was undoubtedly the first place he'd go looking for her.

No phone. No one to trust.

A familiar voice from the past flitted through her head.

You can hate me if you need to. I deserve it. Just know if you ever need anything, I'm here for you.

He was the last person she wanted to see, but possibly the only person she knew who could help her out of whatever mess she seemed to have gotten herself into.

A shot of adrenaline pushed her forward through the trees.

"Gideon, I hope your offer still stands."

Chapter Three

Gideon Wright came fully awake in an instant. He heard the normal creaks and groans of the nearly seventy-year-old house his grandparents had purchased as newlyweds. His eyes swept the room. He was alone, just as he was every night. But something was off.

The lights.

He'd done a complete upgrade of the security system upon inheriting the house. No matter how much he'd tried to convince his grandma Pearl that hardware store locks were not sufficient security, she'd resisted upgrading her home security, insisting she didn't want to live like she was in prison.

He'd installed deadbolt locks on all her doors and snuck two security cameras around the perimeter of the house, but otherwise honored her wishes until after Gran had passed away.

Now, the house boasted a top-of-the-line security system. The outdoor motion-detector lights were set to go on only if someone or something four feet or taller broached the perimeter of his property. It could be a deer, but his instincts told him otherwise.

He rolled out of bed in one smooth motion, and retrieved his gun he kept in his bedside table, without making a sound. Not one of the oak floorboards creaked as he made his way down the stairs to the main floor of the house. The security lights in the backyard were still on, but the house alarm hadn't tripped, so the intruder hadn't made it inside the house. Yet.

He peered through a rear window, careful to stay to the side, and out of the line of sight. Darkness shrouded the rear of the small yard despite the security lights. He made a mental note to add more lights back there as his eyes scanned over the yard.

A gust of wind rustled the naked branches of the large maple tree and he watched as what he'd initially taken to be a shadow broke away from the tree and slunk forward along the edge of the fence.

Gideon couldn't imagine who would be dumb enough to break into the home of a security expert and former marine, but whoever it was, he'd be more than happy to educate them on the error of their ways. He disengaged the house alarm, then stalked through his small living room. He slipped through the sliding glass doors and pressed his back to the side of the house. His bare feet fell on wet grass and another gust of wind swept over his umber skin as he inched his way to the corner of the house and peeked around. A body still slunk along the fence, creeping closer and closer to the back door.

As the intruder's foot fell on the first step of the patio, Gideon pounced, running flat out toward the would-be burglar.

The intruder's head snapped up.

Recognition washed over him faster than his brain could signal his legs to stop moving.

He crashed into the woman he'd once known better

than he'd known himself. A black computer bag skittered across the patio.

Gideon twisted so that he took most of the impact when they landed in the wet grass, but he still felt the air whoosh out of Mya's lungs. Sprawled on top of him, she groaned.

"Mya? What are you doing here? Are you okay?" He ran his hands over her arms and back. Somewhere in the back of his mind, he registered how familiar her body was to him, even though it had been years since he'd touched her.

"Help. Please." Her thin voice sent a stab of fear through him that only sharpened when her dazed eyes met his.

He pushed the hair from her face and nearly gasped at the sight of her. The beautiful brown eyes he still regularly dreamed about were unfocused. Cuts and scrapes marked the smooth brown skin on her face and arms. Through his thin cotton tee, he could feel her tremble, whether from the cold or shock, he couldn't be sure.

Her eyes fluttered closed.

He sat up, cradling her to his chest as he got to his feet. "Hang in there, baby. I'm going to get you to a doctor."

Mya's eyes sprang open. "No." Her voice was little more than a mumble, but he could hear the tremble of fear there. "No doctors. No police. Just you, Gideon. Only you."

The words sent his heart thumping in his chest. He pushed the swell of emotions down. Mya was clearly in some kind of trouble. Big trouble if she'd come to him. He couldn't let lingering feelings get in the way of helping her.

He looked down at her scraped and mud-splattered face as he carried her into his house.

And he would help her. And make whoever had done this to her pay. That was a promise.

SUNLIGHT WAS ALREADY streaming through the kitchen windows when the hinges on the door to the guest room creaked. Several moments later, the lock on the hall bathroom snapped shut. The shower came on.

Gideon pressed the power button on his little-used coffee maker and leaned against the far end of the kitchen counter. He wanted to see Mya the moment she started down the stairs. And to be honest, gauge her reaction to seeing him after all these years.

He'd helped her clean up and gave her some old sweats to wear after he'd gotten her inside. Although her scrapes and bruises were superficial, she was dehydrated, hungry and nearly frozen through. He'd swallowed the rage burning in his chest at the sight of her injuries and heated a bowl of chicken soup. She had only a few mouthfuls before her eyelids drooped and he'd helped her to the guest room.

He hadn't gone back to bed. He'd set up a few additional security measures just in case whoever Mya was afraid of came looking for her. They were more like booby traps, but he'd have plenty of advance warning of any unwanted visitors.

Then he'd set about finding out everything he could about Mya's life since their divorce twelve years ago. Not that he'd ever lost track of her. He knew she'd obtained her medical degree and a PhD in biomedical sciences. More than a little pride had swelled inside reading the glowing articles about the importance of the research she was doing at TriGen Labs, the private cancer research lab established by Irwin Ross. TriGen's mission statement stated its primary focus as discovering a treatment, and ultimately a cure, for glioblastoma brain cancer.

Gideon had never met Irwin Ross, but the undertone in several of the articles he'd read made the man sound somewhat like a brilliant eccentric. Mya had begun as an intern at TriGen in her last year of graduate school and became one of two full-time researchers after she got her doctorate. Based on an archived web page he'd found for TriGen, Irwin had retired to West Virginia last year, turning over TriGen and its research to Mya.

Head of her own lab at thirty-five. He had always known Mya was destined for things far beyond the reach of the boy next-door. Which was one of the reasons he'd asked for the divorce. He loved her too much to let his issues hold her back.

The water shut off overhead, and he heard the bathroom door open.

Ten minutes later, Mya descended the stairs barefoot, his baggy sweats held up by a never-worn braided belt he'd found in the back of his closet. She was still the most beautiful thing he'd ever laid eyes on.

She stopped at the foot of the stairs and eyed him warily, a pretty flush on her bronze-colored cheeks.

"I put the coffee on if you want some." He reached into the cabinet overhead and pulled down a mug.

"Yes, thank you." Mya crossed the short distance to the kitchen island with a pronounced limp.

"Do you need help?" He set the cup down and reached for her.

She waved him off. "No, it's not that bad. I just banged

my knee up a little last night," she said, sitting on one of the two stools at the small island.

"In the fire?"

Mya narrowed her eyes at him. "You've been busy."

His nighttime search had also turned up a newly posted article on the website of a local news blog about the devastating fire at TriGen Labs. The authorities suspected arson. That explained why Mya's clothes and hair had smelled of smoke when he'd found her, but dozens of other questions remained. Like, who or what had scared her so badly she'd sought him out.

He passed her the cup of coffee and held her gaze. "You showed up in my backyard, hurt, smelling of smoke and I am a private security specialist."

His heart stuttered at the smile she gave him. "I know. My mother is still bragging about you protecting the president."

Mya's mother, Francine Rochon, was a second mother to him growing up. He called her once a week and took her to dinner whenever a job brought him to Orlando.

"Hardly," Gideon said, the corners of his lips tipping upward. "My team and I were so far away we never even saw the president."

Mya sipped her coffee, her smile widening. "Well, when my mother tells it, you saved the man's life and you two are BFFs now." She paused. "She's proud of you."

The simple sentiment sent a warm sensation coursing through him. He loved Francine as if she were his own mother, but Mya hadn't shown up on his doorstep to gab about her mom.

"You haven't answered my question. Did you get hurt in the fire last night?"

She took another sip of her coffee and shook her head. "It was after, when I was running from the cop."

His chin jerked up. It was rare for anyone to catch him by surprise, but Mya had always burst through the walls he put up around his emotions. It didn't appear that time had changed that at all.

"Start from the beginning and leave nothing out."

He eased onto the stool next to her and listened as she described returning to work after a late coffee break, overhearing a man on the phone telling someone that he'd started a fire in her lab, and trying and failing to put out the fire. Tension radiated from her as she recounted what she'd gone through. As she told him about fighting off the "maybe cop" and running through the woods he beat back the urge to find the man who'd kidnapped her and hurt him badly.

"That's why you didn't want me to call the police or take you to a hospital last night?"

She nodded. "I don't know if I can trust the police."

He understood her concern and, given the circumstances, shared it. "Can you describe the police officer?"

"Dark blond, blue eyes. About my height." She was taller than average for a woman at five feet eleven. "He wore a police uniform."

Which meant nothing since anyone could get one with a few clicks off the internet.

"I know a detective I can trust." When she didn't look convinced, he added, "The police need to know about the kidnapping attempt."

Her eyebrows knitted. "Okay, if you trust this detective I'll talk to him."

"Why would someone target you and your lab?"

Her gaze drifted away, and she chewed the bottom

corner of her lip. Her tells hadn't changed over the years. She was considering how much she wanted to tell him.

"I can help you best if I know all of it."

Mya sighed. "I don't know for sure. Medical research, pharmaceuticals, it's a cutthroat business. Not enough money to fund everyone's research and the biggest rewards go to those who develop successful treatments first."

"And when you say the biggest rewards…"

Her eyebrows went up. "Millions and millions of rewards."

Which meant millions of reasons to eliminate the competition.

"And knowing you, your research is both successful and a cut above your peers."

She raised her mug to her lips, but he didn't miss her wide smile. When she lowered the mug, a frown replaced her smile. "I know most of the people doing research in this area. They are my colleagues. I can't say I'm friends with all of them, but I can't imagine any of them going to these extremes to destroy my research."

"What are you working on?"

She hesitated for a moment. "A treatment for glioblastoma." At his curious look, she clarified. "Brain cancer."

"And it works?"

Mya's eyes lit with excitement, sending a shot of electricity straight to his groin. "I'd been struggling for a while, but last week I figured out the last piece." She reached out and covered his hand with hers on the soapstone countertop. "There's still a long way to go. I've got to test it in clinical trials, have it peer reviewed—I'll need to partner with a larger lab or pharmaceutical company but…"

"You've made a breakthrough in the treatment of brain cancer. So, we aren't just talking about millions of dollars here, but billions. Possibly more."

Mya frowned. "I know what you're thinking, but no one would go as far as setting fire to my lab. We're scientists, for goodness' sake." She rubbed her temples.

She might not be willing to face it, but scientists were human. It wouldn't be the first time greed led someone to do something criminal. Or deadly.

Gideon reached for his phone. "Let me call the detective I know." He also needed to bring the West Investigation team in.

She gave a small smile. "Thank you for helping me. I wasn't sure…after the way our marriage ended and so much time has passed."

He squeezed her hand. "I'll always be here for you." It didn't escape his notice that those were the same words he'd said to her after their divorce was finalized. He'd meant them then, and he meant them now.

Their gazes locked for a long moment. Mya slid her hand from under his. "I should go get dressed. If it's okay, could we stop by my townhouse before we go see your detective friend?" She slid off the stool.

Gideon rose. "That's not a good idea. It's the first place someone looking for you will go."

"As nice as this ensemble is," she said, holding her hands out to her sides and making a three hundred sixty–degree turn, "I don't think I can wear it all day."

He grinned. "You have a point."

"And I want to make sure my server is secure."

"Your server?"

"My research backs up to a personal server. It's a little unusual, I know, but Irwin didn't trust saving our research to an outside system. I guess some of his paranoia rubbed off. When he retired and turned things over to me, it just seemed best to keep doing what he had in place."

"There are better, safer ways to secure data. I'll help you when this is all over."

Her chin went up. "I didn't ask for your help." He shot her a pointed look. "Not with securing my research."

"Still stubborn."

"And you still think everything needs to be your way. I'm not a soldier at your command."

A feeling of déjà vu swept over Gideon. They'd butted heads over her independent streak more than once when they were married.

"I don't want to fight. If you don't want my help securing your research, fine. Do you still want my help to find whoever's targeting you?"

She hesitated before nodding.

"We'll go to your townhouse, get your things, then go see the detective." He gave her another pointed look. If he was going to protect her, she needed to understand that there would be no time for arguing. "In and out in five minutes. If I say we're leaving, we're leaving. No questions. No complaints. Agreed?"

After a long pause, she nodded. "Agreed." She slid off the stool and headed upstairs.

Gideon watched her go. They'd both always been too headstrong for their own good. It was one of the major reasons their marriage failed. But he didn't care if he was overbearing or pushy. She might not think her colleagues had it in them to attack her, but somebody did.

But from now on, they'd have to get through him first.

Chapter Four

Mya dragged a sweater that was probably three sizes too small for Gideon but that she swam in over her head. Wearing his sweatpants, even just for the short drive to her house, was out of the question, so she slipped back into her dirt-and blood-stained slacks and muddy boots. Her hair still smelled of smoke and ash, but at least the shower had whisked away the last traces of soot from her skin.

She looked at herself in the mirror hanging inside the closet door. The bump on the side of her head would take a few days to go away completely, and the scrape on her cheek could be covered with concealer. She rotated her aching shoulder. Nothing two, or maybe three, pain pills couldn't handle. All in all, not too bad considering what could have happened.

And that thought made her pulse skip.

Water beat a steady rhythm through the pipes in the house as Gideon showered. A memory floated to the front of her mind—slipping into a steaming shower stall with him soapy and wet. His silken hands gliding over her hip before roaming farther south.

The memory sent a shudder coursing through her.

"Knock it off," she admonished herself. She was here

because she needed help. Having her heart broken by Gideon Wright once was more than enough.

Mya descended the stairs for the second time that morning, this time carrying her laptop. She had more than enough problems on her proverbial plate at the moment. The last thing she needed to be doing was lusting after her ex-husband.

Mya put the images of Gideon's wet body out of her mind and dialed Brian's number. Just as it had when she'd called last night to inform him of the fire, the call went to voicemail. She left another message, asking him to return her call as soon as possible, then called Rebecca a second time. As with the call to Brian, she had to leave a message. She couldn't imagine they hadn't already heard about the fire in the lab, but she was the boss, and she wanted to reassure her troops. Hopefully, they'd return her calls quickly.

Mya popped two slices of whole wheat bread in Gideon's toaster and dug around in her oversize purse until she found what she was looking for, a flash drive.

She had spent seven years working with Irwin Ross, a giant in the search for cancer treatments, but a man most would generously describe as peculiar. When he'd retired, Mya had inherited the lab, all his notes and the server where he kept his research.

Mya checked her voicemail and email and found messages from several board members. She dashed off a quick email explaining the lab fire and promising to set up a conference call. She'd have to set up a conference call with the board members and investors soon, but at the moment she didn't know much more than they'd get from the news.

And there was something much more important she needed to deal with first.

Irwin would have a fit if he knew what she was doing. Under normal circumstances she wouldn't keep her research on a flash drive—it was far too easy to lose those little suckers—but desperate times. She'd done her best not to show it, but Gideon's suggestion that the potential financial gain from her treatment had made her a target had shaken her. She wasn't ready to go into a full-on panic but taking extra precautions to make sure she didn't lose her life's work didn't just seem prudent, it was necessary.

She copied the final portion of the treatment to the drive while she ate the toast. Once the files were saved to the drive, she roamed the house for a good hiding spot for the drive.

Under the ficus tree in the dining room? No, the dirt might damage the drive. Tape it to the back of a kitchen drawer? Too obvious. Under the armchair in the living room? Again, too obvious.

The shower shut off upstairs. She trusted Gideon to help her unravel whatever situation she'd gotten into, but her research? That was another story. Maybe more of Irwin's cynicism had rubbed off on her than she'd like to admit. Or maybe it was just her current situation, but caution seemed well-advised at the moment.

She walked from room to room, examining and rejecting hiding spots until she opened a door off the kitchen and stepped into the laundry room. Her eyes landed on the ironing board and she smiled. Her mother's favorite stories. Three-year-old Mya hiding her mother's pearl earrings. After searching high and low without success, Francine had given the earrings up for lost. It wasn't until she'd gone to do her ironing that weekend and heard a rattling in the ironing board's legs that she'd found her earrings and several items she'd yet to notice missing.

The rubber cap on the leg of Gideon's ironing board resisted, but Mya finally worked it off and slid the flash drive inside. She replaced the cap and exited the laundry room just as Gideon strode into the kitchen.

His eyes narrowed with suspicion. "Everything okay?"

"Fine. Just trying to clean up a bit." She crossed to the kitchen table and held up her laptop. "Do you have a safe where I can leave this?" As a security specialist, odds were good that he had a safe somewhere in the house.

Gideon led the way back up the stairs and into his bedroom. His room wasn't much larger than the guest room. The musky scent of his aftershave wafted over her as soon as she crossed the threshold.

She scanned the room, her eyes landing on a framed print she recognized from Grandma Pearl's living room hanging over the dark wood sleigh bed against the wall opposite the door. A matching dresser stood a few feet away. The room, like Gideon, was unabashedly masculine.

Gideon crossed to the closet doors. Mya followed him into the small walk-in closet and noted the safe tucked in a corner. She handed him her laptop. He put it inside, re-secured the door, and turned.

The air was electrified. Her heart lurched. She struggled to contain the emotions swelling inside. From the way his gaze raked over her, she suspected Gideon was struggling with the same problem.

He cupped her cheek and she stepped into his touch.

She pursed her lips, her heart beating wildly in anticipation of his kiss. A kiss that didn't come.

Gideon let his hand drop to his side and took a step back. "The code is Grandma Pearl's birthday in case you ever need to get in when I'm not around. We should get going to your house." He turned on his heel and left the bedroom.

Mya followed him, her entire body flushed with humiliation. She didn't meet his eyes as they got into his Tahoe. The smell of leather and aftershave tickled her nose, quickened her pulse and heightened her discomfort.

"My address is—" Mya began, focusing herself on the task at hand rather than her own embarrassment.

"I got it."

Mya slanted a glance at him. She supposed she should have expected as much. She'd heard the firm he worked for, West Security and Investigations, was the best at what they did. No doubt the same research that had turned up her professional accomplishments and the fire at TriGen had spat out her address.

He certainly looked the part of the elite private investigator. He'd changed into a cream-colored shirt and black wool pea coat that accentuated his broad shoulders and well-defined chest. She couldn't help feeling a little like Beauty and the Beast, only she was the beast.

The Gideon of today was a stark contrast from the ten-year-old boy she'd met over twenty years ago. Shorter and skinnier than most of the other kids in their fifth-grade class, painfully quiet and new to the school, Gideon had quickly become a target for teasing and bullying. Not long after he'd started at the elementary school, Mya had found Kenneth Rickshaw and his two minions playing a game of keep-away with Gideon's backpack.

She'd caught the backpack midair and swung it into Kenneth's solar plexus. As a bona fide "nerd" herself, she'd been Kenny's target and had learned that, like most bullies, he was a coward at heart. Kenny and his crew had skulked away, and she and Gideon became inseparable, especially once they'd learned they lived only a block apart from each other.

Over the subsequent years, Gideon had shot up to six foot four and cultivated layers of muscles that attracted more than a little female attention. The baby fat in his face melted away, revealing chiseled cheekbones and a square jaw. The reticence that he'd developed in middle school made him mysterious and alluring in high school. Mya had noticed how attractive her best friend was, but there'd been nothing more than friendship between them. Not until their senior year.

She snuck another glance at Gideon, a deep sigh slipping from between her lips.

"You sure you're alright?" he asked, shooting her a curious look.

"Fine." She focused her attention out the window again.

While Gideon had chosen to remain in Queens, she'd purchased a tri-level townhouse close to the TriGen lab on the New Jersey side of the Hudson River. "Why are we taking the scenic route?"

"I want to make sure we're not being followed."

Gideon glanced in the side mirror, for what must have been the twentieth time since they'd left his house.

She studied the cars driving by looking for any that seemed suspicious. "There's no way anyone could know I stayed at your place last night."

"You said the man who set the fire in your lab was

looking for you. We don't know how much they know about you. I'm not taking any chances."

Everything Gideon said made sense. Even so, it was hard to wrap her mind around the conclusion. Her heart hammered against her ribcage. "Someone is after me."

Gideon shot a glance across the car, holding her gaze. "And they are very serious about it. The police officer, or whoever it was, had a car that either was or resembled a police cruiser enough to fool you. When we get to your townhouse, it's best we get in, get you enough clothes for a day or two and get out."

"A day or two?"

"You can stay at one of West's safehouses until we're sure you're safe." Gideon cleared his throat. "Or you could stay with me. In the guest room."

She turned back to the window without answering. Gideon was no doubt right that staying at the townhouse was too dangerous. But staying another night at his place? That could be dangerous in a very different way. Despite the divorce and the intervening years, she felt the same pull toward him she'd felt all those years ago when she'd dreamed of a future together.

Gideon's evasive maneuvers had led them blocks from the TriGen lab. "We're right by the lab. Take the next right."

A frown bought his eyebrows together. "Are you sure?"

Mya inhaled and let it out slowly. "I just…need to see."

Moments later Gideon stopped in the empty parking lot, and she got out of the SUV.

Police tape flapped uselessly from the flagpole in front of the building. The usually impeccably manicured front landscaping was a mess of trampled flowers and muddy puddles.

Gideon stood at her side.

Mya shielded her eyes against the sun with one hand and looked up at the third floor. All the windows on that level had been shattered, either by the fire or by the firefighters, Mya wasn't sure. Black soot painted the brick exterior.

She was grateful that most of the damage appeared to be limited to her lab and that no one was hurt, but it was clear the building would be uninhabitable for some time.

"It's all gone." She covered her mouth with her hand in an effort to stop the sob that threatened to break through.

"You can rebuild. You're safe." Gideon wrapped his arm around her shoulders. It was a gesture made awkward by how comforting and familiar it was, even after all the years that had passed.

"I wish it were that easy," she said, stepping out of his grasp as a red sedan turned into the parking lot.

She felt Gideon tense at her side, but she recognized the car. "It's my research assistant, Brian."

The declaration didn't seem to do anything to relax Gideon.

Brian bounded from the car, leaving the door open and the engine on, and strode to where she and Gideon stood. "Mya, thank God you're okay." Brian pulled her into a hug. It was surprising given they weren't close, but it was an unusual situation. Over his shoulder, she saw Gideon glower.

Mya pulled back from Brian's arms. "I left you a message last night and this morning." Her words came out testier than she'd intended.

Brian shot a glance at Gideon before focusing back

on Mya. "I forgot to charge my phone. I don't use it that much, so I didn't notice until this morning."

"Awful timing." Disbelief dripped from Gideon's words.

Brian turned narrowed eyes on Gideon. "It turned out to be. Are you going to introduce me to your friend, Mya?"

"This is Gideon Wright. He works with West Investigations."

One of Brian's eyebrows went up. "You hired a PI?"

"Gideon's a friend but, Brian, you should know that the fire wasn't an accident."

Brian's eyes widened. "Not an accident? What do you mean?"

Mya gestured vaguely toward the fire-ravaged building. "You know I stayed after you left last night."

"You wanted to look at the results from the last round of research again before you left for the night. Even though we've both been over it a dozen times." Brian rolled his eyes.

Mya knew her need to review and rereview the data got under Brian's skin, but she was the boss. "Yes, well, I stepped out not long after you left to get coffee and when I returned there was a stranger in the lobby. He didn't see me because I'd come in from the side, but he was on the phone telling someone that he'd set fire to the lab. I ran up there to try and put it out, but it was too far along."

"Mya, you could have been killed."

Mya held up a hand, stopping the rest of what Brian would have said.

"That's not all. After the police cleared me to go home, I was almost kidnapped."

"She *was* kidnapped," Gideon growled.

"What! What exactly are you saying?" Brian's voice went to a decibel most sopranos couldn't reach.

She described the fake cop and the mad dash through the woods to get away.

"This is incredible. Was it the same man who set the fire?"

She shrugged, wishing she could answer that question. "I don't know. I never saw the face of the man in the lobby."

Brian dragged a hand over his face. "Well, what are we going to do now?"

"What time did you leave the building last night?" Gideon asked.

Brian's frown deepened. "A little after six."

At that moment, Mya realized just how lucky she'd been. She'd left to get coffee right after Brian and had returned at about six twenty. If she'd been a few minutes later leaving or a few minutes earlier returning, she'd have likely run right into their fire starter. What would have happened if she had? The possibilities made her gut clench in terror.

"Did you see anyone when you were leaving?" Gideon asked Brian, pulling Mya back into the present.

Brian shook his head. "No one. It was Sunday. All the ground floor businesses had already closed. The parking lot was pretty much empty. Only a few cars and nothing stood out."

"What about the man who posed as a police officer to kidnap Mya? Does he sound familiar at all? Or maybe someone unfamiliar hanging around the building lobby or waiting in the parking lot. He wouldn't have wanted to draw attention to himself."

It was the same question Gideon had posed to her earlier that morning, and the answer was the same. There were just too many people in and around the building on any given day to remember anyone in particular. Especially if that person didn't want to be remembered.

"Brian, have you heard from Rebecca? I haven't been able to get in touch with her either," Mya said.

Brain blanched. "Me? Why would I have heard from her?" His eyes darted away from Mya's.

"You're lying," Gideon said.

Mya shot a frown at Gideon. He didn't take his eyes from Brian's face, but she was sure he'd caught the look. She turned back to Brian. "I thought she might have heard about the fire and gotten in touch with you since she hadn't called me."

"I'm not lying. I haven't heard from her."

Like Gideon, Mya wasn't sure she believed Brian but couldn't think of a reason he'd lie about talking to Rebecca.

Brian's fitful gaze landed on the building. His tone softening, he said, "I guess it will be some time before we'll be up and running."

The weight of all she needed to do—call the board members, check in with Detective Kamal, notify the insurance company—sent a headache pounding behind Mya's eyes.

She rubbed her temples. "I have to talk to the board and our investors. I'll try to get them to authorize a temporary space for us and let you know as soon as I know."

Brian nodded and plodded back to his car.

"He seems tightly wound," Gideon said after Brian was inside the car and out of hearing.

Mya slanted him a look. "Pot meet kettle."

Gideon's expression remained impassive. "Does Brian forget to charge his phone regularly?"

"I don't know. It doesn't really sound like him but—" Mya shrugged "—it happens to all of us."

From Gideon's expression, she surmised he didn't agree.

A smile quirked the ends of her lips. "It happens to most of us then."

A ghost of a smile flitted over his face before vanishing quickly. "We should go."

"What about my car?" Mya pointed to her car, still parked where she'd left it last night.

"You have the keys?"

My nodded.

"When we get to my offices, I'll send a couple of the guys to pick it up for you."

They returned to his SUV and made their way to her townhouse.

"You tensed when he hugged you," Gideon said as they left the lab behind.

She wasn't surprised Gideon had picked up on that.

If asked, she would have categorized Brian as more colleague than friend. Their working relationship was good, but there had been quite a bit of tension between them when she'd first been appointed director of the lab the prior year.

"Brian has worked at the lab longer than I have."

Gideon nodded. "You got promoted over him to director and he resents it."

"I wouldn't say resents," she said slowly. "It has to be difficult for him, but the board wanted someone with a medical degree and a PhD for the director position and

Brian doesn't have a medical degree and never finished his PhD thesis."

Gideon was silent for several minutes. "The man who set fire to your lab was looking for you. He expected you to be there. That could have been because someone told him you would be."

Mya twisted in her seat. "Brian? No way." She and Brian had their differences, but she couldn't believe he'd burn down the lab and target her.

"We have to examine all possibilities. Who is next in line for the directorship if you can't do the job anymore?"

"I don't know. Brian still hasn't completed his PhD, I don't even think he's trying any longer."

"But in the interim? Your investors or the board members might appoint him to serve as interim director which would give him a chance to show he could do the job."

That might be true, but Gideon didn't know Brian. "Why would Brian set the lab on fire if his plan was to run it?"

It was a gigantic hole in the theory that she could see Gideon wasn't sure how to get around.

He clenched his jaw. "I don't know. What I do know is that someone targeted you, specifically, last night." He shifted his gaze from the traffic in front of them to her face. "And until I know who, everybody is a suspect."

Mya was still contemplating what she should do when he finally turned the car down the small alleyway behind her townhouse.

"Do you have the garage door opener?" Gideon asked, turning the car into her short driveway.

"It's still on the visor in my car at the lab. I can punch in the code, though."

"I'll do it. I don't want you to get out of the car."

She gave him the code. He got out, punched it into the security box, and was back in the car in less than thirty seconds. They glided into her one-car garage. Gideon shut off the engine and jumped out again, this time hitting the button on the wall to close the overhead garage door.

Instead of getting back in the car, this time he walked around to her door. She lowered the window.

"Stay here until I clear the house."

She frowned, unhappy with the order, although she knew letting Gideon make sure all was well inside was the smart thing to do. She handed him the key to the house.

No matter how much you wanted them, discoveries didn't work on anyone's timetable. She'd had years of practice cultivating patience as a scientist. Still, it seemed like Gideon had been in her house for far longer than necessary to ensure her small tri-level home was free from interlopers.

Unwilling to wait any longer, Mya slid from the car and entered the lower level. The garage door opened into a small vestibule with the stairs leading to the primary living spaces. To her left, the basement—a nine-by-thirteen-foot space she used primarily for storage and housing the small private server that stored her research.

She took a step inside the basement and stopped. Her stomach lurched, bile rising in her throat.

Rebecca, the lab's receptionist, lay with arms and legs outstretched on the floor. Her eyes focused sightlessly on the popcorn ceiling. The dark red pool of blood congealed around her head left no doubt that she was dead.

Footsteps pounded down the stairs.

"I told you to stay in the car," Gideon barked.

Mya turned from him, pointing at the form sprawled on her basement floor. "Rebecca… I don't understand? Why is she in my house?"

Gideon wrapped an arm around her shoulder and attempted to steer her from the house. "We'll figure that out, but we need to leave and call the police now." He reached for the door.

"Wait!" Mya twisted from under Gideon's arm and slid by him.

Her eyes scanned the basement, once, twice, her heart dropping as she realized that the murder wasn't the only thing that had happened at her home.

Gideon placed a hand on her shoulder. "Mya, we need to leave."

She heard the words as if they were coming at her from underwater.

"The server with my research. Gideon, it's not here. It's gone."

Chapter Five

Police cruisers lined the narrow back alley behind Mya's house. Yellow police tape blocked off the entrance to the driveway, and a white coroner's van was backed up to the open garage.

Detective Kamal had arrived a half hour earlier and, after briefly speaking with them, had asked them to wait.

Gideon punched in the number of a direct line within the West Investigations offices.

"West Investigations. James West speaking."

He didn't waste time with formality. "Mya and I found TriGen's receptionist dead in Mya's basement. She'd been bludgeoned."

He got along with all his coworkers, but out of everyone at West, James was probably the person he was closest to. Maybe it was the military thing. After putting Mya to bed last night, Gideon had called James to let him know about her sudden appearance and request for help.

James let out a curse. "She okay?"

He shot a look several steps to his left where Mya sat with her feet hanging out of the passenger side of the Tahoe. He'd moved the car onto the street before the police arrived, not wanting to get boxed in by the ambulance.

"She's hanging in there. We need to know everything there is to find on the receptionist." He recalled her name from the staff directory on TriGen's website. "Rebecca Conway."

"On it."

Gideon cast a second glance at Detective Kamal. The detective had been throwing suspicious glances their way since she'd reemerged from Mya's townhouse.

"Could you also give Brandon a call?" Brandon West was the only son of James West Sr., West Investigations' founder, who didn't work for or own an interest in the company. He'd chosen a legal career over the family business, but West Investigations was one of Brandon's biggest and most loyal clients.

"Either of you under arrest?" James said.

"Not yet, but I don't like the way the lead detective is looking at Mya."

"Done. Listen, I was going to bring this up when you got into the office, but it looks like things are moving fast. Do you think you're the right person for this case? I mean, will you be able to maintain perspective where your ex-wife is concerned?"

He felt his jaw tighten and counted to ten before answering. "I've got it under control."

James sighed heavily on the other end of the line. "Just think about what I've said. I know your first priority is protecting Mya, but you might not be the best person to do that right now."

Gideon gripped the phone so tightly he feared he might crush it. "I'm not handing over this case. I won't let anything happen to Mya."

He heard James mutter something that sounded like "pigheaded" and "man in love" before he ended the call.

James's concern that he wouldn't be able to maintain

the objectivity necessary to protect Mya stung, all the more because he knew there was some truth to it. He was still in love with her. He'd never denied it, at least not to himself. Love had not been an issue with them. He'd loved her since he was ten years old. If only things could have stayed that simple when they'd grown up and married.

Gideon stretched his neck to the right then left, working out some tension that had settled there in response to finding the body and the call with James. Normally he was a stickler about not mixing business with personal. But ensuring Mya's safety was nothing but personal and there was no way he was going to turn the job over to anyone else. Even if that meant he had to give up his job at West Investigations.

Mya looked up as he stepped back toward the car. She gave him a tentative smile. "Calling for reinforcements?"

"You could say that. Called in to the office to let them know what happened and to get them started on a background check on your receptionist."

Mya's eyes widened in surprise. "A background check on Rebecca?"

He kept his voice low so he wouldn't be heard by the officer manning the crime scene perimeter. "We need to figure out why she was in your house. You have any ideas?"

Mya shook her head with fervor. "None."

She began to moan quietly and leaned forward, letting her head fall between her knees. "I think I'm going to be sick."

"It's going to be okay, sweetheart." He crouched down, rubbing her back. "It's just the adrenaline flowing through your body. Just breathe slowly." He reached across her and turned the heat in the car up to its maximum setting while he continued to rub her back. "That's it, sweetheart."

"She okay?"

Gideon glanced up to see Kamal watching them.

"Adrenaline dump."

The detective nodded sagely. "I want to talk to you both down at the station. These officers can drive you." Kamal gestured to the two uniformed officers standing behind her.

"We'll meet you at the station," Gideon answered.

Kamal smiled tightly. "I'd prefer if my officers drove you."

Gideon straightened. "Is either of us under arrest?" He knew Kamal couldn't force them to go with the officers if they weren't in custody. She couldn't even force them to speak with her.

He watched as Kamal mentally debated how far to push the issue. "I'll meet you at the station then," she finally said.

He hopped in the SUV and immediately hit the redial button on his phone.

"James West."

"James, we're going to need Brandon at the police station. Right away."

"So, YOU DON'T know what Ms. Conway was doing in your house?"

"As I've said before, no. I have no idea why Rebecca was in my home." Mya forced herself not to shrink from Detective Kamal's piercing gaze.

"There isn't any sign of a break-in."

Mya stared at the detective blankly.

"Do you have any idea how Ms. Conway got into your house?"

Mya gave the same answer that she'd given the prior two times Detective Kamal had asked the question.

Mya felt her forehead crease. After a moment of thought she said, "I don't know."

"There was no sign of a break in at your townhouse," Kamal shot back.

Mya threw her hands up. "I have no idea what to tell you. Maybe Rebecca stole my keys and made a copy. It wouldn't be hard to do. I leave my purse in my office while I work."

Detective Kamal shot a dubious look across the table. "And you didn't change the code in months?"

"No, why would I? I trusted Rebecca." She hadn't changed the code since she'd set it the day she moved into the house. Something she was sure Gideon, and probably Detective Kamal, would note as careless.

Mya reached for the glass of water. A scene from one of the TV cop dramas popped into her head. The TV detective was able to collect the bad guy's DNA from the soda can he'd drunk from during the police interview.

Well, she had nothing to hide, she thought, finishing the last of the water and setting the cup down on the table. She'd assented to be interviewed without an attorney and she'd supply her DNA or anything else the detective requested. She just wanted the police to find out whoever had killed Rebecca.

"Surely you can understand why that's difficult to believe. A woman you work closely with is found dead in your house. The server with your research is missing. And all this happens just hours after your research lab is set ablaze and you know nothing at all about why any of it is happening or who could be doing it?" The thinly veiled accusation sliced like a paper's edge through skin.

Not for the first time, Mya questioned whether she should have listened to Gideon and waited to speak to Detective Kamal with an attorney. Detective Kamal had assured her that she was free to leave whenever she wanted, but Kamal's questions, repeated over and over, made it clear that the detective thought she was some-how involved in everything that had happened over the last day.

"I don't know what to say to that, Detective." Mya folded her hands in her lap and squeezed them together to stop the slight tremble there. Even though she knew she was innocent, it was intimidating to be in a police interview room, under the bright lights, so to speak.

She really wanted to have Gideon by her side, but he'd been whisked away to give his statement not long after they'd arrived at the police station.

Detective Kamal's eyes narrowed. "You could tell the truth. That's all I ask."

Irritation pricked at the back of Mya's neck. She sus-pected that was exactly what the detective intended, so she did her best not to let it show.

"I am telling you the truth. I returned to my house this morning intending to pick up a few things, and that's when we found Rebecca."

Detective Kamal looked down at her notes. "And last night you sought out your ex-husband after escaping a kidnapper dressed like a cop? Do I have that correct?" Incredulity dripped from her words.

"Yes," Mya snapped.

Detective Kamal's brow went up. "You've been divorced from Mr. Wright for twelve years, but you went to him instead of the police?"

"Gideon is a security specialist. I didn't trust the police, after what happened last night." She couldn't help herself from taking the dig at the cops.

So, she'd kept up with what was going on in her ex's life. It hadn't been hard with her mother dropping news about Gideon's life into most of their conversations.

"I guess that distrust of the police is why you didn't call us and report this alleged attempted kidnapping?" Detective Kamal flipped the pages of her notepad, ostensibly looking for Mya's past statement on the topic, although she didn't buy the hapless routine. The detective was as sharp as a newly honed knife. Mya wouldn't have been surprised if she remembered every word that the two had exchanged since meeting the night before.

"You've got your very own personal security guard now," Detective Kamal peered at her.

"We planned to call a detective friend of Gideon's after I'd picked up a few things from home. Obviously, that plan changed."

One sculpted eyebrow went up. "And who is Mr. Wright's detective friend?"

Mya exhaled. "I don't know."

Detective Kamal's lips twisted into a smirk. "Let's go back to last night and the fire. The man you saw in the building, can you describe him for me?"

"I told you, I never saw him. I only heard his voice."

Detective Kamal laid her pen across her notepad. "The security cameras in the lab were destroyed. Before the fire," the detective said, emphasizing the last sentence. "I only have your word that there was a man. And no one on our police force fits the description of the police officer you claim offered you a ride home last night."

Anger stiffened Mya's spine. "I'm not claiming anything. A man dressed in a police uniform said he'd been sent to take me home."

"And you just got in the car with him?"

"He was a police officer! Or at least I thought he was. And you'd said you were sending someone to take me home. There was no reason not to believe him."

Detective Kamal's eyes narrowed. "There's no need to yell, Miss Rochon. I'm just trying to make sure I'm clear on what you say happened."

Mya wanted to yell at the detective again. It wasn't what she said happened. It was what actually happened.

A knock from the other side of the door broke the charged silence in the interview room. Detective Kamal excused herself and stepped out of the room.

Mya took several deep breaths and gathered her emotions. She'd been giving her "statement" for the past two hours. They weren't covering any new ground, and she was tired and hungry. Detective Kamal had made sure to emphasize that she was here voluntarily and could leave whenever she wanted. Well, she wanted to leave now, and she planned to make that clear to the detective the moment she returned.

She needn't have worried.

Detective Kamal returned to the interview room a minute later, a scowl twisting her lips. "Thank you for your time, Miss Rochon. I have all I need from you at the moment."

Mya stood, her prior determination to put the detective in her place swept away by Kamal's sudden change in attitude.

Gideon waited in the hallway. The sight of him calmed her nerves while setting off a whole new set of emotions. She'd have to think about what that meant later. A man she'd never met strode down the corridor toward them.

"Mya, this is Brandon West. He's an attorney."

Brandon extended his hand. "Pleasure to meet you."

May shook his hand. "I'm guessing I should thank you for getting Detective Kamal to back off."

"Don't thank me. You shouldn't have talked to Detective Kamal without me," Brandon said. "I assure you it's only temporary if Kamal doesn't come up with a suspect she likes better than you. But don't worry. West Investigations has me on retainer and I'm told you are now my most important client."

Mya felt herself deflate. "I had nothing to do with anything that's happened."

Gideon's eyes darkened, and his jaw tightened. He stepped in closer to her, the warmth from his body a much-needed comfort in the dank police hallway.

Brandon held both his hands out in front of him in a surrender motion. "I believe you. Gideon says there's no way you're involved. That's more than enough for me."

Detective Kamal exited the interview room then, her notebook tucked under her arm. She shot a glare at the group before turning and striding away down the hall.

Gideon's word may have been enough for Brandon, but there was no doubt in Mya's mind that it wasn't enough to convince Detective Kamal.

Not by a long shot.

Chapter Six

James West Jr. stood as Gideon held the door to the conference room open for Mya to enter first. James looked uncomfortable in an expensively tailored suit that made it perfectly clear how he'd earned the nickname Tank. Six-five and as wide as a compact car, James was definitely a gentle giant. James, who'd only recently left the military, was at loose ends, trying to figure out his next move and working for his family's private investigation firm.

"Mya, this is James West, co-owner of West Investigations and one of my bosses."

James offered his hand. "I don't know about that. Gideon knows more about how this place ticks than I do. I just try not to embarrass myself too much."

Gideon rolled out a chair for Mya at the long oak conference table and waited until she'd settled before he took the seat next to her.

James settled his large frame back in his seat on the other side of the table.

"I've briefed James," Gideon started, "but it would be helpful to both of us if you took us through everything again, starting with what happened at the lab last night."

Mya took a deep breath and plunged in, explaining staying after Brian and Rebecca had gone home, taking a coffee break and coming back to find a strange man in the lobby talking about having set a fire in the lab.

Her hands shook as she described running away from the faux cop through the woods and continued to shake during the description of finding Rebecca dead and the server housing her research gone.

Although he'd heard the story previously, had lived the last portion of it, anger fired through Gideon's blood listening to Mya tell it again. What if she hadn't gotten away? What if he hadn't been home when she'd needed him? What if she'd gone home and had been there when whoever had killed Rebecca arrived?

He knew what-ifs were pointless. They needed to stay in the here and now to find the person behind this, but, at the moment, fear and anger controlled his thoughts. An involuntary growl rumbled in Gideon's chest.

Mya turned curious eyes his way.

James's expression never changed, but Gideon caught the slight shake of his head. He took a deep breath and forced himself to relax.

Mya had fought back, saved herself, and anybody who wanted to get to her now would have to contend with him and all the resources of West Investigations.

Gideon forced himself to listen as impassively as he could as Mya carried on explaining how they'd found the body of Rebecca Conway, the lab's receptionist, in her basement and the server missing.

James shook his head. "A server in a basement."

"I'll fix it after we're sure she's safe," Gideon said.

Mya's cheeks pinked. Her back straightened, sending the oversize sweatshirt he'd lent sliding off one shoulder revealing smooth tawny skin. "It worked just fine for Irwin."

"Irwin Ross? The prior director of TriGen, right?" James scratched notes on the pad in front of him.

"Yes." Mya nodded.

"I did a little digging into your work after Gideon called. Most people agree Irwin Ross is a genius who advanced the treatment of cancer during his thirty-plus years with TriGen but never quite reached the goal of finding a cure."

"Irwin is brilliant. He taught me everything I know."

James's eyebrows arched up. "My sources say you're even smarter than Ross. The rumor is you've figured out how to turn his research into a workable cure."

"She is, and she did," Gideon answered, pride threaded through his words.

"Not a cure," Mya interjected quickly. "A treatment that looks very promising, but it wouldn't cure cancer." She cocked her head and viewed James with a narrow gaze. "How did you know about the treatment? That's confidential information. We haven't publicly reported it yet."

"Then someone who works with you has been talking because it was one of the first things that came up when I started asking about you and TriGen," James said.

A wave of apprehension swept through Gideon. He didn't like where this appeared to be heading. Not after finding a dead TriGen employee in Mya's house.

"The first parts of the formula are on the missing server."

"The first parts?" James said.

"Yes. The treatment has three parts. Irwin worked out the first two parts before he retired. A few weeks ago, I finally figured out the last piece."

James tapped his pen against his cheek. "So, whoever has your server has most of the treatment but not all."

"The first parts are useless without the final piece," Mya said. "It's what makes the other two parts work."

"Given how aggressive Mya's pursuers have been thus far, it's not likely they'll give up," Gideon said.

James nodded. "I agree. Our first course of business should be ensuring Mya's safety." He tapped a few keys on the laptop, then spun it one hundred eighty degrees. "We have a couple of available safe houses open right now."

Gideon reached for the computer, the urge to lock Mya away somewhere safe nearly overwhelming.

Mya grabbed his wrist and looked from James to Gideon. "Hang on. I can't go into hiding. I have a lab to rebuild. I need to meet with the head of the foundation that supports TriGen. And I have a handful of private investors who will be wondering what's going on—"

Gideon felt his shoulders tense. Mya didn't seem to understand the danger she was facing. "Mya."

She shifted in her chair to look at him head on. "Gideon."

He remembered that tone. It was the one that meant she was gearing up for an argument.

Well, so was he.

"Your safety has to come first. You can do whatever you need to from the safe house." His response held a healthy dose of impatience.

"You have a safe house that comes fully equipped with a cancer research lab?" Mya asked, her words heavy with sarcasm. "I heard you guys were the best, but that would be something."

James snickered, and Gideon shot a glare across the table.

"Look, this isn't up for discussion," Mya said, sitting back in her chair. "I'm the client, right? So, I decide."

She might have been the only person who'd ever bested him in an argument, largely because she was one of the only people, outside of his fellow marines, he'd ever cared enough to argue with. But this was one argument she was not going to win.

"You're not a client," Gideon growled. "And I'm not taking money from you."

She stood, sending her chair rolling backward. "Then we're done here. I'll find another security firm to help me."

She turned toward the door.

Gideon reached out and took her hand before she took a step. "Let me keep you safe."

Their gazes caught and held for a long moment before she gently pulled her hand from his.

"It's not going to work, Gideon. There's just too... much between us now."

Her words were as painful as a fist to the kidneys. He drew in a breath and let it out slowly. "We'll do it your way."

Her eyes narrowed. He couldn't blame her for being suspicious. He wasn't one to give up easily, but there was no way he'd chance leaving her welfare to another firm. West Security was the best, and no one would care more about keeping her safe than him.

"For now, and as long as it doesn't compromise your safety, we'll do it your way."

Mya studied him for another long moment, then extended her hand. They shook on it as the door to the conference room opened.

Tessa Stenning, one of the other private investigators, poked her head around the door. "Sorry to interrupt, but I bought some of my own clothes for Miss Rochon to borrow. I thought she might feel better in something more comfortable."

"Thanks, Tessa." Gideon watched Mya follow Tessa from the room before turning back to James.

"I don't know where I got the idea you working with your ex-wife could be a problem," James deadpanned.

Gideon sat without answering.

"I'm going to ask you again, are you sure you're going to be able to handle providing security for your ex-wife?"

"I'm a professional."

James smirked. "Yeah, that little exchange looked very professional."

Gideon glowered at his friend.

"Look, you may be the Ice Man—"

Gideon's glower deepened. He hated the nickname, and his coworkers knew better than to use it to his face.

James continued, "But you are human, and you obviously still care about your ex. That's going to affect how you do your job."

"I'm not handing over this case."

James sighed. "I've got to be in the office covering for Ryan while he's out with the new baby, but I'll do what I can from here. If you need backup, call. If I can't do it, I'll send someone else." He pinned Gideon with a weighty stare. "I mean it. The first sign of trouble, call. No matter what you say, your objectivity is shot here. I know taking you off would be pointless. I'm not even sure Mya would let me despite her earlier bravado, but I won't let it get her, or you, killed."

Gideon clamped down hard on his back teeth to keep what he wanted to say from spilling out. He knew James was only looking out for him, but it still rankled. "Mya will be staying at my place."

James barked out a laugh. "She might just wish she'd agreed to the safe house."

She might just, Gideon thought. Because whether it was at a safe house or his house, he wasn't going to let Mya out of his sight.

MYA STEPPED OUT of the stall and examined herself in the bathroom mirror. Not bad. Definitely better than Gideon's sweats, although she hadn't minded the woodsy smell of aftershave that clung to his sweatshirt.

It reminded her of all the mornings they'd spent getting ready for the day in the tiny bathroom of their apartment—she hunched down so she could see herself in the lower half of the mirror as she applied mascara while he shaved using the top half. They'd dreamed of one day having the luxury of a bathroom with his and hers sinks, but truthfully, she'd loved the intimacy of their tiny little home.

Tess gave her an appraising look. "I wasn't sure they'd fit but it looks like they do."

"They'll more than do. Thank you."

Tessa waved away the thanks. "No problem. I bought a few other things—a couple other tops, another pair of pants, and a jacket—just in case you aren't able to get into your place for a few days. And I brought my makeup bag." She held up a black vinyl case. "Not that you aren't stunningly gorgeous without it, but I know I don't feel myself without at least a little lip gloss and mascara."

Mya shot the other woman a grateful smile. "Thanks. I spend all day in a lab, so I don't really have to wear makeup to work, but I just love the way it makes me feel so I do it, anyway."

"So, you and Gideon were married?" Although they were the only two women in the restroom, Tessa continued to address Mya through the mirror.

"It was a long time ago."

Mya smiled, her mind going back to her eighteen-year-old self and the whirlwind that led her and Gideon to the altar. "We were so young. Just out of high school." She fastened the button at the top of the blouse Tessa had lent her. "I'm a scientist. I make careful, well-thought-out decisions based on data." Mya laughed. "The data's not great on marrying right out of high school but…"

She could still hear her mother's voice warning her and Gideon against marrying so young. As much as Francine loved them both, she hadn't wanted them to make the same mistakes she had. But Mya had known, in her heart and in her soul, that Gideon was the man she was supposed to spend the rest of her life with.

She should have stuck to the data. Data didn't lie.

"Getting married at eighteen is still the most impulsive thing I've ever done." And it was still the decision that had felt the most right in her whole life.

Tessa's fawn complexion was quite a bit fairer than Mya's brown skin so covering the scrape on her face would have to wait, but Mya dug through the makeup bag until she found a deep red lip gloss that would work for her.

"Still, it's hard to imagine Gideon married," Tessa said. "No offense."

"No offense taken." Mya chuckled. "Gideon isn't the easiest person, especially when you live with him. But you won't find anyone more loyal or thoughtful or caring."

"So, there's still something between you two then." Tessa wiggled her eyebrows.

Mya felt heat rise in her cheeks. The conversation had gotten off on a bit of a tangent. "No, I just meant—"

"What happened between you two?"

She considered telling the pretty PI to mind her own business, but there was something endearing about Tessa's brashness.

"We were really just too young." Mya swallowed hard. She hadn't intended to mimic the words Gideon had used when he'd told her their marriage was over. Not intentionally, anyway. But she'd replayed that moment over in her head a million times in the twelve years since their divorce. They'd slipped out and she could tell they'd hit their mark.

"Hmm." Tessa studied her. "Based on the look on your face, I'd say you weren't the one who ended the marriage. I can't see Gideon straying, so what happened?"

What had happened? She'd come home one day during her last semester of university and just before he was scheduled to deploy, and he'd announced that he loved her but didn't want to be married anymore.

And she'd frozen. All the words she might have used to talk him out of leaving fled from her brain. He'd already packed a bag and by the time her brain thawed, he'd been pulling out of the parking lot of their apartment.

"He didn't want to be married anymore."

She swiped mascara over her eyelids and hoped Tessa would chalk the glassiness in her eyes up to the makeup.

Tessa laid a hand on Mya's shoulder. "I'm sorry. Feel free to tell me to butt out."

Mya forced a smile. "No, it's okay, really. It was a long time ago." Had she said that already? She felt like a broken record.

And there was an upside to Tessa's nosiness. "Do you know if Gideon is seeing anyone, you know, a lady friend or whatever?"

A lady friend or whatever! She may as well have asked Tessa to pass Gideon a note. Do you like Mya? Check yes or no.

"My boldness may have given you the wrong idea. Since I started working at West a year ago, I'm pretty sure the only thing Gideon has said to me that hasn't been work related is 'nice to meet you,' 'good morning' and 'good night.'" Tessa waved one hand dramatically. "Oh, I forgot he said 'thanks, Tessa' when I bought you those clothes." Tessa waved a hand at Mya. "I'd be the last to know whether he was dating."

Mya laughed. "He can be a bit taciturn."

One of Tessa's eyebrows went up. "His nickname around here is Ice Man, so…yeah. But he's also a man I'd want watching my back when it's on the line." Tessa gave Mya's shoulder another squeeze.

"Thanks again for everything," Mya said, forcing a smile onto her face as they exited the ladies' room.

"As I said, not a problem." Tessa led Mya back to the conference room.

Through the glass door, Mya could see James and Gideon, heads together, looking at something on the laptop's screen.

Even with a wall between them, Mya could feel Gideon's intensity.

As if he knew she was watching, Gideon lifted his head, his dark gaze locking on hers.

Tessa's gaze swung from Mya to Gideon and back. "You know that question you had about Gideon and lady friends? Based on the data I currently see, Gideon only has eyes for the lady I'm standing next to."

Chapter Seven

"You're looking awfully comfortable at the head of the table." Ryan West's right eyebrow went up at a sharp angle.

After Mya and Tessa left the conference room, James had initiated a video conference call with his brother and president of West Investigations to update him on the firm's newest case. Although Ryan was technically on paternity leave, his first child having made her appearance just three short weeks ago, he couldn't stand to be completely out of the loop. From what Gideon could tell, James didn't mind having his younger brother looking over his shoulder. In fact, he seemed more than a little relieved.

"It's not the worst job, playing boss for a few weeks." James chuckled, leaning back in the leather executive chair.

"Yeah, well, don't get too comfortable. And speaking of not getting comfortable, did you get my email about the new job?"

This was the first Gideon had heard of a new job. James too seemed to be searching the recesses of his brain.

Managing West Investigations seemed to be a never-ending series of emails, phone calls, video chats and meetings. Technically, James and his youngest brothers, Ryan and Shawn, were co-owners of the firm their semi-retired father, James Sr., had started. The only brother with no ownership interest was Brandon, who as an attorney had decided there were too many potential conflicts if he was part owner of a private investigations firm. But James had only recently begun working at West full-time. Gideon could only imagine how difficult it was to stay abreast of all the different cases the firm handled at any given time.

"Carling Lake," Ryan offered by way of reminder.

"Oh, yeah, right. Carling Lake." James scowled. "Where the—"

Ryan shot a warning look through the computer's screen as the tiny bundle cradled in his arms shifted.

Little Cicely was well on her way to being the most spoiled three-week-old this side of the Hudson River, but it would take some time for her many uncles to temper their language in her presence.

"Where might this undoubtedly lovely place be?" James asked.

Ryan rolled his eyes.

Gideon fought a smile. There were times the West brothers made him happy he didn't have siblings, but he knew any one of them would die for one of the others. It was the same kind of bond Gideon shared with his fellow marines.

"The Pennsylvania mountains," Ryan answered.

This time it was James who shot a sour look at his brother. "Why me?"

Ryan gently swung the pink bundle in his arms from side to side. "I'd planned to assign Gideon but with what you've told me, there's no way to be sure Miss Rochon's situation will be settled in time."

While Gideon generally took whatever assignments Ryan gave him, he couldn't help being grateful he'd dodged this one. While he enjoyed the great outdoors—camping and fishing were two of his favorite hobbies—the mountains in midwinter held no appeal.

"I know you've been...struggling a bit since you came home," Ryan said. "Working in an office isn't what you're used to."

Transitioning back to civilian life wasn't easy, Gideon knew from experience. And James had been in the military several years longer than he had. He seemed to be dealing with the change well but looks could be deceiving.

James's brow furrowed. "Have I done something wrong? Have there been complaints?"

"No, nothing like that," Ryan answered. A tiny fist burst from the pink blanket, followed by a sleepy-sounding mewl. Ryan hitched his daughter closer and swayed lightly. "But you're my brother. I know you, and I can see that you're restless."

Gideon opened his mouth to say that he'd take the job. Mya could go to Carling Lake with him. Getting her out of town wasn't a bad idea anyway.

James spoke before he uttered a word, though. "I'm fine. I don't know that I want to make this a permanent position, but I'm happy to help out while you have some bonding time with your new family."

"And I appreciate it," Ryan said. "Nadia and I both do. This would help me out. I'm returning to the office next week, and this assignment in Carling Lake would begin at the end of the week. I need someone who can blend in with the other community members."

"And you think I'd blend in in the community?"

"You like all that outdoorsy stuff, fishing, hiking and hunting," Ryan answered. "It's a small town but economically dependent on tourism. You should have no problem posing as a visitor looking for some R & R."

From the look on his face, James wasn't convinced. Before he could relay those thoughts to his brother, Cicely let out a wail.

Almost immediately, the door behind Ryan swung open and his wife, Nadia Shelton West, entered the room.

"You should have called me. I would have taken her from you while you were on your call." Nadia leaned forward into the camera and waved. "Hi, James. Gideon."

"Nadia."

"Hi, beautiful." James winked at his sister-in-law in a bid to get a rise out of his brother.

"Don't flirt with my wife," Ryan growled before turning to Nadia. "I didn't want to wake you." He let her scoop the squalling infant from his arms, pressing a kiss to the side of her neck as she did. Nadia dropped a kiss of her own onto Ryan's lips before leaving the room.

A twinge of jealousy and…longing stabbed Gideon in his gut as he watched. Ryan and Nadia were perfect for each other. They'd had their difficulties but had worked through them and were building a life, a family together.

It had been a long time since Gideon felt like he had a shot at anything similar. He hadn't even considered it since his divorce from Mya. His life had only been about work and Grandma Pearl and after her death, work had completely taken over.

But now, Mya was back in his life.

No. He couldn't let himself think that way. Mya needed his help. That was all. Once she had her research back and he was sure she wasn't in any danger, she'd go back to her life and he'd go back to his.

He shook off the thoughts and focused on the task at hand. Carling Lake.

"So, you don't have to decide right now," Ryan was saying to James. "Just think about it. I'll send you all the information I have on the assignment and a few links on the town. Just give it some thought."

James promised he would, and they signed off the video call as Tessa and Mya reentered the conference room.

Gideon let his eyes roam over Mya's lithe body. She'd changed into a pair of snug jeans and a red blouse, but he couldn't help thinking she'd looked sexier in his old sweatshirt. And imagined how much better she'd look without any clothes at all. He shifted in his seat and squelched the train of thought before it led to a visibly uncomfortable place.

Mya slid into a chair on the opposite side of the table from him and James. Tessa grabbed bottles of water from the mini-fridge in the corner of the room and took the seat next to Mya.

"What can you tell us about Rebecca?" Gideon asked, focusing back on business.

"She's worked as the receptionist slash file clerk slash admin for the last ten months or so. Our prior receptionist moved out of state." Keyboard keys clacked softly as James took notes on the conversation.

"How did you come to hire her?"

Mya's forehead furrowed in thought. "I think she was a friend of a friend of Brian's."

James stopped typing. "Brian your research assistant?"

"Yes." Mya nodded. "Although he is much more than that. He worked alongside Irwin for several years before I joined the team."

Gideon's eyebrows went up. "You mentioned that before. Tell us about your relationship."

Mya shook her head. "Brian is great. Meticulous, detail oriented with a deep knowledge of the science behind cancer treatments. We work well together."

"But?" Gideon prodded, searching Mya's face. He'd felt like there'd been something there earlier when she'd spoken about her relationship with Brian. Something she hadn't wanted to share with him. A part of him feared she was going to say she and Brian were more than just coworkers.

He knew he didn't have a claim on Mya, but that didn't stop jealousy from swelling in his chest. "You said he didn't have the right education background, but it felt like there was something you weren't saying."

Mya's gaze skittered across the room. "There's a lot that goes into running a successful lab. Irwin and the board didn't think he had the right temperament for the director's position."

Tessa smirked. "That's something you should be able to understand, Gid."

Gideon sent Tessa a biting look, but she just smiled back beatifically.

"Let's get back to Rebecca."

"There's not a lot more I can tell you. Brian said he knew someone who might work in the receptionist position. It seemed like it would be a good fit since Rebecca is…was studying for an associate's degree in chemistry."

Gideon's spine prickled. "You said it seemed like it would be a good fit. It wasn't?"

"Rebecca wasn't a bad employee," Mya hedged. "It's just that there were some definite gaps in her knowledge. I'm not disparaging her—she picked things up quickly, and she was definitely interested in our research, but I guess I expected she'd know more than she did."

A smile tipped his lips upward. "Not everyone is a genius like you."

He watched her face flush. "I'm not a genius."

"You love your work, though."

"I do. I know not everyone is fortunate enough to find a career that they enjoy, and that's important work. I know how lucky I've been, especially as a Black woman in the sciences, to have had Irwin Ross as a mentor. It definitely opened doors that may have never been opened for me otherwise."

"I never doubted you would do it." And he hadn't, especially once he'd stopped being an encumbrance. "I knew you would change the world one day."

She smiled, and it nearly stopped his heart. "I think we both share that 'wanting to make a difference' gene."

"I don't know about that."

Mya cocked her head to the side, a smile curving her lips. "You don't think being a marine, serving your country and defending democracy around the world makes a difference?"

"A bit of an exaggeration."

"Not at all."

James cleared his throat. "I've got an address on Rebecca Conway. Not much more online, though. No social media hits at all, which is unusual for someone her age."

Mya frowned, her expression betraying confusion.

"That is weird. Rebecca was always on her phone during her breaks and coming into work."

Gideon frowned. "Do you know if she had a boyfriend? Any family nearby we could talk to?"

"She has mentioned a roommate, although I'm not sure I'm comfortable questioning her loved ones so soon after her death."

"Normally, I'd give the friends and family some time, but I'm not sure we have time in this case. Whoever is after you and your formula has already committed arson and more than likely killed Rebecca. We need to find out who that is and right now Rebecca is our best lead."

"What do you mean?"

"We need to know why she was in your house. Was it just a sad coincidence or something else?"

"Something else? You can't think Rebecca had something to do with the theft or arson?"

"Right now, I'm suspicious of everyone."

Mya shook her head in disbelief. "I definitely heard a man's voice at the lab last night."

"Maybe Rebecca was working with the guy you saw? The money that you were likely to make from licensing the formula, that's the kind of money that could lead someone to make really bad decisions." The look Mya gave him said she wasn't buying it. "For argument's sake, let's say Rebecca was planning to steal my formula. Why go through all this? I mean, she had access to it at the lab. Why not just slip in one evening and take it?"

"Because then you and Brian would know who had stolen it and you'd get the police involved. She'd never be able to sell it, even on the black market. The theft would be too high profile for someone to eventually pass off as their own."

"I don't know, Gideon." Mya's reddish-brown locks skimmed her shoulders as her head shook back and forth. "It just sounds so far-fetched. And it still doesn't explain why Rebecca was killed in my house."

"Have you ever heard the saying 'there's no honor among thieves'? Maybe Rebecca was supposed to get the first parts of the formula while her accomplice got the final portion from you and destroyed the lab. But the accomplice double-crossed Rebecca instead."

Mya closed her eyes and let her head fall back against the leather chair she sat in. "I feel like I'm in an action film. A bad one."

He cocked an eyebrow. "You hated action movies when we were together."

She opened one eye and looked his way. "They've grown on me."

"I think you start with Rebecca's roommate." James said. "You'll probably get more reliable information about her day-to-day life from a roommate than a grieving family."

Gideon agreed. A twenty-four year-old woman was likely keeping any number of things from her family.

Mya chewed her bottom lip. He could see doubt, and worse, fear, in her eyes.

He spun her chair until it faced his. "We will figure this out. I promise."

Chapter Eight

Rebecca lived in a garden-style apartment complex with four buildings arranged around a small courtyard and surrounded by an asphalt parking lot. Management had given the boxy tan buildings a faux Venetian facade that did little to hide the structure's utilitarian nature. Someone had haphazardly wound white lights around the thin tree in the courtyard as a nod to the season. Located in a working-class neighborhood near two junior colleges, Gideon doubted the residents cared.

Gideon rounded the Tahoe, his eyes scanning the parking lot for threats. He met Mya at the passenger door. She pulled leather gloves she'd borrowed from Tessa over her hands and yanked her skull cap down over her ears.

The sun was out, but it was losing the battle against the nearly freezing temperature.

They walked to the gate surrounding the complex. Gideon pressed the buzzer for Rebecca's apartment three times before a scratchy voice came over the intercom.

"Yes?"

"Felix Ucar?"

"Yes. Who is this?"

"My name is Gideon Wright. I've got Mya Rochon

here with me. Do you have a moment to talk to us about Rebecca?"

There was quiet at the other end of the intercom. Half a minute passed, and then the gate buzzed and opened. Gideon and Mya followed a twisty path to building B. Rebecca and Felix lived in apartment 402. Mya started toward the elevator embedded in the tiny alcove next to the stairs.

Gideon caught her arm. "Let's take the stairs."

Mya's jaw slackened. "It's four flights."

"I know, but we don't know exactly what to expect. I don't want to be stuck in a little box."

She didn't look happy about it, but she started up the stairs with him.

Gideon angled himself so that he was slightly ahead of her as they ascended. He'd run a quick background check on Felix Ucar before they'd left West's offices. He appeared to be a typical part-time student, full-time office drone. So far, there was no reason to suspect Rebecca's roommate had any involvement with the lab fire or her death, but Gideon knew better than to let his guard down. An innocent appearance could cover a multitude of sins.

Felix opened the door on the first knock. His blond hair stood on end, and even at twenty-five, he hadn't quite lost the look of a teen stuck on the cusp of adulthood. Wide, bloodshot eyes swung between Gideon and Mya.

"The police were by to question me earlier today."

"We aren't with the police, Mr. Ucar," Mya answered.

Felix moved a questioning gaze to Gideon.

"This is my friend Gideon. The police may have mentioned that I was attacked, and my lab set on fire last night. Gideon is helping me sort out who would do something like this."

Felix assessed them for another moment, then opened the door wider.

Matted tan carpet covered the floor. The apartment's design esthetic appeared to be little more than broke twenty-somethings. The furniture was mismatched, and the eggshell-white walls were bare. The space's sparseness made the large flat-screen television in the corner of the room even more conspicuous.

They declined Felix's offer of water and settled in on the ancient leather couch. Felix pulled a chair from the kitchen into the living room and settled in across from them.

"I'm sorry for your loss," Mya said.

"I guess I should be saying the same to you. God, I can't believe it." Tears pooled in Felix's eyes. "I mean, I've never known anyone who was murdered before."

"It's always difficult to lose a loved one. If you don't mind, maybe you could tell us a little bit about Rebecca."

Lines formed across the curve of Felix's nose. "What do you want to know?"

"When was the last time you saw or spoke to her?"

"The cops asked me that too. We spoke on the phone yesterday around 6:00 p.m. I'd gotten paid and was feeling like treating myself a little, so I stopped off at Francesca's, an Italian place a couple blocks from here." Felix snatched a tissue from a box on the coffee table between the couch and his chair. "I called Rebecca to see if she wanted me to grab her something for dinner. She loves... loved that place."

Gideon waited for Felix to blow his nose before continuing. "And did she?"

"What?"

Gideon beat back his impatience with the younger man and posed the question again. "Did Rebecca want anything from the restaurant?"

"Oh, no. She said she wouldn't be home until late."

Mya scooted to the edge of the couch. "Did she say why?"

"No, but she sounded winded. I asked her if she was alright, and she said yeah, she was about to be as alright as anyone could possibly get."

"Did you ask what she meant by that?" Mya followed up.

Felix shrugged. "Not really."

Gideon took out his phone. "Could you give me her phone number?"

"Rebecca's number?"

At Gideon's nod, Felix rattled off a phone number. Gideon entered the number on his phone.

"Rebecca was cool, but she always had something going on, you know."

He saw Mya glance at him out of the corner of her eye before she asked, "Something like what?"

Felix's gaze skittered to the front door. "I don't know, really."

Gideon leaned forward, keeping his eyes trained on Felix for several uncomfortable seconds before Felix finally met his gaze. "You must have meant something."

"I don't want to talk bad about the dead."

"Mr. Ucar, I don't know if the police mentioned it, but Rebecca was found in the basement of my house. She may have been a victim of being in the wrong place at the wrong time. If that's the case, my life could be in danger. If you know something that could help us figure out who killed Rebecca, please, you've got to tell us."

Felix sighed. "I don't *know* anything. Not for sure. Rebecca was a nice girl and supersmart, but she wanted more than she was willing to work for—you know what I mean?"

"Not exactly." Mya's expression reflected her confusion. "Rebecca was a really good worker."

"Sure, sure." Felix waved the hand holding the used tissue absently. "But I mean, she was always looking for easy riches, you know. Like she tried selling travel club shares."

His lips twisted with displeasure. Felix clearly didn't think much of Rebecca's career choice.

"What are travel shares?" Mya asked.

Felix rolled his eyes. "I told her it sounded like a pyramid scheme, and like, everybody we know is in school or just graduated. Who has the time or money to travel? But Rebecca just said that was the beauty of it because by pooling our money, we would all save and get to go to cool places."

"I take it the venture wasn't successful."

Felix snorted. "Ah, no. She got the job at your lab not long after. I think she had to buy a bunch of the travel shares to get started with the company, and she needed the job at your lab to pay off the debt."

"Rebecca only worked at the lab part-time. She probably would have made more as a research assistant to a professor on campus."

Felix tilted his head to one side. "They only hire students for those positions."

Gideon stole a glance at Mya before addressing Felix. "Rebecca wasn't a student?"

"I mean, she used to be. That's how we met. I needed a roommate, and she answered an ad I posted in a student's only chat. But I don't think Rebecca finished a whole year. And I know for a fact she wasn't currently enrolled."

"What did she study while she was in school?"

"She was an English major. That's another reason I was surprised she took the job at your lab, but I guess a job is a job. I work at a bakery. I don't even like sweets."

That would explain why Rebecca hadn't known as much about chemistry as Mya had expected. It also raised the question of why she'd been so interested in Mya's research.

"If you're working at a bakery and Rebecca had debts to pay off, how did you two swing that new flat-screen?" Gideon motioned toward the television.

Felix raised a hand as if on a swear. "I didn't afford it. That's all Rebecca."

Gideon's stare hardened on Felix's face. The young man shifted nervously. "Look, when she came home with the new fancy coffee maker at the beginning of the month, I just figured she'd gotten her Christmas bonus early or something."

Gideon glanced at Mya. She shook her head in the negative. If Rebecca had come into some extra money, it hadn't come from her job at the lab.

"But then the TV showed up," Felix continued. "No way a bonus paid for that."

"Did you ask her about it?" Gideon pressed.

"Yeah, I mean, of course." Felix scratched his nose. "She just said not to worry about it. Her exact words were, 'it didn't fall off the back of a truck.' And she laughed."

"And that didn't make you suspicious?"

"Look, I pegged this as a don't ask, don't tell kind of situation. I got to watch a flat-screen instead of the old clunker I got in my room, and Rebecca paid for cable."

Felix had little else to add, and they wrapped up the conversation minutes later.

"Now what?" Mya asked when they were back in the car.

"Now we find out where Rebecca got her influx of cash."

Mya's phone rang.

"It's Brian," she said, answering the phone on speaker. "I'm sorry. I haven't found us a lab space yet. Actually, I don't know when I'll be able to do that. Have you spoken to the police?"

"They called, but I didn't answer. I don't know anything about the fire." Brian's words came out in a rush.

"Brian, I've got some bad news—"

Gideon laid a hand over Mya's. He shook his head when she looked his way. He didn't want her to mention Rebecca's death if Brian didn't already know. Gideon wanted to speak to the man in person and gauge his response.

"Ask him to meet you," he mouthed silently to Mya.

She frowned and spoke into the phone, "Where are you? Can you meet me somewhere now? There's something I need to tell you."

"I—I can't right now." Tension oozed from the voice on the other end of the phone. Brian had been anxious when they'd run into him in the TriGen parking lot earlier that morning, but this was next level.

Gideon couldn't help but wonder what had gotten the man into such a state.

"Meet me at 1:00 p.m. tomorrow at Prospect Park," Brian said.

"Can't you meet sooner? It really is—" The line went dead. "Important," Mya finished to dead air.

"That was strange." Mya tucked her phone back into her purse.

"He's hiding from the police." Gideon guided the Tahoe through the streets toward his house.

"I wouldn't say hiding."

He glanced across the car at her. "I would, and did. You can bet Kamal has been looking for Brian. If he hasn't spoken to the police yet, it's because he doesn't want to. What I want to know is why?"

Mya massaged her temples in the seat next to him. "There's got to be a reasonable explanation."

Gideon worked his jaw. For Brian Leeds's sake, he hoped so.

Chapter Nine

Mya opened her eyes and blinked at the darkness. She'd gone straight to the guest room, pleading exhaustion, when she and Gideon made it back to his house. She'd intended to rest for only a few minutes. But when she rolled to her side, the clock on the bedside table read 7:20. She'd slept for nearly an hour.

Mya stretched and swung her legs over the side of the bed. It was both strange and familiar waking up in Gideon's childhood bedroom. She and Gideon had had hundreds of sleepovers in this room growing up. As a single mother, Francine Rochon had had to work two and sometimes three jobs to keep a roof over their heads and food on the table. Grandma Pearl had stepped up to help, becoming as much of a grandmother to Mya as she was to Gideon—picking both kids up from school, providing dinner, and ensuring homework got done. Grandma Pearl had always waved away the few dollars Francine tried to pay for babysitting saying it was easier to watch two kids than one. But Pearl's heart had so much love inside she couldn't stop it from spilling over onto anyone who came into her orbit. Mya had cried for a full week when Pearl died.

Mya splashed some water on her face and descended

the stairs, the smell of lemon and rosemary beckoning. She'd noted the renovations that Gideon had done on the house earlier, but now she noticed just how much he had changed.

Grandma Pearl's design esthetic had encompassed color, bold prints and eclectic furnishings. Every room had been a different color, and the couches, tables and shelves had been a mishmash of thrift store finds and handed-down antiques. House plants sat on every surface and in every corner. And pictures of Gideon, his father and even one or two of Mya had smiled out from frames in every room. Pearl's home had been awash in life.

Gideon's tastes appeared to run completely counter to his grandmother's. Seemingly every wall in the house was painted a builders' grade gray, designed to be pleasing to the greatest number of people possible. The living room and dining room were showroom perfect without a single painting on the walls or a photograph in sight. It didn't look as if Gideon had ever so much as set foot in either room.

Mya headed for the kitchen expecting to find Gideon there and was surprised to find it empty. The lemon smell led her to the oven where a roasted vegetable medley warmed.

Through the French doors leading onto the patio, she watched a light snowfall leaving a mist of white on the patio table and chairs. Gideon stood in front of a propane grill in a thick black sweater.

He glanced her way, his gaze landing on hers with enough interest that her entire body flushed hot. He hadn't lost his ability to say more with a look than most men could with a thousand words, but she no longer trusted herself to interpret his expressions.

Something intense flared in his eyes—desire? Or was that only wishful thinking?

Gideon had been nothing but professional since she'd shown up uninvited and in a truckload of trouble on his doorstep. And yet, she couldn't help but wonder if, despite everything, this could be the start of a second chance for them. She hadn't known what to say when he'd asked for a divorce years ago, and if she was honest, pride had played a part in not fighting for their marriage after he walked out. But, at this moment, it was clear to her. What she wanted. Gideon.

Something on the grill sizzled violently, drawing Gideon's attention and breaking the moment.

She grabbed the white afghan from the back of the living room couch, and wrapped it around her shoulders before stepping out onto the patio.

"It's freezing out here," she said, taking a half step away from the door.

Gideon shot an amused look over his shoulder. "Then go back inside."

She ignored him. "Can I ask why you're grilling in subzero temperatures?"

"It's not that bad." He turned back to the meat on the grill. "I felt like steak tonight, and the only way to properly cook steak is on a grill."

"There are thousands of restaurants that would disagree with you," Mya answered, pulling the afghan more tightly around her.

Gideon shot another look over his shoulder. "Then there are thousands of restaurants doing it wrong." He clicked the tongs in his hand. "Go back inside. Relax. Meat is almost done. I'll be in in a minute."

Mya frowned. She didn't enjoy being ordered around,

but she wasn't an outdoorsy person under the best of conditions. And freezing temperatures and snow were far from the best of conditions, in her opinion.

She went back inside but ignored Gideon's instruction to relax. She headed for the small wine rack tucked under the countertop island and pulled out a merlot to go with dinner.

She opened cabinets until she found his wineglasses and poured them both a glass.

The French doors opened, and Gideon stepped into the kitchen carrying a covered tray as she carried the glasses to the kitchen table.

"That smells wonderful."

"Exactly. Cooked on a grill." Gideon set the meat on the table and went to the oven for the vegetables while Mya grabbed plates and utensils.

Exhaustion had taken precedence over eating when they'd arrived back at Gideon's, but now she was ravenous. She ate two-thirds of the food on her plate without stopping to utter a word.

"I'll make sure we eat earlier from now on," Gideon said. Having chosen to eat at a much more civilized pace, he still had quite a way to go before making it into the clean plate club.

Embarrassment heated her cheeks. "I'm not sure why I'm so hungry all of a sudden. I'm used to leaving work late and eating even later."

Gideon took a sip of wine before speaking. "You've been through a lot in a short period of time. Your body's been running in part on adrenaline. That takes a lot of energy."

"I guess, but you know, waking up in your old bedroom was the most refreshed I've felt in a long time. I think it's because this house has always been a sanctuary for me. Grandma Pearl always made me feel like I was home when I was here."

Gideon smiled. "There were never any visitors in Grandma Pearl's house. Only family."

"She was a special woman." It had been years since Grandma Pearl passed, but Mya felt a familiar lump growing in her throat. She knew Pearl wouldn't want to be remembered with sadness, so Mya kept her building emotions at bay. "You've made a lot of changes to the house."

Gideon looked around as if he were looking at the space for the first time. "Yeah, Grandma Pearl tended to the big issues, but she didn't see much need for upgrading the interior."

Mya let her gaze flow over the stainless steel and a white-marbled kitchen. "You've definitely changed things."

Gideon frowned. "You don't like it?"

"No, everything is beautiful," she rushed to assure him. And it was. It just lacked personality.

"But…"

"It's not very homey. It looks—" Mya shrugged "— well, it looks like you went to a furniture store, pointed at a couple showrooms and had everything there delivered."

"I don't spend a lot of time at home." He poured more wine into both their glasses, then took a sip.

"No. I guess you never really have." She hated the bitterness in her voice, but she couldn't help it. He'd hurt her deeply when he'd left. Time had softened the edges of that wound, but it hadn't healed completely. She wasn't sure if it ever would.

An awkward silence fell over the table.

She drank a long gulp of wine. Then she figured, since she'd already made things awkward, why not ask the question she'd been dying to have answered?

"I was surprised when my mom told me you'd left the military. I'd thought you were in for the long haul."

He froze, his eyes on the empty plate in front of him. "Things change."

The cool response lit the fuse of frustration in her. Gideon had given her the impression that the military, the multiple tours and his dedication to making a career in the service was the impetus for their divorce. But a little more than a year later, he'd declined to re-enlist. "What things changed?"

Gideon remained silent so long she'd begun to think he wasn't going to answer. Slowly, he raised his gaze to hers. His brown eyes were several shades darker than normal and clouded. "I'd seen too much to stay."

The words hung in the air between them. Mya wasn't sure how to respond.

A moment later, Gideon rose, picked up their plates and carried them to the sink.

An ache drummed in Mya's chest, as much for the pain she'd seen in Gideon's eyes as for what had been lost between them. There was a time when they'd talked to each other about everything and anything. Now, she wasn't sure what to say.

She carried their empty wineglasses to the sink and stood beside Gideon, watching the naked branches of the maple tree sway slightly in the wind.

"You remember when we tried to build a treehouse in that tree?" Mya pointed to the large maple occupying most of the small backyard.

Gideon gazed through the window over the kitchen

sink, a smile on his face. "Of course. I don't know what we were thinking trying to make a treehouse out of what were basically twigs."

"It made perfect sense to our eleven-year-old selves. It's a wonder we didn't break our necks."

"If I remember correctly, you fell out of the tree, and twisted your ankle."

She laughed. "I did. Trying to make a door out of that gigantic piece of wood we found next to the house."

A frown twisted Gideon's lips. "My dad was so mad."

"Your dad?"

Major Garret Wright was an ephemeral presence in Gideon's life, leaving the child-rearing to his mother after his wife passed away.

"He was home on leave. Grandma Pearl was out somewhere, and he was supposed to be watching us, but of course, he wasn't."

Mya shook her head. "I don't remember that. I remember Grandma Pearl fussing and making me fudge brownies."

Gideon's scowl disappeared, replaced by sadness. "There were no fudge brownies for me. The major made me clean the house from top to bottom, and I couldn't watch TV for the rest of the month until he left for duty," Gideon said, referring to his father by his military rank the way he had since they were teens.

Despite all the years that had passed, indignation at Gideon's punishment swelled inside Mya.

"That wasn't fair. Building the treehouse was my idea."

"The major never cared much about fair. As far as he was concerned, I should have known better. It was a man's job to protect the women in their lives, so said the major."

Mya made an indelicate noise. "So, you come by it honestly. But you weren't a man. You were a boy. He was supposed to be watching us."

She reached out, placing her hand on his arm when he moved to step around her. "It doesn't matter now," he said.

"It matters to me."

Mya reached out and cupped his cheek, even as warning bells went off in her brain. She was crossing an emotional boundary with no guarantee she'd be able to turn back if the terrain proved perilous.

Gideon closed his eyes, leaning into her and pressing a soft kiss to her palm.

She stepped closer, rising on her toes to meet his bowed head, and brushed her lips against his.

Gideon wrapped his arms around her, pulling her even closer, and claimed her mouth in a scorching kiss. She parted her lips and deepened the kiss, keeping herself completely in the touch of the man she'd never stopped loving. Would never stop loving.

The evidence of Gideon's desire pressed against her belly. She slid one hand under his sweater, tracing a path up his spine while using the other hand to pull up on the hem.

Gideon wrenched his lips from hers and stepped back. "This can't happen. I need to maintain my focus if I'm going to protect you."

Mya laughed, but the sound was thin and bitter. His rejection stung. She turned her back to him. "You keep telling yourself you're pushing me away for my own good, but you're pushing me away because you're scared. And we both know it."

She turned back to face him, but Gideon was gone.

Chapter Ten

A crisp wind blew in off the man-made lake in the center of Prospect Park. It was unseasonably warm, enticing more people to venture out to the park than Gideon would have liked given the circumstances.

Despite the warm weather, the temperature in his immediate vicinity was glacial. Mya hadn't said more than a few words to him all day. Not that he blamed her. Their kiss last night had been incredible, but completely inappropriate and unprofessional. He'd spent a good chunk of the night kicking himself for having let it happen, although a big part of him hadn't wanted to stop.

He'd even begun to entertain the notion that James might be right about turning Mya's case over to someone else—before discarding the idea. Her safety wasn't something he'd ever trust to someone else. If that meant they'd stroll the park in icy silence, waiting for Brian Leeds, so be it.

Gideon caught a flash of red in his peripheral vision and tensed, ready for attack. Seconds later a spandex-clad man with thinning hair and earbuds rounded the curve. The jogger passed without a glance in their direction.

Mya strolled next to him, her arm hooked around him,

her body tucked into his side. They looked like lovers out for a stroll, exactly the impression he'd intended in case anyone watched.

This wasn't the time for introspection. Several of his colleagues had been strategically deployed in and around the park, their job to keep an eye out for Leeds and anyone else who might pose a threat to Mya. Gideon's job was to be her first line of protection. He had to focus on that.

They'd arrived at the park ten minutes before ten and begun their leisurely stroll around the lake. It was now five after ten, and there was no sign of Leeds.

The knot that had been in his solar plexus since waking this morning tightened. He didn't like the feel of this.

He'd tried to talk Mya into letting him meet Leeds alone, but she'd categorically rejected the idea.

She'd pointed out that Leeds would be expecting her and that he was unlikely to talk to Gideon, who was a stranger to him.

He'd countered that he was very good at getting people who didn't want to talk to him to do so. And Mya had responded that Leeds wasn't some shady criminal that Gideon had plucked from the street.

He'd only grunted in response to that argument. Leeds could very well be a criminal for all they knew. He was clearly involved with whatever was going on or knew something about it. Why else would he insist on this clandestine meeting in the park?

Mya had only narrowed her eyes and said, "I'm going."

It had been a long time since they'd parried back and forth. He'd forgotten what it was like. And how often it was fruitless. He may have been the hard-nosed marine, but Mya always seemed to get what she wanted.

"Any sign of him?" Gideon asked, seemingly to no one in particular. The earpiece he wore was all but invisible.

"Negative," Tessa answered from her perch in the small parking lot that abutted the park.

"Negative," James said.

Gideon and Mya had already walked past James twice. He sat on a bench on the opposite side of the lake, an open book in hand.

Although he was a West, West Security and Investigations, James had only been working at the firm since leaving the marines six months earlier. Still, Gideon was confident that nothing going on in the park at the moment had escaped James's keen eye.

And Gideon was glad for it. There were more people out at the park than he'd expected on a December morning.

He let his gaze skip over the people. A man and a woman, not a couple though, at least not anymore, sitting at one of four picnic tables, their hands wrapped around take-out coffee cups. A man stood at the lake's edge, staring out over the water. Another in an expensive wool overcoat, walking along the gravel path, his eyes glued to his cell phone. A woman with stocking-clad legs stuck into heavy boots and an oversize handbag bouncing against her hip strode purposefully toward the park entrance.

Gideon let his gaze linger on the male pedestrians a bit longer than the others. He knew better than to dismiss the women out of hand, but statistically, you were more likely to be attacked by a man than a woman.

Gideon glanced at Mya. She pointedly avoided looking at him, although he was sure she could feel his gaze on her. They'd always been in tune with each other, and nothing over the last two days suggested that bond had been broken by time—quite the opposite, much to his consternation.

He knew she was angry with him. More than that, he'd hurt her. He hadn't been trying to. That was the last thing he'd wanted. It was why he'd insisted on letting her go, but regardless of his intentions, he had.

Mya's gaze rolled over the lake, the nearby flower garden, the curve in the jogging path, and the children's playground before starting all over again.

They passed James for the third time, and the knot in Gideon's stomach tightened.

"I don't like this. I think I should get Mya out of here."

Mya looked at him now, although the look in her eye wasn't one he liked to see there. "I'm fine. He's only ten minutes late. Maybe he hit traffic. Let's give him a little more time."

Gideon knew James and Tessa had heard them, but neither responded.

He'd give Leeds one more stroll around the lake, and then he'd throw Mya over his shoulder and carry her from the park if he had to. Ignoring his gut was something he'd learned better than to do. In his line of work, listening to his gut had saved him more than once, and he wasn't about to start ignoring it when Mya's life was on the line.

They strolled past the large gazebo that stood at one end of the oblong lake and began the final one-eighty.

A gust of wind sent a ripple over the lake's surface. The water shimmered under the sun's rays.

Gideon glanced at his watch. Fifteen minutes late. Even if there had been traffic, Leeds should have been here by now. He was putting a lid on this when they reached the path, whether Mya liked it or not.

Laughter rose from the playground as they passed, then gave way to the wail of a screaming baby. A harried-looking brunette hustled over to a nearby stroller and lifted the squalling baby to her shoulder. Clad in a yellow snowsuit, Gideon couldn't tell if the kid was male or female. The wailing receded, and the mother turned her attention back toward the children playing on the nearby jungle gym.

"It's time to call—"

Gideon fell silent when Mya squeezed his arm. "That's him. That's Brian."

Leeds hurried along the gravel path toward them. There was no relief at the man's arrival. If anything, the man's ragged appearance set Gideon's instincts on edge. His coat flapped open, his reddish-brown hair looked as if he'd been pulling on it, and he sported a five o'clock shadow.

"Look alive, gang," Gideon mumbled, knowing James and Tessa would hear him. West's equipment was top-of-the-line.

"Damn. He must have parked on the street." Tessa's voice came through the earpiece along with a rustle of fabric and the sound of a car door slamming closed. "I'm on my way into the park via the north entrance."

Leeds's gaze landed on Mya and his body straightened a fraction, his step quickening. Then he noticed Gideon. He hesitated but continued his march in their direction.

Leeds drew to a stop about six feet in front of them.

"Why is he here? I would have thought it went without saying that you should come alone, Mya."

"She goes nowhere alone," Gideon barked.

Mya shot him a glare. "This is Gideon Wright. He's a friend in personal security services."

Leeds's face registered surprise. "A bodyguard?" He nodded. "You really are smart. I wish I had a friend like him."

"What do you mean, Brian? What is going on?"

Leeds ran a hand through his hair. "Oh, God. I don't know where to start. I didn't know. Not at first."

Gideon didn't like how twitchy Leeds was. Or how out in the open they were, standing not far from the flower garden entrance. "Why don't you come back to my office and you can explain it to us?"

"I'm not going anywhere with you." Leeds shook his head. Gideon noted the man's hands trembled. Brian Leeds was terrified.

Gideon caught sight of Tessa heading for them out of the corner of his eye. He gave the slightest shake of his head, and she strolled past.

"You have to understand something," Leeds pleaded. "I'd been working with Irwin for a long time before you came along, Mya. Irwin wasn't just my boss. I thought of him as a mentor and friend."

"I do understand," Mya said, taking Leeds's hand. "Irwin was the same for me."

"Yes and no," Leeds continued. "Irwin was your mentor, but it became clear early on you were the heir apparent. Even though I put in all those years working with him before you came along," Leeds spat before drawing in a deep breath. "Look, I get why Irwin chose you to succeed him as director of the lab. I'd have been miserable at glad-handing donors and investors. But it wasn't easy to be passed over like that."

"What did you do?" Normally, he wouldn't interrupt a suspect in the midst of giving a confession, but someone was targeting Mya, and they were sitting ducks standing out in the open like this.

Leeds shot a glare his way, then pointedly looked back at Mya, ignoring Gideon. "Irwin asked me to keep him informed on our research. I know he wasn't technically part of the team anymore, but I didn't see the harm."

Mya dropped Leeds's hand. "The harm is that doing so breaks the confidentiality clause in your contract and puts our research in jeopardy."

Leeds's face reddened, but he didn't back down. "Irwin knew most of it, anyway. He figured out the first two parts of the formula."

"So, you talked to Irwin Ross about Mya's progress. How much did you tell Ross?" Gideon asked, impatiently.

"All of it. I sent him copies of our most recent research results," Leeds said. "There's something else I have to tell you."

"What else?" Gideon pressed. That Leeds shared information with Ross couldn't be the big secret that Leeds wouldn't share over the phone.

Something Leeds said moments earlier tugged at Gideon. *I didn't know. Not at first.*

Didn't know what? Leeds had to have known that he was sharing confidential information with Ross, so what had he been referring to?

Gideon studied Leeds. "What did you mean when you said, 'you didn't—'" He didn't finish the question.

A motorcycle engine revved loudly. Too loudly. Someone appeared to have missed the large sign posted at the entrance declaring vehicles were prohibited in the park.

A black Suzuki tore a path from the entrance toward where they stood.

Ice-cold panic rose in Gideon's chest. The driver was headed straight for them and accelerating fast.

The driver's right hand rose. Sunlight glinted off the silver gun he held.

"Gun!" Gideon screamed.

A loud crack wrenched the air.

Leeds's eyes clouded with confusion. Blood blossomed across the white sweater visible beneath his open coat. A fraction of a second later, another crack sounded, and Leeds jerked backward, his body freezing in place for a long moment before falling to the ground. There was no question he was dead. Open eyes stared up at the sun, a bullet hole between them.

Gideon curled his body around Mya's and propelled them both forward toward the thicket of trees that lined the nearby flower garden entrance.

Another loud crack split the air, followed almost immediately by a child's scream.

Dear God, no.

A second crack sounded, sending bark from the tree he'd just pushed Mya behind sailing past his face.

"Stay down!"

Mya's entire body shook, but she nodded.

He poked his head around the tree's trunk in time to see the biker plant one foot on the ground and turn the bike abruptly. Gravel flew as the driver gunned the bike back toward the park's entrance.

James rounded the curve of the lake, running full-out, but there was no hope of him catching a Suzuki on foot.

"Don't move," Gideon called to Mya and stepped out from behind the tree, sweeping his gun in front of him.

The park was chaos. Mothers huddled with their children behind the playground equipment, the kids' cries tearing a hole through the panicked adults and calls made to 911.

He noticed Tessa at the playground area, scanning the occupants for injury. The play area was some distance away, and he could only hope that none of the bullets had traveled that far.

Leeds was beyond hope, unfortunately. Gideon went to his knees beside the body and felt for a pulse he knew wouldn't be there.

"I've got a lot of terrified moms and kiddos, but no injuries here," Tessa said.

"I'm on my way back," James said. "Lost the biker when he gunned it through a red light. I've already called it into the police, but they won't find the guy."

That went without saying. Whoever had killed Brian Leeds and tried to kill Mya had known what they were doing.

And they'd keep trying until they got it right.

Chapter Eleven

The first officers on scene secured the park and had all the witnesses or those who'd stuck around at least corralled in the park grounds keeper's offices. Mya had felt Detective Kamal's gaze homed in on her the moment the detective arrived. The look in the detective's eyes was withering. It had been more than an hour since the detective had taken Mya's statement, but Kamal had asked them to stick around in case she had further questions.

Now Mya and Gideon waited, the delay rustling nerves. Several of the witnesses detained had begun to complain to the officers assigned to watch over them.

Mya watched through the window as Detective Kamal exited through the park gates and headed toward the office. She was intercepted by a tall, slender man who Mya could tell was a cop simply from the way he carried himself. The man and Detective Kamal exchanged a few words, then the man turned on his heel and strode away.

Gideon rose as Kamal approached, and Mya followed suit.

"I appreciate your patience," Kamal said, coming to a stop in front of them and flipping her notepad to a clean page. "We've got quite a mess here."

"My colleague and friend was killed right in front of me."

Detective Kamal lifted her eyes from the notepad and met Mya's hard stare. A long moment of silence passed between the two women.

"Of course. I didn't mean to give the impression I was making light of the situation. It is a very serious, which is why I'd like to ask you—" Detective Kamal's gaze turned on Gideon "—and Mr. Wright a few more questions."

Mya felt Gideon's already taut body tense even more beside her. "We've already told you everything we know."

"Bear with me for just a little longer," Kamal answered, though she'd already shifted her gaze to Mya. "Now, you said Mr. Leeds called you yesterday and asked you to meet him in the park? He had something important to tell you about the fire at your lab and the theft of your research, correct?"

Mya nodded. "Brian didn't say what he had to tell me when he called, but of course, I suspected whatever he wanted to say had to do with the lab."

Detective Kamal flipped a few pages. "And he got to the park and told you he'd been sharing your research with…" Detective Kamal flipped another page.

"Irwin Ross. He's the prior director of the lab."

"Right, Mr. Ross. And he devised the first part of the formula that's now missing."

"Yes."

"So, the three of you are talking. West has two more operatives milling around." Detective Kamal gestured vaguely to where James and Tessa stood talking a few feet away. "Suddenly, a motorcycle comes barreling into the park, and the driver shoots, and Mr. Leeds is dead."

"That's what happened," Gideon said, impatience ringing in his words.

Mya fought the urge to sigh. They'd been over this already. "I know it sounds strange, Detective, but I'm sure the other witnesses have confirmed it's the truth."

Detective Kamal scratched behind her ear. "Oh, they have, more or less. Everyone saw something slightly different, but that's to be expected."

"So why are we still here?" Gideon nearly growled.

"Well, Miss Rochon said it. Strange that in the last two days, everyone involved with TriGen Labs has been killed. Everyone except you, Miss Rochon. Any thoughts about that?"

Maya felt her jaw clench. "Your premise is faulty, Detective. Everyone involved with the lab has not been killed. We have investors, board members—"

Kamal interrupted. "Yes, but of the lab's current active employees, you are the only one remaining."

"What are you getting at?" Gideon said.

They all knew exactly what Kamal was hinting at. Whatever was going on clearly had something to do with the research they'd been doing at TriGen. The lab was the only thing Brian and Rebecca had in common. Mya was the last woman standing. She knew that alone made her the prime suspect.

"I had nothing to do with Rebecca's or Brian's deaths, the destruction of my lab or the theft of my research. You said yourself the other witnesses in the park this morning confirmed what Gideon and I have already told you. The man on the bike shot at Gideon and me, as well."

The detective's lips twisted. "You could have hired

someone. I can't help noting how good a shot this man on a bike was when it came to shooting Mr. Leeds, but that he missed both you and Mr. Wright. Fortuitous for you two, wouldn't you say?" Kamal's gaze bore into Mya. "As for the call between you and Mr. Leeds, I have only your word that Mr. Leeds set up this meeting today."

"You have my word too. I was in the car, and Mya had the phone on speaker."

"And I've let you look at my recent call log. You can see Brian called me."

Kamal cocked an eyebrow. "Yes, but that's all the log tells me. It doesn't tell me what was said or who said it. And frankly, Mr. Wright, the word of an ex-husband who acts more like a current husband won't get Miss Rochon very far."

Gideon's already steely gaze hardened on the detective.

"I've made some inquiries about you and your research," the detective carried on. "Not everyone believes your formula is the breakthrough you've held it out to be."

Anxiety knotted Mya's stomach. The scientific community wasn't immune to gossip and jealousy. She'd heard the nasty rumors and had ignored them, knowing her research would speak for itself. Apparently, Detective Kamal didn't feel the same way.

"In fact, some people think you're fabricating the whole thing."

Mya fisted her gloved hands. "Some people? I thought the police dealt in facts? The fact is that I can prove my formula works, so it doesn't matter what anyone thinks."

One of Detective Kamal's eyebrows rose. "Only you

can't prove that without the first part of the formula and research, now can you, Miss Rochon?"

"What are you getting at, Detective?" Gideon growled.

Detective Kamal ignored Gideon's question. She pulled her phone from her pocket and tapped the screen three times. "Do you recognize this piece of paper, Miss Rochon?"

The detective turned the phone around and held it out toward Mya. Gideon leaned into her so he could see, as well.

The photograph on the screen showed a scrap of paper, one ragged edge torn. Mya didn't recognize the piece of paper, but she recognized the five numbers scrawled on it.

She looked up at Gideon, knowing that her face reflected the shock she felt. "Those numbers. That's the code to open my garage door."

Gideon's jaw tightened.

Mya swung her gaze to Detective Kamal. The detective tucked the phone back in her pocket, a frown curving her lips. "We found that piece of paper under Rebecca Conway's body. You want to tell me how she got the code to get into your house?"

Mya was almost too stunned to speak. "I—I don't know. I never shared it with her."

"Never? Never sent Miss Conway to pick something up from your house? Store something in your garage?"

"No. Rebecca was the lab's receptionist. Not my personal assistant, Detective."

"What is it you're trying to say, detective?" Gideon interjected.

Kamal glared. "We will look into it, but in my experience, the most obvious answer is usually the correct answer."

"And what do you see as the most obvious answer in this situation?" Gideon countered.

Detective Kamal flipped her notebook closed and turned to Mya. "You can see how this looks from my perspective, Miss Rochon. You supposedly find a miracle cure, one that no one has seen and several knowledgeable people believe to be bogus, only to have a significant portion of the research that would prove it stolen, your lab destroyed and both of the people who you work with killed all within forty-eight hours."

Mya's hands went to her hips. "Are you accusing me of something, Detective?"

Gideon dropped a hand on her shoulder, angling his body so he was slightly in front of her. "We've answered all your questions and there's nothing more we can help you with right now."

Detective Kamal's gaze narrowed until Mya felt as if she was caged, something she had no doubt Kamal would like to see. It was clear the detective thought she was responsible for everything. The lab fire, the theft and Brian's and Rebecca's deaths.

After a long minute, Detective Kamal spoke. "You can go. But don't go far. I will be seeing you soon, Miss Rochon."

Chapter Twelve

"What the hell happened?" Ryan West's voice carried through the speakerphone in the center of the conference room table. Although he was still technically on a one-month paternity leave, there was no way they could not brief the head of West Investigations on a murder and the attempted murder of a West client, both of which had occurred in the presence of three West employees. Predictably, Ryan had not been happy to hear about the situation.

Gideon slid his chair closer to Mya's. He hadn't let her out of his sight since leaving the park. The urge to wrap his body around her like a coat of armor was nearly overwhelming. Even now, fear of what could have happened roiled his stomach and sent bile into the back of his throat. He'd been over the events of the morning a hundred times in his head. If Mya had been shot, if he'd lost her out there at that park today... The thought squeezed around his chest like a vise, stealing his breath.

"How did the shooter know Brian and Mya would be at the park at that time?" James's voice pulled Gideon's attention back to the conversation at hand.

"The shooter must have followed Brian to the park." West's IT people had done a thorough scan on Mya's laptop and cell phone looking for bugs and tracking apps and had found nothing. He'd driven Mya to the park in his Tahoe and knew the SUV wasn't bugged and that they hadn't been followed.

Mya and Leeds's meeting provided the perfect opportunity to get to both remaining TriGen employees at the same time.

Gideon glanced at Mya.

And it had almost worked.

"It seems clear to me that whatever is going on here has to do with Miss Rochon's research. Someone wants the people who have worked on that project gone."

Gideon studied Mya, concern racing through him when he saw the grayish pallor of her face. She hadn't said much since leaving the park, and he found he wasn't as good at reading her as he used to be. Was she worried that her faith in him and West to keep her safe had been misplaced? She'd come close, too damn close, to being shot this morning. And that was on him.

"The question is why? I mean, obviously, your formula is worth a great deal," Tessa said, turning to Mya, "but wouldn't anyone who just miraculously appeared with it be outing themselves as a thief?"

Mya shook her head slowly. "Not necessarily. Ours isn't the only lab working on this kind of research. Someone with the right knowledge could use what Irwin and I have already done to recreate the research and formula. It would be nearly impossible to prove they hadn't come up with it legitimately."

"Who else is doing similar research?" Gideon asked.

Mya gave them the names of two labs, and James made a note. "I'll get started looking into these labs and their employees."

"You should also look at Nobel Pharmaceuticals and Shannon Travers." Disapproval oozed from Mya's words.

A corner of Tessa's mouth hooked up. "I take it you don't care for Ms. Travers or Nobel Pharmaceuticals."

"Nobel is one of the leading pharma companies in the Northeast. Shannon leads the research and development division."

"Not really an answer to my question." Tessa pointed the pen in her hand at Mya.

Mya frowned. "We were in the same PhD program and often in competition."

Gideon noted that she still hadn't answered Tessa's question and he knew that Tessa had noted it, as well.

"She's impressive," James said, reading from the laptop screen in front of him. "Thirty-nine and already the vice president of development at Nobel. I've got a couple of glowing articles here about her brilliance and her meteoric rise."

"Probably the work of Nobel's marketing department." Mya stood and braced her hands against the back of her chair. "Shannon is a viper whose achievements come in part from having flexible ethics and very little shame." The discussion had put the color back in Mya's face, alleviating some of Gideon's immediate concern for her. But it had also raised an obvious question.

"Do you think her ethics are flexible enough that she'd kill to keep you from getting to a cure before Nobel?"

Mya cocked her head, a thoughtful expression covering her face. "I know Nobel is also working on a treatment for glioblastoma. From what I've heard through the grapevine, they might be pretty close." The expression on her face darkened. "I hate to say it but Shannon…there's nothing she wouldn't do to advance her own interests."

"But someone clearly is—" Gideon watched Mya's eyes widen with alarm. He rose to face her. "What is it?"

"I just realized that I'm not the only one still alive who worked for TriGen. Irwin." The fear in Mya's eyes was searing. "He doesn't work for TriGen anymore, but he developed the first two parts of the formula."

Gideon understood where she was going with the line of thought. "And Leeds admitted he'd been keeping him in the loop since you took over. Ross could be in danger."

"Irwin lives off the grid now. His cabin isn't easy to get to."

"You should warn him. Just to be safe."

Mya reached under the table for her purse. "I'll call him now."

Gideon watched her grab her phone and retreat to the corner of the conference room to make the call. He was glad she hadn't stepped out of the room. Even though they were in West's offices with a dozen of the best trained private investigators and bodyguards in the business, he didn't want Mya out of his reach.

James turned to Gideon. "How do you want to handle this?"

Gideon pulled his gaze from Mya. "Whoever is after this formula has to have the ability to confirm it works or have someone on tap who is able to do so. That makes the list of people Mya gave us our best bet."

"I've got more information on Rebecca Conway's background. She looks like your typical struggling early twenty-something—" Tessa's brow went up "—if you don't look too closely, which of course I did."

Gideon felt his heartbeat speed up. "What did you find?"

"Rebecca Conway, resident of Sarasota, Florida. She works at Walmart and still lives with her parents."

The wrinkles on James's forehead deepened. "A job at Walmart? Are you sure you have the correct person?"

Tessa shot a disgruntled look across the table at James.

"Did you get Ross?" Gideon queried Mya as she sat next to him.

She shook her head. "It's not that easy. Irwin doesn't actually have a phone. I have to call the general store and leave a message for him with the owner. He usually passes on the message when Irwin comes in for supplies, but I stressed that it was important and Phil Gatling, the manager, said he'd drop by Irwin's cabin on the way home tonight and give him the message."

Gideon beat back his irritation at the inefficiency of such a system. "So, it will be tomorrow at least before you hear from Ross."

"Hopefully." Mya smiled wearily. "Irwin is kind of quirky."

"You mentioned that before." Tessa twisted the plastic top off the diet cola she'd carried into the room with her. "What did you mean?"

"Irwin has had to face a lot in his life. He started medical school in his thirties after he already had a wife and two sons. While he was in school, his oldest son was diagnosed with glioblastoma. There wasn't much that could be done. Of course, we hadn't yet met back then, but that was a defining incident for Irwin. I mean, it would be for anyone. I know his marriage fell apart, and he rarely saw his younger son. I think the son developed a drug habit as a teen and served some time in prison. Irwin pretty much dedicated the rest of his life to finding a treatment and cure."

"Why did he retire then?" Gideon asked.

Mya sighed. "It was framed as a retirement, but the

investors and the nonprofit that provides the bulk of our funding pushed him out. Irwin was never great with keeping the investors up-to-date and dealing with the glad-handing part of running the lab." Mya looked down at the table. "He pushed a lot of that stuff off on me."

So, at some point, the investors realized they had two geniuses working for them and didn't need to put up with a mad scientist at the helm. Mya didn't say as much, but the guilt swimming in her eyes spoke volumes.

"What do you know about Rebecca Conway?" Gideon asked, changing the subject back to Rebecca.

Mya looked surprised. "Just what I've already told you and what her roommate told both of us yesterday."

"Did you do a background check on her before she started working for you?"

Mya's chin went up. "Of course. It's TriGen's policy. Brian handled her paperwork, but she must have checked out."

"Whoever set up the alias did a good job. A standard check wouldn't have aroused suspicion," Tessa said.

James nodded. "That's probably why Detective Kamal hasn't mentioned it."

"Or she knows and is too focused on Mya to look into it."

James's brow shot up at the note of bitterness in Gideon's tone.

West worked with local law enforcement frequently, and the investigators were encouraged to maintain professional relationships with the officers they came in contact with despite their sometimes conflicting interests.

But Gideon couldn't help it. He not only didn't like Detective Kamal, but he also didn't trust her.

"Regardless, we should let the cops know about Rebecca," James said.

Mya leaned forward, her gaze sweeping among the three people at the table. "What a minute. What are you three talking about?"

"It appears your receptionist wasn't who she said she was." Tessa looked pointedly at James. "Most of what pops on her background is actually the history for a twenty-one-year-old Rebecca Conway who lives in Sarasota. I could only confirm the existence of your Rebecca Conway going back eight months or so."

"A month before she came to work for TriGen," Gideon said, not at all liking where this seemed to be heading.

Mya looked shocked. "That can't be. Brian said she was a friend of a friend. He knows her." Mya paused. "Knew her," she added softly.

"Do you know how long he'd known Rebecca before she came to work for you?" Tessa queried.

Mya shook her head. "No. I don't think I ever asked."

"Then he could have been taken in by Rebecca's ruse too."

"Or," James said pointedly, "we know Leeds was keeping things from Mya. Maybe this is another one of those things."

Mya dropped her head into her hands. "None of this makes any sense. It was dishonest of Brian to break confidentiality and talk to Irwin behind my back, but he had no reason to lie about Rebecca."

"Like I said, maybe he didn't," Tessa offered. "But the quality of the alias suggests Rebecca either was a pro or was working with one."

"A pro?" Mya's face telegraphed her confusion.

"A professional con artist," Gideon clarified. "We need to get to the bottom of it. Tessa, keep digging into Rebecca's background and start looking into Brian. Where did the two connect? Did they have contact outside of work? Do they have any friends, family or acquaintances in common? You know the drill."

"I'll get started on trying to figure out who our shooter is," James said. "I've got a friend at the transportation authority that owes me a favor. Maybe a traffic camera got a shot of the bike's license plate."

"What do you plan to do?" James directed the question to Gideon, but he ignored James for the moment.

He turned in his chair to face Mya. "Kamal implied that you've orchestrated all this as a way to hide the fact that your research is a failure."

Mya's lips flattened into a tight line. "You can't possibly believe—"

"I don't, not for a minute." And he didn't, but that didn't mean others didn't believe just that. "But we need to figure out what Brian wouldn't tell us."

Mya eyed him curiously. "How are we supposed to do that?"

He could think of one way, but Mya wasn't going to like it.

Chapter Thirteen

"So, let me make sure I understand this. You're planning on breaking into Brian's house, but I am forbidden," Mya practically spat the word, "from going with you?" She couldn't believe he'd actually used the word *forbidden* like she was a misbehaving child.

She wasn't even sure she wanted to go with Gideon on this particular outing. Watching Brian get shot, and being shot at herself, had shaken her more than she was willing to admit. But she hadn't made it to where she was by letting anyone tell her what she could and couldn't do. She wasn't about to start now.

"Gideon's visit to Leeds's place isn't exactly above-board. It's best to keep you out of it."

Mya shot a quelling glance at Tessa. "I'm aware breaking and entering is illegal."

"Which is why it's best if you stay here," Gideon growled.

Mya took a step toward him and pinned him with a look. "Just in case you get caught?" she said.

"I won't get caught. I know how to get in and out of a space without leaving a trace."

Mya smiled, clapping her hands together. "Great. Then I'll just do whatever you do, and I should be fine."

Gideon's voice dropped low, almost menacing, but she recognized the fear in his tone. "You need to stay out of this."

"Whether I stay here or not, I am in this, whatever it is. Someone is trying to kill me. Has killed two people close to me and stolen my life's work. So, I am very much in this."

They stood, locked in a hard stare, a battle of wills, for a long minute.

"You follow my lead. Without question," Gideon said through clenched teeth.

It was dark by the time they left West's offices. The drive to Brian's was tense. Gideon was upset with her for insisting on coming with him. She knew the safest thing would be for her to hole up in one of West's safe houses and let Gideon track down the person or people behind whatever was going on. But she just couldn't do it. She had spent the last seven years of her life developing this treatment. Nobody cared about getting it back more than she did.

Gideon parked on the street adjacent to Brian's house and turned to Mya. "I didn't see any cops, but that doesn't mean much. I'm sure they've already been here and searched."

Mya frowned. "Wouldn't they have already taken anything that might lead them to Brian's killer, then?"

Gideon's eyes roamed over the quiet street. "Anything obvious, yes."

"But we're looking for things that aren't obvious?"

"Yes," he said, looking at her. "Kamal is looking for evidence that will lead her to a killer because she doesn't believe your research has been stolen."

There was a lot Mya could say to that, but she just pressed her lips together and let Gideon go on.

"We are looking for evidence of a theft," Gideon finished.

"Under the assumption that finding whoever stole my research is the killer," Mya said in understanding. "I get it."

"Good. Let's go. The longer we sit here, the more likely someone sees us." Gideon's eyes searched the street through the windshield again. "We go in, see if we can find anything that would shed some light in your situation and head out. Agreed?"

"Agreed."

"Put your gloves on and keep them on until we're back in the car." Mya did as told. "When we're inside, try to touch as little as possible."

They got out of the car, and Gideon put his arm around her shoulders. He leaned his head in close as they made their way down the sidewalk. The warmth from his body stole over her and her heart gave an involuntarily jolt.

"Keep your head down. Hopefully, if anyone sees us, they'll just think we're a couple out for an evening walk."

Mya did as he asked, and they walked quickly, though not fast enough to draw attention to themselves.

Blow-up Santa Clauses and candy cane lights decorated many of the front laws on the street. Several of Brian's neighbors had gone all out, stringing lights from their houses and trees.

A light glowed on the main level of the house to the right of Brian's home, illuminating two teens. Neither of them looked away from the television as she and Gideon passed.

Brian lived in a modest two-story home. A green un-adorned wreath on the front door was the only acknowl-edgment of the season.

Gideon picked the locks on the front door quickly and let Mya slide by him into the house. Even though the sun had set more than an hour earlier, it still took a moment for her eyes to adjust to the complete darkness inside the house. The blinds on the windows were all the way down, making it impossible for anyone outside to see inside the house. That was good for their purposes.

"Don't turn on the lights. We don't want to attract at-tention." Gideon turned on a small pin light and swept it over the space. There wasn't much to see. The house was laid out in shotgun style, the living room leading to the dining room leading into the kitchen. From the front door, they could see into each of the three rooms.

"Where do we start looking?"

"You take the sideboard in the dining room, and I'll search the living room."

They both went to work, but it took only a couple of minutes to determine there was nothing of value to be found.

"Upstairs?" Mya whispered, pointing to the ceiling. Gideon nodded. They split off at the top of the stairs, Gideon moving left and her taking the room to the right.

Brian's bedroom, as it turned out. It felt invasive to be searching his bedroom, even though she knew he'd never return. She pushed away the awkwardness. If there was something here that could help them find out who'd done this, they needed to try.

The blinds had also been pulled low in the room, but enough moonlight filtered around the sides that she could make out the items in the room. The furnishings were modest, a queen-sized bed, matching bureau and nightstand. The attached bathroom was small but clean.

Mya started with the closet, but except for some questionable sweater choices found nothing of note.

She moved to the nightstand next, her eyes falling on the framed photo facing the bed. Rebecca and Brian gazed at each other in obvious affection.

"Gideon, come look at this," Mya hissed. Remembering his admonishment to touch as little as possible, she pulled her phone from her pocket and snapped a photograph.

"What is it?"

Mya pointed to the photograph. "It's Rebecca and Brian."

Gideon studied the picture. "You didn't know they were dating?"

"No. Neither of them said anything to me, and I never noticed anything other than professionalism between them."

Gideon motioned for her to follow him across the hall. "There's something off about this room."

A double bed pressed against one wall while a desk faced the adjacent wall. Nothing stood out as amiss to her. "What's strange about it?"

Gideon pointed his flashlight at the floor. "Look at the windows."

The plastic blinds on the two windows in the room were only halfway down, allowing a glimpse of the siding on the neighboring house through one window and Brian's backyard through the other. One of the room's windows was also dressed with a single blue-and-white curtain. It took only a moment for Mya to understand what Gideon found unusual.

"That is kind of weird. Why hang a curtain on the window that looks out onto a wall but not any of the others? And in the guest room but not in the master bedroom."

Gideon went to the window, staying out of the direct line of sight. He ran his hand over the satin material, starting from the top and working his way down until he was on his knees. "There's something here."

Mya joined him at the window, making sure to stay to the sides so she wouldn't be seen, just as he'd done. She watched as Gideon worked two fingers between several popped stitches at the bottom of the curtain and pulled out a piece of paper that had been folded into a small square.

"A postal receipt." He held the paper out. "The package dimensions are about right for sending a packet of papers without folding or bending them. Could be the receipt for sending your research to Irwin."

Dim light from the streetlamp outside the window illuminated the paper enough that she could read the writing.

Mya shook her head. "That's not Irwin's address."

The line where the recipient's name was supposed to go was empty, but the address was in New Jersey, not that far from where they were now. She didn't recognize the address, but she recognized the handwriting.

She gripped Gideon's bicep. "Gideon, Brian didn't write this. This is Rebecca's handwriting."

He frowned. "Why was it hidden in Brian's curtains?"

"Maybe Rebecca hid it there?" Mya said, but that explanation didn't feel like the right one.

"It's more likely Brian hid it there. If you're right

about him and Rebecca being in a relationship, he could have discovered it while he was with her."

"But why take it?"

"Maybe he recognized the address," Gideon answered.

"We need to know whose address that is, and what Rebecca sent." Mya looked up from the paper in Gideon's hands.

His dark eyes bore into hers. The soft light filtering in from the windows cut across Gideon's chiseled jaw. She ached to touch him. They stood close enough that she'd only have to tilt her head upward to meet his lips.

She pursed her lips.

Gideon dipped his head.

A car door slammed outside the window.

Gideon put his index finger against his lips. They pressed their backs to the wall next to the window. Mya tightened her grip on his arm. He leaned forward to peer out the window, a move she mimicked, ignoring the sharp look he sent her.

A uniformed police officer strode to the front door of the house. He pounded on the door, then tried the lock.

Her heart pounded so loudly she was sure the cop could hear it from outside.

She saw the beam of his flashlight fanning over the lawn before he rounded the side of the house.

"What do we do?"

"Sit tight. Someone might have reported seeing a light inside or hearing something, but it's more likely he's just making sure the place is secure."

They stayed frozen next to the window for what seemed like an eternity. The officer finally reappeared at the front of the house and headed back to his car. After a quick glance back at the house, the police cruiser pulled away from the curb.

Gideon grabbed her hand. "Time to go."

They hustled down the staircase, but when Mya turned toward the front door, Gideon pulled her gently toward the back.

"We can't be sure he isn't waiting farther down the street to see if someone comes out. We'll cut through the backyard."

They let themselves out through the back door and stole through the neighbor's yard. They were lucky the complex appeared to be one that didn't allow fences, but that also increased the odds that someone would see them.

They made it to the car without being stopped. Gideon circled the block.

"Looks like you were right," Mya said as they passed Brian's street. The police cruiser was parked several houses down on the opposite side of the street from the house, the officer they'd seen visible behind the wheel.

Mya held her breath as they passed, but the officer's gaze was fixed on Brian's front door. He didn't so much as spare the passing SUV a glance.

"Where to next?" she asked.

"My place. I want to do some research. See if we can't connect that address to a name."

"I can't believe Brian and Rebecca were betraying my trust and I didn't even suspect." Betrayal ripped through Mya's chest. Gideon reached across the car's console and squeezed her hand. "We don't know anything for sure. Let's get home, share what we found with the team and go from there, okay."

She returned his squeeze, her smile tight. He made it sound easy, but she knew in her gut whatever was going on was much more complicated than they realized.

Chapter Fourteen

Gideon spent the drive back to his place silently berating himself for having taken Mya with him to search Leeds's home. If the officer had decided to check inside the house or if there had been a second cruiser watching the back door, they'd be in jail right now. And it would be damn hard to protect Mya if he was locked up. Not that he was doing a great job of it, anyway.

As soon as they got back to his place, he'd lay down the law. The best way, maybe the only way, he could ensure she was protected was to set her up in one of West's safe houses, and that was just what he was going to do. Even if he had to lock her inside.

Gideon glanced at her in the passenger seat. After an initial rush of words that he attributed to adrenaline, she'd fallen silent. Although she still seemed to read his moods fairly well after twelve years apart, he was rusty on reading hers. He couldn't tell if this was an exhausted silence or one that was going to come back to bite him.

He'd barely closed the door before he got his answer.

"What's wrong with you?" Mya tossed her coat over the banister and plunked her fists on her hips, and glared at him.

He took off his jacket and turned his back to her to

place it on the coat rack by the door. "There's nothing wrong with me."

"The hell there isn't. You brooded all the way home."

Mya's reference to his place as home plucked at his heart, and for a brief moment, he thought about what it would be like for this to really be her home. With him.

He turned around but didn't look her in the eye. "I was just thinking about the case." He tried to move around her to the stairs, but she stepped in front of him, blocking his way.

"No, you weren't. The muscle on the side of your jaw was twitching. You're angry. Why?"

"Why?" The anger he'd internalized bubbled over. "What we did was dangerous. We could have been arrested, not to mention what would have happened if the guy who shot Brian, who shot at you, had shown up."

Mya's face softened a fraction. She placed a hand on his chest. "That didn't happen."

His heartbeat quickened at her touch. "It could have. I should have known better." He covered her hand with his and looked into her eyes. "I do know better, but I let my feelings for you cloud my professional judgment."

A fraction of a second passed and then she stepped in close. "Your feelings for me?"

Her second hand joined the first over his heart.

"Mya—"

"Do you still have feelings for me?"

"You know I do. That doesn't change anything."

"It could." Her gaze sent blood surging to his groin. "I want it to."

Mya slipped her arms around his waist and went up on her toes. She placed a feather-light kiss along the line of his jaw, first on one side of his face and then the other.

"Mya—" Her name seemed to be the only word he could get out at the moment. Not that it mattered. She moved her mouth over his, cutting off any discussion.

She steered them backward until his back met the wall. She deepened the kiss, her mouth hot, eager and devouring.

Emotions ricocheted through him. Anger, frustration, desire.

Desire quickly took precedence.

His hands went under her sweater, and with a flick of his wrist, he undid the clasp on her bra. It had been so long, too long, since he'd held her in his arms. He savored the feeling of smooth bronze skin, the curve of her hips and the well of the peak of her breast.

She stepped back from him long enough to tug her sweater over her head and toss it and her bra to the floor. His shirt landed next to hers a second later. He cupped her right breast then bent his head to take one perfect brown nipple into his mouth, teasing it into a hard peak.

A husky moan tore from her throat, and his erection pulsed. He shifted to take the other breast, wrapping his arm around Mya's waist to keep her upright.

Her hands slid between them and unfastened his belt, then the button on his jeans. Her hands slipped under his waistband and around to cup his buttocks, pulling their bodies even closer.

His lips never left hers as he propelled them both toward the living room. He lowered her onto the couch then stepped back, letting his jeans and boxers fall to the ground.

Mya's eyes raked boldly over his naked form, her eyes darkening with lust when they reached his manhood.

"You're beautiful," Mya said with a touch of awe that had him throbbing for her.

He grabbed a condom from his wallet and sheathed himself before pulling her back into his arms a fraction of a second later. He made quick work of her pants, and then there was nothing at all between them.

He pressed his pelvis to her body, drawing another sexy moan from her lips. "Are you sure?"

She tilted her head and looked into his eyes while hooking one leg around his waist. "Absolutely."

He trailed kisses down her neck. "I've missed you." In one motion, he hooked his arm around her, lifted and dove into her.

For one moment, everything stilled as emotion and sensations, both old and new, swept over him. Mya's head fell back, exposing more creamy chocolate neck to be devoured.

He started to move inside her, slowly and deliberately while suckling at her neck. Her nails dug into his back, and she wrapped her legs tighter around his waist, pulling him in deeper.

Desire built into an inferno quickly. It took only minutes before the first spasms rolled over Mya. Every muscle in his body strained to hold back his release, but he was determined to draw the moment out as long as he could.

"Gideon," she cried out.

The sound of his name entangling with her cries of ecstasy drove him into her harder and faster until he couldn't hold back any longer. He felt her clench around him a second time, and they both fell over a precipice he wasn't sure he could ever come back from.

MYA WOKE SLOWLY, the realization that she wasn't in her own bed or in the guest room bed coming on in stages. She was in Gideon's bed. After their explosive coupling downstairs, they'd moved to his bedroom and continued to reacquaint themselves. She remembered waking during the night and watching him sleep. It was the most relaxed she'd seen him since he'd tackled her in his backyard.

It was still dark outside. The clock on the bedside table read 4:27 a.m.

Mya rolled over and reached for Gideon but found the bed empty. The pillow was still dimpled, but the sheets on his side were cold to the touch, leaving her unsure how long he'd been up.

She swung her feet over the side of the bed and grabbed a clean T-shirt from Gideon's dresser before padding barefoot into the hall.

The house was comfortably still. She started down the stairs at the same time Gideon emerged from the kitchen, headed toward the front door.

"I have to say I've never had a man sneak out of his own house to avoid the morning after awkwardness."

Gideon turned toward the stairs. "I wasn't sneaking out."

Whatever barriers she'd broken through the night before had been rebuilt and, it seemed, reinforced.

Mya sighed and sank down to sit on the top step. "Then what are you doing?"

Gideon moved to stand at the bottom of the steps. He looked up at her. "James is outside. He's going to stay with you until I get back."

Cool air seeped through the light T-shirt Mya wore,

raising goose bumps on her arms. She tucked her knees up under the shirt, bringing them to her chest. "Until you get back from where?"

"I've just got some things to take care of at the office. I shouldn't be too long."

"You've never been a good liar."

His expression hardened. "Look, I made a mistake taking you with me to Leeds's last night. You're safer staying put, out of sight."

Mya pushed to her feet. "I thought I made it clear. I am a part of this investigation. Where you go, I go."

He climbed the steps until they were face-to-face. "And I thought I made it clear I wouldn't do anything that would lead to you getting hurt. I broke that promise yesterday. I won't do it again."

"Are we still talking about breaking into Brian's house or our activities after?"

"Both."

She crossed her arms and watched his eyes dart to her breasts before focusing on her face again. "You know, the sexy alpha male stuff gets old real quick. I'm not some helpless damsel in distress."

"You came to me for help."

"Help!" She threw up her hands. "That implies both of our involvement, not you taking over, making all the decisions, or locking me in a tower while you go slay the dragon."

Gideon's eyes softened. "I'm just trying to protect you."

"The best way to do that is to trust me." She waited for a beat, hoping her words would sink in this time. "Where are you going?"

Gideon's jaw clenched. "To find out who lives at the address we found in Brian's files last night."

Mya turned and headed for the guest bedroom. "I'll get dressed."

"I'm already later than I wanted to be."

"Five minutes," she said, snapping the bedroom door closed behind her.

It took her six minutes, but when she came down the stairs, Gideon was waiting by the front door.

"James still out there?" she asked, putting on her coat. She would have liked to grab a cup of coffee, maybe a piece of toast, but she didn't dare mention that to Gideon.

"No. I told him you'd be coming with me."

From the sour look on his face, she surmised they had said more, but again she didn't push.

Gideon already had the address plugged into his phone's GPS, but Mya did an internet search for it as he drove.

The address was for a Tudor-style home just over the county line in Westchester. Mya scrolled through the links returned by the search and discovered the home had sold to its current owner two years earlier for a little over a million dollars. Nearby homes were currently selling for nearly twenty percent more.

"Looks like a nice house," she said, continuing to scroll on her phone.

"Do you recognize it at all?"

She used two fingers to zoom in on the photo. The exterior of the home was gorgeous, but it didn't ring any bells for her. "No, and no one I know could afford a home like this."

"Not even TriGen investors?"

"Well, of course, the lab's investors probably could,

but I've never had the pleasure of being invited to any of their homes." She slanted a glance across the darkened interior of the car. "You think Brian was sending my research to one of the investors too? Why? I send quarterly reports and, under the investment agreement, any of them could have demanded to see the data and research backing up those reports."

"Maybe they didn't want you to know they had seen the data."

"Why?" Mya asked again, confusion clouding her caffeine-deprived brain. This was making about as much sense as everything else that had happened over the last three days, which was not much sense at all.

"I don't know. It's all just speculation. That's one of the reasons I want to know who lives at this address."

"I'm sure West employs a computer whiz or four. They couldn't find out who lives there without us having to make a trip to Westchester at the crack of dawn?"

Gideon cocked an eyebrow. "I wanted to leave you at home."

She raised her hands. "I'm not complaining, just stating a fact."

Gideon didn't look convinced when he said, "The house was bought using an LLC."

"Very Kim and Kanye." She noticed the ghost of a smile that ticked the edges of Gideon's mouth. "What? I read that's how celebrities buy houses, so they don't have creepy stalker fans showing up in their rose bushes every day."

"Well, I don't think we'll find Kim and Kanye, but you never know."

"Hope springs eternal." Mya grinned.

That got a smile out of him.

They made good time since it was still early.

The Tudor was as impressive in real life as it was in the photos. All the homes in the neighborhood were. Large homes on ever-larger lots that screamed wealth and privilege, many covered with showy decorations. Mya cringed at the thought of how much electricity the block consumed each evening.

Gideon parked several doors down from the Tudor and leaned his seat back.

"So, what do you do on stakeouts?"

Gideon shook his head. "This isn't a stakeout. We're just observing a house."

"Which is the definition of a stakeout," Mya said pointedly. "Accurate description is important in scientific research."

One of Gideon's eyebrows ticked up while the other went down. "We're not curing cancer here."

Mya grinned. "We kind of are, at least treating it, if the person who lives in that house has my server and we get it back."

Gideon leaned over the center console. His aftershave hit her, sending her stomach fluttering and a memory from the night before rippling through her. "Mya? You still with me?"

She shook herself out of the memory. "Of course. What were you saying?"

"I said all we're going to do is watch. If someone comes out of the house, I'll take a photo, and we can go from there. Neither of us is leaving this car, understand."

"Okay. Okay, I get it." She leaned her seat back to match his and settled in.

The residents in the houses began to stir and start their day. Lights came on and cars backed out of garages carrying their owners to the high-powered jobs that paid for the opulence.

"Can I ask you a question?" Mya asked after several more minutes of boring suburban domesticity.

Gideon slanted a glance her way. "You can ask." He turned his gaze back to the Tudor.

"When you said you left the military because you'd seen too much, what did you mean?"

Gideon's eyes stayed trained forward. She didn't repeat the question. She hoped he'd answer, but if he didn't, she wouldn't push.

"I watched five of my friends get blown to pieces by an IED."

Mya wasn't totally surprised. She knew many soldiers returned to the States with scars from the war. Every fiber of her being wanted to whisk away the pain she saw in Gideon's eyes at that moment.

"Oh, Gideon. I'm so sorry." She grabbed his hand and squeezed. "It happened during your second deployment, didn't it?"

"Yes, how did you—"

"You weren't the same when you came back that time. Quieter. You were always quiet, but I guess *morose* is the better word."

"I didn't know how to handle it. I didn't handle it well at all."

"I wish you would have talked to me."

"I'm sorry if I made you feel like there was something wrong with you or the divorce was your fault. It took me a long time to work through that. Not sure I'm done working through it, actually."

"Why did you tell me? I would have helped you through it."

He shot a quick glance at her. "I didn't want to lay that on you."

"I was your wife. I wanted to help you with whatever you were going through." Her voice dropped almost to a whisper. "I still do."

"Mya—"

The door to the Tudor opened, cutting off what Gideon was about to say. He lifted his phone and engaged the video.

A woman swaddled in a pink robe and slippers walked to the end of the driveway and bent down to retrieve the morning paper.

When she turned back toward the house, Mya got a good look at the woman's face.

Shock quickly gave way to anger as she stared at Shannon Travers.

Chapter Fifteen

"I don't understand why we don't confront Shannon right now. We know she's behind all this. She has my research." Mya slammed her palm down on the conference room table.

Gideon fought to keep his frustration at bay. This was why he preferred to work alone.

"We don't know that," Gideon snapped.

James and Tessa pushed through the conference room doors. They steered clear of the end of the long table where he and Mya stood.

"Of course we do. Rebecca was sending my research data to her. When she found out I was getting close to proving my treatment worked, Shannon must have decided to take matters into her own hands."

"All we know is that Rebecca sent something to her. It could have been love letters for all we know."

"Rebecca was seeing Brian."

Tessa pointed her finger at Mya. "That doesn't mean she wasn't also involved with Shannon."

"Let's start with what we know about Shannon Travers," James interjected reasonably. He sat in the chair at the head of the table. Tessa sat next to him.

Gideon sat on the opposite side of the table next to Mya.

"I've already got the basic background on Travers, but any color you can give us on her, stuff that wouldn't come up in a background check, would be helpful."

Mya folded her hands atop the table. "Shannon is a self-centered, egotistical, manipulative witch."

"I can tell you really like her," Tessa deadpanned.

Mya shot a wry smile across the table. "I already told you we were both in the same PhD program. We were never friends, but Shannon somehow convinced herself that I stole the postdoc job with Irwin from her."

"Why would she think that?" James asked.

Mya shrugged. "Because she's deranged?"

James shot a look across the table. Mya swept her arms open. "Okay, I'm sorry." She rose and went to the mini-fridge in the corner of the room. "Both of us concentrated our studies on finding improved treatments for cancer patients, but at the time, I wasn't focused on glioblastoma specifically. Shannon was."

"What made you change your mind?" Gideon asked.

Mya carried four bottles of water back to the table and reclaimed the seat beside him.

"Irwin. He was so passionate about the work. It inspired me."

Tessa grabbed one of the bottles Mya set on the table and twisted its cap off. "So, you went to work for him."

"Shannon and I both applied for an internship at his lab, and Irwin chose me."

James read from the screen of the laptop in front of him. "It doesn't look like Shannon had a hard time finding another job. She's worked for Nobel since getting her PhD. Promoted steadily over the last several years." James looked at Mya.

"What can you tell us about Nobel Pharmaceuticals?" James asked.

Mya sighed. "They are the leading pharmaceutical company in the Northeast region. And they're also working on a treatment for glioblastoma. That's why I'm sure Shannon must be behind what's been happening. We need to confront her."

James's eyes narrowed. "It's a big leap to go from a professional feud to arson and murder."

"You don't understand how driven and malicious Shannon is. And you said it yourself, Gideon, people will do a lot of things for the kind of money my treatment will bring in if it's proven to work."

Gideon couldn't argue that point, but he still wasn't ready to go in completely on the theory that Shannon Travers was behind all this. "I still think we need more before we confront her."

Mya's posture stiffened, her lips angling down in a scowl.

"You both make valid points," Tessa offered. "We don't have enough to accuse Travers of stealing Mya's research, much less being involved with the deaths of her coworkers and the attack on Mya. But if Travers is involved, whether willingly or not, confronting her may push her to make a mistake that we can use against her."

Gideon frowned at Tessa. "Or confronting her lets her know we are on to her, and she destroys any evidence there might be that she is behind this."

"It's a risk, but there are always risks," James said. "If Shannon Travers is involved, it won't be easy for her to get rid of all the evidence."

Crap. Gideon didn't like it. They had nothing concrete, just speculation and grudges. But it wasn't the first time he'd played a hunch, although usually, they were his hunches.

Mya turned to him. "I'm going to talk to Shannon, with or without you."

Double crap.

"We'll go see if Ms. Travers will speak with us. But listen, you can't lose your temper when we do. She's not likely to tell us anything either way, but if we come on too aggressively, we'll never get another shot."

Mya raised her right hand. "I will be on my best behavior."

Chapter Sixteen

Mya looked out the passenger window as Gideon navigated them through a part of Manhattan most tourists never saw. A woman in a houndstooth coat typed on her cell phone and dodged a man pushing a baby stroller. The man glared, but the woman didn't look up from her phone. Seconds later, Gideon drove through the intersection, leaving both the man and the woman behind.

Traffic was light, and they made it over the George Washington Bridge in good time. They were in Jersey before Gideon spoke, "What's the deal between you and this woman?"

Mya glanced at him from the passenger seat. "There is no deal."

"All this animosity developed solely over the job with Irwin." She heard the skepticism in Gideon's voice.

Mya shrugged. "A very prestigious job, although Shannon didn't have too hard a landing. I know people who'd kill to have her job." The minute the words left her mouth, Mya wished she could take them back. The sentiment hit far too close to home under the circumstances.

Gideon's eyes remained trained on the road ahead. "So, she's a genius too."

"I hate that term, but I'd say she's at least as smart

as I am." She hated the begrudging way the words fell from her mouth. "Maybe more if ruthlessness counts as intelligence."

He drummed his fingers on the steering wheel. "It's often mistaken as intelligence."

Mya smiled. "Have you become a philosopher in the last twelve years?"

He shot a lopsided smile her way. "I just call it as I see it, as always."

For a moment, she saw the nineteen-year-old who'd gotten down on one knee at Rockaway Beach and declared his love with a ring she still treasured more than all the expensive jewelry she owned.

Gideon hadn't brought up the night they'd spent together, and despite herself, Mya couldn't help feeling uncharacteristically insecure. She knew one incredible night didn't necessarily mean anything. The problem was, she wanted it to mean something. She wanted it to mean he was as open to giving their relationship a second chance as she was.

But wishing wouldn't make it so.

The Nobel Pharmaceutical headquarters was a flashy new building constructed primarily of glass. In the lobby, a twelve-foot Christmas tree commanded the eye and oversize bulbs hung decoratively from the glass ceiling. Holiday music played softly over the speakers.

They hadn't called ahead, and Mya was surprised when Shannon immediately agreed to see them.

Shannon hadn't changed much since their days as students. She was still tall with an ethereal quality that led people to want to protect her when they really should be more concerned about protecting themselves from her. Her angled blond bob was lighter than it had been the last time Mya had seen her, and small wrinkles creased her sandy-colored skin around her eyes and mouth.

"Mya, what a pleasant surprise." Shannon rose from her chair but didn't approach. Her light blue eyes flashed, not exactly in welcome, but more like curiosity as Mya and Gideon entered the spacious office.

They'd crossed paths enough times over the years to have perfected a professional facade, but hugs and warm greetings they'd never share.

"I'm sorry, I don't have a lot of time today. I'm sure you can't imagine the pressures involved in running a large research lab." Shannon sneered.

TriGen might not have been as big as Nobel, but Tri-Gen's reputation was second to none thanks to Irwin's pioneering efforts and their work was no less meaningful. Her treatment proved that. And she'd done it without the help of multiple research assistants, interns and various administrative personnel.

"Yes, I'm sure it's tiring finding ways to let others do the work while you take the credit." A better woman might have let the barb pass without comment, but old habits were hard to break.

Out of the side of her eye, Mya thought she saw the slightest of smiles flicker across Gideon's face. It was gone before she could be sure, though.

Shannon gave a forced chuckle. "You've always had a peculiar sense of humor." Shannon's gaze moved to Gideon. Based on the men Shannon had been linked to in the society section of the local paper, Gideon was not at all her type. He was attractive enough, but Shannon's last boyfriend, a tech millionaire, had a lean body obviously sculpted by a personal trainer, most likely with a little help from a surgeon. The man was five years their junior and looked as if he hadn't ever done a day of manual labor, quite possibly the polar opposite of Gideon.

Still, Shannon had eyes, and she looked her fill. For his part, Gideon remained expressionless.

"Who's your friend?" Shannon said as a seductive smile spread across her face.

They hadn't discussed how Gideon would introduce himself. Instinct had Mya wanting to keep the fact that he was her ex from Shannon. Whether that instinct derived from the idea that Shannon would be more open if she believed Gideon was a somewhat neutral participant in the conversation or if it was born from something more personal wasn't something Mya felt comfortable examining. She took the easy way out. "I've hired West Investigations to help figure out what is going on."

Shannon waved them toward the guest chairs across from the sleek desk.

"Yes, I was so sorry to hear about the destruction of your lab."

"That's one of the things we're here to talk to you about," Mya said, sitting.

"I'm not sure how I can help, but I'll do my best to try."

"If you heard about the lab, you might have also heard that several attempts have been made on Mya's life in the last several days," Gideon said.

"I'd heard about the fire at your lab, and the death of your receptionist, of course. Has something else happened?" Shannon answered.

"A man on a motorcycle shot at us yesterday. My research assistant Brian was killed." Mya leaned forward in her seat, her gaze trained on Shannon's face looking for a reaction.

Shannon pressed a hand to her chest, her eyes widening slightly. "Oh, my goodness. I'm so sorry to hear that and sorry for your loss." If she was acting, she was good.

"Are you behind it?"

Mya surmised from the sharp look Gideon sent her, he didn't agree with the direct approach. But Shannon wasn't a person you could do subtle with. Deceit and subterfuge were second nature to her.

"Behind... You can't possibly think..." Shannon's eyes grew wider. She shot an innocent look toward Gideon.

"Cut it out, Shannon. Your little show won't work on Gideon, and I already know it's a load of crap."

Shannon's gaze landed on Gideon with new interest. "Gideon. The ex-husband?"

Mya wasn't surprised that Shannon knew about her marriage to Gideon. Keep your friends close and your enemies closer and all that. She kept up on the comings and goings in Shannon's life. She knew Shannon had also married, had a child and divorced since they'd graduated.

Shannon's eyes scanned slowly down Gideon's body and back up again. "For a genius, you're pretty stupid to let such an...attractive man get away from you."

Mya fought the urge to smack the woman.

Reminding herself that distraction was Shannon's goal, Mya pulled her back straight. "The murders of my coworkers? What do you know about that?"

Shannon's sultry smile dropped away as her gaze snapped from Gideon to Mya.

For a brief moment, Mya could see the unadulterated hatred brewing there. "You can't barge into my office and accuse me of murder."

"We're just asking questions," Gideon said. "No one is accusing anyone."

Mya caught his pointed look out of the side of her eye, but she knew Shannon was far too manipulative for subtlety to work on her.

"We found a packing slip in Rebecca Conway's handwriting with your home address." Mya was almost positive she'd seen Shannon flinch at the mention of Rebecca's name, but the moment passed so quickly she couldn't be completely sure. "What did my receptionist send to you?"

There was no mistaking the anger on Shannon's face. She snorted with derision. "I don't know your receptionist or anyone named Rebecca. Now I want you both to go."

Gideon laid a hand on Mya's thigh, stopping her from shooting back a response that would no doubt have had Shannon calling security.

"We'll leave, but I'm sure the police will be asking you the same questions," Gideon answered.

The expression on Shannon's face was as far from flirty as one could get now. "Why would the police want to talk to me? I have nothing to do with any of this."

"Come on," Mya said incredulously. "I know you started the rumor that my formula doesn't work. If you didn't tell the cops yourself, you made sure they heard the lie."

A cold smile curved Shannon's lips. "I did no such thing, although I can't deny I too heard that rumor. From a reputable source, I might add." Shannon leaned back in her leather executive's chair and folded her arms across her chest. "If it's true, it would seem to me you had more reason than anyone to destroy the lab and keep those who knew about your failure quiet. Is that why you're here? To divert suspicion from yourself onto me? If so, it won't work."

"You haven't answered the question," Gideon said.

"I don't even know these people. Why would I want to kill them?" Shannon's mouth twisted into a snarl. The alluring facade she wore to fool the masses had fallen away to reveal the real Shannon underneath.

Gideon's face remained passive. "If Mya's formula wasn't a failure, that means she found a cure before you and Nobel."

Shannon scoffed. "That's a big if."

"It's a fact. And since we're talking rumors, I've heard that your board of directors is not happy with the cost and progress of several of the bigger projects you've spearheaded in the last year. Maybe you know that getting bested by my tiny lab would have been the last straw."

Shannon rose. "The only straws I see are the ones you're grasping at. Now, I believe I asked you both to leave."

They rose. When she reached the door, Mya turned back.

Shannon watched, a smug smile on her face.

Mya held Shannon's gaze. "If I find out you had anything to do with any of this, losing your job will be the least of your worries. I promise you that."

MYA TOOK A long hot shower when she and Gideon got back to his home. They'd stopped by a big box store after leaving the Nobel offices and she'd picked up a more clothes and staples. She dressed one of her new outfits and returned to the main floor to find him freshly showered as well, cooking dinner, a bottle of red wine breathing on the kitchen counter next to where he stood chopping peppers.

Mya hadn't asked what he was making. It didn't matter; it smelled divine, and she was starving. With everything that had happened during the day, she'd only had time to grab a bag of chips from the vending machine in West's offices.

She opened her laptop and got to work figuring out how to save her career. She brought everything she still had regarding the treatment up on the computer screen. Trying to recreate her work would be difficult without a lab or Brian's help but she was willing to try because if she didn't do something quickly, TriGen might not survive.

After leaving Shannon and getting back to West's offices, she'd had an hour-long conference call with TriGen's board members. To say they were jittery would have been the understatement of the decade. They'd hashed out language for a press statement and she'd convinced the board to wait and see what the police investigation turned up before making any big decisions. But she knew she couldn't hold them off forever.

"Dinner will be ready in fifteen," Gideon said, stirring something in a large pot. "How's it going?"

Mya glanced at the computer's clock. An hour had passed with no progress.

"Not great. Trying to reproduce years of work…and I don't even have Brian to help jog my memory," Mya mumbled, surprised by the ball of emotion that had formed in her throat.

"Were you two close?" Gideon strained boiling water from the pasta he'd been cooking.

"No, not really. You heard what he said in the park.

Brian was a terrific assistant, but there was always that little bit of resentment toward me for getting the job he thought should have been his."

"Seems like he was more resentful than you thought."

"I know. I'm trying to understand it. Irwin devoted his life to the lab and this research, and I can understand him having difficulty letting go of it and Brian's loyalty to him."

"But it's still a betrayal by two people you trusted."

Mya felt herself deflate. "Yes. Although, there's a silver lining. The notes Brian shared with Irwin will be a big help at reconstructing my research."

Gideon's phone rang.

"Hey, got a minute?" James said on the other end of the line.

"Sure," Gideon said, stirring the food before turning the burner down to its lowest setting. "I've got you on speaker. Mya is here with me."

"Good, she should hear this too. I've dug up some info on Rebecca Conway. Or I should say Rebecca Calcott."

"She changed her name." Gideon carried his cell phone to the table and sat down.

"I can't find any kind of legal name change on the record, but sometime in the last year, it looks like she got false identification and assumed the name Rebecca Conway." The sound of computer keys tapping came over the line.

"Rebecca Calcott of Cumberland, Maryland, graduated from the public school system with a 4.0 grade point average and enrolled in a local community college. From an archive social media post, it appears she did have an interest in the sciences."

Gideon's phone chimed. Mya peered over his shoulder as he opened a text message with a screenshot of a social media post from Rebecca Calcott excitedly sharing her college class schedule with her online friends.

"Looks like she was enrolled in advanced biology and chemistry classes besides the core freshman curriculum," Gideon said.

"That would explain how she could feign interest in the lab's work," Mya said.

"I contacted the school and was told that Rebecca dropped out before she completed a full semester," James said.

Gideon frowned. "Any sign how Rebecca went from straight As and advanced biology to college dropout in just a few months?"

"Can't answer that. But I can send you her mother's address and phone number. Marie Calcott. She's a home health aide and still lives in Cumberland." Gideon's cell phone chimed. Mya leaned over his shoulder and eyed the address in the text from James.

"I tried calling. The police had already notified Marie of her daughter's death. She called me a few names I won't repeat and hung up on me."

"We'll give her some time and try her again," Gideon said. "We need to find out how Rebecca Calcott went from Cumberland coed to Rebecca Conway, TriGen receptionist. And why."

"I don't know if we'll have any better results, but I'll give it a shot," James said, ending the call.

"This situation just keeps getting stranger," Mya said, chewing her bottom lip.

"Do you know anyone in Cumberland, Maryland?"

Mya shook her head. "I didn't know Cumberland, Maryland, existed until a few minutes ago."

Gideon's gaze was intense. "It seems like someone there knows you."

Her phone vibrated before she came up with an answer to that. "It's Irwin." She connected the call while willing her pulse to stop racing.

"Mya, my dear. How are you? I got your message."

"Everything is a mess. Someone set fire to the lab. It's gone. And…" The sob escaped before she could fight it back.

Gideon reached for her hand and squeezed. His strength helped her pull it together and continue. "Brian and Rebecca have both been killed. We think by the same person who set fire to the lab."

"I had no idea."

Mya wasn't at all surprised that Irwin hadn't heard the news. He might have been using Brian to keep up with what was going on at the lab, but he was a hermit at heart. Besides having no phone, Irwin had also resisted getting internet access or even a television. His primary contact with the outside world came through his weekly visits to the small town at the base of the mountain and his friendship with Phil Gatling, the manager of the general store.

"Irwin, before he was killed Brian told me he'd been sharing my research with you."

There was silence on the other end of the line.

"I know it was a breach—" Irwin started.

"Of contract and of trust," Mya said, her voice hard. She didn't want him to think that what he and Brian had done was okay, but there were bigger concerns to deal with at the moment. "But you may be the one person on Earth capable of helping me right now. Do you still have the copies of the research Brian sent to you?"

"Yes," Irwin answered guiltily.

Her heart beat excitedly.

"Irwin, I need whatever notes Brian sent you." She explained the break-in at her home and the stolen server.

"Of course. Anything you need. I can have Phil send it express mail."

"No. This may be all that's left of our work. We'll come to you. I don't want to take any chances."

"We?"

Mya glanced over at Gideon. "I've hired a personal security firm. There've been multiple attempts made on my life in the last several days. It looks like whoever has stolen our research wants to make sure there's no one left alive who can prove it's stolen. Irwin, you could be in danger."

"I'm sure that's not the case. Aside from you and Phil, almost no one knows who I am or where I live."

"Maybe you should stay with a friend for a while," she said although she knew it was a futile effort.

"I'll be fine. Don't you worry about me, dear."

Mya ended the call and turned her attention to Gideon.

He swung the laptop to face him. "What's Irwin's address?"

She pulled up her contacts on her phone and read off the address for Gideon. "It's about an eight-hour drive. I think we should leave now."

Gideon glanced at the clock on the stove. "It's nearly seven."

"If we leave now, we can get a room on the way and stop by Rebecca's mother's place in the morning before heading to Irwin's."

"If Marie Calcott hung up on James, what makes you

think she'll talk to two strangers who show up on her doorstep uninvited?"

Her chair scraped the floor as she rose. She paced the length of the table then turned to look back at Gideon. "I don't know, okay. Maybe she won't talk to us, but that's not a reason not to try."

Gideon shook his head. "I promised you I wouldn't put you in danger again."

"We aren't breaking and entering. We'll knock on the woman's door. If she slams it in our face, we'll leave. What's dangerous about that?"

From his look, she could tell he was about to tell her exactly what could be dangerous about that.

"Please, Gideon. We could get answers to who exactly Rebecca was, and I can get my formula and prove to Detective Kamal, Shannon and the scientific community that the treatment works. The police won't have any reason to suspect I'm a murderer."

"More importantly, if the success of your research becomes public knowledge, whoever's behind all this won't have an incentive to keep targeting you. They'll no longer be able to pass off your research as their own."

"So, we'll leave now?"

"Go pack a bag."

Chapter Seventeen

Gideon drove south on I-95, questioning whether he'd made the right decision letting Mya talk him into starting this trek so late in the day. He'd run the plan by James, who had supported the idea. James had pointed out that the information on Rebecca was their best lead to figuring out who was behind the theft and attack. And getting the research notes from Irwin and proving that Mya's treatment worked was the fastest way to turning Kamal's attention away from Mya.

Mya slumped against the passenger window, and her breath came in a steady rhythm. She'd fallen asleep not long after they'd crossed the New Jersey-Pennsylvania border.

The peacefulness of sleep had erased the tiny worry lines that creased her forehead during the day. She'd done her best to hide it, but he could tell the stress of the situation was getting to her by the slope in her shoulders and the weakness of her smile.

He'd missed that smile.

A memory from the previous night, Mya smiling up at him as he braced himself above her, sent a flash of longing through him. He shouldn't have let last night happen, but he wasn't sorry it had.

Mya was right that his house didn't feel like a home. It hadn't since Grandma Pearl died. Not until last night. Falling asleep with Mya in his arms again felt like getting back a part of himself that had been missing for the last twelve years.

He glanced at her sleeping form in the seat next to him and reminded himself that he was there to protect her. Nothing more. The past had to stay in the past, and last night couldn't happen again.

His phone rang through the SUV's Bluetooth system, jarring Mya from her slumber.

"I got something for you on your shooter," James said without preamble.

Gideon watched as Mya stretched into full wakefulness.

"We're listening," Gideon said.

"My source in the police department said they found the bike abandoned in an alley about a mile from the park. There's no camera in the alley, but the cops pulled a photo from the traffic cam on the corner. A couple minutes after the bike enters the alley, a man exits carrying a motorcycle helmet, no bike. They tracked him using the cameras for a block before losing him on a side street. I just texted the photo to you."

The phone chimed.

Gideon pulled off the road and unlocked his phone with one hand.

He breathed in Mya's sweet scent as she leaned over the middle console to view the photo on the phone's screen.

The photo showed a large man, at least as tall as Gideon's six foot four. He was heavyset and wore all black, just as the person who'd shot at them had. The camera had caught the man in profile, and the photo quality left much to be desired. Nothing about him seemed familiar to Gideon. He couldn't even say this was the man who had shot at them.

But Mya studied the photo with open scrutiny.

"You recognize him?" Gideon asked.

A shadow of recognition touched her face. "Not really. Maybe? Something about him seems familiar, but it's not a good photo, is it?"

"It's the best one of the bunch, trust me," James said. "I sent two more pictures the cops pulled to your email. Maybe together they'll ring a bell."

Gideon tapped the email icon on his phone's screen.

"There's something else. Hang on a sec." The sound on the other end of the phone faded for a moment, then James's voice returned louder and closer than before. He'd gone off speaker. "I had Brandon make some inquiries about Nobel.

"Nobel is staring down the barrel of an SEC fraud investigation," James offered.

Mya's eyebrows jumped into her hairline. "Fraud?"

"Looks like they've been shading the true results of some of their clinical studies in their quarterly reports to the shareholders."

"You're kidding me?" Mya's eyes were wide with disbelief.

"Not even a little," James shot back.

Gideon's mind raced. "The execs in the crosshairs?" If Brandon could dig up this information in only a few hours, there was no doubt in his mind that the executives at Nobel also knew. How did that play into the attacks on Mya and her lab and colleagues?

"Brandon didn't know which of the company executives were under scrutiny," James said.

"If Nobel is lying to its investors and the public about their research, there's no way Shannon isn't involved." Mya wrung her hands. "In fact, I'd peg her as the ringleader."

"Brandon expects the SEC will announce its investigation in the next couple weeks."

"So, if Travers knows about the investigation, she may be feeling pressure on the one side to show Nobel's glioblastoma treatment is a success and on the other side from the SEC," Gideon mused out loud.

"Might make someone desperate enough to steal." Skepticism laced James's voice. "But kill? It's a leap."

"You don't know Shannon. There's not a leap she wouldn't make to advance her own interests."

Moments after ending the call with James, Gideon turned the Tahoe into the parking lot of the Motel 6. He circled twice, noting the doors that had cars parked in front of them before pulling to a stop in front of the lobby.

A single string of Christmas lights hung limply around the entrance door. Inside they roused the clerk from the handheld video game he'd continued to play even after they'd walked into the lobby. The motel had done the very least as far as decorating for the season went, placing a foot-high Christmas tree at one end of the check-in counter and a matching menorah at the other end.

"Name," the clerk said in a bored tone.

Gideon had done his best to make sure that they weren't followed as they left the city, but he'd still had

Mya make the reservation under West Investigations just to be on the safe side.

"We'd like a corner room on the ground floor. Double beds," Gideon said. From the looks of it the motel was sparsely occupied but a corner room meant he'd have only one possible neighbor to keep an eye on.

The clerk looked at him from under a mop of curly bangs. "Corner rooms cost thirty dollars more."

Gideon was tempted to demand to see the hotel policy stating this premium, but he was too tired to argue over thirty bucks. He paid, and the clerk handed over the keys to the room.

They got back into the car, and Gideon backed into a parking space in front of their assigned room. He grabbed both of their bags from the Tahoe's trunk, and Mya carried her purse. He inserted the keycard in the door, waited for the red light to switch to green and held the door open.

The faint smell of vanilla bodywash tickled his nose as Mya passed into the room ahead of him. Gideon fastened the safety bar on the door, then turned back to the room, letting their bags slide from his shoulder to the floor. "That's not double beds."

The king-sized bed covered with a comforter in various shades of gray took up most of the room, a large flat-screen television on the wall facing it.

His eyes searched the room as if a second bed would appear somewhere and he'd just missed it. A small round table with a single chair had been shoved into the corner between the bed and a large window that looked out onto the parking lot. A door next to the dresser connected to the adjacent room.

"No, it is not," Mya said, sitting on the edge of the bed and easing her boots off.

"I'll go get us another room." Gideon turned back toward the door.

Mya's hand on his arm stopped him.

"It's not worth the trouble. We'll just share." She pushed the duvet to the foot of the bed.

Gideon hesitated. "I don't know if that's a good idea."

His vow not to repeat the previous night rang in his head. Sharing a bed with Mya without touching her sounded like a form of self-torture.

Mya sighed. "Gideon, we slept next to each other for four years." A slow smile stretched her lips. She leaned back on one elbow. "I can control myself if you can."

She watched the desire flame in Gideon's eyes.

"You're playing with fire." Despite his warning, his eyes darkened with obvious desire.

"Am I? Whatever was there between us all those years ago, it's still there."

"We aren't stupid teenagers anymore."

"Exactly, we both know what we're doing. I want you, and I think you want me too. Am I wrong?"

For a fraction of a second, doubt crept in, but then Gideon growled low and sexy and stalked toward the bed.

She slid back to make room for him, and he crawled onto the bed, positioning himself over her. His mouth met hers, and the fire he'd warned about moments earlier ignited. She kissed him back with equal fervor. She was determined to show him, with every inch of her body, that there was nothing she wanted more than him at that moment.

Gideon pulled her shirt over her head, then made

quick work of sliding her jeans from her hips. He let his unhurried gaze roam over her. The reverence she saw swimming in his eyes left her feeling equal parts powerful and seductive.

"You don't know how many times I've dreamed of having you back in my bed." Gideon ran his hand up the inside of her thigh, stoking the growing flames of passion inside her.

"About as many times as I've dreamed of being there, I'd guess," she answered, reaching to pull him closer.

She kissed him again, not wanting to think about the past or the time they'd wasted.

After a long moment, Gideon pulled back. "I don't want to hurt you again."

"You won't."

She had no expectations beyond this moment. No thoughts about the future or what sleeping together now might mean for their relationship.

She moved her hands to his waistband, tugging open the button on his jeans. He stepped away long enough to shed his clothes and sheath himself before returning.

Gideon ran a finger lightly up the inside of her thigh. Mya moaned at the pleasure his touch elicited.

She wrapped her legs around his waist and relished the feel of his weight atop her. The sensations rumbling through her blocked out everything except the feel of him.

She ran her hands over the hard edges of his body, matching the tempo of his movements with zeal.

Her muscles soon clenched around him at the same time his body tensed and he moaned, "Mya."

Gideon buried his face in the side of her neck as they both struggled to catch their breath.

Mya felt boneless, more relaxed than she'd been in… well, since she could remember. She didn't want it to end.

Gideon rose and went into the bathroom before quickly returning to bed. He pulled the duvet up over them with one hand and her in close to his side with the other.

"You okay?"

"More than," she answered. "You?"

His grin was both sweet and roguish. "Excellent."

A stab of pain pricked her heart as she returned his smile. She rested her head on his bare chest so he wouldn't see the swell of emotion she was feeling.

They lay there, quiet, arms and legs entwined. Gideon's drowsy declaration pulled Mya back into wakefulness. She felt his heartbeat slow, his breathing evening out.

She was hovering on the cusp of sleep when Gideon whispered a lethargic, "I love you."

Mya didn't react, knowing he wouldn't have said the words if he'd thought she was still awake. Another realization hit her as she slid into sleep. She'd lied to herself. Had lied to Gideon.

Because she didn't only want "right now." She wanted forever, and she wanted it with him.

And that meant she was well on her way to being hurt all over again.

Chapter Eighteen

Gideon hovered in the state between wakefulness and sleep when the slap of footfalls outside the motel room brought him fully awake in an instant. At five twenty in the morning, all bets were on this not being a friendly visitor.

He grabbed his gun from the nightstand and listened on high alert, adrenaline coursing through his veins.

The footsteps had stopped, as far as he could tell, directly in front of the room.

Mya stirred beside him. He covered her mouth with his hand, and her eyes flew open. He brought his lips close to her ear, the act momentarily bringing back memories of hours earlier when he'd done the same thing for an entirely different reason. He pushed those thoughts away and focused every cell in his body on protecting the woman next to him.

"There's someone outside the door. Slide off the bed and get into the bathroom. Hurry."

Gideon moved onto his knees next to the bed, and Mya rolled off after him. She gathered her clothes quickly and closed the bathroom door behind her.

He pulled on his jeans, shirt and shoes without setting down his gun.

Whispers broke the silence outside the door seconds before a brick shattered the large window that faced the parking lot. A glass bottle, flames leaping from its top, hurtled through the window after the brick. The bottle shattered against the rough gray carpeting.

A smoky haze filled the room, fire shooting across the floor as the fire spread along whatever flammable liquid had been inside the bottle.

They had to get out of there, but he knew that was exactly what their attackers wanted.

The smoke detectors went off, setting off the overhead sprinklers. The fire flashed angrily and continued to spread.

They were trapped.

Stay in the room and burn to death or walk outside and likely be shot.

Gideon's gaze darted to the door connecting their room to the one next to them. He opened the bathroom door and reached for Mya. "Come on. We've got to get out of here."

He unlocked the door opening into their room, but the door opening into the other room was locked from the other side. It gave way after three hard kicks.

Mya grabbed her laptop bag and they rushed into the adjoining room. The door to the room rattled violently.

Gideon barely had time to process that there was someone kicking the door from the outside and to push Mya into the bathroom before a man crashed through the room door.

The man held a gun out in front of him.

Gideon dove at the man before he could get off a shot. In a room as small as the one they were in there was no telling how a bullet would ricochet. He couldn't take the chance of one going through the bathroom door and hitting Mya.

The gun clattered to the floor and slid under the bed. The man swore.

Gideon rose with his gun outstretched, but the man charged before he came fully to his feet.

They hit the carpeted floor with bone-shaking force. His gun skittered across the floor, hitting the closed bathroom door with a thump.

He got a good look at the man's face—the dark, soul-less eyes and square jaw were a match for the man in the picture James had texted him earlier. Then the man's meaty fist connected with Gideon's face, pain searing his cheek. He blocked the second punch and landed a couple of his own.

Smoke from the next room was already floating through the connecting doors, and the alarm still blared. The entire motel had to be awake. Where were the cops?

Gideon grappled with the man, coughing as the smoke from the fire made its way into the room.

He noticed the bathroom door creeping open, drawing Gideon's attention from the fight. The man's fist landed on Gideon's jaw, snapping his head back.

Mya poked her head out of the bathroom, her hand extended toward the gun.

The motion drew the man's attention. He snarled, lunging toward Mya.

"No!" Gideon grabbed the man around his knees, taking him to the ground. A solid right hook to the face left the man dazed, but Gideon knew it wouldn't last long.

He scrambled to Mya, taking the gun from her shaking hand. He turned, putting himself between her and their attacker, but the man was already on his feet and almost through the hotel room door.

Gideon fired, but the shots went into the wall. A moment later, a car door slammed, and the sounds of tires squealing carried into the room.

He ran to the door in time to see a dark sedan fishtail out of the motel parking lot.

Guests peered out of cracked doors and around curtains.

He could make out the sound of sirens, finally, but they sounded as if they were coming from the opposite direction from which their assailant's car had gone.

By the time the cops sorted the whole thing out and got a team mobilized, their assailant would be long gone.

Chapter Nineteen

"Sounds like our vandal is escalating, Sheriff." The pudgy deputy who had been taking their statements tipped his hat back and looked toward his boss.

Mya, Gideon, a deputy and the sheriff stood at the far end of the motel parking lot, next to Gideon's Tahoe. He had moved the car before the fire department arrived so they'd have clear access to the room, and so the Tahoe, which had escaped damage from the initial firebomb, wouldn't be the victim of any secondary damage.

"Maybe." The sheriff looked as if he'd been in bed when he'd gotten the call about the situation at the motel. His gray-brown hair was matted on the left side, and a crease from a pillow still showed faintly on his skin. He wore the same mud-colored pants as his deputy, but a green-and-red sweater peeked out from underneath his half-zipped jacket. Despite his roused-from-bed appearance, the sheriff's eyes were sharp, and they studied Mya and Gideon suspiciously. "Can you walk me through what happened one more time?"

The sun was just cutting through the darkness as Mya began describing, once again, what had occurred. Or rather, what she and Gideon had agreed to tell the police had occurred.

In the minutes before the police and fire trucks had arrived on the scene, Gideon had instructed Mya on what to say when they arrived. They were on their way to visit a friend in West Virginia. Stopped here for the night. They have no idea who threw the Molotov cocktail through the window. The room next to them was supposed to be empty. Say nothing about the situation back home with the lab or murders, Gideon admonished, and nothing about the formula.

Mya wasn't comfortable lying to the police, but Gideon had convinced her that if they told the whole truth, they'd be stuck in town for days, if not longer, while the sheriff investigated.

So, she'd done what Gideon asked and given the deputy a statement that was, if not the whole truth, a version of the truth.

Gideon was probably right about one thing. Whoever attacked them was long gone and, if West had yet to figure out his identity, the sheriff had no chance of doing so.

It was better for them to give their statements and get to Irwin's as soon as possible. Recreating her research and publicizing it was the only way to end this madness.

She finished telling the story and fell quiet. The sheriff looked to Gideon, his expression asking whether Gideon had something more to offer.

"That's exactly what happened, Sheriff."

If Gideon was feeling any of the same anxiety about lying to the police that she was, he was doing an excellent job of hiding it. She'd stuffed her hands in her coat pocket, in part to ward off the chill but also to hide the fact that they shook more than the test tube mixer at her lab.

The sheriff and Gideon's gazes locked and held for a long moment.

Conversation from the firefighters floated back as they were preparing to leave. It was light enough now that a handful of guests and townspeople milled about behind the police tape, watching the firefighters pack up. The hotel clerk had called his manager in, and the man was not happy. He was loudly haranguing one of the other sheriff's deputies about the cost of the damage and the lawlessness that the sheriff's office had allowed to go unchecked in town.

The sheriff finally backed down. "Excuse me for a moment. You two stay right here."

"He doesn't believe us," Mya said once the sheriff and deputy had stepped out of hearing distance.

Gideon put his arm around her and drew her into him. His warmth was a welcome balm against the cold. "He's suspicious. That might be his natural state, he is the sheriff, or he could think something's off."

If he was any kind of sheriff, he knew something was off, Mya thought. They hadn't been able to explain who the man that attacked them in the adjacent room was or why he'd fled. And they'd overheard the very loud manager say that no one was checked into that room.

After a few minutes, the sheriff returned. "Y'all are free to go. I'm sure Kelvin—" the sheriff's chin jutted in the direction of the motel's manager who was still waving his arms and fussing at the deputy "—will set you up with another room."

"We won't be needing a room. May as well get on the road, get ahead of traffic," Gideon said.

"Wait, a minute. That's it?" Mya asked, surprised.

She felt Gideon tense beside her and knew she'd made a mistake, but the sheriff's sudden change from suspicious to just letting them walk away was a shock.

"Unless there's something else you'd like to tell me?" The sheriff's intense green eyes locked on Mya's face.

"No. I just—"

"Deputy Snodgrass is right. We have been having a bit of trouble with vandalism and destruction of property around these parts in the last several months. It's mostly been harmless stuff, broken windows, and dirty words spray-painted on walls." The sheriff took a pair of leather gloves from his pocket and pulled one glove on, then the other. "The last couple incidents though, have been more serious. This isn't the first fire. Perp probably thought no one was in that section of the motel. Everyone knows Kelvin likes to fill the rooms closest to the lobby first. Saves him a few steps if someone needs a towel or has some other problem with the room."

Gideon didn't believe that for a minute. The Tahoe was parked in the space right outside the room. Of course, the sheriff didn't know that.

The sheriff turned to look at Gideon. "Our firebug likes to tag the place somewhere the fire isn't likely to get it. That's probably why he was in the adjacent room. You probably scared him half to death when you busted through that door."

Gideon's eyes went dark and menacing. "I hope so."

"Well, hopefully, your description will help us catch this guy."

Mya slid a glance at Gideon. That was a vain hope.

"We have your contact information," the sheriff said,

stretching his hand out to Gideon. "If we have any further questions—"

The two men shook hands. "You know how to reach us."

"Ma'am." The sheriff tipped his chin and walked away.

Mya slid into the passenger seat and buckled up. "That was a sudden change in attitude."

Gideon's eyebrows rose. "And a good one for us. Let's not question it."

Mya felt heat climb up the back of her neck. "I'm sorry. I wasn't trying to raise the sheriff's suspicions. It's just his change toward believing us was so abrupt."

"Don't worry about it. The deputy probably convinced him the easiest answer was most likely correct."

Mya followed Gideon's gaze out the front windshield. The motel manager was now talking to the sheriff, but the sheriff's gaze was locked on the Tahoe.

Gideon started the ignition. "But we'd better get out of here before the sheriff changes his mind."

THEY WERE LUCKY the town was suffering from a spate of vandalism. Gideon wasn't sure the sheriff would have let them leave so easily otherwise. As it was, he was pretty sure the sheriff hadn't completely bought their story. There were enough holes in it to drive the town's fire truck through, but the sheriff had no way to prove the story not true, and that had saved them a lot of trouble.

What he had to figure out was how someone could have followed them from the city without being seen. He'd kept an eye out for a tail as they'd left the city limits, but he hadn't been as vigilant once they'd crossed state lines, figuring if they'd had a tail, he'd have made it by then.

Another possibility sprang to mind.

He hit the steering wheel with this palm.

Mya startled. "What?"

"We need to make a quick detour."

"Detour?" Her voice rose in surprise. "Why? Where?"

"We need to change cars. This one could have a tracker on it. That could be how our fire starter found us at the motel." Gideon mentally kicked himself for not having considered that Mya's pursuers would have placed a tracker on the Tahoe. By now, the person pursuing her had to know he was sticking close to her. He'd been so focused on making sure her phone and computer didn't have spyware or a tracker, he hadn't considered he might be the one leading Mya's attackers to her.

"You really think—"

He shot a sidelong glance at her. "I don't know, but I'm not willing to take the chance."

Mya's expression darkened. "It was Shannon. She could have had someone place the tracker on your car while we were in her office."

That was a possibility, but it wasn't the only one. Mya's history with and animosity toward Shannon clouded her judgment about the woman. She wanted Shannon to be the responsible party, so she viewed everything that had happened through that lens. He didn't have the same luxury, not if he wanted to keep Mya safe.

Gideon turned a serious gaze on her. "You don't know that. Focusing on one person without evidence can be dangerous. Might lead us to miss something vital." If he was right about a tracker being on the Tahoe, he'd already put her in danger. He wouldn't let it happen again.

Mya's gaze cut across the car. "But you do think that the attack at the motel is related to all the other stuff that's happened, right?"

"Unless there's a reason other than your formula for someone to try to kill you?"

Mya snorted. "Not that I know of—"

A clinking coming from the Tahoe's engine interrupted their conversation. The chassis shook like an earthquake, starting with a slight rumble and quickly growing into full convulsions. Gideon pulled to the side of the road as smoke began seeping from under the hood.

"What's wrong with the car?"

Gideon didn't answer and instead focused on the road behind them. It was clear of any vehicles, but that didn't mean it would stay that way. He scanned the trees on either side of the highway and saw nothing, although he knew that didn't mean no one was out there.

He kept the Tahoe in pristine condition; he'd taken it in for service last week. It seemed like their attacker had done more than just install a tracker. He was setting them up for an ambush.

Stay with the car or bail out? Either way, he and Mya could be walking into a trap.

"I'm going to come around to your side of the car. When I open your door, I want you to get into the cover of those trees as quickly as you can." Gideon pointed to the trees lining the side of the road.

Mya looked at him with fear in her eyes. "Gideon?"

"Trust me." He held her gaze, willing her to see the single most important truth in his life. That he would lay down his life before he'd let any harm come to her.

He exited the driver's side of the car. He stopped at the trunk and moved the two guns in the safe installed in

the boot of the Tahoe to his overnight bag before sling-
ing it over his shoulder. He studied the tree line and road
one more time before opening Mya's door. They were
alone for the moment, but every instinct he possessed
screamed they wouldn't be for much longer.

Fear swam in the eyes that met his own. "Run for
the trees. Don't stop. Don't look back. I'll be right behind you."

Mya hopped out of the car and sprinted for the trees.

He followed, his boots slipping on the rocky terrain.

It wouldn't take long to find the Tahoe along the side
of the road. Gideon wanted to put as much distance between them and the car as he could before that happened.

"Gideon, what's going on? What happened to the
car?" Mya asked.

He didn't answer. For one, he didn't know exactly
what had been done to the car, although he had his suspicions. But more importantly, it wasn't their pressing
problem at the moment. He still wasn't sure whether
they were walking away from an ambush or into one.

After a few moments, they'd made it deep enough
into the trees that he was sure they couldn't be seen.
He changed directions, so they were moving parallel to
the highway.

He listened for sounds of other humans stalking
the trees—the snap of twigs underneath a boot, heavy
breathing, the sound of a bullet being chambered.

Thankfully, all he heard were the usual woodland
creatures and sounds.

They'd put a good bit of distance between them and
the Tahoe, but he had no idea how far they'd have to
walk before they got to safety. He'd tried his phone, but
he couldn't get service. He didn't want to chance walk-

ing closer to the road. No service also meant no GPS, so they kept moving, edging into the woods a little deeper whenever the trees thinned out.

They hiked through the trees. Mya didn't complain. In fact, she had said nothing to him since he'd failed to answer her question, but he could see exhaustion was catching up with her. Despite the cold weather, sweat trickled down the sides of her face, and she'd unzipped her jacket.

Mya stopped short, hunching over with her hands on her knees. "Gideon, I've got to stop. I need to rest."

She'd surprised him by keeping pace for this long. They'd been walking, nearly running, through the trees for forty minutes now.

He eased their bags onto the ground. "Just for a few minutes. We need to keep moving."

The daylight peeking over the tops of the trees made it easier for them to navigate the dense foliage, but it also made it easier to be spotted.

Mya eased down onto the trunk of a fallen tree. "I take it you don't think whatever is wrong with the car is an accident?"

"No—" his eyes pierced the trees "—I don't."

Mya pressed her palms against her knees. "What do you think happened?"

"Later." Gideon reached for the bags on the ground and slung them onto his shoulder. "Let's get moving." He reached to help her up.

MYA PULLED AWAY from him, her mood changing swiftly from anxious to irritated. "Don't you dare brush me off. I'm in this too. It's my life at stake."

"I know that," Gideon replied sharply. "And I'm trying to keep you alive." He started walking.

Mya fell in step beside him. "So, this is how it's going to be again. My God. I'd have never pegged you for a coward."

"Now is not the time." His tone was even, but his words came out through clenched teeth. Irritation etched lines in Gideon's face. Too bad because she was angry and sick of biting back all the words that stood between them.

"It's never the time." Her thighs strained with the effort to match his stride. "You're pulling away from me because of last night." She stopped walking. "You keep doing this. Letting me in just a little then pulling away."

Gideon stopped short but didn't look at her. "Last night was—"

"Amazing." Mya grabbed his arm and turned him to face her. "It was absolutely amazing. And I'm not just talking about sex. You opened up to me, and I'm not sure you ever did that while we were married. You've always kept everything inside—what you're thinking, what you're feeling. But a relationship, a marriage, can't survive like that."

"We're not married anymore."

Mya squared her shoulders. "I heard you last night." Surprise lit Gideon's eyes as she continued. "I heard you say you loved me. Did you mean it?"

The silence seemed to last an eternity before he finally answered. "You want me to open up. Okay, here it is. I'm not standing here in these woods with you because of a promise made twelve years ago. I'm here because there is absolutely nothing I wouldn't do to protect you. I loved you at nineteen. I loved you the day I signed the divorce papers. I love you now, and I will love you until my last breath."

Her heart raced. It was everything she'd ever wanted to hear from him, but she knew it wasn't enough. Not if they were to have a second chance that had a shot at lasting. "I love you too. I still want to be with you. But love is not enough. You have to decide to take a chance. You can be the Ice Man with everyone else, but not with me. I deserve more."

"You do. That's why I asked for the divorce. My time in the military, the things I saw." He shook his head. "It messed with my head, and you shouldn't have to deal with that."

Her heart softened. She cupped his cheek. "I was your wife. I would have done everything I could have to help you."

"Mya—"

"I want us to try again."

He leaned his face into her palm. "We've been down this road before."

She reached up and cupped his cheek. "I'm scared too, Gideon, but I want to try again."

Her heart pounded, both with longing for him and fear that he'd reject her entreaty.

Gideon closed the inches between them, and this time, instead of pushing him away, she pulled him to her.

His mouth met hers, and he kissed her hungrily. She closed her eyes and melted into the kiss, meeting his fervor with her own. She opened her mouth beneath his, and he wrapped his arms around her waist, bringing their bodies as close to each other as they could get in their bulky winter clothes. Despite the freezing air whirling around them, an inferno was building in the pit of her stomach.

This could be a new beginning for them. They weren't dumb kids anymore. They'd both matured, achieved success on their own. They'd learn from the mistakes of their past and build something that would last this time. She knew they could do it as long as they were open with each other.

Gideon stilled, and doubt flooded her. Was he pulling away again?

Mya opened her eyes, prepared to go another round. Gideon put a finger to his lips, the distress on his face sending fear shooting through her.

He pulled her behind a large pine tree and put his lips to her ear. "There's someone out there. When I tell you to, run. Don't stop and don't look back."

Mya hadn't seen him pull his gun, but it was in his hand now. Staying low, he moved to her left, taking cover behind a large evergreen.

Mya peered around the tree trunk. She could just make out the shape of a person, a man, from the size. He was the same height as the fake cop who'd attempted to kidnap her and had the same dirty blond hair again. The sensation that she'd seen him before tickled the back of her brain.

A branch snapped, and Gideon pivoted, firing off three shots in rapid succession.

"Run!" he yelled, pushing her toward a thick bramble.

She weaved through the trees, not sure where she was going but not looking back, just as Gideon instructed. She prayed he was right behind her.

Several more shots rang out, and she pumped her legs faster. The forest floor pitched downward suddenly, and she struggled to stay on her feet as she slipped and slid down the slope. She stumbled over tree roots, but a vise clamped around her arm before she slid all the way to the ground.

Gideon hauled her to her feet. "We have to keep going."

They slid down the incline and burst through the trees into a small parking lot at the back of a line of buildings. They ran around the building and found themselves at one of the rest stops along the highway.

Just a few days before Christmas, it was fairly busy with people getting an early start on their holiday travel. The sight of them, dirt laden and out of breath, drew a few curious stares.

Gideon wrapped his arm around her, leading her into the line of travelers going in and out of the building, his gun once again tucked away in the waistband of his jeans.

Mya glanced over her shoulder as she stepped into the warmth and relative safety of the rest stop. She didn't see anyone coming from the direction of the trees, but that didn't mean much.

Had their pursuer simply blended into the crowd as they had?

Chapter Twenty

Mya washed up in the rest stop ladies' room, fighting to control her racing thoughts. How had she ended up more or less bathing in a rest stop sink, her research gone, running for her life? Most importantly, who was this man trying to kill her? And why did she feel like she knew him somehow?

The plethora of emotions she'd cycled through over the last several days all crashed down on her at once. She wasn't a crier by nature, but the impulse to sink to the floor and sob almost overpowered her.

She splashed water on her face with trembling hands. Stress. From the situation and from the emotions churning between herself and Gideon. Their confrontation in the woods had felt like a breakthrough of sorts, even if he had been right about it not being the right time or place. They definitely had more pressing matters to deal with.

Mya exited the restroom to the sound of holiday music and found Gideon waiting for her just outside the door.

"What are we going to do now?" Mya asked.

"We're going to get a new car. A major rest stop like this is bound to have a rental car place somewhere nearby. West has corporate accounts with most of them, and if they don't, I'll just use my corporate card."

"We can use mine. You shouldn't have to pay for a rental."

He shook his head. "No. It would take significantly more pull to have a trace on your credit card than to put a tracker on the Tahoe, but I don't want to take the chance. We don't know who we're dealing with, but if it is Shannon or someone else involved in Big Pharma, it's clear they have the resources." He glanced over at her. "There's no way they'd get by West's security."

"This is all so crazy. Switching cars and Molotov cocktails. Brian and Rebecca murdered. All for what?"

"People will do all kinds of things for the kind of money TriGen stands to make off your treatment."

A cashier at the rest stop directed them to a rental car company a quarter mile away. The morning's events followed by a trek through the woods left Mya exhausted but she kept pace with Gideon.

They arrived just as the office opened. It didn't take long to fill out the paperwork and get the keys for a nondescript green four-door Chevrolet sedan.

He was signing his name to the contract when Mya gasped. He dropped the pen and reached for the gun tucked into his waistband.

But he, Mya, and the clerk were still the only ones in the office, and a quick scan of the parking lot showed it was also clear.

Mya's gaze was locked onto the television hanging on the wall behind the clerk. The bottom of the screen was cluttered with the usual breaking news announcements, but Detective Kamal stood behind a cluster of microphones on the screen.

"You mind turning that up?" Gideon asked the clerk.

"At this time, we believe the murders of Brian Leeds

and Rebecca Conway are related to each other and to the fire at TriGen. We continue to investigate," the detective was saying.

Off-screen, reporters began yelling questions at Kamal before she'd looked up from the paper she'd been reading. "Detective, our sources say that you are about to arrest TriGen director, Dr. Mya Rochon. Is that true?"

Kamal's expression was withering. "When we arrest a person for these crimes, we will announce it."

"But is Dr. Rochon a suspect?" the reporter called out.

Detective Kamal glared. "The doctor is a suspect. Excuse me." She turned away from the microphones and headed up the steps to the doors of the police station. The television shot moved back to the in-studio anchor.

"How could she say that? I can't—" Mya couldn't catch her breath. It felt like she'd been punched in the chest.

Gideon shot her a look and shook his head.

The clerk, who'd had his back to them watching along, turned back to face Gideon and Mya. "Everything okay?"

"Fine." Gideon hoisted their bags onto his shoulder once more. He grabbed the keys to the rental with one hand and her elbow with the other, and he shepherded her out the door. Mya made no effort to resist. All she could think about was Kamal's words. She was a suspect in a murder.

"I can't believe this," Mya said once they were in the car. "She all but called me a murderer on television!"

"Calm down." Gideon adjusted the mirrors in the car and turned over the engine. "Let's find a place to get breakfast, and I'll call James, see what's going on."

They drove about a quarter mile before Gideon pulled

into the parking lot of a diner with a retro design too appealing to be genuinely old.

Mya's stomach grumbled, but she ignored it, impatiently waiting for Gideon's call to West's offices to connect. It took only seconds, but it felt like hours.

"Have you seen the news?" James asked as soon as Gideon identified himself.

"Just a little while ago. What the hell's going on back there?" Gideon demanded.

"Detective Kamal is determined to pin this on Mya. I've talked to our police sources, and they say Kamal is convinced the fire and murders are all Mya's attempt to cover up the fact that her research is a failure."

Mya struggled to comprehend what she was hearing. "Without any evidence."

"Kamal confirmed the weapon used to kill Rebecca was the award found next to her. It had Mya's fingerprints on it."

Gideon swore. "Of course it did. It's her award."

"And that's what the prosecutor said when Kamal took it to her to get a warrant for Mya's arrest." Mya felt like all the air had been sucked out of the car. Kamal wanted to arrest her. Panic roiled her stomach.

Gideon reached for her hand and squeezed. "Brendan's keeping an eye on things, and I'll let you know if anything changes." He kept hold of her hand as he filled James in on the attack at the hotel and being pursued through the woods. "We've switched cars. I need you to get someone to pick up the Tahoe." Gideon glanced up at the sky. "We should get to Ross's house by early afternoon." Assuming the weather held.

Gideon ended the call and turned to face Mya. "I don't want you to worry."

Mya stared out the front windshield of the sedan. "Sure, I won't worry about being arrested for murder." A choked, desperate laugh escaped her lips.

"Mya, look at me." She turned to face him. "You aren't going to be arrested. We will get your research notes from Ross and prove your treatment works. Kamal's theory falls apart if the treatment works. Mya, baby, are you listening to me?" Gideon's tone took on a note of desperation.

Mya swallowed hard and forced herself to focus on his face. Some of the hysteria swirling inside of her subsided. He was an anchor, keeping her from tipping over into a full-blown panic attack.

She nodded.

"Come on," Gideon said, bringing her hand to his lips for a kiss. "Let's get something to eat and make a plan."

OVER BREAKFAST, GIDEON and Mya agreed the best course of action was to continue with the plan to speak with Rebecca's mother before heading to Irwin's cabin. Proving the treatment worked had taken on greater urgency, but Kamal's insistence on pinning the murders on Mya at the expense of finding the real killers lit a fire in Mya. If Kamal wouldn't get justice for Rebecca and Brian, then it was left to her to make sure they got it.

As Gideon drove the gravel drive cutting through the trailer park, a long-forgotten memory floated to the surface of Mya's mind. The one and only time she and her mother had gone to Louisiana to visit Nana Mimi, her maternal grandmother. Nana Mimi had lived in a mobile home park much like the one they currently drove through. Her mother had promised there would be a lot of kids to play with and there were. Mya had made several friends in the first days.

The friendships hadn't lasted long.

She and her mother were supposed to stay for the entire summer, but a week after they arrived, her mother and Nana Mimi had gotten into a huge argument over what Nana Mimi called their wicked city lifestyle. The next morning her mother had packed their suitcases, and they'd boarded a Greyhound back to New York.

Mya shook herself back into the present and noticed residents eying the car from front porches and from behind dusty windows as it passed.

Gideon stopped the rental in front of a white single wide. A wreath proclaiming "Merry Christmas" hung on the front door. The curtains at the window facing the front fluttered.

"Someone's home," Gideon said, turning off the engine. "I think you should do the talking if she lets us inside."

"Really?" She didn't even try to hide her surprise. He'd barely wanted to let her out of the house over the last several days. Now he wanted her to question Rebecca's mother. "What's the catch?"

Gideon chuckled. "No catch. I think questions about her daughter will go down easier if they're asked by another woman, especially one who worked with and cared about her daughter."

"That makes sense. Any questions in particular you want me to ask?"

"Just try to elicit as much information as you can. We aren't totally sure what might be helpful. I do want to show her Shannon's picture, see if she recognizes her."

Mya exhaled a deep breath. "Okay." She reached for the door handle.

"Hey." Gideon reached out and swept a finger gently along her cheek. "Don't worry. I'll be right there. I'll jump in if you need me, but I know you can do this."

His touch was reassuring. The curtains at the mobile home's front window fluttered again.

They hopped out of the car and climbed the stairs of the small porch.

Gideon rapped on the screen door.

The main door opened a crack, and a dishwater blonde peeked around its side. "Yes?" Marie's blue eyes reflected suspicion.

"Miss Calcott? My name is Mya Rochon. This is Gideon Wright. I worked with your daughter, Rebecca."

"I know who you are. Rebecca spoke about you often."

From the woman's expression, Mya couldn't tell whether that was a positive or negative, so she plowed on. "I want to express my condolences for your loss."

"Thank you, but I doubt you came all this way to convey condolences. What do you want?"

"Could we come in, please? We just want to talk."

"I have to get to work."

"Please? We just want a few minutes of your time," Mya implored. She couldn't help but be glad they hadn't called before coming. There was no way Marie would have agreed to talk to them over the phone. As it was, it was going to take all the charm and finesse she possessed to convince the woman to invite them in. Mya changed tacks. "I care about Rebecca and I want to find out who did this to her. That's why we're here. Mr. Wright is a private investigator. I've hired him to help find Rebecca's killer."

Marie's expression didn't change, but she opened the door a little wider. "Isn't that a job for the police?"

"The police have multiple cases to investigate," Gideon answered. "This is the only case I'm working."

Marie eyed them for another moment before reaching out and flicking the lock on the screen door. "Come in." She held the screen door open and allowed them to pass into the house.

Marie waved them to the well-worn sofa and flopped into one of two chairs at the round table set against the opposite wall.

"What do you want to know?" Marie drummed her finger against the tabletop.

Mya shifted on her couch. "I only met Rebecca seven months ago when she applied for the receptionist job at TriGen. Anything you can tell us about Rebecca before she moved to New York might be helpful."

"Rebecca is, was, smart, ambitious, but she was so impatient and more than a little entitled though who can say where she got that from. I mean, look around, I don't got much, but I worked for every bit of it."

"I'm sure you did."

"I tried to instill the right values in her. Study hard, work hard, earn your way in this life. Some of it got through, I think. Boy, was that girl smart. Got all As all the way through high school. I'm not ashamed to say I was more than a little proud."

"Of course you were. It's an accomplishment for both of you."

"You're right about that. I can tell neither of you have kids, but it's no easy feat raising one by yourself," Marie said.

"You're right that we're not parents, but Gideon and I

were raised by single parents, so we know it's not easy," Mya responded, hoping to build rapport with Marie. "Do you know why Rebecca left college?"

Marie grabbed a cigarette from the pack of Marlboros on the table and went to the rear window. "Some irony, huh? I work in healthcare, yet I'm hooked on these little killers." She pushed the window sash up. "Rebecca didn't leave school. She was kicked out. Never went to class. Failed all the tests." She took a long pull on the cigarette and held it for several seconds. "Entitled," she finally said, expelling cigarette smoke with the word.

"What did she do after she left school?"

"For a while, nothing. Not until I made it clear she had to get a job or get out. She worked at the public library for a while. Shelving books, reading to the kids, that kind of thing. Then one day, she said she was leaving."

"Did she say why?"

"There was nothing here for her, she said, which, to be honest, I couldn't argue against." Marie blew out another plume of smoke. "She said she was going to try a city like Philly or DC. Someplace where she could work and go to school part-time. Although, I suspect the school part was entirely for my benefit. I'd been on her case to go back to school."

"It does look like she took a few classes at a university in New York."

"That's good, I guess. That girl was too smart for her own good." Tears pooled in Marie's eyes.

"We know this must be hard for you. Just a few more questions."

Marie glanced at the watch on her wrist. "Only a few. I got to leave for work soon."

"Do you know how Rebecca ended up in New York?"

At the other woman's confused expression, Mya added, "You said Rebecca left Hagerstown with plans to go to DC or Philadelphia. What made her change her mind and move to New York?"

"Oh, well, I don't think it was so much of a change in mind as it was she'd set her mind to moving to a city. Probably any city would have done. I don't know for sure why she chose New York. Maybe just that that was where the bus was going."

"Do you remember the exact day she left?"

"Oh, yeah. February 14. I tried to talk her into waiting a month or two until it was warmer. I mean, who wants to move in the winter? But she wanted to go on Valentine's Day. Said it was a day when people got engaged and started new lives. She wasn't getting engaged, but it was the start of a new life." Marie sucked on the cigarette. "I don't go in for all that romantic claptrap, but I didn't want her to leave here on an argument so…" Marie shrugged, flicked the nub of her cigarette out the window, and closed the sash.

"I'm sorry, I've got to go to work."

Mya rose from the couch with Gideon by her side. She gave him a nod. He reached into his coat pocket and pulled out his phone. "Just one more question. Do you recognize this woman?"

Gideon called Shannon's photo up and held the phone out. Marie took it, turning it so she could see the picture right side up.

Marie's eyes lit with recognition. "'Course I know who she is. Shannon. She looks just like she did when she was growing up." From the frown on Marie's face, it didn't appear she had fond memories of little Shannon.

Mya had a hard time keeping herself from cheering.

She could feel it. This was the connection they'd been looking for. Proof that Shannon was behind everything that had happened.

"She and my Rebecca are cousins on Rebecca's father's side. Rebecca idolized Shannon. Rebecca cried for a week when Shannon moved away." Marie handed the phone back to Gideon. "I tried to keep the girls in touch, but—" Marie shrugged again "—you know how it goes." Marie's gaze darted between Mya and Gideon. "Why? What does Shannon have to do with this?"

Chapter Twenty-One

Gideon followed Marie's white Altima out of the trailer park and onto the highway. Marie sped off the moment the Altima's tires met the pavement. But she'd been happy enough to be late to work in order to dish about Shannon.

"Interesting family," Gideon said, eyeing the distant taillights on Marie's car.

"What's the saying? Every family is dysfunctional in its own way."

Gideon shot a glance across the car. "According to Marie, Shannon was a devil intent on leading the little angel Rebecca astray."

"Pretty much tracks with grown-up Shannon, in my experience. You know what this means, right? This is the connection we needed to prove that Rebecca was working for Shannon, and Shannon is the one behind Rebecca and Brian's murders."

"It's a connection. We'll pass it on to Detective Kamal and get started digging up the evidence we need to prove Travers is involved." Kamal wouldn't be able to ignore the relationship between Rebecca and Travers, but it didn't prove Travers was behind the theft and murders.

Mya studied his face with a frown on her own. "You still don't believe Shannon is behind this?"

"I follow the evidence, and right now, we don't have enough to say definitively who is, or isn't, behind the attacks."

He knew she didn't understand why he wasn't as willing to commit to one theory just yet. It was looking more and more likely that Shannon Travers had something to do with the events surrounding Mya in the last several days. But he knew how dangerous jumping to conclusions could be. He wasn't willing to take that chance when Mya's safety was at risk.

Frustration radiated from Mya. They spent the rest of the trip in near silence. When she spoke to him again, it was to give directions to Ross's cabin. His GPS was top-of-the-line, but the old mountain road wasn't always marked, and a light snow had started falling as they drove.

"Slow down. You're coming up on the driveway."

Gideon tapped the breaks and squinted out the front windshield. Mya pointed to the right. It took him a moment to see the dirt path that opened off the main drag. If Mya hadn't been pointing her finger at it, he would have missed it altogether.

He made the right turn and eased the car down a road that was only slightly wider than a footpath. West would pay a fee for the scratches being made on the side of the car by the overgrown trees and brush. The sedan bounced the two hundred yards down the dirt-packed road through woods before the trees gave way to a clearing. An unremarkable wood cabin sat at its center.

A man Gideon recognized as Irwin Ross from the file West had compiled stepped out onto the porch as they pulled up. Ross looked more like a lumberjack than a brilliant scientist.

Mya exited the car the moment Gideon shifted into Park and bounded into the man's arms. He moved more deliberately, sizing up the man in front of him. Ross was tall and muscled, no doubt from working the land around the cabin, but obviously well into his senior discount years. His long gray hair was pulled back in a braid. As Ross descended the stairs, Gideon noticed a limp and wondered whether the older man had gotten it before or after he'd moved to his cabin hideaway. Ross caught Gideon's eye, the cautiousness in them letting Gideon know Ross knew he was being sized up and that he was doing some sizing of his own.

When Gideon got close enough, Ross extended his hand. "Irwin Ross."

Gideon took Ross's outstretched hand. "Gideon Wright."

"Y'all come on in. I've made us lunch," Ross said, turning for the cabin.

Mya's laugh bounced off the trees. "Y'all? I think West Virginia is rubbing off on you?"

Ross grinned. "When in Rome, as they say."

Ross hooked his arm around Mya's shoulders and pulled her into his side like a father welcoming home his progeny. Ross turned Mya toward the front of the house, and the two climbed the steps to the house, leaving Gideon to trail behind.

The inside of the cabin was just as sparse as the outside. A dark-colored couch and a single end table faced a television that had to be at least a decade old. The living room opened onto a kitchen so small, the three of them wouldn't have fit in it at the same time.

"Come on in. Have a seat." Ross waved them toward the square pine dining table he'd set up in the small amount of floor space between the couch and the kitchen. "I made a stew. Figured with all the traveling, you'd need something that sticks to your ribs."

Ross filled two bowls with stew and set them onto the table with thick slices of bread he'd baked himself. He'd eaten his lunch while he was waiting for them to arrive, but he joined them at the table and nursed a cup of coffee.

Mya had given Ross a quick summary of the fire at the lab and told him about Rebecca's murder when they'd spoken on the phone, but as they ate, she filled in the details and described the attack at the hotel.

"And you have no idea who the man was who shot at you?" Irwin said.

"West was able to get a traffic cam photo, but it was too grainy to identify him," Mya said.

"The hotel attacker was the same height and build as the motorcycle driver, so it's a safe assumption it's the same guy," Gideon said.

"Good. Good. That should make it easier for the police to find him," Irwin said.

Mya shared a look with Gideon. "We didn't tell the sheriff about the earlier attacks."

"What? Why not?"

"Because we didn't want to get stuck answering questions for days. I needed to get to you and get whatever parts of my research Brian shared with you."

"Yes, about that. I'm sure you're upset with me for going behind your back."

"Irwin, we don't have to—"

"Yes, yes, we do. I turned over the lab to you because I knew you'd do what I hadn't been able to do. Find a cure for the horrible disease that took my son. And you did, a thing for which I will forever be grateful." Irwin reached across the table and took both her hands in his. "I want you to know that I always believed in you. My checking up on you, chalk it up to a lonely old man, reliving his glory days."

Mya gave her mentor's boney hands a squeeze. "Your research is the foundation of the treatment. If it hadn't been for everything you taught me and all the work you put in before we even met, there's no way I'd have found a successful formula."

"That's kind of you to say, but you'd have figured it out. That brain of yours wouldn't quit until it did." Irwin slid his hands from hers and slapped them down on the table. "Now enough patting ourselves on the back. You'll want to see those notes."

Irwin stood.

Gideon did the same. "I have a few calls I need to make."

"Well, then you'll need to go down the mountain to Phil's store. No cell phone tower reaches way up here, but Phil will let you use his Wi-Fi connection."

Gideon frowned. He was sure they hadn't been followed. Not only had he been on guard the entire time since picking up the rental car, but there was no way anyone could have followed them up the mountain or down Irwin's drive without being seen. Still, he didn't like the idea of leaving Mya alone. He doubted whoever was out there planned to give up, and even without a tracker on their car, it wouldn't be hard to figure out where they were headed. It might take whoever was after them some time, but they'd eventually discover Ross's location. He'd need to address the issue with Ross before leaving. It was probably not safe for him to stay in this isolated cabin, at least not until they'd proved Mya's treatment was a success.

Mya rose and came to stand by his side, placing a hand on his arm. "I'll be fine. Irwin and I are going to be talking shop for a while."

Irwin chucked. "Don't worry, son. The only way to this cabin is by going past the general store. If you're down there, you'll be the first to know about anyone heading this way." Irwin pulled open one of the kitchen drawers and took out a revolver. "And if they should get past you, I know how to use this bad boy."

Gideon still wasn't convinced, but he didn't have a choice. He needed to check in with James and make sure Kamal hadn't somehow secured a warrant for Mya's arrest.

"Go. The sooner you make your calls, the sooner you'll get back here." She gave Gideon a little push toward the door.

He headed back down the mountain, the snow still falling lightly, a clutch of nerves twisting his stomach. He needed to check with James, and it wouldn't take him long, but leaving Mya... They'd been apart for twelve years, but in less than a week, he'd grown so he didn't want to let her out of his sight. And not just because of everything that was happening at the moment.

His argument with Mya may have been ill-timed, but she was right. He was a coward when it came to their relationship. He'd told himself that he was being mature, letting Mya go so she could achieve her dreams, but he'd allowed his insecurities and fears to ruin the relationship he'd valued most in the world. But now, she was offering him a second chance. He would not make the same mistakes again.

Twenty minutes after leaving Irwin's cabin, Gideon pulled the sedan to a stop in front of a rundown building that was little more than a shack. He tried making his call from the car, but there was still no signal.

He got out of the car and went into the store.

A grizzled bear of a man looked up from the magazine he'd been reading behind the counter. "Can I help you with anything?"

"I just wanted to make a call." Gideon held up his cell phone.

The clerk squinted at him. "You visiting Irwin?"

Gideon's instincts went on alert. "Yes."

The man nodded. "Figured. We don't get strangers up here that much, but since Irwin used to be one of you fancy people…"

Gideon wouldn't have described himself as a fancy person, but everyone was entitled to their own opinion. "Irwin said I could get phone service in the store."

"Yep. Have to use the Wi-Fi, though." The man tapped a piece of paper taped to the side of the cash register. "Password's right here."

Gideon didn't care much for using other people's Wi-Fi connections. May as well just give them any personal information from the phone, but since he didn't keep personal information on his phone and had little choice at the moment, he logged on to the store's network.

Phil busied himself with arranging items at the far end of the checkout counter, but the tilt of his head made it clear he was listening to his only customer's conversation.

"Where are you right now?" James bellowed the moment the phone call connected.

"I'm at the general store near Ross's cabin. What's going on?" Gideon's pulse picked up the pace. "Did Kamal get the warrant for Mya's arrest?"

Phil's eyes widened, and any pretense at not eavesdropping fell away.

"Is Mya with you?"

The urgency in James's voice sent Gideon's stomach into freefall. "No. I left her at Irwin Ross's cabin. What the hell is going on, James?" He paced the store wishing there was better cellphone coverage in the mountains.

"IT cleaned up the photo of the motorcycle and ran it through facial recognition detectors. We got a hit on the name Adam Ross."

"Adam Ross?" Gideon said.

"Irwin Ross's younger son. I looked up that tattoo you sent. It's a prison tattoo, though lucky for us, not a very common one. It's found in prisons in Kentucky and northern West Virginia." Papers rustled on the other end of the phone. "I remembered Mya mentioning that Irwin had two sons. The older son's death spurred Ross's research. Adam has been in and out of prison on drug related charges for the last fifteen years."

"I take it he's currently out."

"Earlier this year. Served every bit of his last prison sentence too. No time off for good behavior. Cops suspect him of killing a man while he was inside, but you know how that goes. No one wanted to testify."

Gideon ended the call and sprinted to the car. The snow had begun to come down heavier, but Gideon pressed the car to move as fast as he dared, but he wasn't familiar with the curvy mountain roads. The last thing he needed was to drive off into a ditch or over the side of the mountain.

If James was right and Adam Ross was behind all this, he didn't do it on his own. Adam wouldn't have known that Mya had found a cure. Irwin must have told his son and explained what it could mean for them both.

With Mya, Brian and Rebecca out of the way, Irwin could step in, either under the pretext of reconstructing Mya's research or simply claiming that he'd never stopped working on finding a solution and had finally been successful. Everyone who could prove that the work wasn't his would be dead.

"Any idea where Adam is now?" Gideon asked.

"No, but I have notified the sheriff up there. Their offices aren't close to where you are. It will take them at least an hour to get to you."

Mya didn't have an hour. Irwin was smart. He had seen his chance to get Mya alone and had taken it. It would be a lot easier for Adam and Irwin to deal with him and Mya separately.

If Adam wasn't living with Irwin in the cabin, he was probably somewhere nearby. Since Irwin and Adam hadn't been able to take him and Mya out before they'd arrived at the cabin, they'd have determined that they'd have to do it there and make some excuse for their disappearance.

Mya could already be...

He turned a curve and saw the opening for Irwin's driveway.

"Hang on, Mya, baby. Just hang on for me a little while longer."

Chapter Twenty-Two

Mya flipped through one of Irwin's old research note-books. They'd cleared the table of lunch, and Irwin had carried a box containing several years' worth of his old research notes from his spare bedroom. Her laptop was on the table, the research from her flash drive open on its screen.

Irwin had never been one for computers. When she'd worked under him at the lab, one of her responsibilities had been to input all the information he scratched into his notebooks that day into the system. Thankfully, she was used to his cramped writing and barely decipherable notes in the margins of the pages. Between his notebook, her research notes Brian had sent to him, and the research she had on the flash drive, Mya was sure she could reconstruct the treatment and show it was viable.

"Irwin, this is wonderful. It's just what I need." She leaned over and threw her arms around him, giving him a quick hug before turning back to the notebook in front of her.

Irwin chuckled. "I'm glad I could be of help." He cleared his throat. "So, you're back with your ex?"

Mya stopped flipping and looked up at her old mentor. In all the years they'd worked together, they'd never talked too much about their private lives. He knew she'd been married, and she knew how the death of his elder son had gutted him and that he blamed himself for his younger son having turned to a life of crime. It had taken years for them to share that much information, and it had come out only in drips and drabs. This was the first direct question about her personal life she could ever remember Irwin asking.

"Well, I wouldn't say we're together. I mean, physically we are here at your cabin together, but not together, together, you know what I mean." She felt like a teenager again, explaining to her mom that Jeffery Jordan wasn't really her boyfriend. She could feel the heat rising in her cheeks.

Irwin's laughter filled the small space. "I have no idea what you mean, actually. The man has driven you over three or four states to get information he doesn't understand. Trust me, you two are together, whether you know it or not."

Mya didn't know what to say to that. "Um…well, do you mind if I…" She pointed toward the hall, hoping he'd get her meaning.

"Sure. It's the second door on the left."

Mya escaped to the small bathroom. She didn't know what she and Gideon were to each other. She'd meant every word she'd said, but if they gave their relationship another chance, she knew they had a long road ahead of them if they wanted it to last this time. And she did. She really wanted their relationship to go the long haul this time. But that definitely seemed like something she should share with Gideon before she shared it with anyone else.

Mya washed up and exited the bathroom. From the

hallway, she could see that Irwin's chair at the table was empty. Her eyes went to the door's spare bedroom.

He had mentioned a second box of notebooks.

She should grab the box while she was here.

Irwin's spare room had always doubled as storage, but it seemed as if he'd collected a few more things since the last time she'd visited. Despite the cramped nature of the room, all the boxes inside were stacked neatly, with their contents written in black marker across the side of the box.

She found the second box of notebooks and turned to leave the room. Her gaze fell on a photograph on top of the dresser. A thirty-years-younger Irwin, his arms slung over the shoulders of two young boys standing on either side of him. One of the boys was a carbon copy of Irwin. The other looked more like the woman standing a little apart from the males in the photo—Irwin's late wife.

Mya peered at the photo, a small gasp escaping her lips when the image of the second boy merged with a much more recent image in her mind.

The man who'd attacked her and Gideon at the motel and in the woods. The same man who'd shot Brian and kidnapped her the night the lab caught fire.

Irwin's younger son, Adam; his name came to her now that she was staring at his picture.

The box she'd been holding fell onto the scratched hardwood floor with a thump.

Mya's mind whirred with questions. The most pressing of which was what to do now?

Should she go back out there and pretend all was well until Gideon returned? Could she pull that off? Or would it be safer to lock herself in a room or even try to run?

She was sure Adam was the man who had attacked

her several times now, but she had no proof that Irwin was involved at all.

As if drawn there by some unseen force, her gaze landed on a rectangular black box on the floor in the corner of the room.

Her server.

Her body froze, but every brain cell in her head fired simultaneously. What was her server doing in Irwin's cabin?

There's something else I need to tell you...

The last words Brian had said to her before he'd been gunned down in the park.

And then she knew, without any doubt, what Brian had figured out.

Irwin was behind everything.

"I wish you hadn't come in here."

Mya whirled around.

Irwin stood in the doorway, holding the gun from his kitchen drawer.

"Why?" Shock, disappointment and fear wrestled inside her for dominance.

Irwin sighed heavily. "Why? You know I've asked that question so many times in my life. Why did my son have to get glioblastoma? Why did he have to die? Why did I allow myself to be pushed out before I succeeded? Why? Why? Why? You know what I've learned? The whys get you nowhere. I may not have been smart enough to come up with the treatment, but I am smart enough to steal it from you."

"So, it's all about money. That's it?"

"It didn't start out that way." Irwin sounded almost sad. "I sacrificed my entire life, my family, for this treatment. But then the board members of the laboratory I built from the ground up decided just like that—" he snapped his fingers "—that I was too old to cross the finish line."

Irwin's face twisted into a scowl. "So, I decided to take what was rightfully mine."

Mya scooted farther away from her former mentor. "I thought you only cared about people. I thought you wanted to make a difference and save lives."

"Only? No. But lives will be saved. Differences made. I'm sorry you won't be around to see it. I'll give you some credit, of course. You were almost there. Terrible that your young life was snatched from you before you could finish your work. But of course, isn't the world just so lucky that your old mentor is still firing on all cylinders." Irwin's smile was chilling. "I'll just step in and come up with the last part of the formula which you have so kindly delivered to me."

"No one will believe that," Mya spat, tears threatening. She beat them back. She wasn't about to give him the satisfaction of her tears, even if they were tears of rage.

Irwin's usually kind eyes narrowed, darkened. "They will. Like you said, it's all about money. And there's too much money to be made with this treatment for people to ask too many questions." He shook his head as if she were a small child, just learning how cruel the world was. "Anyway, everyone who can prove my story isn't true will be long dead by the time I make my miraculous discovery. Come on."

Irwin motioned with the gun in his hand for her to come out of the room. He stepped back into the hall, his eyes never leaving hers, to allow her past. Irwin limped behind her.

Mya turned to face him in the living room. "Why did you kill Rebecca and Brian?"

"Rebecca?" Confusion clouded Irwin's face for a moment before clearing. "Oh, the receptionist." He shrugged. "We would have had to deal with her at some point. I sent Adam to get your server. She was in the wrong place at the wrong time."

So, Rebecca hadn't been working for Irwin, and it still wasn't clear why she had been in her house.

"Adam. He was the man dressed as a cop who tried to kidnap me after the fire at the lab and the shooter at the park. That's why it felt like I knew him. I recognized him from the photos you used to keep in your office."

Irwin ignored her and instead walked to the window and peeked through the slats of the blinds.

"So now what? You're going to kill me in your living room? Gideon will be back any minute."

Irwin scowled. "Yes, I didn't anticipate you dragging your ex-husband into this. Unfortunate, but he'll have to be dealt with too. I guess all my little deceptions are going to come out now." Irwin motioned for her to sit.

She sank down onto the edge of the couch without taking her eyes off the gun in Irwin's hands.

"I have a landline in my bedroom. Only a fool would completely forgo technology in this day and age." Irwin shot her a pointed look. "But it suited my purposes to be believed such a fool. While you were in the bathroom, I called Adam, my younger son. To be honest, I was a little surprised you hadn't put things together faster." Irwin shook his head, a look of disgust twisting his face. "Adam has always been a disappointment, even as a hired thug. No matter, I've found I'm pretty quick on my feet. He will only have to follow my instructions this time."

The rumble of a car making its way toward the cabin came from outside.

Mya prayed it was Gideon but knew it could just as easily be Adam. Even if it was Gideon, he'd have no idea what he was walking into.

She didn't dare take her eyes off Irwin long enough to turn to look out the window behind the couch, but Irwin took several steps forward, leaning to the side to glance out the window.

It was now or never. If it was Gideon on his way up the driveway, she had to warn him. And if it was Adam, her best chance of escape was to make it into the dense woods surrounding the cabin before Adam or Irwin had a chance to react.

Mya leaned back and kicked out, her foot connecting with Irwin's injured leg.

He let out a howl, dropping the gun and falling onto his side.

Mya wasted no time springing from the couch and lunging for the laptop, still open on the kitchen table. She grabbed it at a run and sprinted for the cabin door.

She hit the front porch just as a shot thundered. Shards of wood splintered from the door behind her, but she didn't stop.

Gray clouds hung overhead, bringing with them snow that was heavier and colder than the light flakes that had followed her and Gideon up the mountain earlier.

A pickup truck rounded the last curve of the driveway, coming into view.

Adam.

Mya willed her legs to move faster and closed the

short distance between the cabin and the woods without looking back. She plunged into the trees, praying she could put a good distance between herself and Adam. There was no doubt in her mind Irwin would send his son after her. He'd come too far to let her get away.

The snow had left the forest floor slick and muddy. Mya zig-zagged through the trees, attempting to avoid the densest part of the foliage while staying to the areas that provided cover. She'd never been the outdoorsy type, and yet this was the third time in less than a week she'd run through the woods.

Running for her life.

Chapter Twenty-Three

Gideon pulled the car to the side of the road right before the curve in the street gave way to the cabin. As much as he wanted to get into Irwin's cabin, driving up to the driveway would make him a sitting duck for whoever was inside.

Adrenaline spiked in his body and he fought the urge to bolt toward the cabin. He stepped out of the car and into the quickly rising snow. He made his way to the house, keeping to the tree line of the property.

A rust-covered pickup truck sat in the driveway, validating his decision to approach the cabin with stealth.

He'd taken stock of the cabin when he and Mya arrived earlier. The only way in was through the front door, a safety hazard, but an effective ambush position. His best bet was to use the element of surprise. If he was lucky, Irwin and Adam weren't yet aware that he was on to them.

Gideon studied the front windows of the cabin for a minute more, hoping to see some activity inside that would give him an idea of Irwin and Adam's positions.

The interior of the cabin was eerily still.

He climbed the steps of the porch, careful to stay out

of the line of sight of the windows and that his footsteps fell silently against the wood planks.

At the door, he waited, listening for movement or sound from inside. There was nothing but silence.

Gideon inhaled deeply, training and instinct sharpening his senses for what was to come. A swift, well-placed kick sent the door crashing in. He stepped inside, his gun outstretched in front of him, sweeping from left to right as he catalogued the empty living area and vacant kitchen.

Seconds ticked by and no one appeared, solidifying his fear that whatever plan Irwin had for Mya he'd already put in motion.

Gideon approached the hallway slowly, clearing the bathroom and one bedroom before making his way to the farthest room in the cabin, the room he presumed was Irwin's bedroom. He reached for the doorknob but before he touched it the door was jerked open.

He had a second to take in Irwin's previously genial features now contorted with rage and desperation before the older man lunged at him. An innate aversion to shooting a septuagenarian cost him precious seconds.

Irwin slammed into him as he pulled the trigger, sending his shot wide, and knocking his gun from his hand.

They hit the hallway floor in arm's reach of the gun but with Irwin on top. The older man was surprisingly strong, landing a punch that exploded behind Gideon's eye.

Gideon grabbed Irwin's wrist, twisting until he cried out, most of the fight having gone out of him quickly.

Grabbing his gun, Gideon got to his feet, jerking Irwin along with him. He frog-walked the man into the living room and pushed him onto the couch.

"Where's Mya?"

A devious smile slid over Irwin's face, but he said nothing.

If Mya was in the cabin, she would have made herself known by now. He glanced through the window at the blanket of snow now falling. She was out there, he knew it in his gut, and she wasn't alone.

"Where's Adam?" Gideon asked.

The smile on Irwin's face slipped. So, he hadn't anticipated they'd figure out who his accomplice was. Not that that mattered at the moment. The only thing that mattered right now was finding Mya and making sure she was safe. But he couldn't leave Irwin unguarded. There was no way he'd give the man the opportunity to get away after all he'd done.

Gideon holstered his gun then stalked across the room. He watched surprise flash across Irwin's face in the seconds before his fist connected with Irwin's jaw.

The punch sent a jolt up his arm but was effective in knocking the older man out. He secured Irwin using a length of rope from the front porch before racing from the cabin.

The snow was falling fast but the faint outlines of two sets of footprints could still be seen heading into the trees behind the cabin.

Gideon took off at a run in the same direction. Mya was tough, a fighter. She'd be okay. She had to be.

He didn't know if he could live with the alternative.

MYA HAD HOPED her nonlinear path would make it difficult for Adam to follow, but it was also making it difficult for her to know how far she'd run or if she was running in circles. The last thing she wanted was to be heading back toward the cabin.

Branches slapped her face, and snow soaked through her sweater and jeans. She slogged through the trees, her feet sinking into the muddied snow, the laptop growing heavier and heavier with each step. She just needed to find a neighboring cabin or a road where she could hitch a ride to the base of the mountain. Somewhere with a phone that she could use to call Gideon.

She stopped to catch her breath, pressing her back against an oak tree. Her teeth chattered. If she stayed out here for much longer, she'd run the very real risk of getting hypothermia, but there was no way to know how close or far she was from another cabin. And going back to Irwin's was out of the question. As long as she had the laptop, she had a chance. She wouldn't let Irwin have it.

She started forward again just as a voice broke through the trees.

"Girlie, you better get yourself back here!" She couldn't see him, but Adam couldn't be too far away if she could hear him.

Her own footsteps and branches snapping under them were the only sounds that broke the silence. She didn't hear anyone chasing her, but that didn't mean they weren't there.

Without warning, the trees gave way to a clearing. The space wasn't large, about twenty feet wide, but it ended in a cliff, leaving her nowhere to run except back the way she'd come.

She looked over the edge into a large lake, small waves rippling the water's surface. She gauged the drop—fifteen, maybe twenty feet. Not bad, but she didn't know how deep the lake was, and she wasn't the strongest swimmer in the world. And the water was bound to be frigidly cold.

Branches cracked behind her. She was out of time.

Mya turned back toward the trees as Adam Ross stepped into the clearing. She could see it now, the resemblance between the man in front of her and the young man she'd met years earlier. She could even see the resemblance between him and Irwin, the calculation and deviousness in both their eyes.

Adam pointed a gun at her. Not the one Irwin had. This one was silver and much bigger. "Give me the laptop."

Mya listened for the sounds of the cavalry coming, hoping that somehow Gideon had realized she was in danger. But the only sound she heard was the pounding of her heart, which seemed to block out everything else. It was futile. Gideon had no idea she was in trouble, and by the time he did, she'd most likely be dead.

At least she'd told him she loved him. They wouldn't get the future she'd hoped for, but he'd know how she felt. How she'd always felt about him.

"No." Mya took two steps backward, each one bringing her closer to the cliff's edge.

Her thoughts raced.

He held the gun higher. "I will shoot you."

She wouldn't give him the laptop, but there was nothing stopping him from just shooting her and taking it.

Unless.

Mya glanced behind her, inching backward until she reached the edge of the cliff. She held the laptop out over the side. "If you do, this will go over the side of the cliff with me, and everything you and Irwin have done will be for nothing."

"You wouldn't," Adam snarled, the smile on his face grotesque. "That's millions of dollars you've got there in your hands."

"There is no way in hell I'm letting you or your father get their hands on this treatment."

"Put the gun down, Adam."

Mya nearly cried at the sound of Gideon's voice. He stepped out from the shelter of the trees, five feet from where Adam stood.

Adam's gun didn't waver. He spoke without taking his eyes off Mya. "You won't shoot me. Not before I shoot her."

"I wouldn't bet on it if I were you," Gideon growled.

Adam's lips twisted in a creepy semblance of a smile and Mya knew he was too far gone.

"I think I'll take that bet," Adam said.

Mya took one more step backward, her feet finding nothing but air as a gunshot echoed through the trees.

For a moment, she felt as if she was floating. She turned her gaze on Gideon, their eyes meeting and in an instant conveying all the words and emotions they hadn't found the strength to share with each other.

Then he was gone.

Air rushed at her, slapping her hair against her face.

A moment later water closed over her head and there was nothing but darkness.

Chapter Twenty-Four

Gideon discharged his gun at the same time as Adam, his bullets hitting their mark. Two bullets slammed into Adam's chest.

Gideon was running for the cliff's edge before Adam's body hit the ground. There was no need to stop and check for a pulse. Adam's sightless eyes stared up at the falling snow. Tucking his gun in his waistband, Gideon jumped over the side of the cliff.

Water crashed over his head and tugged him toward its murky depths. He kicked as hard as he could, propelling his body upward.

When his head broke the surface of the water moments later, he found Mya treading water several feet away.

He swam over and pulled her against his chest, recalling that she didn't like the water and was only a fair swimmer. They made it to the banks of the bank of the lake. "Are you okay?" He ran his hands over her arms, her back. Every place he could reach while keeping them afloat, reassuring himself that she was in one piece.

She clung to him. "I'm fine. What about you? Adam?"

"Adam is dead. And I'm going to need to recover

from the heart attack you gave me when you went over the side of that cliff."

She pulled back so she could look into his eyes. "It was the only way. He was going to pull that trigger no matter what."

"But your research. Everything you worked so hard for was on that laptop."

Mya smiled, and his racing heart slowed, finally willing to accept that she was unharmed. "It's all good. Just remind me that I need to do some ironing when we get back to your place."

He had no idea what she meant, but as long as she kept smiling at him like that, he was a happy man.

Mya spent the weeks following Irwin's arrest answering countless questions about the events that took place at Irwin's cabin from the sheriff in West Virginia as well as Detective Kamal. She'd also had to spend some time reassuring TriGen's jittery investors, a task that was made easier once she showed them that the treatment worked. Luckily, the police had quickly returned her server and she'd retrieved the flash drive from Gideon's ironing board. She finally had all the pieces of her research. And Gideon and the techs at West had helped her securely store it so it wouldn't be lost again.

The investors had insisted on a media tour to rehabilitate TriGen's image. The story had gone national, taking on a dramatic movie-like quality. And although Mya didn't relish the attention, she agreed with the board it was best if they controlled the narrative. The onslaught of positive press had allayed nearly all of the board's and investors' concerns about her leadership. And it seemed their apprehension over the deaths of two TriGen employees ended at the point where profits became a reality.

It left a sour taste in her mouth, but at least they'd agreed to pay out a bonus to Rebecca's and Brian's estates. Whatever they might have done, they'd both contributed to the success of the treatment and had paid a hefty price for their mistakes.

Adam hadn't survived being shot on the mountain. Whether it was the loss of his second son or the loss of any hope of taking credit for finding a treatment for the disease that had taken the first son, Irwin had elected to cooperate with the police. He'd explained that he'd convinced Brian to keep him updated on the treatment's progress.

The closer she got to making the treatment work, the more Irwin grew to believe he was the one deserving of the accolades and a greater share of the wealth that would come with success. When Brian reported that it looked like Mya was successful at making the treatment work, Irwin and Adam had hatched a plan to steal TriGen's research and claim it as his own. Irwin had enlisted the help of his son Adam, to eliminate the three people who could prove otherwise—Mya, Brian and Rebecca. It was just horrible timing that Adam made it to Mya's townhouse at the same time as Rebecca. He'd slipped in after her and found her attempting to steal the server to give to her cousin, Shannon. Killing Rebecca right then hadn't been part of Adam's and Irwin's plans, but it had worked out for them since it threw suspicion on Mya.

Rebecca and Brian's betrayal stung, but Irwin's betrayal had cut deeply. Mya had attempted to visit him in prison, to understand why he had gone to such unthinkable lengths, but he'd refused to meet with her.

Shannon Travers had been charged with theft for her part in having Rebecca funnel her TriGen proprietary research. But that was the least of her problems. The federal government had filed charges against Nobel and a number of its executives, including Shannon—for shareholder fraud and other corporate crimes. Nobel undertook its own media blitz blaming everything on Shannon.

Mya couldn't help feeling just a little bit sorry for her former classmate. As much as she hated to admit it, Shannon had a brilliant scientific mind that could have been put to life-changing use. Instead, she had let avarice and jealousy prevail.

Mya shook off thoughts of Shannon and opened a box of protective goggles. She stacked them next to the gloves in the supply closet of her new lab.

She'd been able to convince one of the local universities to allow her the use of a vacant laboratory, a conversation that had gone much better than she'd expected with the renewed support of her investors. Partnering with the university had worked out in more ways than one. She'd found a new assistant one day over lunch, a brilliant woman at the end of her postdoc who had come highly recommended by several professors at the university. It would take time before Mya could trust her given what she'd just gone through, but together they were working night and day to start up the new lab.

Gideon's job had also kept him working long hours. But they spent as much time as they could together, including nearly every night at his house, although the last three nights Gideon had insisted they sleep at her place.

She hadn't questioned it, happy that he was just as comfortable in her space as she was in his. But it appeared he missed sleeping in his own bed. He'd sent her a text after lunch asking what time she planned to knock off for the night and to drop by his place when she did.

The front porch light was on when she arrived, but there didn't appear to be any lights on in the interior of the house. Gideon's Tahoe was in the driveway, and since they'd exchanged keys several weeks ago, she let herself into the house.

"Gideon?"

There was no response, but a faint glow of light drew her toward the kitchen. The French doors were open onto the back patio.

As she drew closer to the doors, she could see that white lights had been strung around the posts of the pergola. Paper lanterns hung from the overhead slats, and large vases of red and white roses sat on pedestals of varying heights, creating a narrow rose petal-strewn path to the patio's edge.

Mya started down the path, curious as to exactly what was going on. She was at the halfway point when Gideon stepped out from the shadows, looking more handsome than she'd ever seen him in a dark blue bespoke suit. He held another dozen red roses in his hand.

She had to remind herself to breathe.

"What is all this?" she asked.

"Do you like it?"

She did a three-sixty, taking in all the lights, soaking up the romance of the moment, before turning back to him. "It's gorgeous, but what's it all for."

"It's all for you," Gideon said, holding the roses out to her. She took them, the butterflies in her stomach fluttering.

"I wanted to do something special for you. The last time I proposed, it was less than romantic."

She locked her knees so they wouldn't give out. Had he really just said he was proposing again? The setting certainly was romantic enough for a proposal, but her brain didn't seem to be able to keep up with current events. Her heart was, though. It pounded in her chest, and it was a fight to keep the tears that threatened from spilling over onto her cheeks.

"This time, I wanted it to be special," Gideon continued. "Something you'll remember for the rest of your life. Something you'll tell our children about."

"Our children?" She wasn't able to hold the tears back any longer. They fell freely.

Gideon swiped his thumb over her cheek, whisking away the tears. "Our children. I got you a ring, but I wanted to give you something else."

He slipped his hand in his pocket, and the strings of light and lanterns that had been strung through the large maple tree in the backyard sprang on.

A full-sized treehouse sat amongst the branches.

"You built me a treehouse," she managed between tears.

"I had to hire a contractor. It took a little architectural magic to make it happen."

Mya reached for his hand and squeezed. "You built me a treehouse," she repeated in amazement.

"You want to see inside?"

She climbed the ladder.

A blanket was spread out on the floor, and champagne chilled in a bucket next to two flutes.

Mya tucked her legs under a heated blanket as Gideon ascended the ladder and sat across from her.

"This would have worked a lot better when we were kids," he said.

"I still can't believe you built this for me."

Gideon slid the champagne to the side and drew her in close. "I'd build you a dozen more if that's what you wanted. You deserve to have everything you want, and I want to be the man to give it to you. Because you've given me everything. Your love, loyalty and trust even when I didn't deserve it. Even after I pushed you away."

Tears streamed down her face again. "Gideon," she choked out.

He pressed a finger against her lips and pulled a red velvet box from his pocket with the other hand. "I've loved you for most of my life. You are the most important, the most precious thing to me in the entire world. I know I don't deserve another chance, but I'm asking you to give me one. Will you marry me?"

She was crying so hard she could barely see the massive square-cut diamond he slipped on her finger.

It didn't matter. Her answer would be the same whether he slipped a sparkly rock or a barely there chip on her finger.

"Yes. Absolutely, yes."

She sank into his kiss, wishing it would never end.

Gideon pulled his mouth from hers and pressed his lips to her earlobe. "What do you say we christen this treehouse?"

That sounded like a good idea to her.

* * * * *

A COLTON
INTERNAL
AFFAIR

JENNIFER D. BOKAL

To everyone who serves their community with fidelity, bravery and integrity—this book is for you.

To John, always, for being one of those people.

Chapter One

Grace Colton sat in the passenger seat of the patrol SUV. Sweat snaked down her back, and the straps of her Kevlar vest were heavy on her shoulders. Beside her, Brett Shea drove. His black Lab, Ember, was secured at the rear. The dog snuffled at the grate between kennel and seat, before letting out a soft whine.

She knew exactly how the dog felt.

Despite the fact that it was mid-September, summer still had Grave Gulch in its clutches. The dashboard glowed green in the darkened auto. Although it was 9:37 p.m., it was still seventy-eight degrees outside.

The air conditioning blew a weak stream of cooled air into the cabin, and Grace leaned into the vent. Tendrils of blond hair, which had hung limp around her face, fluttered. Sitting back, she shifted her rig. Grace knew every piece of equipment she wore and had taken the time to check each item before her shift began. Body camera on her chest. Mic head on the shoulder. She also wore extra ammo, a sidearm, a Taser, a collapsible baton, and a radio attached to her utility belt.

Brett took a left at an intersection. At the end of the block was Grave Gulch Park. A crowd of people—approximately fifty by her estimation—stood at the property's edge. Their chanting was unmistakable.

"Hey-hey! Ho-ho! Chief Colton has got to go!"

Grace winced.

"It's a hell of a thing," said Brett, turning left at another intersection. "Our job is to keep people safe, despite the fact that they hate us right now."

"I always thought that cops were the good guys," she said, her mouth dry. "It's why I joined the force—to do good and protect my community. But what do you do when the department is doing bad?" The conversation ebbed, and Grace glanced out the window. It had been revealed that Randall Bowe, a former GGPD and CSI analyst, had doctored evidence for years. His false findings had put innocent people in jail and let guilty ones go free—namely, a serial killer, Len Davison. The community was rightfully outraged, but that also meant the many Coltons in the department were also under fire.

She began, "It's just..." With a shake of her head, Grace said, "Never mind."

"We've got to know each other pretty well, working to catch that catfish last month. It's not like you to be speechless." He gave a quick chuckle to show that he was teasing, at least a little.

He was right. Usually, Grace was overflowing with words. "It makes me." She paused. "Well, upset." She glanced out the window again, seeing only her reflection in the glass. Like she had said, she'd become a cop to be on the side of right. Right now, everything in law enforcement seemed to be wrong. "I get that things happen, and the cops aren't always right. We're just as much Bowe's victims as the whole city."

"Hey, don't let these protesters get you down. It's this damned heat that's got everyone on edge. Isn't that right, girl?" Brett asked, addressing the dog.

Ember gave a happy bark.

"See, even she thinks it's the heat."

Grace gave an exaggerated eye roll, then glanced at Brett. He wore the same uniform as Grace. He had reddish hair, blue eyes and a way about him that made her feel totally secure. It was no wonder that her big sister, Annalise, was head over heels in love with the guy.

Grace had been so focused on her new job with the force for the past year that she hadn't gone on a decent date in months. Yet, she couldn't help but wonder if there was a guy for her.

"It just sucks that everyone's so hard on Melissa. I know she's doing her best, despite everything that's happened." Melissa Colton was the chief of police and Grace's favorite cousin. Honestly, that was saying something. Grace had a lot of cousins.

As an awkward kid in middle school, Melissa had stopped by to take Grace out for ice cream. Grace still remembered sitting in the passenger seat of Melissa's car, for the first time in her life feeling cool. From that day to this, Grace had been totally devoted to her older cousin.

Melissa was smart, dedicated to the GGPD and willing to work long hours to see that justice was served. In short, she was everything that Grace wanted to become.

Melissa had even found her own true love—Antonio Ruiz. Had most members of the Colton clan found their happily-ever-after? Except for Grace, that is.

"You and Melissa are pretty tight," said Brett, his words breaking through her reverie.

"She's my role model, that's for sure."

"She's a good lady."

The chanting protesters could still be heard. Sadly, Grace knew that they had a right to be upset. Still, the fact that much of the anger was directed at Melissa sat like a rock in her gut.

Glancing down an alley, she saw it, and her heart froze midbeat.

"Stop the car." A person, clad in a dark hoodie and jeans, had his hands on a window. He wore a backpack. From his build, she could guess the person was male.

"What is it?" Brett asked, his foot dropping onto the brake.

"I hope it's not trouble," Grace replied, her door already open. She pointed toward the figure, who stood near the window. Sure, it could be the homeowner, locked out of his house. Still, she was more than a little suspicious. "Sir," she said, directing her words to the man in the alley. "Do you need assistance?"

Even from where she stood, Grace could see his shoulders go rigid. He froze, his hands on the window. For a moment, she thought he was going to address her.

Without a word, he sprinted down the narrow alley.

Grace cursed. "I'll go after him on foot," she yelled over her shoulder to Brett. "You come around the block."

If Brett answered, Grace didn't hear what he'd said. She sprinted toward the figure, doing her best to ensure her footfalls remained loud on the quiet street.

The person glanced at Grace. She glimpsed the face:

it was a male. Caucasian. Dark mustache. Then, he pivoted and sprinted to the far end of the alley.

Heart racing, legs pumping, Grace ran after the suspect. "Stop," she called out. "Grave Gulch Police." Sure, she was a rookie cop, not even on the force for a year. Still, her training was fresh, so she knew what to do.

The first rule of policing: be clear as to what she wanted and to whom she was speaking. She tried again. "You, sir, in the black hoodie and backpack. Stop!" she called again. "Police."

The man never broke his stride.

Grace activated the mic on her shoulder. "This is Officer Colton. I'm in pursuit of a suspect in a possible breaking and entering." She gave her location.

Her radio chirped. The voice of the dispatch officer broke through the static. "Ten-four, Officer Colton. Do you have a description of the suspect?"

She recalled that single second when the man had looked her way. "Caucasian male," she gasped. "Black or navy-blue hoodie. Dark mustache. Height approximately five feet ten inches. One hundred and sixty to one hundred and seventy pounds."

Rule two: always get film of any interaction with the public—especially if the incident could end up in court. Slapping the control on her chest, Grace turned on her body camera.

Adrenaline raced through her veins. It gave her a surge of power, and she closed in on the suspect. Yet, the end of the alleyway loomed large.

Was Brett waiting with the SUV and Ember?

God, she hoped so.

Turning as he ran, the suspect glanced over his shoulder. His eyes were wide, and his nostrils flared.

How was she supposed to read his expression?

Was he afraid?

Angry?

Slipping the pack from his back, he whirled it around. The bag sailed through the air, coming right at Grace's chest. On instinct alone, she shifted her body and lifted her arm to block the blow. The bag connected. For a moment there was a flash of pain as the bag hit her, then an explosion of white filled her vision and agony rocketed through her wrist, her hand.

The bag hit the pavement with a metallic clatter. Grace stumbled, slowed and sidestepped the backpack.

Pushing the discomfort from her mind, she sprinted the last few yards. Bursting onto the sidewalk, she stopped short. There was no Brett, no Ember, no police SUV.

What made matters worse, the suspect was gone.

CAMDEN KINGSLEY SAT at his desk, located in the back corner of the Grave Gulch DA's office. As an investigator with Internal Affairs, he'd been relegated to no-man's-land between a supply closet and a conference room that nobody ever used. Honestly, he didn't mind the solitude. Being set apart allowed him to remain neutral—investigating the investigators.

Despite the large window that overlooked the street, the room was dark, illuminated only by the computer screen. A file filled the monitor, complete with a photo of a dark-haired man. A list of identifying information—name, date of birth, sibling, spouse—accompanied the picture. Camden didn't need to read anything: long ago he'd memorized every word.

Staring at the man's dark eyes, Camden asked, "Randall Bowe, where in the hell are you?" For years, Bowe had worked as a forensic scientist for the Grave Gulch PD. During a murder trial several months prior, it was discovered that Randall had tampered with the evidence that implicated the accused, one Everleigh Emerson, when she was actually innocent.

After that trial, there'd been a review of all of Bowe's cases. And that's when the crap really hit the fan. When his crimes came to light, Bowe went on the run.

Aside from finding the forensic scientist who was on the lam, Camden's job was to discover what really had happened with Bowe. Sure, Bowe was trying to punish his wife for having an affair. He planted evidence in cases where he thought suspects had cheated on their romantic partners or rewarded faithful spouses.

It was a twisted retribution yet, there was one question that had plagued him from the beginning. What did the rest of the GGPD know about Bowe's misdeeds? It was the same question he'd asked himself every day for months now. So far, he didn't have an answer.

"Knock, knock," came a voice at his doorway.

Camden looked up. District Attorney Arielle Parks stood on the threshold. The DA was in her midfifties and kept her blond hair short. She wore a dark green blouse and an ivory skirt; both were creased from a long day at the office.

"What's up?" he asked, his eyes burning with exhaustion. "You're here late."

"I was just about to say the same thing to you. What are you working on?"

"Randall Bowe," he said with a sigh. As part of IA, Camden operated independently of all other city agencies. Since many of his cases ended up in court, he worked closely with Arielle.

The public was outraged about the whole Bowe debacle—and Arielle was a favorite target of the protesters. "Have you found anything?" she asked, her voice hopeful.

Camden shook his head. "Nada."

"Listen, it's almost ten o'clock. You should go home. Even people who work for Internal Affairs need to sleep sometime."

"I'm almost done," said Camden. He was the only Korean American man on the force. Sure, he sometimes felt that he had to prove himself. Yet, his long hours had more to do with his need to uncover the facts—any personal sacrifices be damned. "I'll be out of here in ten minutes, half an hour tops."

The light from his monitor reflected off the lenses of Arielle's signature tortoise-rimmed glasses. The older woman could have been looking at nothing or anything. The effect was slightly disconcerting. "What're you hoping to find?"

Camden paused and looked back at his computer. "The truth," he said.

"Are you any closer?" Arielle asked. She stepped into his office. The motion sensor turned on the overhead light.

Camden squinted at the glare.

"I keep wondering…" he began.

"What about?" Arielle asked, taking a seat on the opposite side of the desk.

That was one of the things he admired about the district attorney. She was as hungry for the truth as Camden. Did he really want to share his suspicions with the DA yet?

All the same, he was the one who'd alluded to his concerns. If he didn't want Arielle involved, he should've just kept his big mouth shut.

"We all agree that Bowe changed a lot of evidence on a lot of crimes," said Camden. He shifted his monitor so Arielle could see the screen. He pulled up an electronic copy of the initial arrest report of Everleigh Emerson. She'd been charged with murdering her estranged husband. Bowe's findings—fibers and hair on the murder weapon—were the cornerstone of the indictment.

The case went to trial. It seemed like an easy conviction for Arielle's team at the DA's office. Then, it came to light that Randall had fabricated the evidence linking Everleigh to the crime.

In the end, all charges were dropped.

Justice had been served.

The truth had won out.

It's just that the Emerson case—along with dozens more—left the Grave Gulch DA's office looking bad. The police department looked worse.

"What am I supposed to see now that I haven't before?"

"I keep asking myself *what if*," said Camden.

"Okay. What if?"

"Bowe's wife cheated on him. That's a fact."

"True."

"He forgives her to a point. But decides to punish those he sees as unfaithful spouses by falsifying evidence. Or to vindicate himself by altering reports to exonerate criminals who were faithful."

Arielle nodded. "Also true."

"He contacted Melissa Colton."

"True again."

"I just keep thinking." He paused. "What if Bowe wasn't working alone?"

Arielle's head snapped back, as if she'd been slapped. "What are you implying?"

He'd bet money that the district attorney knew. Still, Camden said, "What if Bowe had help from someone in the GGPD? What if it was Chief Colton?"

Arielle gave a short laugh. "You're kidding, right?"

Camden leveled his gaze at the district attorney. His stomach was tight, a rope tied into a knot. "I wish I was," he said, "but he hasn't been in contact with anyone else."

"Have you found any evidence to connect the chief to the investigations?"

"That's just it," said Camden. "Her name is all over the Emerson arrest warrant." He clicked open another file and one after that. "Her name is on all of these arrest warrants. And before you say it, I'll point out the obvious. She is the chief of police and involved in most every arrest."

"We know what motivated Bowe—his hatred of those who cheated on their spouses. What would Chief Colton get out of sending innocent people to jail?"

"I guess that's the biggest puzzle piece that's missing," said Camden. "A motive. I might be wrong. Still, I wouldn't be doing my job if I didn't ask the questions."

Arielle rubbed the middle of her forehead. "Keep digging, and keep me personally informed of anything you find. Don't talk to anyone else. The last thing we need is for your theory to get leaked to the press." She stood.

Of course the DA would be worried about the media, the public image, the voters. Only a few months prior, ADA Evangeline Whittaker had faced serious public outcry. She'd been the prosecutor on one of the cases where Bowe had provided evidence. Despite the fact that Evangeline wasn't part of the DA's team anymore, the episode was still a stain on the office. More than that, Evangeline was gaslit and made to believe that she'd witnessed a crime on the streets. To him, it seemed like the whole town was on edge, albeit for good reasons. Yet one more incident could be too much. Camden said, "Discretion is my middle name. Anything else?"

Arielle began to shake her head. She stopped. "Actually, there is. Go home. Get some rest."

Camden laughed. "I can do that, too. Is there anything else you need that's work-related?"

"Sure, we all just need to hope that the GGPD isn't involved. This town's a tinderbox. One more scandal with the police and Grave Gulch is going to go up in flames."

PULSE POUNDING, BREATH ragged and short, Grace stood at the end of the alley. She scanned the street. Cars, parked at the curb, lined both sides of the road. A single streetlight, at the end of the block, threw a puddle of light on the sidewalk. The street was filled with busi-

nesses—a laundromat, a hairdresser, a barbershop—
all of them closed for the night.

Yet the truth was undeniable. Aside from Grace,
the street was empty.

The suspect had inexplicably escaped.

The block ran perpendicular to Grave Gulch Boulevard. Across the street was Grave Gulch Park. The
wide lawn was surrounded by a wrought iron fence
and protesters.

With a shake of her head, Grace turned her attention
back to the matter at hand and the suspect who seemed
to have vanished. Too bad she didn't believe in magic,
which meant one thing: the guy must still be nearby.

She moved along the sidewalk, her steps slow and
light. Grace paused at the fender of a car. Peering into
the space between the bumper of one auto and the next,
she saw nothing but pavement.

Slowly, she moved to the next car and the one after
that.

There was a rustling noise, like leaves in the wind.
She stopped. A shadow moved. It was her man.

Having hidden in the doorway of a business, the
suspect darted onto the sidewalk.

"Stop." Still following protocol, she pursued and
called out, "Grave Gulch Police."

The suspect didn't even slow, not that she'd expected
any different.

She hit the mic on her shoulder. "In pursuit of suspect," she said, sprinting after the man and passing
two people loitering at the entrance. "He's headed for
the park's western entrance. Advise Detective Shea."

Dispatch responded, though their unintelligible
words were nothing but noise.

At that same moment, the suspect turned. There was something in his hand. A flash of silver that caught the light. Grace could see a barrel. A trigger. He held a firearm, trying to aim at her as he ran.

"Gun!" she shouted, alerting anyone who might be nearby. "Take cover."

For Grace, time didn't slow as much as it shattered into a million pieces. She held her own sidearm, yet she didn't recall taking it from the holster. The suspect's weapon came up inch by inch. She understood that it was a small handgun.

Before the suspect had the chance to fire, Grace stopped, aimed and pulled the trigger.

There was the report of the gun. The flash of a flame was followed by the scent of a match-strike.

The suspect spun in a drunken circle. He staggered backward two steps, before falling face-first onto the concrete.

Bile rose in the back of Grace's throat. A couple—a man and woman she had barely noticed before—stood at the end of the block.

"Grave Gulch Police," she said to the couple. Her hands trembled, and her throat closed on the last word. "Stay where you are."

The woman began to wail. "Omigod, omigod, omigod!"

"Dude, you shot him," said the man. "You shot him!"

The young man approached the suspect, who lay on the ground, moaning. Grace exhaled. Thank goodness the shot wasn't fatal.

"That man's armed and dangerous," Grace said. Following all the safety procedures she'd been taught,

Grace kept her own firearm pointed at the ground. She approached at a run. "Stay away from him."

The man knelt next to the suspect.

"For your own safety," said Grace, "you need to step away."

"Or what?" the young man sneered, while getting to his feet. "You'll shoot me, too?" He grabbed his girlfriend, still wailing, by the elbow. "Let's get out of here."

The couple ran.

Lying on the ground, the suspect held his shoulder. Blood from the bullet wound leaked through his fingers. "I've been shot. I've been shot. Why'd you shoot me?"

"Where's your firearm?" Grace asked.

He continued to cry out. "I've been shot. I've been shot."

"Your gun." That was another rule. Make sure any suspect has been disarmed. "Where's your gun?"

"I've been shot." He gritted his teeth and spoke through the pain. "My shoulder. You shot me in the shoulder!"

Grace had paid attention to every word said at the police academy. She listened to every piece of advice given by senior officers. But nothing had prepared her for this moment. The sour taste of panic rose in the back of her throat. As if chaos was an animal, she could feel its eyes watching her in the dark—ready to pounce.

She scanned the sidewalk. A pool of blood surrounded the man. Yet, there was no firearm lying on the ground. Did the suspect have it still? What was she supposed to do next?

Grace knew. She had to get the suspect into custody.

"Put your hands where I can see them." She looked down the barrel of her gun, placing the suspect's chest in the middle of her sight.

"Put my hands where? How? I can't even move my damn arm." The suspect looked at Grace for the first time. "Aw, damn, I got shot by a little girl."

"Put your hands where I can see them." Her jaw was tight, and her words like flint.

The suspect lifted his palms. They were both covered in blood. She removed a set of flex-cuffs from her utility belt. One-handed, she slipped it around the suspect's wrists, before pulling the ends tight.

"Where's the gun?" she asked again. She slipped her own handgun back into the holster. Until the firearm was secured, not much else mattered.

"I don't have a gun." The man's face was greasy with sweat. The front of his hoodie was wet. The coppery stench of blood hung in the air.

"Do you have any other weapons?" she asked, slipping on a pair of sterile gloves. Starting at his shoulders, she patted the suspect down. The man didn't have anything with him—not a wallet, and most definitely not a gun.

Standing, she actuated the mic on her shoulder. "There's been an officer-involved shooting," Grace said, before giving Dispatch the address. She ended with "Send an ambulance."

"An ambulance is on the way," the operator replied.

From her training and limited time in the field, she knew what needed to be done next. From her utility belt, Grace removed a wad of gauze.

"I'm going to apply pressure to your wound now," she said. "It'll help stop the bleeding until EMTs can treat you properly." A ragged rip in his hoodie made the bullet hole easy to find. She pressed the gauze onto the wound. Sure, she'd shot the guy. Still, he was part of the community she'd sworn to protect and serve. It was an oath that Grace took to heart. "What's your name?"

"Robert," said the man, his teeth gritted. "Robert Grimaldi."

"Mr. Grimaldi, can you tell me what you did with your firearm?"

"What firearm?"

"The one you pointed at me," said Grace.

"I never pointed no gun at you. Never."

Her patience was thin, yet she refused to be drawn into an argument with Grimaldi. Drawing in a deep breath, she counted to three and exhaled. "We both know that's a lie. Where's the gun?"

"How old are you?" asked Robert. It was then that Grace noticed the absolute silence. The protesters, little more than a block away, had stopped chanting.

Before Grace could wonder what that meant, there was a single *whoop* of a siren and the flash of blue and red lights. Brett stopped his SUV next to where she knelt on the sidewalk.

"What happened?" he asked, jumping from the driver's seat.

"Mr. Grimaldi drew a weapon, and I fired before he had the chance to shoot. He doesn't have the firearm on him now," said Grace.

"Anything else?" Brett asked.

Grace pointed her chin toward the alleyway. "He also threw his backpack at me."

Grimaldi said, "The little-girl cop is lying about the

gun. I don't have a gun. I didn't have a gun. And you won't find a gun because it don't exist."

"We'll see about that," said Brett. Then to Grace he said, "I'll take Ember and do a search. If he threw the gun away or dropped it, Ember will find it."

Three more police cruisers approached, their sirens wailing and lights flashing. An ambulance followed. Police cars parked at the end of both streets, creating a barricade.

But it was too late.

She now understood what had happened with the protesters. Her pulse slowed, turning sluggish in her veins. They'd heard the gunshot and come—en masse—to investigate. More than four dozen people now stood just beyond the patrol cars. They no longer held protest signs. Now, they all had cell phones. What was worse, they were recording the incident. Dread pooled in her stomach.

A duo of EMTs approached. One carried a stretcher, and the other had a medical kit. "We can take over from here, Officer," a tech said.

Grace stepped to the side. Her head swam, and her legs were weak.

"What's going on?" one of the protesters yelled. "What happened? Did you shoot that guy? Hey, lady, I'm talking to you."

"Just ignore them." Brett grabbed Grace by the elbow and led her to the side. As they walked, he spoke. "It was a legitimate shoot. He drew a weapon. You had no choice but to fire. Let's go and find that backpack and then the gun."

It seemed that Robert Grimaldi had noticed the protesters, too. It didn't matter that he still lay on the ground, or that he was being treated by the EMTs. He yelled to the crowd, "The girl cop shot me. And for no reason."

The mob began to boo.

It was then that Grace knew an undeniable truth. Sure, things had been bad for the Grave Gulch Police Department before tonight. Yet, because of her, it was about to get a whole lot worse.

Chapter Two

Police dogs on leashes sniffed the ground. Blue and red lights atop cruisers strobed. Grace knew that most of the force had been called to look for Grimaldi's missing gun.

So far, nothing had been found.

Sitting on the rear bumper of an ambulance, Grace's heart thumped with each flash of the lights.

An EMT stood at her side and examined her injured arm. "Can you open and close your hand?" he asked. His echoing voice sounded like it came from the opposite side of a canyon. Moreover, she felt as if she were watching the events unfold and not actually a part of the action. From somewhere in the back of her mind came a single word. *Shock.*

She'd seen it before in victims of car crashes and crimes alike. It was a detached disbelief that something awful had occurred. Just putting a word to the sensation thrust Grace back into her own body.

The EMT watched her. She knew he'd spoken yet couldn't recall what he'd said. "I'm sorry. Can you say that again?"

"Can you move your hand?"

Grace spread her fingers and then closed them to a fist.

"Can you roll your wrist?" the EMT asked, rolling his own.

She imitated the motion.

"Any pain?"

Grace shook her head. "It's a little sore, but nothing I can't handle."

"It doesn't appear that you have any broken bones. Still, you might want to follow up with your doctor, especially if your discomfort worsens."

"Thanks," she said. The EMT packed up his med kit.

A barricade, a wooden sawhorse painted yellow with GGPD stenciled in black, had been set up at each end of the block. From where she stood, Grace could see that the group of onlookers had grown to more than one hundred. Beyond protesters and gawkers, there was also a TV crew from nearby Kendall.

Melissa approached as the EMT left. She wore a blue windbreaker with a badge embroidered on the chest. She also wore jeans and a T-shirt. Her brown hair hung loose around her shoulders. Just seeing Melissa calmed Grace.

Grace knew the truth. Melissa wasn't at the scene to offer personal support. Rather, the other woman was the chief of police, and it was her job to be on the scene of a shooting.

"How's the wrist?" Melissa asked.

"Nothing's broken."

Melissa nodded. "Can you tell me what happened?"

Brett approached with Ember and waited as Grace began to speak.

Grace had already repeated the story several times.

Still, she said, "I saw the suspect, Mr. Grimaldi, at a window. I identified myself as a police officer. It was then that he ran. In the alleyway, he threw his backpack at me. It struck me in the wrist when I batted it away." She drew in a deep breath, trying to slow her racing pulse. "He exited the alley, which is where I lost sight of him. As it turns out, he ducked into a doorway," she continued, pointing to the spot. "As I approached, he ran again. It was then that he drew his weapon. I fired. He went down. There was a couple, a man and woman, at the end of the street. They approached Mr. Grimaldi. I told them to back away. They didn't at first but left as I approached. I placed Mr. Grimaldi in custody and called for backup and medical care." Looking at Brett, she concluded, "That's when Detective Shea arrived."

Melissa turned. "Brett?"

"It all went down as Grace said. She pursued the suspect on foot while I brought my SUV around the block. There were protesters in the street, and it slowed my response. By the time I arrived, Grimaldi was down."

"What about the couple?"

"I saw a man and woman running down the street."

"So you arrived after Mr. Grimaldi was shot?"

"That's correct," said Brett.

Melissa continued. "You didn't see his gun? Or Grace firing?"

Dropping his eyes to the pavement, Brett ran his fingers through the fur on Ember's head. "I did not."

Melissa tensed her jaw. "Anything else?"

"We recovered the backpack." Brett continued, meeting Grace's gaze. "Grimaldi's driver's license was inside, as well as two laptop computers, a smartphone, jewelry—watches, rings, a diamond bracelet—and lots of cash. My guess, Mr. Grimaldi was routinely looking for open windows and letting himself into people's homes. We've already gotten calls about some of the missing items."

"Tell me about Grimaldi," said Melissa.

Brett held Ember's lead with one hand and his phone in the other. Using his thumb to navigate, he held up a screen. It was filled with a rap sheet. "He has a pretty long arrest record. Robbery. Larceny. Selling a controlled substance."

"What about his gun?" Melissa asked. "Have you found that yet?"

Brett shook his head. "No."

"You have Grimaldi's criminal history. Has he ever been arrested with a gun before? Are there any weapons charges in his file?"

Brett glanced at the screen and then wordlessly, shook his head.

Grace's knees threatened to buckle. No gun? What was going on? Was this all some ploy to make the department look bad? Could this be another attack on the police by Randall Bowe? Or maybe it was one of those Bowe sent to jail. The witnesses had been more than a little hostile. Had this whole incident been a setup from the beginning?

At the same time, Grace had another thought—worse than the first. What if she'd been mistaken? What if Grimaldi never had a weapon to begin with?

She drew a shaking breath and recalled those seconds before she pulled the trigger. "He was armed," she said, her voice a croak.

"What's that?" Melissa drew her brows together.

Grace cleared her throat. "Grimaldi was armed. He

had a gun. He pointed it at me." She paused. "I know what I saw."

"Get a CSI team down here for a thorough search. If the gun is out here, we'll find it," said Melissa. Her green eyes held an unmistakable look of concern.

If? "It's out here," said Grace, her voice stronger than she felt. She scanned the street. It was overflowing with cops. "Somewhere."

"And if it's not?" Brett asked.

Were Brett and Melissa really questioning what she saw? "Grimaldi had a gun."

"Let's just keep looking, okay?" said Melissa.

"Sure thing, boss," said Brett. He clicked his tongue, signaling Ember to follow.

"Before you go, I need you to do something else," said Melissa.

Brett stopped. "Whatever you need."

"This investigation has to be done by the book," said Melissa. "Officer Colton's firearm has to be examined by Forensics. Can I ask you to place it in an evidence bag? The body camera, too?"

Brett removed two evidence bags tucked into a pocket of his utility belt.

At the academy, every cadet had been warned that this day could come. If a gun was ever fired in the line of duty, that firearm would have to be analyzed and compared to the bullet. It made no difference if the officer admitted to firing or not.

Her throat tightened around a hard kernel of indignation. She was being wronged, but she knew her job and was determined to remain professional. Saying nothing, she handed over both her gun and her camera.

"For now," Melissa continued, "let's get back to

headquarters. From there, we'll evaluate the body-cam footage you caught. That'll at least prove that Grimaldi was armed. Grace, you ride with me. Brett, we'll meet you there."

Despite the heat, Grace started to shiver. She followed Melissa to the car. Her cousin slipped into the driver's seat of an SUV, Grace into the passenger seat. Melissa maneuvered to the end of the block, where a police officer lifted the crossbeam of a barricade.

A light shone through, blinding Grace with the glare.

A reporter pressed her face next to the glass. "I'm Harper Sullivan from Kendall, I have some questions for you." A man stood behind her. A camera, along with the light, was perched on his shoulder.

Melissa said nothing.

The reporter continued. "Chief Colton, do you have any comment about what happened tonight? Is this case related to the Len Davison case? Or Randall Bowe? There was an officer-involved shooting. Is this the officer? Does she have any comment?"

Gripping the steering wheel with white knuckles, Melissa stared through the windshield. "Just look ahead," she whispered. "And don't say a word."

Tense, Grace faced forward and looked at nothing. The crowd parted as the SUV nosed forward. It took only a minute before they were on an empty street. Grace glanced in the side-view mirror. All the protesters and onlookers were behind her. She exhaled. "What in the hell was all that?"

"It'll be okay." Melissa smiled, but her brows were drawn together in concern.

"Thanks for saying so, but…" Grace shook her head.

"But what?"

"Just never mind," said Grace. "It's not important."

"I might be the chief of police and your boss, but I'm also your cousin. Don't tell me to 'never mind.'"

Just moments before, Grace had had too many thoughts to even know what to think. Now, her mind was blank. What was she supposed to say?

"I don't think this problem will be over soon." Grace's hands started to tremble. Tucking her palms under her thighs, she continued, "I think that the GGPD is about to be hit by the full force of this town's anger. It's all because…" Her words faltered. She cleared her throat. "It's all because of me."

Without speaking, Melissa drove. Turning a corner, she pulled into a lot at the back of the police department. A spot near the door was empty. A white sign on a post read *Reserved for Chief of Police*. She turned to Grace.

"I'm not going to lie to you," Melissa began. "You're going to have to be strong. The public doesn't like to see police shoot anyone."

"Of course not," she said, interrupting. "Nobody wants to have force used."

Melissa started again. "There's going to be questions you'll need to answer. My guess, there will be an investigation. Be honest, but don't answer a question until it's asked. You don't want to provide the IA investigator with details they can use against you."

Grace tried to swallow, but her throat was closed. "Don't give any information unless asked."

"Once we see what's on your body camera, a lot of the furor will die down, I'm sure." She turned off the motor. The silence was total. Grace could hear her own breath and the resonance of her own heart.

Melissa continued. "I called Ellie. She'll be waiting to download the camera footage." Ellie Bloomberg was the IT expert for the GGPD and one of the hardest working people on the force.

Grace reached for the door handle. "I can't wait to get all of this behind me. Let's go."

Melissa reached out, placing her palm on Grace's shoulder. "One last thing. You did turn on your body cam, right?"

Grace recalled those few seconds as she raced through the alley. She could feel the pressure of her fingers on the Record button. "I'm positive," she said.

"All right, then." Melissa smiled again. This time the expression was real. "Let's go."

DESPITE WHAT HE'D said to Arielle, Camden worked later than he intended. As he finally parked his car in front of his town house, he glanced at the dashboard clock: 10:42 p.m. No wonder he was tired.

While loosening his tie, he walked slowly to the front door. Stepping into the townhome, his mind was already on a cold beer and a soft sofa.

He twisted off the cap and took a long drink. He sighed. Home, finally. Dropping onto the sofa, he turned on the TV. As the set flickered to life, he wondered about dinner—specifically if the leftover pizza in the fridge was still fresh enough to eat.

A sitcom was interrupted by a breaking-news alert.

A newscaster from a station in Kendall stood near a police barricade.

Camden recognized the street at once. It was in

downtown Grave Gulch, about a block from the city park. Blue and red emergency lights flashed in the background. The reporter wore a yellow blazer. Holding her microphone, she looked into the camera and began speaking. "This is Harper Sullivan. I'm in downtown Grave Gulch, where a department beset by scandal can add another disgrace to the list. A police-officer-involved shooting."

The screen filled with footage of a man on a stretcher. His shoulder was encased in a white bandage, and his arm rested in a sling.

The chyron at the bottom of the screen read *Robert Grimaldi shot by Grave Gulch Police Officer.* "She just shot me for no reason," said Grimaldi, speaking into the camera. "The girl cop said I had a gun, but I don't got no gun."

The newscaster appeared in profile. "Why would the police officer think that you were armed if you weren't?"

"I dunno," said Grimaldi. "She's inexperienced, I guess. That, or maybe she's a liar…just like the rest of them."

Then, the victim was wheeled out of the camera's shot and into the back of a waiting ambulance.

The picture on the screen changed once more. This time, there was footage of two women in an SUV. Camden recognized one. It was the chief of police, Melissa Colton. The other was younger, blonde, pretty, in uniform. He'd never seen her before; still, he bet that she was the girl cop Grimaldi had mentioned.

The video in the car continued, as did the voice of the reporter. "Do you have any comment about what happened tonight? Is this case related to the Len Davison case? Or Randall Bowe? There was an officer-involved shooting. Is this the officer? Does she have a comment?"

Neither of the women in the police vehicle flinched.

The camera cut back to the reporter for a live shot. "There you have it. A citizen of Grave Gulch, Robert Grimaldi, shot by the police without warning or reason. And the police have nothing to say. This is Harper Sullivan, sending you back to your regularly scheduled program."

Setting his beer on a side table, Camden cursed with frustration. An officer-involved shooting would be his case, for sure. It was more than his interrupted night. He reached for his cell phone at the same moment it began to ring. The caller ID read *Arielle Parks*.

"Why am I not surprised," he muttered to himself before accepting the call. Without a greeting he said, "I saw it on the news."

"Good god, Camden. This is the last thing we need in Grave Gulch." He agreed with the DA, but knew she'd called to do more than complain. She continued, "I just got off the phone with the mayor. He wants you on the case."

"Understood. I'll head over to police headquarters now." Camden paused a beat and waited for Arielle to say more. "Everything okay?"

She gave a tight laugh. "The mayor's furious at everyone. It's not even my department and he chewed me out." He could well imagine Mayor Abels yelling at Arielle. The picture wasn't pleasant. "What are we supposed to do now?" Her tone was sharp. "*Someone...*" she drew out the word "...has to be held publicly accountable once and for all. It's for the public good."

Camden's neck and shoulders tightened. "I'm not interested in public accountability," he said tersely. "What I want is the truth."

"Well, the truth is that a man was shot. Was it caused by bad policing or bad training? That's what the people of Grave Gulch deserve to know."

Picking up his messenger bag, he slipped the strap over his shoulder. "What d'you know about the incident? The officer?"

"Her name is Grace Colton. Right now, she's on the way to police headquarters."

Camden turned off his TV and threw the remote onto the sofa. "Colton? As in she's Chief Colton's—what, sister?"

"I think they're cousins."

Detective Troy Colton was assigned to the Randall Bowe case, and Camden had worked with him more than once. Troy was a good guy. Still, Camden had to ask, "Is everyone in that police department related to one another?"

"Not quite. But there are a whole lot of them," said Arielle.

Camden stepped out of his town house and pulled the door closed behind him. The night air was oppressive, and he began to sweat. Yet, it was more than the heat and humidity of a summer holding on too long. Two things bothered him. The first was obvious. Camden was worried that with all the family relations in the GGPD, Chief Colton would want to protect her officer. Randall Bowe had tried to frame several members of the GGPD, as well. He had to assume that they'd be wary of anyone not named Colton—or an employee of the police department. What kind of cooperation could he expect?

The second problem was more oblique. An officer-involved shooting was too close to the one that had changed his father's life. Hell, it was the case that had made Camden who and what he was today. A sharp pain gripped his chest along with a memory of his father. Accused of a crime he hadn't committed, his pop had been found guilty, nevertheless. He'd been removed from the force. It was a disgrace that became a part of his father—like a tattoo on his soul.

The aftermath of those events had shaped the rest of Camden's life. In the span of a heartbeat, he saw his father as he was the night he'd been let go from the force. Sitting at the kitchen table, head down, hands resting on a placemat.

A headache started in his temple. Camden didn't have the luxury of wallowing in pity or doubt. He had a job to do and turned his thoughts to the news report and the female police officer in the passenger seat of the SUV. At first, it appeared that her gaze was impassive and without any emotion. But Camden had been wrong. There had been tension around Grace Colton's eyes. Her jaw had been tight. She was worried, perhaps even afraid.

That left Camden wondering: What did she have to fear?

Was she simply overwhelmed?

Or was she afraid of someone finding out what had really happened?

Camden's fists clenched. It was then that he realized he still held the phone to his ear. The DA was on the other end of the call, still waiting for his reply.

"I'm on my way to the police department now. I don't know what happened on that street tonight. Until I get the facts I'm not going to speculate. But there's one thing Grave Gulch will get from my investigation, Arielle."

"Oh, yeah? What's that?"

"The truth."

ELLIE BLOOMBERG SAT in front of a bank of computer monitors. She looked up as Melissa and Grace entered.

"Rough night," said Ellie. Her wavy brown hair was tied into a bun at the top of her head. She wore jeans, a T-shirt and a pair of flip-flops.

Grace ignored the comment about her rough night. Instead, she said, "Sorry for making you come into work." She continued, mentioning Ellie's longtime boyfriend. "Mick must be peeved."

Ellie waved away the comment. "He's fine. When I left, he was still in his office on a call with Tokyo or London or something." Sitting taller, she held up a plastic bag. Inside was the camera. "Brett dropped this off and said he was taking the gun for forensic analysis." A yellow-and-black *Evidence* banner ran along the top of the translucent bag. There were also several lines for signatures in the chain of custody. Brett Shea's name was first. Then, Melissa Colton's.

Ellie stood, pen in hand, and wrote her name on the third line.

The camera was small and black and had plastic casing. The lens was smaller than a dime. Recorded footage needed to be uploaded to a computer in order to be viewed. Sure, some of the newer cameras had a built-in screen. But the GGPD's budget hadn't allowed for an upgrade in years.

Ellie studied the bag and chewed on her bottom lip.

Grace didn't like the expression, and her stomach churned. "What's the matter?"

"It looks like this has been damaged." Holding up the camera for Grace to see, Ellie used the end of her pen and pointed. "See this? The Record button is cracked."

Grace sucked in a breath as her heart started racing. "That's impossible. I examined that camera myself before we left for patrol. It was in perfectly good condition then."

"Well, it's not now," said Ellie. "Let me see what I can do, and I'll get back to you."

Grace stood next to Melissa. The older woman placed a reassuring hand on her shoulder. "Let's go to my office. I'll get you a cup of coffee. Tonight's going to be a long night."

Grace's stomach still roiled. Her hands still trembled. She was already jittery. She'd paid attention to all of the academy lectures on what would happen if a cop ever shot a civilian. It's just that in those moments, Grace never imagined she'd be the one to pull the trigger. It didn't help that the gun hadn't been found or that the camera was now broken. What was going on? Could she be the victim of sabotage? It seemed far-fetched, but nothing that happened tonight made any sense.

"Let's get some coffee," Melissa said.

"I don't want any."

"Yeah? Well, I do. Besides, Ellie won't get her job

done any faster if we're watching over her shoulder." Melissa tugged Grace. "C'mon."

Grace relented. They used a set of stairs that led to the main level.

The squad room was filled with more than a dozen desks. In short, there was always someone in there. At night, the GGPD headquarters wasn't nearly as busy as it was during the day. All the same, it didn't mean that it was ever empty. Yet, tonight was different. Every desk was vacant. The silence was total—not even interrupted by the ringing of a phone.

"Where is everyone?" Grace asked. "This place is like a tomb."

"Everyone's out." Melissa's answer was vague— yet not so ambiguous that Grace couldn't figure out what she meant.

"They're looking for the gun," said Grace grimly.

"Among other things."

"What if this is all a setup?" Grace asked.

"Setup?" Melissa echoed.

"Maybe it's someone who wants to make the department look bad." Once Grace began to speak, words flowed out of her like water from a firehose. "Maybe it's Bowe. He hates the department enough. He could have paid all those people..."

Melissa stopped in the middle of the squad room. "Ask yourself one question. Even if this whole scenario could be orchestrated, Grimaldi would never know which cop would find him. How could he be sure that he was shot in the shoulder and not the chest or the head?" She walked to her office and opened the door. "That's a hell of risk to take. For what? Money? Revenge?"

"I guess you're right," Grace grumbled.

"For now, we're going to follow the facts. First, coffee."

Melissa's office was tucked into the back corner of the squad room, a light turned on as soon as Grace crossed the threshold. A large desk sat in the middle of the room, a pile of manila folders filled one corner. One wall was filled with pictures of Randall Bowe. A whiteboard had been tacked to the wall. The names of all his victims had been written in blue marker. Beneath the names were the words *Don't stop until the job is done.*

Grace lifted a smaller picture from the table. It was a selfie of Melissa and her new fiancé, Antonio Ruiz. Melissa smiled at the camera, Antonio looking at her. It was impossible to miss the look of tenderness and dedication on Antonio's face. "This one's new."

"I figured I needed a picture of the two of us."

Grace handed the photograph back to Melissa. More than having movie-star good looks, Antonio was rich. "He's a catch. Plus, he looks like he's completely in love with you."

"I am lucky." Melissa stroked her finger over the picture before setting the photograph on the table.

Grace couldn't help but wonder how two people could find each other and fall in love. Obviously, she knew how Melissa and Antonio met. It was during the investigation into the kidnapping of Grace's nephew, Danny. Danny had been found and returned to his family, so the story had a happy ending all the way around.

But why had they met and fallen in love? Was it luck?

And moreover, why was Grace caught up in this and not in love? Was that luck, too? Good luck for Melissa and bad luck for Grace?

Gesturing to one of two chairs that sat near her desk, Melissa said, "Have a seat. I'll get a coffee started for you."

Melissa started her single-cup brewer. For a moment, the hiss of coffee brewing was the only sound in the room. What was Melissa thinking? What should Grace say? She was usually bubbling over with words, and now, well...

Glancing over her shoulder, Melissa asked, "How are you?"

Slipping her hands under her thighs, Grace said, "Fine. Not great, you know. But I'm fine." She nodded vigorously.

"I've known you your whole life. You're far from fine."

Grace's eyes burned, but she'd be damned before she'd cry—even in front of Melissa. She bit the inside of her lip hard. Still, she couldn't help but say, "I'm worried that I've made things worse for the department. I'm worried that I'm a failure as a cop." She stopped and drew a breath. "I'm worried that I've done the wrong thing or disappointed you."

Melissa stirred in a packet of sugar. She handed Grace a mug filled with steaming coffee. "Drink that."

Grace took a sip. The liquid scalded a raw spot on her lip, and she winced. *Damn, when had she hurt her mouth?*

"For the record, I'll never be disappointed in you, Grace. There's a lot of us Coltons, you know. But you're my favorite little cousin."

Grace smiled. "Thanks."

"Now, really, drink the coffee. Once the adrenaline wears off, you're going to have a hell of a headache.

Besides, you aren't going home anytime soon. Someone from Internal Affairs will be here soon. You'll want the caffeine to keep you sharp."

Grace took another drink. At least she could always count on her cousin. "Yes, ma'am."

Melissa's cell phone rang. She glanced at the screen. "It's Ellie," she said, before swiping the call open and turning on the Speaker feature. "Hey." Melissa set the phone on her desk. "I have Grace here, and you're on Speaker."

"I'm glad she's with you. I was able to access the footage. Come down to the lab. I'll have everything set up for you to review."

"On our way," said Melissa and ended the call. She exhaled and smiled. "If all goes well, then we'll have Mr. Grimaldi on video, pointing a gun at you. This incident will be resolved tonight. By tomorrow morning, your life will be back to normal."

"If all goes well," Grace echoed, trying to summon her cousin's optimism.

Why did Grace feel as if it wasn't going to *go well* at all? And that things wouldn't be *normal* for a long time?

Chapter Three

Grace sat at one of the computer workstations, complete with three monitors. Melissa stood behind her, Ellie on Grace's right.

Clacking on her keyboard, Ellie spoke. "I've got good news and bad news."

More bad news? As if she was in free fall, Grace's stomach dropped.

"Start with the good news," urged Melissa.

"I was able to get footage from the camera." The center screen winked to life and an up-close image of a hand filled the screen. "This is where the video starts. It looks like you got a little over a minute and a half."

"Ninety seconds?" Grace folded her arms over her chest. "I'd swear that the incident took longer." Then she recalled those moments on the street when time seemed to bend. Maybe the recording was right, after all.

"All right," said Melissa, sliding into a chair next to Grace. "Let's see what we have."

Grace held her breath and watched the monitor.

"Is that the body-cam footage?" a male voice asked from behind.

Grace turned, her heart racing. A tall man, nearly

six feet with dark short hair and dark eyes, stood on the threshold. Grace's heart continued to thunder—and it wasn't entirely from the start he'd given her.

"What are you doing here?" Melissa asked, rising from her seat. Her tone was less than friendly. Grace sat up taller. It wasn't like her cousin to be rude.

"I stopped by your office. You weren't there. I figured the next best place to find you was here." The man pointed to the monitor. "You never answered my question. Is that the footage from the body cam of tonight's shooting?"

"It is, and I suppose you want to watch with us," said Melissa.

"It's my job to see everything that you have on this case," said the man. "You know that."

Melissa gestured to the chair she'd just vacated. "Have a seat."

He slid in next to Grace. His hand brushed her wrist as he sat. A jolt of electricity shot up her arm. Was it just nerves? Or had there been something else—something more?

"Camden Kingsley," he said, holding out his hand. "Internal Affairs. You must be Grace Colton."

Grace stared at his palm. "Internal Affairs?" Her voice sounded small in the cavernous room.

"My being here is entirely procedural," he said, rubbing fingertips and thumb together before dropping his palm to the table. "You don't have to worry. I'm only looking for the truth."

Melissa gave a derisive snort.

Yet, Grace thought there was something trustworthy about Camden Kingsley. What was it? And how could she tell after only a few seconds?

He was confident and calm. Without him saying a word, his demeanor spoke of being in charge; even better, he was fair. She rubbed the back of her neck, loosening her tight shoulders. Maybe now, things would turn in Grace's favor.

"Can we see the video now?" Camden asked.

"Sure thing," said Ellie, typing.

The video began to play. There was footage of a man running. The image jostled, as the camera attached to Grace's chest recorded her in the middle of the pursuit. Her labored breath along with the staccato of her footfalls on the pavement were the only sounds in the room.

Mr. Grimaldi turned toward the camera. His eyes were wide.

"You captured a perfect video of his face, Grace. Good job," said Melissa.

"He's going to throw his backpack." Her wrist ached with the memory. "After that, I lost sight of him."

In a few more seconds, they'd all see what happened. Then, there'd be no more questions. No more slights about her professionalism. Better yet, her actions wouldn't stain the police force.

Just as she said, the suspect slipped the bag from his shoulder. Like an Olympic discus athlete, he threw the pack. It whirled through the air.

The camera's audio recorded a curse that Grace didn't remember uttering. The aspect of the picture changed. There was a flash of brick wall. The side of her arm. The black bag, the nylon fibers visible.

The image was nothing but static as the timer on the camera continued counting off the seconds. Then, the screen went black—with no sight of a gun.

As if he'd been sucker punched, Camden's jaw ached. He stared at the computer screen, willing the video to start again. It didn't.

What would follow was a simple mathematical equation. No video equaled more civil unrest. The protests would grow. The calls for reform or defunding the police would become a constant chant. Politics would become paramount.

In the end, the truth wouldn't matter at all. And the truth was that Grace Colton had shot someone, apparently unprovoked.

Moreover, Grace Colton's career with the Grave Gulch police force would be over.

The dull ache became a stabbing pain.

Despite what he'd just seen on the camera, though, there was something about Grace. What was it?

Honestly, he didn't know.

All the same, he knew that this case was worth his time.

In the blackened screen of the monitor, Camden refocused his gaze to the reflection of Grace's face. Her complexion was pale. Her eyes were wide. What was she thinking? How did she feel?

Stricken was the word that came to mind.

Clearing his throat, he turned in his seat and looked at Ellie. "Is there any way you can recover more of the footage?"

She ran a thumbnail between the keys of her keyboard. "I'll see what I can do." Her tone had said much more than her words. Camden knew there was no way in hell she'd find any more of the video.

But he was far from being done for the night.

He really only needed to spend a little time with

anyone before he knew if they were telling the truth—
or not. Everyone had a tell when lying. A shifting of
the eyes. A tapping of the foot.

Grace Colton would be no different.

He said, "Officer Colton, we need to talk about what
happened. Obviously, the video isn't going to help us
right now."

Grace stared at her folded hands. There were two
red dots—hot coals of color—on her cheeks. "I'm not
sure what else to say."

Melissa interrupted. "You don't have to say anything, Grace. You're entitled to counsel. Ask your
union legal rep to come in."

Camden spoke slowly. "I'd like to talk to you now,
while your memories are still fresh." She turned her
gaze to him. Camden could look at nothing other than
Grace's eyes. They were a soft blue, like the sky on
the first warm day of spring.

"There was a couple at the end of the block," said
Grace.

Melissa placed her hand on Grace's shoulder. "You
don't have to talk to IA right now, without your rep."

Grace shook her head. "I don't have anything to
hide. Besides, Mr. Kingsley's right. Now, my memories are fresh."

"Are you *sure*?" Melissa asked, stretching out the
last word. "You haven't even had time to file a report."

Grace nodded. "I'm positive."

"Then, we should make this an official interview,"
said Camden. "I'd like to use a conference room."

Melissa glared. He sensed an argument. She wanted
to protect the rookie cop. But was it as the chief of po-

lice or as a cousin? Moving toward the door, she said, "This way."

Camden was used to terse treatment from officers being investigated. Nobody liked oversight or having their professionalism questioned. But without oversight, there was no professionalism to be had. He stood and waited for Grace Colton to get to her feet. Then, they both followed Melissa Colton down a narrow hallway.

The chief a few steps ahead, Camden walked shoulder to shoulder with Grace. His wrist brushed the back of her hand. He searched for something reassuring to say.

What was he thinking? *It isn't my job to be reassuring.*

He had to admit that Grace was affecting him in ways he dared not examine. It was more than her looks, though she was beyond attractive. It was her reaction to the video. Her shock that the entire incident hadn't been recorded was sincere. In short, Grace needed his protection.

First, reassurance. Now, protection? It wasn't like Camden to get personally involved. All he could hope is that the case was resolved quickly. He needed to get away from Grace before he did something really stupid.

Melissa pulled a door open. "You can use this room."

Stepping across the threshold, an automatic light buzzed to life. A conference table stood in the middle of the floor. Two sets of chairs sat on each side of the table, leaving only enough room to slide into a seat.

"Let me know if you need anything," said Melissa, her hand resting on the handle. "And Grace?"

"Yeah?"

"I'll be right outside."

Grace gave a small nod. "Thanks."

Staying on his feet, Camden waited until Chief Colton pulled the door shut. "Please," he said, gesturing to a chair. "Sit." Grace pulled the seat out from under the table and dropped down with a sigh.

"Long night," he said, lowering into his own chair.

"You wouldn't believe, Mr. Kingsley."

"Call me Camden."

"Okay," she said. "Camden."

"I know you're nervous. Tired. Overwhelmed. I also know that I'm the last person in the world you want to be talking to right now. I want to assure you that I'm only interested in the facts." It was how he began each interview—and every word spoken was true.

"I appreciate it."

Camden kept a small tape recorder tucked into a side pocket of his messenger bag. It was with him at all times for moments just like this. He laid it on the table. The recorder was followed by a pad of paper and pen. "I'd like to record this interview—if that's okay with you?"

"A tape recorder. You don't see those often."

"It was my father's. Since it worked for my pop, I figure it'll work for me." He paused, not bothering to add that each time Camden used the recorder he felt as if he honored his father. Or that it was almost like the old man was in the room with him. "Do I have your permission to record this interview?" He pressed a button, and the Record light glowed red.

Grace nodded.

"Is that a yes?"

"Yes," she said. "You have my permission to record the interview."

"This is Camden Kingsley, Internal Affairs investigator with the Grave Gulch District Attorney's office." He also gave the date and time. "For the record," he said, continuing his well-practiced lines, "can you state your name?"

Leaning forward, she projected her voice toward the tiny tape recorder. "Grace Colton. Officer with the Grave Gulch Police Department."

"There was an officer-involved shooting this evening," he said. "Were you present?"

She nodded. "I was."

"Can you tell me, in your own words, what happened?" What she had to say was important, but Camden was also interested in how she told her story. Was it robotic, like she'd memorized details? Or was it disjointed, with details changing from one version to the next? Moreover, what were her mannerisms? Could she maintain eye contact? Did her breathing pattern change when answering specific questions? Were the facts of her story consistent? In short, Camden was looking for a lie.

She spent a few minutes recounting what he already knew. Camden took notes on it all. She'd witnessed a person trying to open a window. After she identified herself as a police officer, the person ran and she gave chase. Detective Brett Shea, still in the patrol vehicle, had circled the block in order to stop the suspect at the end of the alleyway. According to Grace, Robert Grimaldi had a gun. He'd aimed at her. She ordered him to drop his weapon, and when he didn't, she fired her own. The bullet had struck Grimaldi in the shoulder. Two individuals had been at the end of the block. They'd approached Mr. Grimaldi as he lay on the sidewalk.

Camden's pen quit moving. "I want to come back to the witnesses. What'd they look like?" he asked, interrupting.

Grace inhaled. "It was a man and woman. Caucasian. Late teens maybe or early twenties. The guy had longish hair and a thin beard. The woman was wearing a T-shirt with a concert schedule, cut-off jeans and sneakers."

"Are you sure they witnessed the shooting?"

Grace nodded again. "After Mr. Grimaldi was shot, they approached him. I told them to back up." She paused. Her eyes glistened with unshed tears. She blinked hard. Inhaled. Exhaled. "They did, but not at first. I got closer, and they ran off."

Camden looked at Grace. "Can Detective Shea verify the part about the couple?"

"He saw them running away," she said.

That brought up another important point. "Why'd they run?"

"I don't think they liked the police. The guy said something about cops being bad."

"Did Shea hear the remark?"

Grace shrugged. Then she seemed to remember the recorder. Leaning toward the small microphone, she said, "I don't know what he witnessed. You can talk to him, too. He also confiscated my gun for a ballistics review at the scene."

"I'll get to him soon." Camden leaned back in the chair. So far he thought she was telling the truth. "Could you identify again the people you saw?" Without body-cam footage, the witnesses would be the key to finding out what happened. "I need to talk to them, as well."

"Honestly, I've never seen those two before in my life."

"Would you recognize a picture?"

"Maybe." She touched her bottom lip with her tongue. "Probably."

Camden rose from his seat and opened the door. Melissa stood across the hall. She looked up as he stepped into the corridor.

"You need something?" she asked.

"Can I get a set of mug shots?" he asked. "Male, late teens or early twenties. Caucasian. Long hair. Thin beard."

Melissa rolled her eyes. "That guy sounds like a good bit of Grave Gulch," she said. "You have anything more specific?"

"Someone matching that description witnessed the shooting." Camden couldn't help it. He was sincerely relieved that there'd been witnesses. "Grace thinks she can identify him."

Melissa pushed off the wall. "I'll pull some files and be right back."

Camden returned to the room and closed the door. "Your cousin is going to get some photos for you to look through." He slid into the chair and rested his hands on the table. Grace traced a whorl in the faux wood. "If you can identify the witnesses, then we'll track them down and get their statements."

Grace pressed her palms together, as if in prayer, and rested her forehead on her hands. "That'd be great," she said. "If we can find them."

"While we wait," he said, "tell me about the gun."

"What do you want to know?"

"What kind of firearm did Grimaldi have?"

"A handgun."

"Was it an automatic or a revolver?"

She shook her head. "I think it was a revolver."

"Anything else?"

Grace closed her eyes. "It was silver. I remember the metallic glint on the barrel."

"What do you think happened to the gun?"

Opening her eyes, Grace folded her arms over her chest—a definite defensive move. She shook her head. "I don't know. Grimaldi must've dropped it when he went down. Maybe it skittered under a car or something."

Camden's phone pinged. He glanced at the screen. It was a message from Arielle.

Report on missing gun. Document attached.

He hit the link with his thumb. An official Grave Gulch police report filled the screen. The text was small, but its content was unmistakable. More than a dozen officers had searched for a weapon. Several canine units had been employed. They'd all come up empty.

It meant only one thing. There had never been a gun.

It brought up a new set of questions. Had Grace Colton been mistaken? Or was she lying?

As far as he could tell, she'd been truthful until now. Was she the kind of person who'd get angry and lash out? True, he didn't know her well but still, he couldn't see being anything other than careful and forthright.

His mouth felt as if it'd been filled with ash.

"The street was dark," he said, trying a new tactic. "How do you know that the suspect had a gun?"

"There was a streetlamp near the corner," she said. "Mr. Grimaldi was standing in a pool of light. I know what I saw." She paused. "What's on your phone?"

The room was suddenly hot, and he began to sweat. Shoving the cell into his bag, he mumbled, "A report."

"About me? About the gun?"

Camden twirled the pen between his fingers and back again. He tried to collect his thoughts and decide what needed to be said. "Thing is," he said, deciding on the unvarnished truth, "the police officers searched. Canine units were used. Nothing was found. There is no gun."

Sitting back hard, she sucked in a breath. "That's wrong. I know what I saw…" Her words trailed off as the door opened. Melissa stepped into the room. She held a digital tablet, and a sheen of perspiration covered her brow.

"I created a file on everyone in the system with a description that matches the male witness." Chief Colton set the computer on the table before sliding into the seat next to Grace.

"You saw the report," said Grace. "The one about the gun."

It wasn't quite a question. Not really a statement, either.

Melissa swallowed. Nodded. She tapped on the computer, filling the screen with several pictures. Sliding the device over to Grace, she said, "Let's get a look at these mug shots."

"I know what you both are thinking." Grace leaned

forward in her seat. "I'm young. Inexperienced. It's hard to see in the dark. Maybe you even think that I was mad at Mr. Grimaldi. After all, he threw a backpack at me. He damn near broke my wrist." She wrapped a hand around her injured arm. Her skin was mottled by a purple bruise. "The thing is, I saw what I saw. I might be young. I might not have worked many cases. But I'm not wrong."

"I know," said Melissa. Her voice was small. For the first time, Camden noticed worry lines creasing her forehead. "But without that gun, or any video from your body cam, it's your word against Grimaldi's. I don't have to tell you this, but public opinion isn't going to be in your favor."

Camden reached across the table and pushed the tablet closer to Grace. "Look at the mug shots. See if you can find the witness."

She let go of her wrist and picked up the tablet. She said nothing while flipping through screen after screen. After several minutes, Grace shook her head. "He's not here."

"Are you sure?" Melissa took the computer from her younger cousin and flipped back through the photographs. "What about him? He lives near the park. Matches the description perfectly. Or—" she tapped on the screen "—we can look for his girlfriend. She might be in the system."

Grace took the tablet from the other woman's hand. Placing it on the table, screen down, she shook her head. "The guy I saw isn't in any of the photographs."

"You have to keep looking, Grace." Melissa's voice was getting close to shrill. "What if this couple did more than witness the shooting, but they're actually the ones who took the gun? They had opportunity."

Camden connected the dots. "Not too long ago, a co-worker of mine was placed as a witness to a crime. The evidence had been fabricated. You think this is happening again? Is someone setting you up?"

Melissa and Grace exchanged a look. What had he missed?

"You're asking the same question I did," said Grace. "I know Evangeline. She and my brother, Troy, are an item." She continued. "I did wonder if this whole incident was a setup." She shook her head. "Like Melissa pointed out, the only way for this to work is for the police officer—that's me—to shoot Grimaldi. Even if he's desperate enough to take a bullet, he could've been killed."

Camden nodded. The theory made sense.

Melissa said, "I think that the witnesses may have taken the gun."

It was an interesting theory. "If the couple picked up the gun, it's doubtful they have it still. In fact, we have to assume they might've already dropped it into Lake Michigan."

"Until we find those witnesses, we won't know." Melissa pinched the bridge of her nose. "But if they don't have arrest records, how're we supposed to find them?"

Camden already had an answer to that question. "We use a sketch artist. See if we can get a likeness. Then ask the public for help."

"Help from the public," Melissa scoffed. "Not damn likely. Right now, the whole town hates the police department."

"Do you have any other ideas?" Grace asked.

"No," said Melissa. "None."

"Then, I say we try and get a sketch," said Grace.

Melissa asked, "Did you get a good-enough look for a drawing?"

"I can give a description, sure."

Melissa let out a long exhale. "I hope you know what you're doing, Kingsley. There's a lot riding on finding these witnesses and figuring out what happened to the gun."

Unbidden, the image of his father sitting at the kitchen table came to mind. It filled Camden with a steely resolve to find the truth.

Chief Colton drew in a deep breath yet kept her gaze on the table.

Camden knew what she was going to say. What she had to do. His chest tightened.

"I hate to do this, Grace," she said. "Really, I do. I need to put you on administrative leave for possible use of unlawful force."

"You what?" Grace asked, her voice tight.

"Until we find those witnesses, you can't come back to work. I'll need your badge."

Camden had witnessed this awkward moment too many times to count. He hated each and every episode. Each cop reacted differently. Some cursed. Others cried. A few even threatened lawsuits or violence. All the same, Camden couldn't help but wonder—how had his dad reacted? How would Grace react?

Without a word, Grace stood. She unclipped the badge that was hooked to her belt and set it on the table. Melissa scooped it up, holding it in the palm of her hand as if trying to gauge its weight. Or maybe she was weighing her own words.

"Well, then," the chief said. She cleared her throat. "Before you come back, you'll need to talk to one of the counselors. It's department policy after an officer is involved in a shooting." She pulled a business card from the pocket of her pants and slid it toward Grace. Had she been holding it the whole time? "Give them a call." She paused. "I'll contact Desiree and let you get back to the interview."

Grace stared forward, said nothing. Without a word, Melissa Colton left the interview room.

Camden's throat was tight. Sure, he was affected by the heartbreaking moment between family members. Still, he knew there was more.

If the truth was what he valued most, then Camden needed to be honest with himself. The facts were not in Grace's favor.

He also knew something else. If he felt drawn to help Grace, then this case was the most dangerous of Camden's career.

Chapter Four

Since being hired by the GGPD, Grace had never given the interview room much thought. As she sat across from Camden Kingsley, she mentally christened it the Torture Chamber.

There was nothing here that could hurt her physically. But the tiny room trapped Grace with her thoughts.

She'd shot a civilian.

Her body camera hadn't captured the moment, though, when the suspect had brandished his own firearm.

The gun in question was missing.

There were witnesses, yet their identities were unknown. What was worse, the couple had certainly seen the incident, but they weren't bothering to come forward.

The population of Grave Gulch had turned against the police force, too, and this incident was certainly going to make matters worse.

So, on a day when she had little to make her thankful, she inexplicably counted the Internal Affairs investigator as a blessing.

He'd questioned her for nearly a half an hour. So

far, she'd gone over the shooting three times. Grace started off hoping that this was all a mistake or that she'd somehow been framed. There was no evidence to prove either scenario. It meant one thing: she was in serious trouble.

With each telling, the IA investigator said nothing, only watched her with his dark eyes. At the end, he'd ask her to clarify a point or two. Compare her words from one story to the words used in another.

Obviously, the guy was looking for inconsistencies—a way to trip her up. Grace should feel threatened, yet she didn't. Ironically, she admired his methodical and patient questioning.

In the short thirty minutes with Camden, she'd learned a lot about interrogation. One day, she planned to use the techniques herself—that was, if she didn't get fired.

"Let's spend a little time talking about you," he said.

"What do you want to know?"

"When did you eat last?" he asked.

"At dinner, right before my shift."

"Which was?"

"Around half past five, I guess," she said.

"You guess?"

She tried to reign in her annoyance, but Grace couldn't keep the peevish tone from her voice. "Why does any of this matter?"

"I'm trying to establish your state of mind prior to the shooting. A good bit of how you feel is physical. Were you hungry? Hungover? Mad about a fight with your boyfriend?"

"I haven't had a drink since last weekend. That was a single glass of wine. I was with my sister, Annalise, and cousin Madison. We spent the evening looking at wedding dresses online." She paused before saying, "My cousin is getting married in the spring."

Camden scribbled a note. Grace couldn't help but wonder what she'd said that was so noteworthy. "And your boyfriend?"

"I don't have one."

"Good." For a moment, they stared at each other. Camden dropped his gaze to his notepad.

Was it her imagination, or had Camden Kingsley sat taller when she'd told him she was single?

After clearing his throat, he spoke again. "I mean, it's good that you didn't come to work upset."

Grace tried to remember her day—a time before the shooting. It had only been a few hours ago, yet the memories were lost in a fog. To her, it seemed as if everything had happened years earlier. A flash came to her. She started again. "I broiled a piece of chicken and had leftover rice pilaf. The bagged salad I planned to eat was wilted, so I had an apple with my meal. I finished eating, put my dishes in the sink. Since I was already in my uniform, I left for work. My shift runs from six o'clock in the evening until two o'clock in the morning. I sleep from about three in the morning until ten o'clock. Get up. Run. Breakfast. Errands. You know, the grind."

"Do you find life to be a grind?"

Damn. Grace had been given a single piece of advice for talking to the IA investigator: don't give any information that's not asked for. What had she done? She'd broken the sole rule. Now, Camden had reason to think she was malcontent—or, worse, angry.

"It's just an expression." And then, "What other questions can I answer?"

Camden gazed at Grace. She wanted to look away. Yet, she couldn't. He asked, "Is there anything else you want to add?"

Grace paused. Was there? Sitting in the tiny room it was easy to question everything. Had she been mistaken? Had Robert Grimaldi actually been holding a gun—or not? She brought back those moments in the alleyway. The air, heavy and humid. She'd been damp with sweat, and her uniform clung to her skin. The street was silent, save for the slapping of her footfalls on the pavement and Grace's own labored breathing.

Then, Mr. Grimaldi had seemed to come from nowhere. He sprinted down the street. He slowed and turned. There was a glint of silver in his hand as light reflected off his sidearm.

"I know what I saw," she said. "The suspect had a gun. I wasn't tired. Or angry. Or distracted."

After hitting the Stop button on his recorder, Camden asked, "You okay?"

"Yes," she said. Then, "No, not really."

"You and Chief Colton are related, right?"

He already knew the answer, so why ask? Still, she answered his question. "She's my cousin."

"Must be tough, to have your cousin take your badge."

Was Camden trying to set Grace up? Were his kindness and professionalism actually just an act? "Probably not half as tough as it was for her to take my badge."

"Listen," he murmured and leaned forward. "The investigation will follow the evidence. We will find out what happened." He stopped and swallowed. "One day soon, you will be okay. I promise."

After just a few minutes, she knew she somehow trusted Camden to be honest and uphold justice. Was that wise, especially since Melissa had warned her to be wary? Or was Grace so keenly vulnerable that she wanted him to be trustworthy?

"How long have you been doing this?" she asked. "Working for IA?"

"A while," he said.

"So you've seen a lot, then?"

Smiling, he shook his head. "I've seen more than enough."

His smile stirred her blood, creating a fluttering in her belly. She disregarded the sensation. "Has there ever been a case like mine in Grave Gulch? A shooting with a missing gun? Witnesses who won't come forward?"

Camden tapped the pen on the table. "No," he said. "I can't think of any."

"Anything close?" she pressed, hoping for a crumb of good news.

"There have been times when police officers have fired their guns and the civilian's weapon wasn't found at the scene." He pinned Grace in place with his gaze. "In the end, it was determined that the officer was mistaken. Maybe the suspect did have something in their hand. Because of the angle or the lighting, it looked like a firearm." He paused again, lining up his pen with the pad of paper. "Despite training and experience, mistakes happen."

"What about those police officers?" Her hands were cold. Grace couldn't help it. She was worried. Would

Camden believe the Grimaldi had a gun? And if he didn't, what did that mean for her career? "What about their jobs?"

Why had she even bothered with the question? She could guess the answer—and knew it wouldn't be good. Then again, maybe hope was all she had left.

With a shake of his head, Camden exhaled. "The department had to let them go. You can't hold the public's trust if someone on the force shoots an unarmed person. It doesn't matter if it was an accident. Or a mistake."

Was that what he thought? And would he be right? Had she been mistaken? Dear God, Grace never would have fired if she hadn't been certain. Now, she wasn't sure of anything.

Suddenly, Grace was exhausted. She wished like hell that she still had the cup of coffee Melissa had made. Camden was waiting for her to say something. But what?

The door opened, saving her from having to say anything.

Desiree, Grace's half sister, stepped into the room.

Her curly dark hair was wound into a bun at the nape of her neck. She was casually dressed in a pair of jeans and a hoodie. A leather-bound sketch pad was tucked under her arm. She also carried a metal tin filled with pencils. "Hey, honey. I heard what happened on the news. Stavros sends his love. Danny would have, too. But he's asleep," Desiree said, mentioning the new man in her life and with her two-year-old son.

Desiree was only at police headquarters as the department's part-time sketch artist. Still, emotions—relief and regret—washed over Grace in a wave. She felt her lip start to quiver.

Desiree rushed forward. Pulling Grace from the chair, she wrapped her into a big hug. Enveloped in her sister's embrace, Grace's throat closed. Her eyes burned. She fought with everything in her to keep from crying.

"How ya doing?"

"Ya know." Even Grace heard the tremor of emotion in her voice. "Lousy."

"I'm here for you. You know that, right?"

Grace nodded, not trusting her own voice.

Desiree released her younger sibling. "I got a call from Melissa. She said there were some witnesses to the incident. You need me to do a sketch…" Her voice trailed off as her eyes moved across the table.

"This is Camden Kingsley," said Grace, answering the unasked question of *Who's that guy?*

"Nice to meet you, Camden," said Desiree, offering her hand to shake. "I'm Desiree. Sketch artist. Grace's eldest sister."

"I'm from Internal Affairs," he said.

Desiree's spine went rigid. "IA?" she echoed, still shaking his hand. "Why's IA here?"

"He's doing his job," said Grace. She stopped speaking.

Why was she defending the man who had the power to ruin her career? Heck, he could ruin her life. But she knew his goal was to seek out the truth, even if he didn't believe her. Not yet, anyway.

"I guess we all have a job to do," said Desiree. "Before I get started, do you need anything? A water, maybe?"

Grace slipped back into her seat. Her back ached.

Her head hurt. Her eyes were heavy, and she wanted to sleep for two weeks straight. "Coffee," said Grace. "With sugar, no milk."

"I know how my baby sister drinks her coffee," said Desiree with mock indignation. Her phone pinged with an incoming text. She glanced at the screen and drew her brows together.

Grace's chest tightened. "What's wrong? Is it something with Danny?" she asked. "I can't handle more bad news."

"Nothing's wrong." She smiled. "It's Stavros. I'll call him back when we're done."

Camden rose to his feet. "I could use a coffee, too. You two get started. I'll be back in a minute." He pointed to Desiree. "What do you want?"

"I'm good for now." She set her pad and pencil box on the table. "Thanks for asking, though."

Desiree stood by the table and waited until Camden left the room. "He's really easy to look at. Too bad he's IA."

"Camden's not a bad guy. He's just got a difficult job, that's all."

"A cop getting other people to tattle on cops." Desiree dropped into the chair next to Grace's. She opened the sketch pad to a fresh sheet. "That sounds like a whole lot to me."

"Or he's keeping us all honest," said Grace.

Desiree lifted one brow. "Right. Honest."

"What?" Grace asked. She knew, though. Her cheeks warmed, just thinking about Camden and his eyes.

"What do you mean, *what?*"

"What's up with the look?" Lifting a single brow, she mirrored her sister's expression mockingly.

Desiree swatted Grace's arm. "You know what your mom says. Your face will freeze that way."

"My face," said Grace. "What about yours?"

"You want to see a face?" Desiree asked. She rested her chin on her hands and batted her eyelashes. "That's you looking at the IA guy."

Had her appreciation of Camden—his smile, his broad shoulders, his honesty—been that obvious? Or did Desiree know Grace better than Grace knew herself? "Is not."

"Is too! But don't worry, he is hot."

"Really? I hadn't noticed," Grace lied to her sister. As far as she was concerned, Camden Kingsley was more than good-looking; he might actually be a good person. What was she thinking? She couldn't have a crush on the IA investigator.

"Aren't you worried that your pants will catch on fire for telling lies like that?"

Grace let out a peal of laughter. It felt good to do so and yet the timing was all wrong. Desiree and Grace weren't at home, joking around. She was in an interrogation room at the police station. What was more, *she* was the one being questioned.

"Hey," said Desiree, rubbing the back of Grace's arm. "It'll be okay. I promise."

"You have to tell me the truth. How bad is the media coverage?"

Desiree exhaled and shook her head. "It's bad. That's what Stavros said when he texted me. Even at this hour, the protests are getting worse. People are calling on Melissa to resign."

"No. Melissa can't leave the department. She's the chief of police! Whether Grave Gulch wants to admit it or not, the town needs Melissa."

"The problem is that she's your cousin," said Desiree. "There are a lot of Coltons who work for the GGPD. People are complaining about nepotism."

Bile rose in the back of Grace's throat. Not only had the shooting put Grace's career in jeopardy, but it had further threatened Melissa's, as well.

Grabbing Grace by the wrist, Desiree said, "We will get through this—together, as a family—like always." Patting her arm again, she continued, "Now, let's get this sketch done. The sooner we can get a picture out to the public, the quicker we can find your witnesses."

CAMDEN WALKED DOWN the empty hallway of the police station. True, he'd left to get a cup of coffee, but what he really needed was time. Time to think. Time to regroup. Time to figure out why he was so damn affected by Grace Colton. For starters, she was pretty. No, that wasn't exactly right. Flowers were pretty. Sunsets were pretty. Every time he glanced at Grace it was like seeing the ocean or the Grand Canyon for the first time. In a word, she was breathtaking.

If he was lucky, he'd run into Brett Shea. Then he could ask about the witnesses. Who knew, maybe he'd get lucky twice, and Brett would have something more to add that exonerated Grace.

His phone began to shimmy, and he fished it from the pocket of his coat.

Damn. Maybe his luck had just run out.

"Hey, Arielle. What's up?"

"So what have you learned?"

Above, fluorescent lights buzzed and cast a jaundiced glow. But no coffeepot. What'd a guy have to do to find a cup around here? "There were witnesses."

"What'd they say?" Arielle asked.

"They ran off." He opened the metal door that led to a set of stairs and paused. He did have information for his boss. "Chief Colton put her on administrative leave pending the outcome of my investigation and an evaluation with a counselor."

"As she should," said Arielle. "What else can you tell me?"

"Officer Colton is with a sketch artist now. We hope to have a likeness to share with the public soon."

"*We*?" Arielle scoffed. "Remember whose team you're on, Camden."

"I'm on whichever team is looking for the facts." He owed it to his father to not let politics or public outcry get in the way of the truth. "I'm on the team that won't jump to conclusions."

Arielle spoke. "It's like what the mayor said, the GGPD has messed up. A serial killer is on the loose because their forensic investigator tampered with evidence. Innocent people went to jail because the police failed to do their jobs. Guilty people are on the street."

Camden leaned against the open door. There was no denying that Arielle and Mayor Abels were right. "Sure, but none of that has anything to do with what happened tonight."

"Or maybe it has everything to do with what happened. Is it bad leadership?"

Camden closed his eyes. Hadn't he been wondering the same thing just hours before? Then, he'd met Grace Colton. Had he forgotten about the other facts—focusing only on her blue eyes, her smile, her tight rear and strong legs, and, well, how damned attractive she was?

Which meant what?

For starters, he'd never be able to remain professional and impartial.

"I might not be the guy for this case," he began.

"You're kidding, right?"

"It's just..." He paused. Camden needed to choose his words with extreme care. "Grace Colton has integrity. It's hard to see her as being anything other than honest."

Above, the clang of footsteps drew Camden's attention. He looked up the winding stairwell. Chief Colton was descending.

"I have to go. I'll stay here until the sketch artist is done. We'll regroup in the morning."

"The mayor wants you on this case. Get used to it."

Before Camden could respond, the line went dead.

Melissa stopped on the bottom step. "Everything okay?"

While tucking the phone back into his suit coat, Camden said, "It's Arielle. She's looking for an update."

After a beat, she asked, "How's the sketch coming?"

"I don't know. It seemed like the sisters needed a moment. So, I took the opportunity to come looking for coffee."

"That's something I can help you out with," said Melissa, pivoting on the step. "There's always a pot brewed in the squad room, but you have to be pretty generous to call that stuff coffee. I have a single-serve in my office. I can make you something fresher."

"And a cup for Grace," said Camden. Damn. Even

he heard the eagerness in his tone. Clearing his throat, he followed the police chief up the stairs.

"She's been through a lot," said Melissa, stopping to open a door.

Camden stepped onto the main floor. "Officer Colton seems to be holding up well under all the pressure."

"Don't let the cool exterior fool you. Usually, my cousin is quite chatty."

An image of Grace laughing and talking came to mind—and brought a smile to Camden's lips. He had to get this case reassigned.

As she started brewing a cup, Melissa asked, "How do you take your coffee?"

"Just black," he said. "Grace takes her with sugar. No milk."

Openmouthed, Melissa stared at Camden. He immediately understood his mistake. Knowing how Grace Colton liked her coffee made him look like a lovesick schoolboy. His chest was hot with embarrassment. He needed to fix the problem—and now.

He cleared his throat. "Downstairs, Grace and Desiree were talking. She mentioned it. I guess I just remembered."

Damn. Had he just made matters worse? Now he looked like a lovesick schoolboy who'd also memorized the class schedule of his crush. Clamping his jaw shut, Camden swore to say nothing more.

What was wrong with Camden? It's not like he'd never met a good-looking woman before. It's just that Grace was different. Hell, it felt like he'd been waiting for her to show up for his entire life.

With a smile, Melissa handed him a steaming cup of coffee. "Sugar. No milk."

He took the cup. Yet, he couldn't help but wonder—why the smile? Had he already let on that his interest in Grace Colton went beyond professional?

Chapter Five

"Here you go." Desiree held up her sketch pad for Grace to see.

The rendering was in black-and-white. Yet, her sister had drawn a close likeness to the woman she'd seen on the street. "That's her." Grace sighed with relief. "Maybe the case will start moving in a positive direction."

"That's why I'm here." She flipped to a clean page. "Let's get started on the male witness, and I can get home to my baby."

"Is Mom taking care of Danny?"

"No, Stavros is home with him," said Desiree. "Danny was asleep when I left," she continued. "He should be okay. But I don't like to leave Danny alone for long."

Grace didn't blame her sister. True, she was a protective mother, but there was more. At the beginning of the year, Danny had been kidnapped at a wedding. Then over the summer, a woman had stalked Grace's nephew and tried to steal him, as well. It was a huge blessing that Danny was physically unharmed. Still, the incidents had left their mark on the child.

"How's he doing?"

"Nights are the worst, to be honest. He has nightmares. He doesn't like the dark."

Grace's chest tightened with a pang of guilt. "You've done too much for me already. Go home. Take care of your family. We can finish up in the morning."

"Like it or not, you're part of my family, baby sister. I'm here for the long haul."

Opening her mouth, Grace was ready to argue. The door opened, and whatever she might've said was forgotten. Camden stood on the threshold with a cup of coffee in each hand. He'd loosened his tie, and a narrow strip of flesh was exposed at his neck. Grace couldn't look away.

"Sorry it took so long," he said, setting the cups on the table. "Your cousin had to help me find the coffee." He pushed a cup toward Grace. "Sugar, no milk."

The same fluttering from before filled her middle. "Desiree did a likeness of the female witness." She reached for the coffee. "She was just about to go home and see my adorable nephew."

"I'm not leaving until we're done, Grace," Desiree said. "Besides, I'll stay till you're done, too. After that, you can stay with me."

"No way to both," said Grace, suddenly feeling very young. "I don't need a babysitter. I'll be fine." She took a sip of coffee, as if that somehow proved her point. The caffeine hit her system, and her head began to buzz. Now, she'd never get to sleep tonight. Not that she really thought she'd get much rest—even without drinking the coffee.

She was worried about her job, her reputation, and in a small way the health of Robert Grimaldi.

"I don't think you need a babysitter, either. But here's what we do need to do—finish the second sketch."

Grace sipped her coffee to hide a smile.

"What's that for?" Desiree asked.

"You."

"Me?"

"You sound like you did when we were younger, and Mom left you in charge."

"Are you saying that I'm using my bossy-older-sister voice?"

Grace measured a distance between finger and thumb. "Maybe a little."

"Good. Then, let's get this done."

"Honestly, you can go home." Grace was almost positive that Danny was fine. Yet, she hated that Desiree was worried. And it was all because of her.

Camden sat on the edge of the table, lifting his own cup of coffee to his lips. "Your sister is right, finishing the sketch. Do it now. You'll forget details later."

He was right, she knew. Yet, with him so near she could think of nothing else than, well, him. His dark eyes. His full lips. His thick hair. His features, somehow both strong and refined. In fact, he looked so damned perfect that she'd swear he was an artist's rendering of what a man should be—not simply flesh and blood.

Grace swiveled in the cramped seat to face her sister. "Where do you want to start?"

"The eyes," said Desiree. "After all, they're the windows to the soul, right?"

Grace closed her own eyes. Inhaled. Exhaled. She pictured the street and the young man with a thin beard. She focused on only the man. His face. His eyes.

They were dark brown. Full lashes. Beautifully shaped. Full lips.

No, damn it. In her mind's eye, she saw Camden.

With a sigh, Grace slumped back in her seat. Would she ever be able to prove her innocence? Especially since there was one thing she knew for certain. Grace was drawn to the guy who'd been sent to find out if she was guilty.

What was her problem? Was it because almost everyone in her family had found a person to love? Or was it because Grace hadn't been on a date worth mentioning since joining the force?

"Can I see the sketch you did of the woman?" he asked, interrupting her thoughts.

Desiree handed over a sheet of paper. For a moment, Camden studied the likeness. "I don't recognize her, but someone must. I'll take this to Melissa. At least she can get the picture to the local reporters. They can splash it all over social media. Then I'm going back to my office. We should meet in the morning, Grace. Here. Nine o'clock."

"Nine o'clock," she echoed. "I'll be here."

He took another sip of coffee before rising from the table. Then he was gone.

Grace had been warned about the IA investigator. Yet, that was before she'd met Camden Kingsley. She couldn't help it: she trusted him to do the right thing. Did that make her a fool?

FOR ONCE IN his life, Camden had not been a man of his word. He had not returned to his office. Instead, he'd stayed at the police department and commandeered a small conference room on the first floor—courtesy of Chief Colton.

It had been more than an hour since he'd left Grace Colton with her sister, the sketch artist. The time was now 1:45 a.m. And still he couldn't bring himself to go home.

The metal door that led to the stairs opened and closed with a clang. Camden looked up just as Grace strode past. Desiree was at her side.

The two women couldn't look more different. Desiree, several years older, had dark curly hair that matched her curvy figure. Grace, blond-haired and blue-eyed, was tall and lithe. She glanced into the room as she passed.

Camden's mouth went dry with desire.

"Hey," she said, slowing to a stop. "I thought you were going back to your office. Did you find anything new? Did the gun turn up? Was Ellie able to recover any more of the body-cam footage?"

It was impossible to miss her hopeful tone. He had nothing to offer, unfortunately. Instinctively, his shoulder blades pinched together. Rubbing the back of his neck, he said, "Your cousin offered me this conference room to use. For now, it seemed better to stay put." His words trailed off. What else was there to say? He couldn't admit the truth—that he'd waited around for more than an hour hoping to catch another glimpse of Grace.

Nodding slowly, she exhaled. "Okay, then."

"If there's nothing new, then I'm going to go," said Desiree. "I don't like to leave Danny at home, even with Stavros on duty."

"You know, you're the only mom I know who isn't

even satisfied with a physician watching their child." Grace pulled her sister in for a hug.

"I think a lot of moms are like me. You sure you're okay?"

With a nod, Grace released her sister.

Desiree continued. "You know I'm always here for you, right? You can stay at my place if you want. My kid would love to see you in the morning."

"I'm tempted, but I'm good." Grace gave her sister a wan smile. "Honestly."

"All right, then, I am finally going home." Desiree flicked her fingertips with a small wave.

He'd been charged with finding the truth about Grace Colton. Was there more to the family than what he'd seen so far? Or were they simply a kind and loving family?

Redirecting his gaze back at his open laptop, Camden saw nothing. Was he a heel for staying on the case? Or was he just a guy doing his job?

Grace loosened her hair, shaking her tresses out of the bun she'd worn at the nape of her neck. Golden locks flowed over her shoulders. His fingers itched with the need to touch her. Good Lord! What was the matter with him? *Focus, damn it. Focus.*

"Do you need to speak to me about anything else?" she asked, bringing him back to the tiny conference room.

"It's been a long evening. Go home. Sleep if you can."

"Sleep?" she echoed. "I doubt I'll get much rest."

"You might surprise yourself. We'll get back together in the morning."

She placed her hand on the doorjamb and drew her

bottom lip between her teeth. He waited, wondering what she wanted to say. Or ask.

She exhaled and met his gaze. "Well, good night."

"Yeah," he said. The heavy weight of fatigue dropped to his shoulders. "G'night."

She turned and walked away. He waited until the sound of her footfalls faded to nothing. Camden glanced back at his computer. The monitor was now asleep, and his reflection wavered in the dark screen.

"You have to get off this case," he said to his shadowy self. "There's no two ways about it. If you keep working on this investigation, you're going to ruin her career as well as yours."

He gave a short laugh. He could definitely get the case assigned to someone else if he admitted to Arielle that he'd developed a crush on the subject of the latest IA investigation.

After packing up his computer, Camden stood. Stretched. For the first time in hours, his stomach grumbled with a reminder that he'd skipped his late dinner.

He made his way through the squad room. The waiting room of the police station was empty. Not even a duty sergeant sat behind the front desk.

He walked into the holding area and stopped short. Beyond the glass doors, the street was filled with more than two dozen protesters.

Some held signs that read:
Fire the Chief.
Others read:
Grave Gulch Deserves Better.
Or others:
Police Reform NOW!

A line of cops—all in uniform—stood in front of the doors. No doubt, they were blocking people from entering the building.

Despite the different signs they held, the protesters were all unified in their message. "What do we want?" one person called out.

A crowd of more than two dozen answered in unison. "To fire Grace Colton!"

"When do we want it?" the leader on a bullhorn asked.

Everyone called back with a single word. "Now!"

The sound of a gasp caught his attention. On the opposite side of the lobby, Grace stood near a corner. She'd changed out of her police uniform and now wore a light blue T-shirt and jeans. A duffel bag was slung over her shoulder.

The change in Grace from just a few minutes earlier was remarkable. Yet, it was more than the way her jeans hugged her rear and thighs. Or that the delicate blue of her shirt matched her eyes perfectly. Her complexion was pale.

She looked at him, her eyes wide and her voice small. "What do I do now?" she asked.

The last thing Camden needed was to spend more time with Grace. Was he going to leave her to face that mob alone?

"Obviously, you can't go out those doors." He hustled to her side. God, it felt good to stand next to her. He held out his hand. "Come with me. I'll take you out the back."

She looked from his palm to his face and back again. Without a word, she slipped her fingers through his. In taking her hand, Camden had crossed a line. He'd become personally involved with the subject of an investigation. From here, would he ever be able to go back?

He really didn't care how much damage he might be doing to his career. In the moment, there was only one thing that mattered to Camden: it was Grace.

HEAD BUZZING, GRACE walked down the hallway. Was there really a mob outside the police station? Were they all calling for her resignation? It was almost two in the morning. Good god, they really must hate her. Each fact was a punch to her gut, painful and surprising, and left her ready to retch.

Obviously, you can't go out those doors, Camden had said.

Come with me, he'd offered. *I'll take you out the back.*

Then, he'd grabbed her hand, and now, she was being led through the police station. This whole situation had been nothing short of a nightmare. From the time she'd fired her gun, Grace felt as if she'd been walking in a fog.

She was young, and a rookie to boot. But if Grace wanted to prove her innocence, it was time to wake up. She needed to act, not be led around and told what to do.

She pulled her hand from Camden's grip and stopped in the middle of the corridor.

He strode on for a step or two, before turning to face her.

"You okay?" he asked.

"I'm not sneaking out the back door like a criminal. It makes me look guilty." She pivoted. "I'm going outside. I'll explain to that crowd what happened."

"What? No way. That crowd is peaceful now. What will you do if that changes?" He didn't wait for an answer. "There's a lot of police officers standing in front of the building. What happens to them if things get violent?"

"I…" Grace began. Maybe her plan wasn't as solid as she thought.

"There's a time and place for you to tell your story. Now's not it."

He was right, she knew. Yet, she couldn't think of anything to say.

"Do you trust me?" he asked.

Did she? Melissa had warned her about the IA investigator. Yet, Camden was so different than the man she'd imagined. Maybe she did trust him—at least a little.

She shrugged.

"Come with me. I'll get you out of the building and get home safe." He paused. "Where do you live?"

"I have an apartment a few blocks from here."

"Car?" he asked.

She shook her head. "I walked to work today."

"C'mon," he said. He didn't reach for her hand a second time. "Let's go."

Was he really going to walk her home? Honestly, Grave Gulch was a fairly safe town—or had been, until recently. She'd be fine on her own.

But would she?

She'd seen the protesters at the front door. There was no telling what would happen if they found Grace. "Thanks," she said. "I appreciate the offer."

He opened the back door. The air was still hot and heavy, and sweat gathered at the nape of her neck.

The chanting from the protesters was clear even at the back of the building.

"What do we want?"

"To fire Grace Colton!"

"When do we want it?"

"Now!"

The police station's parking lot had more than a dozen vehicles—both police cruisers and personal cars—parked inside the perimeter. Thankfully, the street was empty. After pulling the door open, Camden said, "Ladies first."

Grace paused before stepping through. "I know you don't have to do this," she said. "You know, help me out." Her eyes rested on his hand. His fingers were long, his nails neatly trimmed. For a moment, she recalled the feeling of his palm in hers. She liked the memory a little too much. Returning her gaze to his face, she continued, "Anyway, I want to thank you."

He accepted her gratitude with a nod. "Let's go before someone comes around the building and sees you."

She slid through the door and paused on the side street.

"This way," said Camden. He led her away from the police station and the waiting mob.

The lights from police headquarters were the only ones on the block. Within a few yards, the shadows moved in, surrounding Grace with darkness. The voices of the protesters faded.

Camden stayed at her side yet said nothing.

She didn't mind the quiet. It gave her time to think. Too much had happened for her to actually have a thought.

Ahead, the light from Mae's Diner spilled onto the

sidewalk. Camden's pace slowed as they passed. He stared at the door.

"What is it?" she asked.

He gave a small smile. "I was thinking that I haven't eaten since lunch. That was—what, twelve—" he looked at his watch, an old-school timepiece with a leather band "—make that fourteen hours ago."

"We can stop and grab a bite." Had she just invited herself to have a midnight snack with Camden Kingsley? What was the matter with her? Grace had to get a grip. "I mean, I can get myself home from here. It's just a few blocks away. You get something to eat."

He'd already turned back to Mae's Diner. "Or we can both stop."

The pull to be with Camden was strong—maybe too strong. "Really, I shouldn't." She hooked her thumb over her shoulder. "I have an early meeting in the morning."

"Yeah," he said, pulling the door open. "With me. We can move back the time if you want. Come in and at least keep me company. Eating alone—and in the middle of the night, no less—is just sad."

There were about a million reasons for Grace to say no. She could recite them all without thinking. It was late. She was tired. She'd had the worst day of her life, and she just wanted it to end. She shouldn't be hanging out with the man in charge of her investigation—especially since she found him so damned handsome.

Yet, her mouth didn't listen to her mind. Grace found herself walking through the door. "I guess I could stay for a little bit..."

A man with sparse hair and a round middle stood behind a long counter. He wore a white apron and a blue shirt. A name tag read *Mike*. "Evening, folks," he said as they walked through the door. "Heck of a night to be out."

"You mean, all the people at the police station?" asked Camden, not letting on that they'd just been inside the building. "Heck of a night."

"Have a seat anywhere you'd like. I'm the only one here, so the menu's pretty limited."

Aside from the counter, the room was ringed with booths, the seats covered in red and gray vinyl. A dozen tables, with chairs set on top, sat in the middle of the room.

Camden slid onto a stool near where the man stood. Grace took a stool beside him. She dropped her duffel bag at her feet. "What d'you recommend?" Camden asked.

"The apple pie's fresh this morning," Mike said. "Not many people ordered, so I'd give you a big slice."

Camden gestured to Grace, allowing her to order first. "I'll take pie and a coffee. Decaf."

"Make that two," said Camden.

"Two pies and two decaf coffees, coming right up," said Mike. "You want that pie heated?"

"Sure," said Camden. And then, "You got vanilla ice cream?"

"Any other way to eat apple pie?" Mike asked.

"Not that I know of," said Camden, slipping his messenger bag over the chair back.

Grace enjoyed listening to the easy banter. It was a nice break from the chaos of the evening. "Same," she said.

"Give me a minute, and I'll be right back," Mike

said, before disappearing through a set of doors marked *Kitchen*.

Grace picked up a set of silverware wrapped in a paper napkin. She twirled it between her fingers. "So," she began, not knowing what to say next, "how'd you end up working for IA?"

"I was a cop first," he said. "State police. I worked a lot with Arielle, and when a position opened up, she helped me get the job."

Grace nodded. She wasn't sure where the conversation was going. Was it right to chat up Camden? No, she decided, she definitely shouldn't try to get chummy with the guy from Internal Affairs.

If it was wrong, why had she even asked about his life?

"My dad was a beat cop in Detroit," he continued. "I grew up admiring him and wanting to be just like my pop. Probably the same reason that you joined the force. I mean, there certainly are a lot of Coltons working for the GGPD."

It was definitely part of the reason why Grace had become a police officer. "There's that aspect," she said. "I admire the hell out of Melissa. Annalise, my other sister, works for GGPD as a canine instructor. You met Desiree, who's a part-time sketch artist. I have a brother who's a detective."

"I know Troy."

"There's a cousin who's with the FBI."

"I've never met Bryce, but I've heard the name."

"So you know that we're very heavy into law enforcement. But…"

"But what?" he asked.

"There's more to the story." She drew in a deep

breath, not completely certain why she was sharing her family's history. "Desiree and I are half sisters. Her mother, Amanda, was murdered decades ago. The killer was never found."

"Wow," said Camden. "That's rough." He paused. "I know how a family's history can influence everyone."

She waited a beat. And then another. Was there something else he wanted to say? Camden stayed silent.

"Anyway," she sighed. How long had it been since Grace had told this story? It had been years, and still she knew all the details. Smoothing a seam on the rolled napkin, she spoke. "My dad was heartbroken. A few years later, he met and married my mom. She was a preschool teacher at the time. Amanda's memory looms large in our house. In our entire family, really. We all want to make sure that justice is done for everybody—even if it never happened for Amanda."

She looked up and met Camden's gaze. He opened his mouth, ready to speak. Before he said a word, the kitchen door opened. Mike emerged, holding a tray with two huge slices of pie and two steaming cups of coffee.

"I made a new pot of coffee for you folks," he said, setting the tray on the counter. "The other one had gotten old." He set a cup in front of Grace. "How'd you both take your poison? Milk? Sugar? Straight black?"

"She'll take sugar, no milk. I like my coffee black."

Mike placed a dish filled with sugar packets next to Grace's cup. Then he set down the plates of pie. "Enjoy."

Grace unwrapped her utensils. Using the side of her fork, she cut off a piece of pie before swirling it through the melting ice cream. She took a bite and chewed slowly, savoring the flaky crust, the spicy cinnamon and the sweet-tart apples.

Swallowing down her bite with a sip of coffee, she couldn't shake the feeling that Camden had been ready to tell her something but changed his mind. It left her wondering about what he'd been about to say…and why she was so eager to hear more about him.

Chapter Six

Camden scraped the last bit of pie off his plate and took the final bite. He hummed with satisfaction. "Delicious."

Grace sat beside him and nodded. "Good idea to stop. I didn't know that I needed a break, but I did." She pushed her plate back with a finger.

A clock above the kitchen doors read 2:37 a.m. Without a doubt, this had been one of the longest workdays in recent memory. Camden was comfortably full and ready for several uninterrupted hours of sleep. Yet, he didn't want the night to end.

"Can I get you folks anything else?" Mike asked. "A top-up on your coffee?"

"I'm good," said Grace, placing her hand over the cup. "It's late. I better get going."

"We'll just take the check," said Camden.

"Two checks." Grace held up two fingers.

"I'll make it easy on you both. You each owe five dollars," said Mike. "And you can figure it out on your own. I never interfere in anyone's love life."

Grace's cheeks reddened. "Oh, we're not a couple."

"Yeah, right." Mike drew out his words.

The last thing Camden wanted was to let things get

uncomfortable for Grace. Despite the fact that he'd had a better time with Grace than on his last three dates combined, they weren't involved. What's more—they never would be in a relationship.

Pulling his wallet from his back pocket, Camden found a twenty-dollar bill. He threw it on the counter. To Mike he said, "Thanks for the pie and coffee." He stood. "C'mon. You're right, Grace. It's late. Let's go."

Grace stood and picked up the duffel she'd stowed on the floor. "You don't have to pay for me," she said. "I'm completely capable. I have a job…" She blanched. He could only guess what she was thinking—*at least, she used to have a job.*

Camden didn't want anything to get weird. "I was the one who invited you. I can cover the tab for coffee and pie." He walked to the door and held it open as she passed. The street was silent. The heat from the day had finally broken, yet the air was heavy with humidity. "It feels like rain," he said.

"Maybe the storm will chase away the protesters tomorrow." She started walking down the sidewalk. "I believe that everyone should exercise their First Amendment rights. Still, it's a little different when a group is calling for me to be fired."

Camden jogged to her side. He wanted to offer her some kind of comfort, to tell her everything would be okay. But would it? Besides, he worked for Internal Affairs. In stopping at Mae's Diner, he'd come dangerously close to crossing a professional line.

They walked the next few blocks in silence. Grace stopped in front of a brick apartment building. Narrow with four stories, it was much like all the other buildings on the block. A set of steps led to a security door. "This is my place." While retrieving a set of keys from her black duffel bag, Grace climbed the short flight of stairs.

"You're okay to get into your place yourself?"

Sliding a key into a security-door lock, she said, "I'll be fine. See you in the morning."

And now what? Did he follow her up the steps? Shake her hand? Hug her? God help him, in a flash he imagined Grace's lips on his own. "Well," he said stepping backward, "I have to get my car from the police department." A rumble of thunder sounded, and a far-off flash of lighting glowed at the horizon.

Grace turned her gaze to the sky. "I think that's the storm you predicted."

Without a backward glance, Grace slid into the foyer. He only caught a glimpse of the cramped space—just a tiled area, with a bank of mailboxes set into the wall. The door closed, the lock engaging with a click.

Remaining on the sidewalk, Camden watched the building. A moment later, a window glowed as a light inside a room was illuminated. It was Grace's apartment—second floor, unit on the left.

A breeze blew, sending leaves skittering down the street. There was the hint of a chill in the wind. Had he been right? Was a storm coming?

Camden turned toward the police station. As he walked, he tried to think of everything he knew about Grace and her case. Yet, his mind continued to wander to another time and another cop who hadn't been given the benefit of a fair investigation.

At the diner, he'd been tempted to share what had

happened to his father. He never spoke about his pop anymore. So why now? Why with her?

It's not that Camden lived like a monk. He dated but nobody had created a spark of excitement for a long time. Grace had definitely awakened feelings that he dared not examine too closely.

Lights over the parking lot of GGPD's headquarters still blazed bright. Fewer cars filled spaces now than before. The protesters at the front of the building were gone. The only sound was the slapping of Camden's shoes on the pavement. He crossed the lot to his car. Using a fob, he unlocked the door. As he slid behind the passenger seat, the first raindrop fell. The storm had finally come.

As GRACE WOKE the next morning, she felt her head throb. Her tongue was thick, and her mouth was dry. Was she hungover? What had she done the night before? The alarm on her phone continued to blare the opening chords of a pop song. With a groan, she rolled over and silenced her phone.

Then it hit like a wave crashing on the shore. Everything from last night came back in an instant. The break-in. The chase. The shooting. And, worst of all, the missing gun and damaged body camera. A cramp gripped Grace's middle. With a moan, she curled into a ball.

Breathe, she told herself. *In through the nose. Out through the mouth.* Just like the yoga teacher had instructed when she, Annalise, Desiree, and her mom had taken that class in the spring.

The controlled breathing, along with the happy memory, settled her stomach. Flopping to her back,

Grace stared at the ceiling. Her curtains were pulled tight. Outside, rain tapped against her window.

In a flash, she recalled standing next to Camden Kingsley on the sidewalk. He had held out his hand and looked to the sky. "Feels like rain," he'd said.

She guessed that he'd been right.

Honestly, she didn't know what to make of Camden. They both knew he had to investigate her—never mind that he spoke only of finding the truth. It was the truth about *her* that he hoped to find. Yet, he'd been kind. Concerned. Almost caring.

He wasn't at all what she'd expected. And it had nothing to do with the fact that he was good-looking. He was distractingly handsome, in fact.

Was Camden really as good a guy as he seemed?

Or was it all an act—like Melissa warned it might have been? Was he trying to get Grace to share incriminating evidence?

There were other worries, as well. Had she really shot someone? Her palm ached with the recoil from her gun and her chest tightened. There was a part of Grace that hoped it was all a bad dream. She knew it wasn't. Being the cop who shot a civilian was now a part of her new reality.

Sitting up, she stretched her arms above her head. There was no sense in lying in bed all day. She had to get up and face whatever came next.

As she set her feet on the floor, her phone began to ring.

Sitting on the edge of her bed, she swiped the call open. "Morning, Mom."

"Baby, how are you? I saw what happened on the news and wanted to call you last night. Your father said to wait. He said that you'd call us when you wanted to talk. But I haven't slept."

Grace's stomach cramped again, this time with guilt, not anxiety. She knew her parents—especially her mother—would be upset. She should've reached out before now. "Sorry for not calling earlier. I didn't get home until after two o'clock this morning. Then it was too late."

"You can call me anytime, you know that."

"Yeah, I do."

"Tell me everything," said her mother. "What happened?"

Grace had only given herself forty-five minutes to get ready. "I have a meeting with the guy from IA in less than an hour. I wish I could talk more, Mom…"

"IA? Why do you have to talk to someone from Internal Affairs? Are they saying that you're in the wrong?"

Rising from the bed, Grace walked down the short hallway to the kitchen. "Nobody is saying anything. Camden is trying to gather all the facts, which is what everyone wants."

"Camden, is it? Well, he's only after one thing—to make you guilty. Watch what you say to him, Grace. Don't let him ingratiate himself with you. I saw a movie on TV last week. Wait, no. It was last month. Or the month before that."

"Mom," she interrupted, "I really can't chat."

"It doesn't matter when I saw the movie. The point is that a police officer gets wrongly accused of stealing from the precinct. Then someone from Internal Affairs gets involved. It's almost like what happened with Evangeline. You remember that, right?"

"I remember, Mom. But really..." she began, trying to get off the phone.

"Oh, yes. The movie," her mother said. "After an investigation, the officer is found guilty. He's fired. His wife leaves him. He develops a drinking problem."

"I don't have a drinking problem, Mom." Grace set her phone on the counter and actuated the Speaker function. With both hands free, she scooped coffee grounds into a paper liner. "I'm running late, though."

"Well, I'll make this short. The guy knows something is wrong. So he launches his own investigation of the investigators. Guess what? It was the person from Internal Affairs who embezzled the money. The police officer had been set up from the beginning."

"That sounds like an interesting movie, but it has nothing to do with me. Internal Affairs didn't force Mr. Grimaldi to run when I told him to stop. Or to pull a gun on me in order to escape." She filled the coffee maker's reservoir with water and started a pot brewing. The nutty aroma filled her kitchen.

"I'm just saying," said her mother, "I don't think that people from Internal Affairs are to be trusted."

Wasn't that what Melissa had said already? And Desiree? "I appreciate your concern," said Grace. "You always look out for me."

"That's because you're my baby, even though you're twenty-five."

"I love you, Mom. But I really do have to go."

"Okay. I'll see you tonight."

"Tonight?" Grace echoed. What was happening tonight?

"Don't tell me you forgot," her mother began. "I

know you got the invitation because I handed it to you myself."

"Umm…" Invitation?

Her mom sighed. "Remember? Your dad and I are hosting an engagement party for Palmer and Soledad. Six o'clock at the restaurant."

Grace's father, Geoff, owned the Grave Gulch Grille. It was one of the nicest restaurants in town. Her mom, Leanne, worked as the hostess—which was perfect for her mother's bubbly personality. More than that, it was a convenient place to celebrate all special occasions. That being said, she'd completely forgotten about the party for her brother and his fiancée.

"You wouldn't believe the outfit I found for Lyra," her mother gushed about Soledad's adopted daughter. "All pink and frills. It has these little bloomers. She'll be adorable."

"That baby could wear anything and be adorable," said Grace, smiling. Actually, the whole family was pretty darned cute.

It really did seem like everyone in the Colton clan was finding love. Of course, Grace knew she'd be the final one to settle down. As the baby of the family, she always was last.

It's just…

Unbidden, Camden's face came to mind.

"So, you'll come to the party tonight?" her mother asked.

While pouring a cup of coffee, Grace opened her mouth, ready to remind her mother that she wouldn't be able to attend. After all, she was supposed to work the night shift for the next month.

Then she remembered. Until further notice, Grace

was on administrative leave. She wasn't expected at work tonight, or any other night. Disappointment, like a boot heel to the gut, hit her hard.

"I'll see what I can do about the party," she said, breathless. "But I really do have to go, Mom."

"Call me later."

"Okay."

"Promise?"

Grace stirred a spoonful of sugar into her coffee. "I promise."

"Love you, baby."

"Love you, too," she said, before ending the call.

After setting her phone aside, Grace picked up her mug and took a sip. Three times she'd been warned about Camden—well, not about him personally. But she'd been warned not to trust anyone from IA.

Did her family want her to be extra cautious?

Or was there something more to Camden Kingsley?

He was good-looking. What's more, he'd seemed like a decent person who was looking only for the truth.

She couldn't help but wonder, what if she was wrong?

What if he was only interested in finding a way to make Grace pay?

Chapter Seven

Camden stepped out of the shower and grabbed his towel from the hook. Running it through his damp hair, he mentally prepared for what he needed to do next. He had to get taken off the Grace Colton case. There was no way he could be impartial, given his immediate attraction to her. Hell, Grace had even shown up in his dreams. She'd been in his arms. His lips had been on her neck. He'd woken hard with desire, something that never happened with an investigation's subject before. In the end, his biases would cost them both.

Wrapping the towel around his waist, he walked to his bedroom. Sitting on the edge of the bed, he lifted the phone from a charger on his nightstand.

After pulling up Arielle's contact, he placed the call.

"Hello. Camden? This is early, even for you. What happened?"

"We have to talk about Grace Colton," he said.

"Okay. Talk."

He paused. Where should he begin? "Last night, there were protesters outside the police station. They were calling for her to be fired. She was shaken by everything, and I offered to walk her home. We stopped at Mae's Diner and spent some time together. She trusts me." He paused. Be direct. Be professional. Be done with this case. "You have to talk to the mayor and reassign the Colton case. I can't work it—not anymore."

"Of course, you can. You've done a good job getting her to trust you. Now, let's see what she shares."

"I'm not setting up anyone." Camden's pulse rose with his temper.

"I'm not asking you to set up anyone. I'm asking for the truth," said Arielle.

Camden exhaled loudly. If he was going to get the case reassigned, he had to do it now. Rip off the bandage quick. Wasn't that the best way? "Someone else needs to take over."

"I can't call the mayor for no reason. Keep me posted throughout the day. We'll talk soon."

The line went dead.

Sitting on the edge of his bed, Camden stared at the phone. He hated that politics was part of his job.

Too much had happened recently for last night's shooting to be ignored. The public wouldn't allow it. Certainly, someone needed to be held responsible for the incident. After all, both the mayor and the DA relied on the voters to stay in office.

It meant only one thing. There was about to be a reckoning at the GGPD, courtesy of the DA's office—and his boss.

THE WEATHER APP predicted scattered showers throughout the day. To Grace, it seemed like fall had arrived overnight. Yesterday's sweltering heat was replaced by cooler temperatures and a steady stream of rain.

Shoving her hands deeper into the pockets of her rain jacket, Grace hustled down the street. With the hood doing a decent job of hiding her face, she couldn't help but be thankful for the storm. To any member of the press who might be lurking around the police station, Grace would be almost invisible.

The station came into view, and she stumbled to a stop. A podium, covered by an awning emblazoned with the GGPD seal, stood on the steps. Satellites, flowers of metal, bloomed from several media trucks that were parked across the street. Half a dozen officers were setting up a microphone. Grace recognized Daniel Coleman and approached.

"Hey," she said. "What's up?"

Coleman had been on the force forever and was like an uncle to every rookie. "Hey, kid. I heard about what happened. Tough break."

"Yeah, tough break."

Did everyone on the force know what had happened?

It was a stupid question to ask. Of course the entire force had heard. Even if they hadn't been part of the investigation. Or assigned to stand on the steps of the station last night. Or if they'd missed the media coverage. They'd certainly heard the gossip.

Yet, Grace wasn't sure if she hated the fact that she hadn't been the one to share her side of the story. Or if she was relieved that she'd never have to tell people what happened. "So…" She rolled her wrist. The gesture took in the tent, the microphone, the press vans. "What's going on?"

"The chief's giving a press conference."

Did it have something to do with last night's shooting? Was there a development in her case? If so, why hadn't she heard already? And if not, what else was going on? For a moment, Grace felt dizzy. Holding onto the podium for support, she asked, "What's Melissa going to say?"

"You know how it goes. They don't tell us street cops nothing." Daniel hooked a thumb toward the front door. "Melissa's been locked in her office with Brett Shea for the last hour."

"I'll let you get back to work." Grace stepped from under the awning.

"See you later, kid. Don't get too down about all of this." He held his hand out to catch the rain. "Just like a storm, it'll blow over."

"If it doesn't?" she asked, pausing. "You know, blow over. What happens then?"

"Me, I've been around a long time. It always blows over."

"Thanks, Dan," she said. With the injection of the older cop's no-nonsense positivity, her spirits lifted. But by the time she walked through the front doors, the mental storm clouds had returned.

She didn't bother checking in with the duty sergeant. Why should she? She'd been put on administrative leave. Grace checked her watch. Nine o'clock. At this moment, she was supposed to be sitting down with Camden, reviewing anything that she'd forgotten or answering new questions. Yet, she couldn't help but wonder: What did Melissa plan to say at the press conference?

She bypassed the conference room commandeered by Camden. Instead, she headed directly to Melissa's office. Who knew? Maybe she'd get lucky and catch her cousin as the meeting was ending.

Water dripped from her raincoat, hitting the floor

and leaving a trail. The door to Melissa's office was stubbornly closed. Pausing, Grace lifted her hand, ready to knock. She stopped at the moment flesh connected with wood. With a sigh, she let her hand drop.

Could she really interrupt?

"Damn it," she muttered, softly kicking the door.

Her phone, tucked into the pocket of her jacket, began to ring. She fished it out and looked at the caller ID. Camden Kingsley.

Her pulse spiked. Why the reaction? Was she nervous about the investigation? Or was she excited to see Camden again?

Pivoting, she swiped the call open. "I'm here," she said, by way of a greeting. "I'm in the building. I'll be at the conference room in just a second."

"Good," he said. "You noticed the podium outside? Any idea what Melissa plans to say?"

"That's actually why I'm late," she said. "I stopped by her office to see if she'd share anything with me."

"And?" Camden asked.

Grace stood on the conference room's threshold, the phone to her ear. "I didn't bother," she said to both Camden on the phone and in person. His dark hair, still damp from a shower, curled slightly at the end. He wore black trousers, a pristine white shirt and a yellow tie. Even in business attire, Camden's strong shoulders and the muscles in his arms were hard to miss. What would it feel like to have him hold her? She swallowed. His dark brown eyes pinned Grace where she stood. She couldn't help it: at the sight of him, her pulse did a little stutter-step. She lowered the phone from her ear. "Melissa's door was shut."

"Damn it," he cursed, ending the call.

"Did any other evidence turn up? Any idea what happened to my body cam?" Grace asked. "Anything about my case?"

Camden shook his head. "No. Sorry."

"Oh." Grace's pulse, racing only moments ago, slowed to a sluggish beat. "I was hoping that Melissa learned something. Maybe she heard from one of the witnesses."

In the narrow corridor, several police officers passed Grace.

"You coming?" one of the cops asked.

"Where?"

"Melissa's press conference," he said, walking backward. "It's about to start."

Grace was supposed to be interviewed again by Camden Kingsley. Yet the IA investigator had already lifted his suit jacket from the back of a chair and slipped it on. "After you," he said.

Without speaking, they walked down the corridor. Several police officers—both those in uniform and those in plain clothes—gathered in the lobby. Grace and Camden took up a spot near the doors. Through the glass panels, they had a perfect view of Melissa, Brett Shea and others from the rear.

The local press stood at the bottom of the steps. Their spot had them sandwiched between the podium at the front and more than two dozen protesters at the back.

Many of the protesters carried signs. From where she stood, Grace could read them all. There was *Ditch the Chief.* Or *Chief Colton Has Got to Go.* Or Grace's least favorite, *Jail to the Chief.*

"Is that Harper Sullivan?" Camden asked. "From the TV station in Kendall?"

Grace peered into the crowd. Sure enough, the dark-haired reporter stood in the drizzle.

She didn't have time to react before Melissa approached the podium.

She started speaking. "I'd like to thank you all for coming today, even though I ordered the rain special—hoping that it would keep the press away." Polite laughter rippled around the group of cops inside and reporters outside. "Let me begin by giving you an update on what happened last night. There was a police-officer-involved shooting in downtown Grave Gulch. While this incident is being investigated by both the District Attorney's office and the GGPD, we need the public's help."

Melissa held up two sheets of paper. They were the sketches Desiree had drawn based on Grace's description of the witnesses. "We have reason to believe that these two individuals witnessed the shooting. Obviously, we are interested in speaking to them immediately. We need to know what they know. The individuals fled the scene, so it's likely that they don't want to talk to the police. But someone knows these two. To let them disappear—all without making a statement—is a gross miscarriage of justice."

Lowering the pages to the podium, Melissa continued. "Copies of both sketches will be provided to anyone who wants them. Also, they have been emailed to all local newsrooms." She sighed. "If anyone sees these individuals, they should contact the police. Questions?"

Harper was the first to raise her hand. "Is it true that the person who was shot, Robert Grimaldi, was unarmed?"

"I cannot comment on an ongoing investigation," said Melissa.

"Is it true that the officer's body cam wasn't used during the incident?" Harper asked.

The cramped vestibule grew warm. Grace started to sweat.

Outside, Melissa exhaled. "Again, I can't comment on an ongoing investigation."

"What's the status of the police officer who fired their gun?"

"She's been put on administrative leave," said Melissa. "Pending the outcome of the investigation."

Harper asked, "Is it true that the officer in question is also your cousin, Grace Colton?"

Grace wished the floor would open up and swallow her whole.

Melissa's voice was a low growl. "No comment."

Daniel Coleman stood in front of Grace. Peering over his shoulder, he whispered, "It'll all blow over, just like a storm. Remember that."

She wanted to believe him. Yet, nothing had been okay—not since she'd seen Robert Grimaldi in the alley last night.

"One last question, Chief Colton." Harper continued, the phone still in her hand. "A serial killer, Len Davison, is on the loose. A crime scene investigator— one who worked for your department—fabricated evidence that both implicated the innocent and exonerated the guilty. Why should the public trust you now?"

"*Well.*" Melissa drew out the single word. "I have a second announcement to make. I can see that the citizens of Grave Gulch have lost confidence in the GGPD and in our ability to keep peace in the city. It's my responsibility to maintain a trust between the town and the police department. I haven't. Therefore, I'll be temporarily stepping down as chief of police."

Gasps rippled around the room.

Grace went numb.

No. No. No! She wanted to scream. This couldn't be happening. Melissa was Grace's cousin, her role model, her protector and champion on the force. How could she be stepping down now, at the exact time Grace needed her most? Melissa continued. "Beginning now, all my duties will be handled by Detective Brett Shea." She concluded, "It's been the honor of a lifetime to lead the fine men and women who make up the Grave Gulch Police Department. I will do anything—including releasing my position—to assure that they're able to do their job. Thank you for your time." Reporters yelled questions. Protesters began to cheer.

Without another word, Melissa stepped away from the microphone. One of the officers held the door as she crossed the threshold. All eyes, including Grace's, were on Melissa.

"You all heard what I said out there. I meant every word. Being chief of police has been an honor and a privilege. But I can't stay. I've become a distraction. Like I said, Brett Shea will be acting chief, and I expect you to keep acting in the same professional and caring manner you do every day. Whether the people out there realize this or not, they need the police."

She paused. "There are a lot of cases to work, but the top priority is to find the witnesses from last night's shooting."

"What about social media posts?" Officer Daniel Coleman asked. "Have the witnesses posted anything online?"

Grace knew it was a good question, but she also knew the answer. Neither one of them had recorded the incident with their phone or shared any information on social media.

"We feel that the witnesses didn't want proof of what happened," Melissa said. "But Ellie will continue to monitor what's being posted."

Brett added, "Our best hope is that someone will recognize the sketches and give us a call."

"On that note," said Melissa, "I'll let Brett take charge."

She walked forward, with Brett at her side. The crowd parted like the Red Sea, and she strode across the squad room, before disappearing inside her office.

Grace was many things—angry, scared, outraged—but confused wasn't one them. True, Melissa had said she wasn't stepping down because of a single case. But that had been a partial lie. She was stepping down because a single incident had proven to be the last straw. It was the police shooting that had happened last night.

It meant that Grace hadn't simply ruined her own life but Melissa's, as well.

Standing taller, her spine filled with a steely resolve. She had to make this all right. She had to find those witnesses.

But how?

DANIEL COLEMAN HELD a stack of sketches. He walked through the crowd, handing them to police officers. "Plaster the city with these things, folks. We need to find this couple and get a statement."

"Hey, Dan," said Camden. "Can I have a couple of those?"

"Sure thing." Dan held out two sets. "I hear that you're looking into last night's shooting."

Camden wasn't surprised that the entire force knew about his role. "You heard right," he said, taking the papers.

"Grace Colton is a good kid, you know."

"You make me sound like Santa Claus. It's not my job to decide who's good or bad. I'm here to find the facts. That's it."

Papers in hand, Camden scanned the entrance. Grace, huddled in a corner, chewed on her bottom lip. The need to reassure and protect Grace came on strong. Despite the fact that he should feel neither, he made his way to her. "That announcement was a shocker." Although he doubted that Arielle or the mayor would be upset.

Grace drew in a deep breath. "I wasn't expecting Melissa to step down, that's for sure."

"Like she said, it's just temporary." Camden didn't know what else to say—or do. Grace looked miserable. His fingers twitched with the need to reach out and touch her. Yet, giving her comfort would be beyond inappropriate.

He'd hoped that a decent night's sleep would rid him of his infatuation with Grace.

It hadn't.

He had to get this case reassigned to another IA investigator and soon. Until then, maybe he could both help Grace and do his job at the same time. "Come with me," he said, heading for the door.

She followed. "Where are we going? Don't you want to interview me some more?"

"We can talk," he said once they stood on the steps. The rain had stopped, but the sky was still gray and the air cool. "We can do more than two things at once." He held up the sketches. "I have an idea of where we can look for the witnesses. There's a neighborhood a few blocks from here where a lot of young adults live. Small apartments. Lots of coffee shops and restaurants. Let's walk the neighborhood and show these. Maybe someone will recognize them."

He handed Grace a set of sketches. Her fingertips brushed the back of his hand. His skin warmed, and his pulse raced.

"Thanks," she whispered, pulling her hand away.

Damn it. There had been something in their touch, something more than a simple attraction. Camden needed to ignore his reaction.

"It's this way," he said, striding down the sidewalk.

Grace jogged to catch up. "So what's next?"

"Hopefully, Ellie can pull something off your body camera after all. If not, it's old-fashioned police work. Let's start here."

He was supposed to find out what happened with the shooting and the couple was an integral part of the investigation. Find the witnesses and find the truth.

Several sidewalk cafés sat in a row. Tables were filled. Some people sat alone and stared at laptops. Others were crowded around a table meant for two. Dozens of people passed them on the street. Camden's blood buzzed in his veins. If the couple Grace saw was anywhere in Grave Gulch, it was in this neighborhood. And if they were here, he'd find them.

"It might be easier if we separate," Grace suggested. "I'll start across the street and at that end of the block." She pointed. "And you can work from here. We'll meet later and compare notes."

"Makes sense," said Camden with a nod. All the same, he hated not being at her side. Or maybe that was the best reason of all to split up.

"I'll see you in a bit," she said.

Camden watched as she called out to a duo—two men with beards and beanies.

"Excuse me." Grace held up the sheets of paper. "I'm wondering if you've seen these two."

"Sorry," said one. "Never seen 'em before in my life."

"Me, either," said the other.

Grace smiled. "Thanks for your time."

Camden felt a smile pull at his lips, as well. The young men didn't know the witnesses, but he liked watching Grace work. She was competent and professional and kind. She moved on to another group, farther away, and Camden could no longer hear what she was saying.

It was time he got to work.

Grave Gulch Coffee and Treats was on the corner. Half a dozen tables filled the sidewalk. At one of the tables, a lone woman wore noise-canceling headphones and stared at her phone.

"Excuse me." He waved to get her attention.

The customer looked up and smiled. "Hello?"

"Sorry to bother you, but I'm wondering if you've seen either one of these people." He held up the sketches.

"Oh, those two. Sure, I've seen them."

Camden had hoped it would be easy to locate the witnesses, but he'd never dreamed it would be *this* easy. "Really? Where?"

The woman held up her phone. The screen was filled with the same sketches he now held. "They're all over the place. Social media. The actual news."

Camden wanted to groan. He didn't. "Have you seen them in real life? Like, around here?"

Pursing her lips, she considered his question. "Not that I remember."

"Thanks for your time."

Camden worked his way up the block. Dozens of times he asked the same question. "Have you seen these two?"

Dozens of times, he got the same answer.

"No. Never."

It was as if these people had disappeared. Or maybe they didn't exist at all.

What if that were true? What did it mean? Was Grace guilty of framing a suspect and an unlawful shooting after all?

Pausing on the sidewalk, he searched for Grace. She walked down the opposite side of the street. He watched as she talked to another group of people, gathered around a bench. They all glanced at her sketches. They all shook their heads.

No luck, either.

She glanced across the street. Her gaze stopped on Camden. She waved.

He didn't want to feel anything. He didn't want his

chest to get warm. Or for his pulse to race. He definitely didn't want his mouth to twitch up into a smile—and yet, they all did.

He waved back. She jogged across the street.

As her foot hit the curb, a few fat raindrops splattered on the sidewalk. Camden glanced skyward. Black clouds roiled, and then a deluge began.

Holding the sketches overhead, Grace ducked into a recessed doorway. Camden followed. The space was just a small square of concrete beneath the building's brick overhang. They were both wedged in tight, her shoulders pressed against his chest.

"That rain came from nowhere," she said, water dripping from her nose. She wiped a hand down her face. The gesture was vulnerable, unpretentious and somehow sexy. "I'm soaked. The damn sketches are trash." She held them up. The paper was waterlogged and shredding. She turned her gaze to Camden. "And look at you. Your suit. It's ruined."

Camden glanced at the clothes. The jacket was stained with water, the hem of his trousers damp and dirty. "It's nothing that dry cleaning won't fix."

"So what do we do now?"

The cafés, busy only moments ago, were vacant. Coffee cups, forgotten in the rush, filled with rainwater.

Suddenly, he didn't care about the investigation.

He watched her lips and wondered what it would feel like to have her mouth on his. To taste her. To touch her. She was so close that he could feel the whisper of her breath on his neck. The floral scent of her shampoo surrounded him like a fog. From where he stood, he could see the swell of her breasts beneath her shirt.

It was then that Camden realized she was watching him, as well. Their gazes met and held. Her sleeve brushed against the tips of his fingers. He wanted to touch her. Hold her.

But he couldn't. Shouldn't.

He swallowed and shifted. The wall was at his back. He was trapped, with no place else to go. Camden wouldn't try to escape—even if he had the chance. His hand brushed her waist.

She drew in a short breath.

"Sorry," he said. "I didn't mean to touch you."

"It's okay," she said, her gaze on the ground. She lifted her eyes. "I don't mind."

He moved closer. She didn't retreat. Camden bent toward her, then stopped.

What the hell was he doing?

It didn't matter that he was drawn to Grace Colton. Standing tall, he smothered a curse behind his hand.

She hitched her chin to the side. "Looks like the rain stopped."

It was a small torture to look at anything other than Grace. Puddles dotted the sidewalk and street. Sodden tablecloths hung limp. Awnings dripped. The downpour was over as soon as it had begun.

She stepped away, and his chest ached.

He'd stopped himself from kissing Grace this time. The question was: What would he do if he got another chance?

Chapter Eight

Standing on the sidewalk, Grace's pulse raced. She was a rookie cop, albeit currently suspended. Yet, she'd had a life beyond the force—one that included her share of former boyfriends and flirtations. In short, she'd been kissed before today.

So, what had happened between her and Camden in the doorway? Why was she drawn to him like she'd never been to any other man?

Had he really been ready to kiss her?

Getting involved with this IA investigator would be career suicide.

Yet, she couldn't lie to herself—she'd thought about kissing him, too.

What was worse, she wouldn't have stopped him if he'd tried.

What did that make her? A horrible person? Desperate? Or was she inexplicably drawn to him because he was the one guy she shouldn't want?

It wasn't like her to make bad choices...well, until she pulled the trigger last night. Still, she knew better than to kiss the IA investigator. Never mind that he was intelligent, focused on finding justice and handsome.

Sun broke through the clouds, and mist clung to the

ground as the puddles started to evaporate. She should say something to Camden. But what?

He still stood in the doorway. "Come on," he said, stepping toward her. "We should go."

She held the set of sketches, drenched and ruined. "These won't do me any good." A recycling bin sat at the curb. She tossed them inside.

He checked his watch. "It's already after eleven o'clock. Let's get something to eat. I skipped breakfast."

Did the guy never eat on time? Grace worked the night shift and still she made time to eat regularly. "You have to get on a better schedule for meals."

"I know. I know." He lifted his palms in surrender. "You're right. But don't keep me from my lunch now. Come on. I know a good pizza place."

Having lunch together was a decidedly bad idea.

Especially since Grace had to admit that she was attracted to Camden Kingsley. She was drawn to more than his good looks: his self-possession, as well. Camden was calm, collected and able to think on his feet. He was everything that Grace—passionate, reactive, talkative—was not.

Besides, they hadn't actually kissed. It was just a reaction to the moment, right?

Still, she needed to get away for her sake—and his.

Tell him you can't go out to lunch. Tell him you have to go.

She knew she was right. She opened her mouth, ready to decline the invite. Instead, her voice betrayed her. "Pizza sounds nice. Which way?"

"Left at the corner, then two blocks down."

"So," she began, as they walked.

"So, what?"

"So what comes next in the investigation? We've showed the sketches. No luck in finding the witnesses, though. The gun is missing. What do you do now?"

"I still have to do some more interviews," he said.

Was he being evasive? "And then?"

"I bother Ellie and see if she's gotten anything else from the body cam."

"What happens after that?"

"I'll look at all the evidence. If there's enough, I'll write a report with my findings. If I need more facts, I'll keep looking." He stopped in front of a restaurant. A green and red canvas awning hung over the doorway. Painted on the glass door in gold and black were the words *Paola's Pizzeria: New York Style Pizza.* Beneath was a similar gold and black skyline of Manhattan. "You ever eat here?"

Grace had grown up in Grave Gulch, but whenever she ate out, she ate at her father's restaurant.

"Never," she said.

"You'll like it." Camden pulled the door open. He smiled as she passed. "Trust me."

Maybe that was another problem. Grace *did* trust Camden.

A counter stood between the dining area and the kitchen. A glass hood covered a long line of prepared pizzas, ready to be reheated by the slice. A large dome brick oven was attached to the back wall.

"Hey, Camden. Good to see you, buddy." A man with dark hair and a graying mustache stood behind the counter. He smiled as they approached.

"How's it going, Stu?" Camden asked.

"Busy. Lots of protesters downtown, and they get

hungry. But I'm not doing as good as you. Are you going to introduce me to your lunch date, or what?"

"I'm not his date. We're, um…" How could she categorize their relationship—especially since she didn't want to admit that *she* was one of the reasons protesters had been out in force?

"This is my colleague. Grace."

"Nice to meet you, Grace."

"Likewise."

"So what'll it be?" Stu asked.

She scanned the line of pizza choices. Buffalo chicken. Margherita. Cheese. Hawaiian. Veggie. She wasn't hungry, but there was something comforting in the idea of sitting down with a hot, saucy and greasy slice of pizza.

"I'll take the lunch special." A slice of pizza, a side salad and a drink. "Cheese."

"Make that two," said Camden.

"But you'll want sausage and pepperoni on your slice, am I right?"

"You are," said Camden.

Stu handed over two empty plastic cups. A drink fountain stood in the corner. "Your order will be up in a minute."

The restaurant had seating for two dozen. Round tables, covered with a checkered vinyl cloth in red and white, filled in the middle of the room. Three booths, all in a row, were placed along the window.

Grace and Camden were the only patrons. Since the shooting, Grace had felt as if everyone knew exactly who she was and what she'd done. What's worse, they hated her for her actions.

She didn't feel judged by Camden, despite the fact that his job was to investigate her guilt.

"Is here good?" Camden pointed to the booth in the middle.

Grace looked up from where she stood, filling her cup with unsweetened iced tea from a metal dispenser. "Works for me."

She approached the table and set her cup down. After stripping out of her sodden jacket, she hung it on the corner of the bench. Sliding onto the seat opposite from Camden, she took a sip from her drink.

Usually, she had an easy time with chitchat. But what was she supposed to talk about with Camden? The restaurant was empty save for the two of them and Stu at the counter. Maybe now was the perfect time to have a candid conversation.

"Last night you said you were only interested in the truth," she began, then felt not entirely certain where to go after such a bold statement.

He'd gotten himself a soda and sipped before nodding. "I am. The truth. The facts. Those are the only things that matter."

"But they're different, aren't they? The truth and facts."

Camden shook his head. "Not to me, they aren't."

"Facts are like a math problem. Two plus two is always four. The truth is what you can convince people to believe."

He took another drink, seeming to consider her words. "I guess you're right, although I never thought of it quite that way."

"Tell me this, then. What's the truth about my case?" Staring out the window, she watched a car drive by.

"Right now, it's my word against Grimaldi's. I say he had a gun. He says he didn't. The gun hasn't turned up, so those facts prove Grimaldi's truth—not mine."

"Basically," he said.

She waited for him to say something. Anything.

He didn't.

Grace continued, "My body cam was broken, so there's no video evidence. There are witnesses, but they haven't come forward. There's a lot of anti-police feeling in the community." She paused and met his gaze. "I'm a cop. I know what kind of narrative those facts create. It makes me look guilty as hell. But here are the facts. I'm innocent. Grimaldi had a gun, and he pointed it at me. If I hadn't fired first, he would've shot me."

Camden wiped a bead of sweat from the side of his glass. He opened his mouth, ready to speak. But Stu approached with a tray of food, and Camden snapped his jaw shut.

The other man set down two salads in bowls, along with two gravy boats filled with dressing—creamy ranch and tangy Italian. He also had two wedges of pizza, bigger than the plates, and he set those down, as well. "How's that look?" Stu asked, tucking the tray under his arm. "Can I get you anything else?" He quickly removed two sets of silverware rolled in paper napkins from the pocket of his apron and set them on the table. "Aside from these," he added.

"It looks great," said Grace. Her stomach clenched in a hard knot of anxiety. She'd never be able to eat much more than a few bites.

"All righty, then. Enjoy."

Stu retreated behind the counter as Camden unrolled his silverware. With the other man out of earshot, he turned back to Grace. "If there's evidence that proves your story, I'll find it."

"And if you don't?"

"I will."

"Do you swear that you won't give up on the case?" Grace asked. "On *me*?" She shoved a bite of salad in her mouth and chewed. Had she really just pressured him to make a personal promise? That was a bad move. "Never mind what I asked. It was wrong." She washed down her salad with a swallow of tea.

"Grace, listen," he began. "I need to tell you something from when I was a kid…"

His phone started to ring, and he quietly cursed. He'd already told her that his dad was a cop. Was there more? Fishing the cell from his pocket, he glanced at the screen. "It's Ellie."

"Ellie?" Her chest was tight. Had the IT expert recovered the missing footage? Was this nightmare about to end? Wiping her mouth with the napkin, she leaned forward. "Let's hope she has good news."

Camden swiped the call open and put it on Speaker. Setting the phone on the table, he said, "Hey, Ellie. I'm here with Grace. What have you got for us?"

"Nothing," she said, her voice flat. "I tried everything I know. But there's nothing more to get off the body camera. I'm sorry."

"Can you tell if anyone tampered with the camera?" Camden asked.

The chain of evidence was well-established. The camera went from Grace to Brett to Ellie. But weirder things had happened recently. Holding her breath, she waited for Ellie's answer.

"The video and physical evidence suggest that the camera broke when Grace was hit with the bag."

Grace's pulse went sluggish. Having footage of Grimaldi pointing a gun at Grace was the only sure way to clear her name. Without it, would Grace have to live with a stain on her reputation forever? A wave of despair washed over her, and she began to sweat. "Sure," she said. "Thanks for trying."

"What else can be done?" Camden asked. "There has to be something."

He was definitely trying to exonerate Grace. She knew that she should be pleased. Yet Melissa's warning not to trust anyone from IA was still fresh.

What did Camden really want? Before Grace could wonder anything more, Ellie spoke.

"I've done all I can." She paused. "I am sorry." She ended the call.

The single bite of salad now sat like a rock in Grace's gut. The phone, screen blank, lay on the table. Camden picked it up and tucked it into his pocket.

Grace pushed the bowl away. Finding more footage on the camera had been her final hope. Now, that was gone. She knew one thing for certain—she'd been defeated. Her eyes stung, yet she refused to cry in front of Camden. "Well, that's a dead end."

"I know that you're disappointed," he began. "But you need to consider some other facts."

She held up her hand, stopping Camden before he got started. "I appreciate whatever you plan to say. But I'm not in the mood for a pep talk."

In fact, there was really only one person Grace wanted to talk to right now: Melissa. She'd know what Grace should do.

Just because Melissa had stepped down from being the chief of police didn't mean that she'd lost any knowledge. Her jacket hung on the corner of the bench. Standing, Grace patted down the pockets until she found her phone. "Give me a second. I need to make a call."

Striding through the restaurant, Grace opened her contacts. She pushed out of the restaurant. After the morning rain, the sun had come out, and the sky was now a cloudless blue.

Melissa answered the call on the third ring. "Grace, where are you? I just heard from Ellie. She wasn't able to get anything else off the body camera."

"Yeah. I heard that, too. Where are you?"

"I'm still at headquarters, cleaning out some personal stuff from my office. I looked for you after the presser, but Coleman said you were gone."

There was a lot more to talk about than just last night's shooting and the lack of evidence. Her cousin had stepped down from being Grave Gulch's chief of police, and it was in part because of Grace. "I took a set of the sketches and canvased a few blocks. I was hoping that someone would recognize the witnesses."

"That's a smart idea," said Melissa. She chuckled quietly. "You always were smart."

"I wasn't the one who thought it up. It was Camden."

"Camden? As in Camden Kingsley? You're working with him? Are you serious?"

Grace bristled at Melissa's incredulous tone. "He's looking for the truth," she said, paraphrasing what Camden had told her earlier.

"He's looking for someone to hold accountable, and don't forget it."

Grace glanced at Camden through the window. He sat at the table, slice of pizza in hand. He took a bite and looked up. Wiping his mouth with a paper napkin, he nodded at her.

Her heart skipped a beat. Despite herself, she smiled. "I haven't forgotten anything." Grace changed the subject. "How are you? You must be devastated about having to step down."

"Actually, I'm not. Antonio and I had a long talk last night after I got home. Even before now, we've been talking about getting married and starting a family. It'd be hard to be chief of police and a new mom all at the same time."

A hard kernel of disappointment lodged in Grace's throat. "Is that it? You're quitting?"

"I'm not *quitting*." Melissa drew out the last word. "I'm taking time to evaluate what I really want."

Grace knew what she wanted. She wanted to clear her name and get back to work. But would the GGPD be the same without Melissa around, even if Grace was eventually exonerated? Would Grace ever find a guy she loved enough to stop being a cop? She thought not, and yet she felt Camden's gaze on the back of her neck. She tried to think of something else to say but had nothing. "I need to get off the phone."

"Chin up, okay? You'll get through this."

"That's what everyone keeps saying."

"Because it's true," said Melissa. "Will I see you tonight?"

Oh, yeah. The party for Palmer and Soledad. She had no place else to go. "I'll be there."

Grace ended the call and folded her arms across her chest. She should go back into the restaurant. But her life was falling apart, and worse, she didn't know how to put it back together.

CAMDEN TRIED NOT to watch Grace as she stood on the sidewalk. Or to appreciate how her jeans hugged her hips and rear. Or that the sun, just beginning to peek through the clouds, turned her hair into a golden halo. He also tried not to wonder what she was telling Melissa—or what advice Melissa was sharing in return.

On all accounts, he failed miserably.

Maybe now was the time to ask Arielle to intervene and get him taken off the case once and for all. He looked around the restaurant, still empty, and removed his phone. Arielle answered his call on the first ring.

"I've got a meeting in two minutes," she said. "What have you got for me?"

"The body camera was damaged. The IT expert can't get any more video off the device."

"That's convenient, isn't it?" said Arielle, her voice dripping with sarcasm. "Chief Colton's cousin shoots a civilian. At the time, she claims that the person had a gun. Then, the camera is so damaged that they can't get any video of the incident."

"Melissa Colton stepped down temporarily," said Camden. His jaw tightened. "She's not able to manipulate the investigation, if that's what you're suggesting."

"And she named Brett to replace her. Interesting, don't you think? Especially since I heard he's involved with Annalise Colton, Grace's older sister." Arielle sighed. "They're all a big family at GGPD. Literally. You have to find out more about what's happening."

"Here's what happening, Arielle. There's a conflict of interest."

"A what?" And then, "You're right, we do have to talk, but not now. My meeting is starting. Stay on the case, and I'll call this evening."

"Arielle," he said, his teeth gritted. "Do not hang up the phone. This is important."

Whatever he was about to say was for naught. She'd already ended the call. Camden muttered a curse in frustration.

Grace opened the door to the small restaurant. She came back to the booth and sat.

He said, "Your pizza's gotten cold. Stu can throw it back in the oven if you'd like."

Grace shook her head. "I'm not really hungry."

"You want to take it to go? We can canvas a few blocks from here…"

"Listen," she began. Grace tightened her jaw. From the resolute look on her face, Camden knew that he wasn't going to like whatever she had to say next. "I appreciate what you're trying to do, really. More than that, I understand you're going beyond what's expected of someone from IA. But…" She exhaled, her breath ruffling her hair. "I should probably just go. There's not much more that can be accomplished by us walking around, you know."

He'd just been asking to be taken off the case. Maybe now was the best time to part ways. Why was his chest suddenly tight?

She asked, "What do I owe for lunch?"

Camden waved away her offer to pay. "I've got this." He held out her plate and bowl. "Take this with you. You don't want to waste food. Besides, what'd you tell me? To get on a regular meal schedule?"

"I guess I did say something like that." Taking both salad and pizza, she stood. "Thanks."

At the counter, Stu wrapped up Grace's lunch and tried to get her to buy a cannoli. Then, without another word, she was gone. He should be happy, or at least pleased, that she'd left. His attraction to her was more than a distraction; it was the best way to ruin his career.

But Camden pushed his salad through a pool of dressing. He took a bite and swallowed, despite the fact that his throat was closed like a fist. Working his jaw back and forth, he wondered if he'd ever see Grace again. Or was she gone from his life for good?

CHASTITY SHOALS LAY on the sofa and scrolled through her newsfeed. She glanced at a post and clicked on the link. The headline read *Police Chief Steps Down Amid Scandal, Police Shooting.*

Her heart pounding, she opened the article and read.

Once again, the Grave Gulch Police Department is forced to investigate one of their own. This time, the scandal has cost Chief Melissa Colton her position—at least temporarily. In a press conference at GGPD headquarters, Melissa Colton spoke to reporters and the public. In her statement, she took responsibility for the police's mishandling of several investigations, including last night's police-involved shooting. Detective Brett Shea will take over the role of police chief until Colton's return.

The officer in question, Grace Colton, has given a statement that Robert Grimaldi, 29, of Grave Gulch, brandished a firearm while she

*was trying to apprehend him. Officer Colton
fired her weapon first. No weapon of Grimaldi's
has been located, despite an extensive search of
the area. Grimaldi claims that he was unarmed
at the time of the shooting. Officer Colton has
been placed on administrative leave.*

*The police report that there were witnesses
to the incident. The7y are asking the public for
their help in identifying the couple. If you know
those pictured below, contact the Grave Gulch
Police Department.*

Two sketches accompanied the article. Her nose was
a little bigger, and Thad's eyes were farther apart. But
without question, the pictures were of Chastity and
Thad.

"Thad." She stood. For a moment, the floor seemed
to tilt. Dark spots danced in front of her eyes. Holding
onto the side of the sofa, she waited for the dizziness
to pass. "You have to come here and see this."

Thad sat at a table. He was huddled over a laptop,
where he worked on his newest project as a game de-
signer. "What is it?" he asked, without looking up.

She crossed the small living room and shoved her
phone in his face. "See?"

He focused his vision on her hand and the phone.
"What is it?" he asked, again. This time, his voice was
sharp with alarm.

"Us," she said. "Our pictures. We witnessed that
shooting. Now the cops want to talk to us…"

"We aren't saying anything to cops," said Thad. He
returned his gaze to his computer.

"We shouldn't have split last night. I told you that."

"Yeah, you told me after we got home, and you drank like half a bottle of wine. It wasn't helpful in that moment."

"Maybe we should call," Chastity began.

"Maybe we shouldn't, and you should let me get back to work."

"No need to be nasty."

"Listen, Chas, I'm sorry. It's just that I'm on a deadline, and you know how that makes me stressed."

She did know that deadlines left Thad stressed. He had a degree in computer programming, but he did so much more than write the codes. In fact, he was more of an artist. And like he always said, *Art can't be forced. It has to be found.*

Still, she didn't like that the police were looking for them.

"What should we do?"

"Well." Thad lifted his arms over head. His shirt rode up, exposing his stomach and his abs. "Do you have classwork?" he asked. "Or you could find a workout video on the internet. Get a head start on the weight you wanted to lose."

She pulled her T-shirt lower over her leggings. "I'm not asking what I should do right now. I'm asking what we should do about the police."

"Oh, that." Thad turned back to his work. "I say we do nothing."

"Nothing?" she echoed. "Where's your civic duty?"

"How many times have you told me that you hate the cops? Or how often have you said that cops are just schoolyard bullies but with badges?"

The single time she'd dealt with the cops came back

to Chastity with a sharp clarity. The memory stabbed her in the chest. She *had* said that before. "A lot."

"Yeah, a lot. So, why aren't you happy that we took the gun? It sounds like the lady cop is up crap creek without a paddle."

"They know about the gun, though." Annoyance, hot and sticky, bubbled up from Chastity's gut. Did Thad really not care about the truth? Or maybe he didn't understand what kind of trouble they'd be in if the police found them and the weapon they'd taken from the scene of a crime. For Thad, everything was like the games he designed. There was always a secret work-around for any problem. Only this time, there wasn't.

Sighing, Thad turned toward her. "They don't know jack. Obviously, we have the gun. The guy—" he glanced at the article on her screen once more "— Robert Grimaldi isn't going to say anything. If he admitted to pointing a gun at a police officer, he'd be in deep, deep trouble. There's no video of the incident—or us. All we have to do is lay low for a few weeks. And also, we have to get rid of the gun."

"Lay low? Get rid of the gun? How're we supposed to do both?"

"We stay in the apartment for a few weeks and keep the gun here. When this story blows over—and it will blow over—we dump the gun in Lake Michigan. Or we ditch it at the town dump."

Chastity could feel the walls of the small apartment closing in on her. "Have you thought about food? How're we going to eat if we're stuck in here?"

"What's the matter with you? Order groceries for delivery. Order food from restaurants online, too. My work is online. Your classes are online. We just moved here at the beginning of the month. The only person we've spoken to more than once is the old man who lives downstairs. I don't know if he remembers us all that well to begin with."

Thad was right. He always was. Chastity slunk back to the sofa and flopped onto the cushions. It's just that she had hoped Grave Gulch would be more than a place to live, that the town would become their home.

For a moment, she let her favorite daydream swirl around her. She pictured the apartment filled with smiling faces of friends they hadn't yet made. Laughter. Light. Happiness. Chastity would stand in the galley kitchen. A glass of wine would sit on the counter, as she mashed avocado for her soon-to-be-famous guacamole.

"Who's hungry?" she'd ask, bowl of chips in one hand, dish of guac in the other.

Thad, while taking both from her, would kiss her cheek. "My girlfriend," he'd announce. "Pretty. Smart. Talented."

The party disappeared as the last tendrils of Chastity's fantasy faded to nothing.

Of course, Thad was right. They only had to stay inside for a few weeks. By then, the whole story would be forgotten.

Still, Chastity couldn't keep from asking a single question. If Thad was right, why did all of this feel so wrong?

Chapter Nine

It was barely past noon. Already Grace was exhausted. It was more than the exhausting night and the fruitless search for the witnesses this morning. Striding down the street from the pizza parlor, she wanted nothing more than a nap, a cup of tea and to see her mother.

Folding her arms against the chill, she knew that she could get the tea and the nap in her apartment. Seeing her mother would have to wait for tonight's party.

Ugh. The party.

Grace unlocked the door to her building and trudged up to the second floor. From there, she entered her apartment.

Pushing the door shut with her heel, she wondered if there was any way to get out of going tonight. Surely, her brother would understand if she needed an evening at home and alone. Yet, while Palmer might understand, her parents would not. She was a Colton—and expected to attend.

After setting her phone and her keys on the counter, she placed her leftover pizza and salad in the fridge. Automatically, she moved to the closet. Hand resting on the knob, she stopped.

Damn. She'd had a jacket on when she left this morning. Now, it was gone.

Obviously, she'd left it somewhere.

In a flash, she remembered hooking it over the back of the bench at the pizza place. With a sigh, Grace knew she'd have to turn around and go back to the restaurant. To her, it seemed like the tea and nap would have to wait forever.

Still, there was something she needed to do. Something she'd been avoiding, until now.

Leaning on the closet door, she searched through the apps until she found the one for the TV station in Kendall. Grace opened the app. The most recent headline hit her like a slap to the face: *Police Chief Steps Down Amid Scandal, Police Shooting.*

Holding her breath, Grace scanned the article. It was short, precise, and while not flattering, nothing had been misleading, either.

A video clip of the news conference, posted by a subscriber, accompanied the article. A white arrow was superimposed on the footage. Grace played the video.

Melissa stood behind the podium. To her left was Brett Shea. At her right was the mayor. Melissa began speaking. *"I'd like to thank you all for coming today, even though I ordered the rain special—hoping that it would keep the press away."* She paused. Chuckles could be heard in the background. *"Let me begin by giving you an update on what happened last night."*

The camera panned the gathered crowd. Those in the back, with their signs. A group of reporters, huddled together, in the rain. Then, the aspect zoomed to the front of police headquarters. Shadowy figures could be seen inside. Grace would have been one of those forms. It was odd to watch the scene unfold. After all, she'd already lived these moments once. Yet Grace was driven by the need to know what was being presented in the media.

Melissa continued to speak, her voice in the background. *"There was a police-officer-involved shooting in downtown Grave Gulch. While this incident is being investigated by both the District Attorney's office and the GGPD, we need the public's help."*

The camera focused in on a person—but it wasn't just anyone. They'd caught Camden in profile. His eyes. His jaw. His hair. His face was as familiar to Grace as her own. Yet, she'd only known him for less than a day.

True, Grace had never been one to believe in luck. She saw success—or failure—as the result of a person's work ethic. Yet, as she watched the video of Camden, it was easy to think that luck—and bad luck, at that—was in control of her life.

How else could it be that she'd met a nice guy, only to have him be the totally wrong person?

Her phone rang, interrupting the pity party for one. She glanced at the caller ID. It was her cousin, Madison. "Hey," she said, after accepting the call. "How are you?"

Madison's voice was full of concern. "I should be asking you the same thing. I saw what happened on the news."

Madison was more than another Colton cousin. She was also one of Grace's best friends. "I can't believe this is happening. I mean," she said and dropped onto her sofa, "I'm always so careful. The guy definitely had a gun."

"Of course he did. It'll just take some time to pull all the evidence together."

"I don't know." Grace sighed as her stomach began to grumble. Maybe she should have eaten something for lunch. "There's no video from my body camera of the incident. Both Brett and I saw two witnesses, but they ran away. Melissa's circulated a set of sketches, but so far...nothing."

"Yet," said Madison.

"I know what you're trying to do. Lift my spirits. I love you for trying, but I need more than positive thinking."

"You might be surprised—" Madison began.

"Hey," Grace interrupted, "how can you be calling me, anyway? Don't you have a classroom full of kids?" Madison, a kindergarten teacher at Grave Gulch Elementary School, lived a charmed life. Aside from having a job she loved, she was also engaged to one of the teachers at her school, Alec Lash.

"It's my planning period," said Madison. "The kids are in lunch, then they have music."

"I'm sure you have more to do than just chat with me."

"There's always something to take care of as a teacher, that's for certain. But right now, you're my top priority."

"I'm just happy to hear your voice." Grace paused. "Let's talk about something that's not me. Have you found a dress yet?"

"Actually—" Madison let out a squeal "—I think I have. I saw it in *Lake Country* magazine this morning."

"Really?" Grace couldn't keep the amazement out of her voice. Madison had been engaged for months yet refused to do anything for the wedding. She claimed that planning began with finding the perfect dress. Until now, nothing had been good enough. All the same, Grace suspected that Madison might not just want a fairy-tale gown but a different Prince Charming altogether. Clearing her throat, Grace forced her voice to be upbeat. "Really! That's so great. Pictures?"

"Hold on a sec, and I'll text you."

"Tell me all about it," said Grace, while switching to Speaker.

"Well, it's white and fancy…"

Grace laughed. "I bet it's both." Her phone pinged with a text, and she opened the picture. With a lace bodice and full train, the gown was stunning. For some reason, the image of Camden wearing a tuxedo came to mind. "That's the most beautiful dress ever. You'll look stunning."

"There's only one problem."

"Uh-oh," said Grace, not surprised at all. There was always a problem with wedding dresses. "What's that?"

"The dress is only available at a boutique that's all the way in Kendall."

"All the way in Kendall?" Grace echoed teasingly. "Kendall's only two hours away. You took me shopping for a prom dress there, remember? You can certainly take that drive to try on a wedding gown."

"I guess you're right…" Madison began, before letting her words fade to nothing.

"Unless there's something wrong with the dress." Grace paused. Should she bring up Madison's constant hesitation? "Or the wedding."

"It's not that…"

"I'll tell you what, tomorrow is Saturday. Why don't

we go and look at the dress? It'll be fun. We can make a day out of the trip. We'll wear cute outfits and have lunch in one of the swanky bistros afterward. What do you say?"

"You'd go with me? Really?"

"Of course I'll go. I'm on administrative leave. What else am I going to do? Besides," Grace continued, feeling happy for the first time all day, "it'll do me good to get out of town and have something to do other than worry about the investigation."

"It's a date." And then, "Listen, I have to go and actually do some prep work. I'll see you tonight, all right? Can you believe that your brother's actually getting married?"

Grace still didn't want to go to the party, but maybe being around her family would help. Besides, Madison was right. Palmer was her brother, and she needed to be there for him—if not for herself. "See you tonight."

Madison ended the call. Grace rose from the sofa. In the kitchen, she filled the kettle. As she set it on the stove to boil, fat drops of water began pelting her kitchen window. Damn. She'd never gone back to get her jacket.

Did she really want to walk in the rain?

Absolutely not.

Opening a search engine on her phone, she found the number for the pizza parlor and called.

"Paola's Pizzeria. This is Stu. What can I get started for you?"

"Hi, Stu. This is Grace. I was in your restaurant with my, um, colleague Camden Kingsley. I think I left my coat. Can you grab it for me? I'll get it later this afternoon, if that's okay."

"Your coat?" he echoed. "I don't see your coat."

"I draped it over the side of the booth where I was sitting."

"I'm looking at that spot, and it's not there."

"Are you sure?" Even she heard that her voice was an octave higher. It wasn't as if the jacket were extremely valuable, or even one of Grace's favorites. But the loss of something personal typified this day: rotten and unfair.

He paused. "I've had some customers since you left, but they all did takeout. Plus, I think I would've noticed a coat just lying around. Maybe Camden grabbed it when he left. Have you called him?"

The kettle began to whistle. She took it from the burner. One-handed, she filled a mug with boiling water. *Camden Kingsley.* Her mind repeated his name as if it was a wish or a prayer. "I'll give him a call. Thanks."

"If it turns up, I'll let you know. The number on caller ID good?"

"It is," said Grace. "And thanks."

The call ended, and she dropped a tea bag into the steaming water. As the tea began to turn the liquid to a dark bronze, Grace set the phone on the counter.

Should she bother Camden about her jacket?

After all, it was just a coat. She had others.

Why the hesitancy to make the call, though?

In truth, Grace knew the answer, even without asking.

The prudent thing would be to avoid him at all costs.

In a short time, her physical attraction to Camden had taken on a decidedly emotional turn. Developing a deeper attraction for the man who was tasked with investigating her was dangerous, dumb and reckless. Despite it all, Grace couldn't deny it: she was drawn to the man investigating her.

TUCKING GRACE'S JACKET over his messenger bag, Camden walked back to police headquarters and made a mental list of everything he needed to do. First on the agenda was to drop off Grace's jacket with Mary Suzuki, the GGPD desk clerk. Second, he needed to talk to Brett Shea. Finally, he had to visit with Robert Grimaldi.

True, Camden was supposed to be neutral. All the same, he couldn't help it: he wanted Shea or Grimaldi to give him something that would exonerate Grace.

Turning the corner, the GGPD building came into view. Brett Shea jogged down the steps.

"Interim Chief Shea," Camden called. "Hold on."

Brett stood on the sidewalk and waited for Camden. "What's up?"

"I'm trying to piece together what happened last night with Officer Colton. You got a minute to chat?"

"Actually," said Brett with a sigh. "I don't. I'm headed to the hospital to interview Robert Grimaldi."

"Sounds like it's my lucky day. I need to speak to him, too. Care if I tag along?"

"I'll drive, and you can talk." Brett's car was parked in front of the building. "Ready to go?"

Brett still had Grace's jacket. He should take it to Mary and move on. Then again, he didn't want to miss his chance to interview Brett and Grimaldi. Shoving the jacket into his bag, he approached the auto. "Let's go."

Camden said nothing as Brett pulled away from the

curb. As the SUV rolled down the street, he began by asking, "What do you remember about last night?"

Brett recounted a story that Camden knew well. The figure in the alley. Grace's chase on foot. Brett coming around the block but being delayed by protesters in the street. He described seeing the witnesses—a man and woman—running away from the scene. Brett ended with "When I pulled up, Grace was providing first aid to Grimaldi. Ember and I looked for the gun, but…" he exhaled and shook his head "…we didn't find anything."

So far, Camden had learned nothing new.

"You know Grace, um, Officer Colton pretty well, right? I heard that you're engaged to her sister."

"Annalise," Brett offered. "She's a canine instructor for the police department."

"What about Grace?"

"Grace is a good person and a great cop in the making."

"In the making?" Camden repeated. The hospital was only a few minutes away from GGPD's headquarters. If Camden was going to learn anything, he didn't have much time. "What do you mean by that?"

"It's just a phrase. But she is young."

"Inexperienced?"

"No, I wouldn't call her that."

"What *would* you call her?" Camden asked. His palms itched. It felt like the truth was so close that he could reach out and grab it.

"Enthusiastic."

"How so?"

"She's very loyal to the police force, for starters. I mean, of course she is. Most of the family works for the GGPD. Plus," said Brett, turning into the hospital's parking lot, "she adores Melissa."

"From what I've seen, the feeling is pretty mutual."

"They're all protective of one another, I'll give you that."

Protective? Protective enough to lie? "Give me an example."

There was a space in front of the hospital's main entrance reserved for law enforcement. Brett maneuvered the big SUV into the spot. He turned off the engine. "I don't know that I have an example, it's just a feeling I get."

"Why?"

"Well, last night Grace was upset by all the protesters."

"When they were standing in front of the building and calling for her to be fired? I'd think anyone would be upset."

"No," said Brett. "Not then. Earlier. Right before she saw Grimaldi. We were driving near the park and the protesters were calling for Melissa to be fired. Grace took it personally. That's what I mean." Looking at his watch, Brett said, "We can talk on the way back, but I made arrangements with the hospital to speak to Grimaldi now."

"Sure. Right." Camden opened the door and stepped from the SUV. He walked next to Brett, his messenger bag over his shoulder. Camden had just gotten his first glimpse into Grace's state of mind moments before the shooting.

Last night, he'd asked if she was upset—specifically, about a boyfriend. She'd told him she was single. Honestly, he'd been satisfied with the answer. Now he knew it'd been a stupid mistake made because of his attraction to Grace.

Yet, what did it mean for the case?

Was there more that he'd missed?

Brett and Camden approached the front doors of the hospital. They opened automatically. A water feature of copper and brass was attached to the lobby's far wall. A semicircular desk stood in the middle of the room. A woman, in a purple shirt with the word *Volunteer* embroidered on her pocket, looked up and smiled.

Despite the pleasant surroundings, Camden knew he was in a hospital. It was unnaturally quiet, and the pungent smell of disinfectant hung in the air.

"May I help you?" the woman asked, her voice as soft and soothing as the bubbling water.

"I'm Detective Shea with the GGPD, also acting chief. This is Camden Kingsley from Internal Affairs. I'm here to talk to Robert Grimaldi. I spoke to his doctor. She's expecting us."

A computer terminal sat below the lip of the desk, and the volunteer tapped on the keys. "Mr. Grimaldi's in East Seventeen. Take the elevators to the second floor. The East wing is the third door on the right. I've sent a message, and the doctor will be waiting for you."

Brett and Camden thanked the woman. The directions they'd been given were perfect, and soon they were shaking hands with Grimaldi's attending physician. Dr. Murielle Shah was a woman who Camden estimated to be in her late fifties. Her dark hair was streaked with gray, and she wore a silk blouse under her lab coat.

Dr. Shah greeted them. "I wasn't expecting two police officers."

Camden held up his official ID. "I'm with Internal Affairs, investigating the shooting last night."

The doctor studied the ID before nodding her approval. "Obviously, Robert Grimaldi's injuries aren't life-threatening. Still, I want to know where my patient will be taken if I release him."

"Dr. Shah," said Brett, "as soon as you say Mr. Grimaldi is healthy enough to leave the hospital, he'll be brought before a judge. From there, it's up to the courts to decide what happens and where he goes. Until then, I need to speak to him about what he was doing last night."

"What about the shooting?" she asked.

Camden bristled at the sharp edges of her tone. "What about it?"

"I can't release a man who's been shot by the police for no reason. What if there's retribution?"

"That's why I'm here," said Camden. He understood the pressure from the public. Still, he refused to be bullied into turning Grace into a scapegoat, even if it'd make a lot of people happier. "It's my job to figure out what happened."

Dr. Shah shook her head. "I don't like this, but I'll let you both speak to him. Fifteen minutes only. I'm keeping him in the hospital until Monday morning. With his history of abusing controlled substances, I want to monitor his pain medication until he's healed enough for only OTC meds. Then, you can take him to court. Fair enough?"

"You're the doctor. We'll do whatever you say."

Because Grimaldi was viewed as a flight risk, police protection had been assigned to the room 24-7. A patrol officer sat on a chair and scrolled through his phone. He looked up as Brett and Camden approached. Shoving the phone into his pocket, he swallowed. "Everything okay, Chief?"

"We're here to talk to Grimaldi. You can take a break if you want. The doc says we only have fifteen minutes, so don't go far."

"Thanks," said the officer as he stood. "I'll be right back."

Even though a police officer was outside his room, Grimaldi was handcuffed to the rail of his bed. A TV hung on the wall. The screen was filled with a sitcom from the '70s.

Grimaldi looked up as Camden and Brett crossed the threshold. The room was little more than a closet—big enough for the bed, the TV and nothing else. The suspect wore a hospital gown. His cheeks and chin were covered with stubble, and his shoulder was immobilized with a sling.

"Get out of here. My attorney told me I don't have to say anything to you."

Attorney? Had Grimaldi already lawyered up? Once a suspect had a lawyer and had invoked their right to remain silent, there was little more for the police to do or say. Luckily, Camden wasn't exactly a cop. "What kind of counsel did you retain?"

"The kind that will sue the ass off the police department. My lawyer came to me. I don't have to pay him nothing, unless we win big." Grimaldi pointed to himself with his thumb. "Did you know that girl cop who shot me was the police chief's cousin? Don't that seem like a crime to you?"

"How's that criminal?" Brett folded his arms.

"Too much of one family working together ain't right. It's...oh, what's the word?"

"*Nepotism*?" Camden offered.

"Yeah, *nepotism*."

"I'm with Internal Affairs." Camden held up his ID again. "And investigating the shooting. I know you said that you don't want to speak to Shea, but would you talk to me?"

"About what?"

"I'm looking into Officer Grace Colton's actions."

Grimaldi said, "I was shot for no reason."

"That must be tragic." Camden kept his tone neutral and reminded himself that he was still after one thing. The truth.

"Tragic, yeah. It was."

"So." Camden paused. "Can we talk?"

"Who'd you say you worked for, again?"

"Internal Affairs."

"You're looking into the girl cop who shot me?" Grimaldi asked. Had his voice cracked? Was it nerves? Pain? Both?

Camden nodded. "I am."

"Okay. I guess I can talk to you. But only if the other cop ain't here."

Brett stepped toward the door. "I'll wait outside."

Camden removed the tape recorder from his messenger bag. He set it on the edge of the bed.

Grimaldi eyed the recorder. "What's that for?"

"To be certain I get an accurate record. Mind if I record what you say?"

"I guess you can use that thing."

Camden hit the record button. "Can you state your name?"

"Robert Grimaldi."

"Tell me what happened last night."

"Like I told you, I was shot for no reason."

"No reason?" Camden echoed.

"I was running. But running ain't a crime."

"Why were you running?"

Grimaldi turned his gaze back to the TV. His left eye fluttered. "Exercise."

"Do you recall if Officer Colton told you to stop?"

Grimaldi kept his eyes on the TV. "No."

"No, you don't recall? Or no, she didn't tell you to stop?"

"I don't recall."

Camden nodded. "Can we talk about the gun?"

"I didn't have a gun."

"Do you own a gun?"

Grimaldi looked back at the TV. His left eye twitched. "No."

"Tell me about the witnesses."

"What witnesses?"

"A man and woman approached you after you were shot. According to Officer Colton, the man spoke to you. What did he say?"

"I don't remember." Grimaldi once again glanced at the TV. Slightly, but unmistakably, his left eye twitched again.

Looking at the TV and the eye twitch: Were those Grimaldi's tells? There was only one way for Camden to find out. "How many homes did you break into last night?"

He looked at the TV. His left eye twitched. "None."

"Can I ask you one more question?"

"I guess."

"Why did you point your gun at Officer Colton? Did you intend to shoot her?"

"I think we're done here." His gaze was trained on the TV. His left eye spasmed. "You take your recorder, and get the hell out of my room."

Those were his tells—and everything that Camden needed to see.

Scooping up his recorder, he left the room.

He strode down the hallway.

Brett caught up with Camden. "How'd it go?"

"Everything that guy just said was a lie. He had a gun. He pointed it at Grace. He spoke to the witnesses."

"So what if he is lying?" They stood in front of a bank of elevators and waited for the car to come up from the lobby. "Can you prove that any of his story is false?"

Camden shook his head. "But he said something else. He said he doesn't own a gun. That's a lie, too."

The elevator doors slid open, and the two men stepped inside. "How do you even know?"

"Everyone has a reaction to their lying. It's their tell. For Grimaldi, he looks away, and his eye twitches."

"Everyone has a tell?"

"Everyone." The elevator doors opened, and the two men stepped into the lobby.

Brett whistled. "Remind me never to play poker with you. How's this going to help Grace?"

"Grimaldi made one more statement, also a lie, but this one should be easy to disprove."

"What's that?" Brett asked as they crossed the lobby.

"He said he doesn't own a gun, but I can tell he does. If I can prove that, then I have him on making a false statement. Also, I can ask him to produce the gun, which he won't be able to do. It might not be a perfect solution, but at least it'll help get Grace out of the jam."

Brett used the fob to start the police SUV. "It'll work in theory."

Now all Camden needed to do was prove it.

Chapter Ten

Camden had spent a fruitless afternoon. First, he called one of his buddies with the state police and asked if Robert Grimaldi had registered a gun in Michigan.

No matches were found.

For Camden, there was no doubt. Grimaldi had lied about owning a gun. Being able to prove that fact could be the difference between showing that Grace had acted appropriately to a threat or having the world believe that she'd misused force.

In order to find the gun, Camden needed to request information from forty-nine other states. So far, he'd contacted three. He glanced at his watch.

It was 6:25 p.m.

Correction: it had been a very long afternoon—and part of an evening.

After powering down his computer, he rose from the conference table. His gaze was drawn to Grace's jacket—the same one she'd forgotten at the pizza parlor. The garment held her floral scent.

He really should just drop off the coat on his way out.

Why, then, was he tucking it into his bag?

He knew the answer to that question without even thinking.

Camden wanted to see Grace again. Still, it was a bad idea—horrible, really. He strode through the squad room and toward the front door.

Mary Suzuki stood at the front desk. Looking up with a smile as he approached, she said, "Evening, Camden. You done for the weekend?"

"Define *done*," he said jokingly.

She laughed. "Always something, right?"

"Right."

"Can I do anything for you?" she offered.

Camden paused. This was the moment. He could give Mary the jacket. Certainly, one of the many Coltons who worked at the department could pick up the coat. From now on, he could put Grace Colton behind him. Shaking his head, he said, "I'm good for now. See you Monday." He pushed the door open.

"See you Monday," she called after him.

The streets were wet, glistening in the light that spilled from the windows of downtown businesses. It was dusk, yet roiling dark clouds blocked out whatever sunset there might've been. The lack of color left the world awash in shades of gray. Camden, in his black suit and white shirt, felt as if he'd just stepped into an old-time movie.

He rounded the building and found his car in the back lot. Slipping behind the steering wheel, he started the engine. Indecision lay heavy, like a rock in his gut. For Camden, it was a foreign feeling. After inhaling deeply, he emptied his lungs in a single exhale. His mind, organized as ever, filled with dozens of ways to remedy the situation. Top of the list: return to the station and leave the coat with Mary. It's what he should have done from the beginning.

Instead, he put the gearshift into Drive and pulled out of the parking lot. Grace's apartment was only a few blocks from the police station. In less than five minutes, he was parked in front of her building. Leaning forward, he stared at her apartment window. The curtains were drawn, yet the glow of a lamp inside turned the fabric golden.

She was home.

Now he had to wonder: Was he really going to stop by, unannounced?

All the same, if he wasn't going to see her, why had he come at all?

After turning off the engine, he pulled Grace's jacket from his bag and stepped onto the sidewalk. At the same moment the door to the apartment building opened. Grace stood on the stoop. Their eyes met. She froze, her hand resting on the door.

She wore a dress in cream and pink. The bodice fitted her breasts perfectly, and the fabric skimmed over her body to the waist. The skirt was full and flowing. He recalled the feeling—only moments ago—that he'd been plunked into a black-and-white movie.

Then there was Grace. The Technicolor wonder on the screen. Her entrance onto the set was the magic that propelled the story forward.

It also made Camden wonder if he'd needed a bit of color in his own life.

"Hey," she said.

Camden shut his mouth. Swallowed. "Hey."

"What are you doing here? I was just heading out."

Damn. "A date?" he asked, his jaw tight.

"It's a family party. I'm waiting for my rideshare." Glancing at her phone, she sighed. "I ordered the car over half an hour ago, and still nothing." She paused. "Did you hear anything about the case? Have the witnesses shown up?"

Camden shook his head. "Sorry. No." He held up her jacket. "You left this at lunch."

"Oh, thanks." She came down the short flight of steps. The skirt flowed around her as she walked. "I appreciate you bringing it by."

She reached for the coat. Her fingertips brushed the back of his hand. Her touch was electric, and Camden's skin warmed. "You look great, by the way."

Grace rotated at the waist, sending the skirt twirling around her legs. "I'm usually a jeans and T-shirt kind of girl. The party is at the Grave Gulch Grill and kind of swanky. So I thought, what the hell? I can dress up for an evening, right?"

His gaze was drawn to the deep neckline of her dress. An image of his mouth on her skin flooded his mind. "Right."

Grace slipped her arms into the coat. "Well, thanks again. I probably should order another rideshare. I don't think my first one will ever show."

Walk away. Just say "Good night" and walk away.

Yet, he couldn't. Camden inclined his head toward his car. "I can give you a lift."

"Thanks for the offer, but I can't be a bother. You were nice enough to drop off my jacket. So already I've taken up too much of your time."

The little voice in his head returned. This time it was accompanied by an alarm that wailed.

After all, he'd offered Grace a ride. She'd declined. He should just leave well enough alone—but he couldn't. "Dropping you off wouldn't be a bother.

Besides, I can't leave you on the street. Alone. It's getting dark."

She lifted a brow. "You think I can't take care of myself?"

"Oh, I know you can. It's just that giving a lady a ride is part of the gentleman's code."

"You're a gentleman?" she asked, lifting her eyebrow yet again. "I didn't know."

Was she flirting? God, he hoped so. Straightening his tie, Camden asked, "Don't I look dapper?"

She laughed. The sound went straight to his soul. "You do look nice." Pausing, she chewed on her bottom lip. "Are you sure that dropping me off won't be a problem?"

"Positive," he said.

He hadn't bothered to lock his car and moved to the auto, opening the passenger door as Grace approached. "Wow," she teased. "You really are a gentleman."

"You sound surprised," he joked in return. Rounding to the driver's side, he slid behind the steering wheel.

"You know the way?" she asked, as he started the engine.

"I do." He pulled onto the nearly empty street and began to drive toward the restaurant.

"Your parents own the Grave Gulch Grill, right?"

"You read that in my file?" She winked to show that she was teasing him, at least a little.

Truth was, he had read her file. But there was more. "I've worked with your brother, Troy. He mentioned it."

She nodded but said nothing. He drove, wondering what she was thinking.

He glanced at Grace. "What's the occasion?"

"My brother, Palmer, got engaged. Mom and Dad wanted to celebrate and welcome his fiancée, Soledad, and their baby girl, Lyra, to the family."

"Sounds nice. Your family seems pretty tight."

Grace lifted a shoulder and let it drop. "I guess."

"You don't seem convinced. You aren't a close crew, or it isn't good?"

"We are definitely very close. It's just…" She exhaled and looked out the window.

"It's just what?"

Before she could answer, his phone began to ring. The caller ID showed on the entertainment screen. Arielle Parks. *Crap.* He sent the call to voice mail.

"You aren't going to answer that?"

Camden tightened his grip on the wheel. "I'll call her once I get home. It'll just be a minute."

"Home?" she echoed. "You mean you don't have plans for a Friday night?"

With a shake of his head, he turned off Grave Gulch Boulevard. "Just work."

A long drive led to the Grave Gulch Grill. Tall trees, the leaves starting to turn from green to golden, lined both sides of the road. Then, the restaurant came into view. It was a large stone building. Inside, lights spilled onto the walkway and the adjacent parking lot.

What would it feel like to show up at a place like this, with a girl like Grace Colton as his date? True, Camden had never suffered from a lack of female companionship. It's just that he hadn't met anyone interesting for several months.

Correction: he hadn't met anyone interesting until he'd met Grace.

Pulling into a space near the door, he put the gearshift into Park. "I'll call you if we get any leads on the witnesses." He knew well enough that Brett Shea would hear first. The Colton grapevine would deliver the message to Grace before Camden was even notified.

"Thanks," she said.

Camden tried to look only at the windshield. Yet his gaze was drawn to her face. Her eyes. Her neck. Her lips.

"I hate to think of you home all alone and bored."

"I won't be bored," he said.

Tilting her head toward the door, she smiled. "You want to join me?"

WHAT IN THE world had Grace just done? Obviously, she'd invited Camden to attend the family party. But why?

He began, "I really don't think I'm your cousin's favorite person."

Now was the moment she could demur. Grace had done the polite thing in inviting Camden inside. It's what her mother—always classy and gracious—would do. He'd declined. She should just go. Why was she still sitting in the car? Why did she feel compelled to ask "Which one?"

True, there were a lot of Coltons. Camden chuckled. His eyes crinkled with his smile. His teeth were white. His jaw was chiseled, and his lips looked strong. Her own lips tingled.

"I was thinking of Melissa," he said. "I guess any of the others might not like me, either."

"Because you're an IA investigator?"

"It's because I'm investigating you."

He wasn't wrong—and they both knew it. "One drink." She held up a single finger.

Camden shook his head. Relief and disappointment washed over Grace until she felt as if she might drown in her emotions.

And then he said, "Okay. Sure. One drink. It's Friday night, after all."

She couldn't help but smile. "C'mon, then. Let's go."

Opening the car door, she headed to the restaurant. The main dining room was one large space. Tables, covered in pristine white cloths, filled the room. Almost every table was filled with customers. The din of conversations was the background music. "I worked here as a kid," said Grace, circumventing the dining area.

"What'd you do?" Camden asked. He walked at her side.

"What didn't I do? I washed dishes. Bused tables. Worked as a server. Hostess. Hell, I did everything but cook."

"You didn't like the restaurant business? You weren't tempted to stay and help your folks run this place?"

"Not for a minute," said Grace with a laugh. "The restaurant has been good to my family. It's put a roof over our head, food on our own table and all of us kids through school. But it's a hard life. Early mornings. Late nights."

"Sounds like being a cop," said Camden.

Grace stopped at the door to the private-party room. She gripped the handle. "Running a restaurant makes being a cop look easy."

He laughed as she pulled the door open. The private-party room was filled with people. High-top tables, covered in blue and burgundy cloths, circumvented the room. Waiters in tuxedos maneuvered through the crowd while holding trays of tapas. A long bar was set against the far wall, and overhead a set of crystal chandeliers glowed. The first person who Grace saw was Melissa. She stood with Antonio and Grace's parents—of all people.

Melissa's gaze fell on Camden with a look that could only be described as frosty.

Then, the two women made eye contact. Grace lifted her brow—not quite a challenge, not quite a threat.

Whatever it was that she meant to communicate, Melissa understood. The scowl was replaced with a smile as she approached. Antonio Ruiz, Melissa's fiancé, stood at her side.

"Grace. Camden. It's good to see you both." She then introduced Camden to Antonio. The men shook hands.

"Camden gave me a ride here tonight," Grace said. "I invited him in for a drink."

"Oh, really?" Melissa drew her brows together. "How kind of him."

For a second, nobody spoke.

"And speaking of that drink…" Camden said, filling the silence. "I'll go grab one from the bar. What'll you have?"

"Draft beer. Thanks."

Grace watched as Camden moved through the crowd, admiring his tight rear with every step.

"Gracc Colton," said Melissa. "What are you thinking by bringing an IA investigator to the party?"

"Whoa," said Antonio, interrupting. "I might let you

two have a private conversation. I'm going to the bar, too. What can I get you, Melissa?"

She sighed, looking tired. "Just water."

"Water it is," he said, before slipping away.

As soon as Antonio was out of earshot, Melissa leaned in close. "An IA investigator. Really? He's investigating *you*."

"It's his job," said Grace, not entirely sure why she was defending the person tasked with establishing her culpability. "It's not his entire being." She paused. "Besides, I trust him to do right by me. I've thought this through…"

Folding her arms across her chest, Melissa said, "I don't know what part of your anatomy you're thinking with, Grace, but it's not your head."

"Excuse me?" asked Grace, feeling her face burning hot. "You don't need to be rude. Or crude."

Holding up her hands in surrender, Melissa took a step back. "You're right. That was out of line, but I'm worried."

Grace was still upset, but she wasn't going to deny the obvious. "Maybe he is a good-looking guy. What of it?" She paused. "You've been on the force for a long time. Have you heard something about Camden? Has he used his looks and charm to implicate someone before?"

Melissa let out a long exhale and moved closer to Grace. "The only time Kingsley gets brought up, it's to mention his honesty."

"So why are you questioning his character now?"

"That's easy. I want to protect you."

"I appreciate that you're always looking out for me." Grace reached for Melissa's hand and gave it a squeeze.

"If I can trust him, you can, too. Or is the problem that you don't trust me?"

Camden stood at the bar, elbow on the wooden top, as he waited for drinks. He glanced at Grace. Smiled.

Just looking at him warmed Grace to her toes. She smiled back.

"I trust you," Melissa said, letting her hand slip from Grace's grasp. "I just want to make sure that you're safe. I can see the way you look at him. Getting involved with Camden can cost you more than your career. Your heart, as well."

"So what if I look? He's a handsome man."

"I'll give you that. Camden is easy on the eyes." Melissa's words trailed off.

"I hear a distinct *but* waiting to come out."

She shook her head. "I don't want to ruin the evening."

"Not saying anything is what's going to ruin the evening. Spill."

Melissa sighed again. "Just be careful, that's all."

It was then that Grace noticed the dark circles around Melissa's eyes. The color in her cheeks looked more feverish than the flush of excitement. Her cousin had made a huge sacrifice in stepping down from her job.

No wonder Melissa was in a foul mood. "I'm sorry about what happened. All of it. You might still be police chief if it wasn't for me."

Shaking her head, Melissa said, "There's so much going on at the department. Me having to step aside was inevitable. I just wanted it to be on my own terms, you know?"

Grace did know. "You look tired."

"I'm definitely fatigued. All the stress, I guess. But, c'mon. Tonight's not the night to dwell on the bad." Melissa linked her arm through Grace's, maneuvering them so they faced the bar. "It's a celebration. Lots of us Coltons are getting married—not just Palmer and Soledad. Tell me the truth, what do you think of Antonio?"

"He's amazing, honestly."

Melissa smiled, all of the weariness in her face melting away. Grace recognized the expression on her cousin's face: it was pure love and joy. "He is kind of amazing."

Grace searched the room for Camden. He was still at the bar. As she watched him, she couldn't help but wonder if she would ever find a love of her own like that.

CAMDEN SCANNED THE private room. The space was packed, just a sea of people. Typically, a crowded party wouldn't have been his thing. He preferred more intimate settings for his socializing, such that it was. Yet, he had to admit, as the music of animated conversations and the peals of laughter swirled around him, the Colton family was a happy crew.

It was totally opposite from his family. Camden was the only child of a father who'd died too soon. His mother, all these years later, was still wrapped in a cocoon of grief. A pang of jealousy filled his chest, gone as quick as it came. Still, Camden couldn't help but wonder what it would be like to be a part of such a large and boisterous clan.

His gaze was drawn to Grace. She stood with her cousin, Melissa, and a group of other women. They all favored each other—hair, eyes, nose—and he assumed they were more of the Coltons.

"Hey, my man," said a familiar voice. "I didn't expect to see you here."

Camden turned toward the greeting. It was Troy Colton, Grace's brother. He was almost as tall as Camden but had broader shoulders. From the looks of his rumpled suit and loose tie, Camden guessed that the other man had come to the party right after work. Then again, Camden had on a suit, worn all day, as well.

"Troy," he said, holding out his hand to shake. The two men had worked on the Randall Bowe case, Troy trying to find the forensic scientist, Camden trying to find out why he got away with so much. "I gave Grace a ride over to the party. She invited me to stay.

"I'm glad she did."

"How's Evangeline?" Camden asked, mentioning the former ADA and Troy's love.

"Busy. She'll be here later and will be happy to see you."

"It'll be great to see her, too."

Then, the conversation moved, as it always did with cops, to work. Troy asked, "What're you working on?"

"Aside from Bowe?" Did the GGPD detective not know that Camden was looking into last night's shooting? Or was he trying to gauge what Camden would say? "I'm working on what happened with Grace."

Troy glanced over his shoulder. He watched Grace for a moment, before turning back to Camden. "How's she doing?"

"Your sister's tough and smart." Camden pressed his lips together before he said anything that might give away his true feelings.

"Any leads on those witnesses?"

"None at all." The bartender slid two beers across the bar, and Camden picked up the glasses. "And what about you? What're you working on these days?"

"All my time is spent on the Bowe case. You know Randall texted Melissa a while back."

Camden did. He nodded and took a sip of beer. "He wants to talk to his brother."

"It's been my job to find him."

"Any luck?"

"None at all," he said, echoing Camden's words. "I've talked to my cousin Bryce. He's with the FBI. Bryce put out feelers with the US Marshals for Randall's brother, Baldwin. So far, nothing's turned up. It's like Baldwin's a ghost or something."

"Who's a ghost?" Another guy dressed in a suit and tie approached the bar. He had sandy-brown hair and blue eyes and looked fit. He was taller than Camden. Was this another Colton? "You know I always love a scary story."

"Camden Kingsley, let me introduce you to my cousin, Bryce." Troy draped his arm over Bryce's shoulder. "Bryce is with the FBI, but don't let the fancy job fool you. He's still an okay guy."

So this was Special Agent Colton? Camden nodded his greetings. "Nice to meet you."

"Same," said Bryce. "Really, what're you two talking about?"

"What else is there to talk about?" Troy asked. "Work. Camden's with the DA's office. Internal Affairs. He's looking into the Bowe fiasco, among other things."

Camden stepped to the side so the other men could order their drinks.

"What else are you working on?" Bryce asked, leaning an elbow on the bar.

"Last night's shooting, for one."

"Grace?" Bryce asked.

Camden nodded. He should've known that he'd be persona non grata before he ever walked through the door, although the Coltons hadn't really treated him like that.

"What've you found out?" Bryce asked.

"Not much more than has been reported to the media." He paused. No, that wasn't right. "Today I interviewed the guy who was shot. Robert Grimaldi's his name and he's still in the hospital. The guy has a tell. When he lies, he looks away, and there's a twitch in the left eye."

"Impressive that you figured it out," said Troy.

"Just a bit of paying attention to his response. Plus, I asked him a question that I already knew the answer to. He lied, and again there was the tell."

"What's all of this mean for Grace?" Bryce asked. "Were you able to figure anything?"

"For starters, I think he's lying about owning a gun. It's not registered in Michigan, but until we find the firearm, we got nothing."

"For the record, I'm glad you're the one looking into last night's shooting," said Bryce. "You're doing the right thing by Grace."

"I'm not sure Melissa agrees with you. She gave me quite a look when I arrived."

Bryce shrugged. "All us Coltons are pretty protective of Grace, Melissa especially. Plus, she must feel some extra responsibility because she's chief of police. Or was until this morning."

"I have to get this beer to your cousin before it gets warm."

"Go. Let me know if you need anything."

Stopping short, Camden turned. "What'd you say?"

The bartender handed Bryce a glass filled with amber liquid and ice. "What'd I say about what?"

"If I need help."

"Oh, sure, let me know if you need help. The bureau has resources. We can help with local cases, but only if the authorities ask."

"What about the gun?" Camden's pulse started to race. "Could you get into the database for other states?"

"I can, but only for a reason."

"Today, I talked to Robert Grimaldi—the guy who was shot. I asked him if he had a gun. He said he didn't own one, but he's lying. I checked Michigan's firearm registry." Camden shook his head. "Nada."

"But he might've bought one in another state. Is that what you're thinking?"

"More like hoping, but yeah."

"You have to come to my office," said Bryce. "Can you meet at eight o'clock tomorrow morning?"

"Got it," said Camden, his head buzzing with excitement.

"I'll text if anything changes."

Grace still stood in the middle of a group of women. Some he recognized—like Melissa, Desiree and Annalise, the K-9 instructor. Others he could only guess were members of the family.

He approached the group, drink in hand.

Grace excused herself from the knot of women. "Thanks," she said, taking the offered beer.

"Nice party. I spoke to Troy and Bryce."

"About?" she asked, taking a sip.

"Work. Randall Bowe. You." He took a drink from his beer. "I think Bryce might be able to help."

Grabbing Camden by his elbow, she pulled him away from the group of women. "Help me? How?"

"The FBI has access to firearm databases for different states. It might be able to tell me if Robert Grimaldi purchased a gun. If he owns a firearm—but can't produce it—it would prove a bit of your story."

"You think that'll work?"

"It's a long shot, sure. Mostly because there are states that don't keep track of gun sales. Or Grimaldi might've stolen a gun or bought a stolen gun."

"Let's hope that, for once, he followed the rules."

"Hello, dear. Who's your friend?" An older woman stepped away from the group of chatting women. She stood right behind Grace. "Are you going to introduce me?"

"Mom, this is Camden Kingsley. He works for the DA's office and gave me a ride to the party." Grace paused. "Camden, this is my mom, Leanne Colton."

"Mrs. Colton, it's a pleasure to meet you. I can see the resemblance between you and your daughter," said Camden, shaking the other woman's hand.

"It's nice to meet a friend of Grace's. But please, call me Leanne."

Camden immediately liked her. She was gracious and kind and obviously cared about her daughter.

Leanne continued. "I'm glad you could join us to celebrate. We are a tight family, but we love our friends, too. Eat lots. I picked out the menu personally."

"Mom does all the customer relations here. Dad is in charge of the kitchen and the business." Grace paused and scanned the room. Camden's gaze was drawn to the hollow of her neck, and his mind was filled with a single question: What would it feel like to kiss her throat? He looked away. "Where is Dad?"

Leanne laughed. "Guess."

"The kitchen," said Grace with a mock groan.

"You should see the cake we have, Camden. Soledad owns Dream Bakes. She and Grace's father have been working on the cake all day. The reveal itself will be an event. I hope you can stay for the whole party."

"Don't pressure, Mom. He was just nice enough to give me a ride. Nothing else."

"I'm not pressuring your friend. I'm *inviting*. There's a difference…"

Camden could tell that the two women had deep affection and admiration for each other. His phone rang. He fished it one-handed from the inner pocket of his suit coat. It was Arielle. Finally. "I have to take this, Mrs.—" he stopped to correct himself "—I mean, Leanne. It was nice meeting you."

Swiping the call open with his thumb, he pressed the phone to his ear. Making his way to a set of glass doors at the back of the room, he said, "Hold on a sec."

Beer in one hand and phone in the other, Camden used his hip to open the door. He stepped onto a patio of gray stone. A short wall, also of gray stone, surrounded the semicircular area. Glass globes, on wrought iron poles, cast pools of golden light. Several seating arrangements filled the space. Nobody from the party had ventured outside, leaving Camden completely alone. After the noisy room, he breathed in the silence.

Setting his beer on the ledge, he stared into the

night. "You still there, Arielle? I had to get outside so we could speak."

"It sounds like you were in the middle of quite a celebration. Where are you?"

"The Coltons are having an engagement party for Grace's brother."

"You got invited? How?" And then, "That's amazing, really. You're doing a heck of a job sticking close to Grace."

Now was the time. He could confess all to Arielle, and she'd have no choice but to remove him from the investigation. If he recused himself, would he still be able to work with Bryce Colton?

No. If he stepped away from Grace's case now, he walked away forever. Could he rely on someone else to follow up with the FBI agent and his offer to help? Or would it be seen as another Colton protecting a member of the family?

"There's more going on right now than me learning what I can about Grace and the rest of the Colton clan."

Like a whisper of pressure on his spine, Camden could feel a set of eyes on his back. Worse, he knew who was watching him.

Turning slowly, he faced Grace Colton. Had she heard what he'd said to Arielle?

Her complexion was pale, almost ashen. Her lips trembled. Yet, there was a fire in her eyes, and he knew: she'd heard. And she was pissed.

"Arielle, I have to go."

"Go?" his boss squawked. "Go where? You've been trying to talk to me all day."

"I'll call you back," he said, hanging up.

Camden let the phone slip from his ear. Standing in the dark, he stared at Grace. "Hey."

"Hey, yourself." She still held her drink. Her hand shook. Beer sloshed over the glass, leaving her sleeve soaked. She'd donned the jacket that he'd kept with him just to give him an excuse to see her again. Now, the coat was going to be his ruin.

Hell, he should have left the coat with Mary at police headquarters.

"Damn it," Grace cursed. After setting the beer on the wall, she wiped her hand on the tail of her coat.

Camden knew there was no way forward other than to tell the truth. "Listen, I know what you overheard, but I can explain…"

"Explain?" She snorted. "I heard plenty. You're spying on my family, trying to make sure that I'm guilty. That, somehow, we're all guilty. But that's where you're wrong. The Coltons might not be perfect, but we're good people…"

"I agree," he said.

"I don't care what you say. Robert Grimaldi had a gun."

"I agree," he said again.

"Wait. You *what*?"

"I agree. Your family isn't corrupt. Maybe a bit unlucky with everything that's happened recently."

"And me?"

"You? You're *really* unlucky. But that doesn't mean you're guilty of shooting an unarmed man."

Grace shook her head and muttered a curse.

Camden knew that she wasn't ready to forgive— or forget.

After a moment, she asked, "What's up, then? I heard what you said, so don't deny it."

"I'm not going to deny anything," said Camden. The truth always won in the end. Moreover, it was well past time that he was honest with Grace. "There are reservations about how the most recent cases have been handled in the GGPD. But I've been trying to talk to Arielle all day. There's something I need to tell her."

"Oh, really?" Grace's voice dripped with derision. "Why's that?"

"I need to be taken off the case."

"Really?" His confession appeared to blunt some of Grace's fury. She drew in a deep breath and sat on the stone wall. "Is it because you're going to have to find me at fault?"

What was Camden supposed to say? He could let Grace think that her case was hopeless—and in a lot of ways it was. But when had lying ever solved a problem?

He shook his head. "It's not that."

"What is it, then?"

Camden turned to face Grace. God, she was beautiful. And strong. And sincere. And kind. In short, she was everything he'd ever want in a woman—even if she'd never be the one for him. "I need to be taken off the case because the truth is…" he inhaled "…Grace Colton, I like you. A lot."

Chapter Eleven

Grace's pulse thundered in her ears. Her heart beat wildly against her chest, a trapped animal trying to break free. "You like me?" She echoed Camden's words.

She found him more than handsome. He was also stalwart, honest and determined. Suddenly, she was aware of how very secluded the patio was. Camden stood so close that she could feel his breath on her neck. The heat of his body warmed her flesh.

She didn't mind being alone or feeling his breath on her skin, like a lover's caress. Yet, what did she intend to do with this moment?

"Is that so hard to believe?" His whispered words disappeared in the dark night.

He sat next to her. His finger was so close to hers that she need only move a little and they would be touching. Was that what she wanted—to hold Camden's hand?

In truth, she wanted so much more. An image of Camden—his lips on hers, his hands on her body—flooded her thoughts. Her mouth tingled with the imagined kiss. Her skin burned with the fantasy of his touch.

She could lean in close and let the fiction become reality.

And then what?

Grace might be a rookie cop on leave, but she wasn't stupid. The best way to ruin her career would be to get involved with Camden.

Still, she sat in the darkness wanting nothing more than to give in to her longing.

No. She couldn't. She loved her job. Even after the last twenty-four hours, she wanted nothing more than to get back to work.

Scooting back, she picked up her beer and took a sip. Maybe the little bit of alcohol gave her some courage. Or maybe it just lessened her reservations. Or maybe it was as simple as the need to tell Grace the truth was paramount. She took another swallow of her beer. "I like you, too. But we can't. You know that."

Camden's head hung. He nodded slowly. "You're right, which is why I've been trying to get taken off the case all day. Until now, that is."

"Now you want to stay. Why?"

"It's what your cousin said about the FBI having tech that the GGPD doesn't. What if we can prove that Grimaldi owns a gun?" He still whispered, but his words tumbled out, a stream rushing over rocks. "I can't trust anyone else from the DA's office to do the right thing. After I see what Bryce can find, I'll recuse myself from the investigation."

"What happens then?" she asked, her gaze on his lips.

"Then we have to go our separate ways. There isn't anything else to do."

He was right. Yet a pain stabbed Grace in the chest.

"Sure." She paused a beat. "You're right."

He reached for her. His pinky stroked the side of her hand. The touch danced along her skin. She wanted to lean in to him, to feel his lips on hers just this once. That would be a step too far.

Camden must've known, too. He stood. "I better go. Thank your mom for letting me stop by the party."

"Should you get behind the wheel? You've had a beer."

He gestured to a glass, nearly full, that sat on the wall. "Only a sip or two. I'll be fine to drive home."

There was nothing else she could say or do to keep him with her even if she wanted. Grace rose, too. Her mouth was dry, and her throat raw. Still, she couldn't let him walk out of her life without saying goodbye. "It's only been a day, really less than twenty-four hours. I already know that I was lucky to have met you."

"Well." Camden stood taller and held out his hand for her to shake. "I guess that makes two of us."

She placed her palm in his. Her hand warmed as a golden glow crept up her arm and lodged in her heart.

They still held hands. "I better go."

"Drive safe." She closed the distance between them.

"I'll let you know if the FBI can find out anything about a gun." Closer still. His palm slipped from hers, and he traced the back of her hand. They were hidden from the party room by the shadows, and his touch was a delicious indulgence.

Was that the moment that Grace decided she didn't care about expectations, propriety or even her career? Or had the decision been made long ago?

Slipping her arms around his neck, she pulled him to her. His mouth was on hers. Hungrily, he claimed her with his kiss. The desire was intense. It registered deep in her belly. Grace opened herself to him, wanting to be devoured.

Tongues. Mouths. Teeth. Camden and Grace embraced, tasted and explored.

Camden's touch trailed under her jacket. His fingertips were hot against the thin fabric of her dress. Her clothes were too tight. The cool night was suddenly too warm. The pain of desire built in her middle.

It was all hands and touch. Mouths and kisses. Longing and passion, at first ignored, had now ignited. She ran her fingers through his hair, pulling him closer. Yet he'd never be close enough.

His arms were around her as he claimed her hungrily with his mouth. Grace was drunk on the sensation. She pressed her body into his. He was already hard. She was wet, and her innermost muscles clenched.

"Camden," she breathed into the kiss. "Oh, Camden."

His touch branded her skin. But Grace didn't care if she got burned. He reached into the bodice of her dress. Inside her bra, he teased her nipple.

"Grace, you are so damned perfect."

"Perfect, huh?" Nipping his bottom lip, she teased. "Perfect how?"

"Perfect breasts," he whispered, rubbing his thumb over her taut nipple. "Perfect mouth." He claimed her once more with a kiss. "Perfect body." His touch moved lower, and he reached up the skirt of her dress and then into her panties.

She'd never wanted anyone the way she wanted

Camden Kingsley. Could she take him as a lover after only knowing him for one day?

At the moment, she didn't care about any personal rules.

She ran her hands over his chest and torso. The muscles of his pecs and abs were unmistakable. What would it be like to have him hold her with his strong arms?

He slipped his finger between the folds of her sex. Grace lifted her leg, wrapping it over Camden's hip, and giving him complete access. He found the top of her sex already swollen and sensitive. He rubbed repeatedly, and Grace's world shattered into a million pieces. Crying out as she came, she knew the noise was captured by Camden's kisses.

Reckless, a small voice whispered from the back of her mind. *This is beyond reckless, and you know it. If you sleep with Camden now, then you'll have to live with the consequences for the rest of your life.*

Her pulse pounded in her ears, drowning out the little words of her conscience. Every inch of her body buzzed, as if she'd been electrified. Yet, it was more than the pleasure of Camden's touch. It was the man. She wanted him. No, she needed him inside her, the personal costs be damned.

Besides, in the darkened corner of the patio, nobody ever needed to know.

She reached for the front of his pants and her fingers trembled as she worked the top button free.

He kissed her again. "Grace, you're driving me wild."

Good. She wanted him to lose control. She wanted

him to need her as much as she needed him. Tugging on his zipper, she pulled down. Grace glanced at Camden, he pressed against the fabric of his shorts. Her hand slipped inside the waistband and she slid her finger over the head of his penis. Collecting a bead of moisture, she gripped him and ran her palm over his length. Closing his eyes, he hissed as her movement took on a rhythm.

Camden held tight to her wrist, stopping Grace. "I'm about to lose it, but I want…" He kissed her lips softly. "I want to be inside you when I do."

"Do you have a condom?"

"I do," said Camden, reaching for his wallet.

He pulled out a foil packet and Grace's knees went weak with longing.

You don't want to live with the work-related consequences of this moment for the rest of your life, the voice in her head warned.

Yet, as Camden placed his lips on hers, she told the voice to shut up.

After rolling the condom down his length, Camden gripped Grace's rear. He lifted her and she let out squeal of surprise and delight. Wrapping her legs around his waist, she pulled aside her panties. The silk of her skirt cascaded down, and then he was inside her. They moved together, hot and frantic. His fingers dug into her flesh and as he thrust into her hard. Grace held onto his shoulders as the wave of desire began to swell in her middle again. Harder. Faster. The pleasure grew and she pulled him closer, took him deeper. Still, she knew that it would never be enough.

She rode the wave of ecstasy higher and higher. It broke, and she cried out with her orgasm.

Camden thrust twice more and growled as he came.

Grace placed her lips on his, her pulse racing and echoing in her ears. Yet it wasn't so loud that she couldn't hear the small voice inside her head.

What have you done, Grace? No matter what happens now, you'll never be exonerated. By having sex with Camden Kingsley, your innocence—along with your professionalism—will always be in doubt.

The truth gripped her by the throat until she couldn't swallow or even breathe. She slipped from his grip and fixed her underwear. It didn't matter that her heartbeat still raced. Or that her lips still tingled. Or even that her body still thrummed.

"I didn't mean for that to happen," she began. Her voice echoed inside her head, the words seeming to be spoken by someone else. All of the stress from the last day seemed to drop on her shoulders. How had she given in to the temptation to have sex with Camden? Never mind the fact that she'd been burning with desire. Now, all she wanted to do was get away. "I'm sorry." She stepped farther away, creating distance between them.

"Don't be sorry." Camden took a napkin from his pocket and dealt with the condom. Looking away, she gave him a moment of privacy.

She picked up her beer from the stone wall and took a long swallow. The alcohol exploded in her stomach like a bomb yet did nothing to stop her racing heart. "I should get back." She backed up, hooking her thumb toward the patio doors. "You know. The party."

Camden nodded. "I better go. If I find out anything about Grimaldi owning a gun, I'll ask Bryce to give you a call."

As if shocked by a faulty switch, she jolted and recoiled at the mention of her cousin's name. Bryce would call, not Camden himself. It was easy to figure out why. Camden Kingsley was about to walk out of Grace's life forever.

His gaze lingered on her face for a beat and then another.

Giving her one last smile, he turned and walked away.

Grace stood on the patio, breathless. Her eyes burned. She watched as he followed a path that led from the patio to the parking lot. The darkness swallowed him, and then he was gone.

As THE FIRST rays of the gray morning seeped through his curtains, Camden rubbed his gritty eyes. Saturday morning already? He'd spent the night tossing and turning, filled with regrets.

Making love to Grace Colton had been a mistake.

Walking away from her had been a tragedy.

His hands still recalled the feel of her body. He hardened with desire. There was more than merely the physical attraction. For years, Camden had observed the life of others, never really caring about much more than uncovering the facts. All that changed when he met Grace.

Was there any way to make a possible relationship between them work?

He shouldn't even bother with the question, though, because he already knew the answer.

Despite how he felt about Grace—or how she felt about him—being together was not in their future.

Setting his feet on the floor, Camden stood and ran

his hand over his face. His lips still held the memory of Grace's kiss. His hands still remembered the feel of her body—muscular yet soft. His phone pinged with an incoming text. It was from Bryce.

Heading to office. Can you still meet?

Thank goodness the other man was an early riser. Camden would have gone crazy if he'd had to spend the entire day waiting for Bryce.

Camden typed out a message and hit Send.

See you then.

Bryce's simple reply:

Text me when you arrive.

Camden showered and dressed quickly, deciding on jeans and a T-shirt. Stepping from his condo, he felt his pulse race as he drove to Bryce's office.

Before he had a chance to send his text, the front door opened. Bryce Colton, dressed in a golf shirt and jeans, stood on the threshold. A holster, along with a gun, was strapped under his arm.

"Thanks for stopping by so early," said Bryce.

Sliding out of the car, Camden used the fob to lock the door. "Thanks for running Grimaldi's name through the database."

"I'd offer my services to any investigation. The FBI is here to help," Bryce said. "But I'm not going to lie, I'm glad you're here. Grace is my baby cousin, and I'll do everything in my power to find out what happened."

Grace. His pulse sped at the sound of her name. The fact that they'd had sex should change everything. Still, he was here.

Stepping into the vestibule, Camden took in his surroundings. The floors and walls were covered in marble the color of ash. A patriotic mural filled the ceiling. Camden couldn't help himself; he was impressed.

A set of dual walk-through metal detectors led to a long hallway. At the end of the corridor stood a bank of elevators.

"You don't have to worry about those," said Bryce, tilting his head to the detectors. "They aren't on when the building's closed."

"You're at work."

"There's always something to keep me busy," said Bryce. "You know how it goes."

Camden walked between the two detectors. For the first time, he wondered if the agent was like him: working constantly because it was a calling. "I do know how it goes."

They took an elevator to the second floor, then walked down a long hallway. Motion-sensor lights clicked on as they approached. The hallway ended at a single door. It would have been unremarkable if not for the FBI seal—scales, a shield, olive branches and a banner with the words *Fidelity, Bravery* and *Integrity*—affixed to the wall.

The door was locked. Bryce keyed in a code on an electronic lock that was attached to the handle. He then scanned his thumbprint, and the latch clicked. Bryce turned the handle, and they entered a waiting room. Pictures of both the president of the United States and the US attorney general hung on the wall. Flags for both the USA and the state of Michigan flanked the framed photographs.

Camden couldn't ignore the thrill that danced along his skin. The whole setup was, well, cool and impressive. It was where important work was done to serve and protect not just the state but the entire nation.

"Right this way," said Bryce. Another door. Another security code and thumbprint scan.

Finally, they were in the inner sanctum of the FBI. It was much like any other office. Workspaces, with desks separated only by partitions, filled a large room. Yet the walls told a different story. A large picture of Len Davison, a man wanted in connection to several serial killings in the Grave Gulch area, was tacked on one wall. It was surrounded by photos of his victims. A timeline of the killings had been scrawled on a whiteboard. Another wall had a picture of Randall Bowe, the CSI investigator who had falsified evidence.

Bryce's cell phone began to ring. He glanced at the screen before opening the call. "Hey, Troy. You're up early."

He was silent for a moment, while the GGPD detective spoke.

"You're kidding, right?" His eyes went wide. Looking at Camden, he mouthed the words *Baldwin Bowe.*

Randall Bowe's brother? Camden's pulse spiked. Baldwin had gone off the radar and been near impossible to find.

"I'm here with Camden Kingsley," said Bryce. "I'm putting you on speakerphone."

Bryce engaged the app and set the phone on the desk.

"Troy," said Camden, "what happened? Baldwin Bowe's been a hard man to track down."

"It looks like he didn't want to be found until now," said Troy. The excitement in his voice was unmistakable. "I'm meeting with him soon and need backup." He continued. "There's a coffee shop near the park. Grave Gulch Coffee and Treats. There are tables on the street."

It was the same place Camden and Grace had shown pictures of the witnesses only the day before. "I know the one."

"Meet me there in ten minutes," said Troy.

"Ten minutes," Bryce echoed, and then the line went dead.

CHASTITY KNEW SHE had a headache before she opened her eyes. Her mouth was dry, and her tongue felt as if it'd been wrapped in cotton. Crap. How many bottles of cheap wine had she and Thad gone through the night before?

He lay beside her. Blankets were draped over his hips. His back was naked, and she traced the outline of his shoulder blade. Groaning, he batted her hand away in his sleep.

Chastity knew two things for certain. First, she'd never get back to sleep, and second, she needed a cup of coffee. A real latte—made with soy milk, by an actual barista—and not the crap they made from instant coffee.

Lying on her back, she stared at the ceiling. Her gaze outlined the water stain that looked like a rabbit. It was early for a Saturday, not much after nine o'clock. If she left now, would Thad even know she'd been gone?

Rolling off the mattress, she rummaged through the clothes that covered the floor. It took a minute to find a shirt without a stain and a pair of pants. After dressing silently, she slipped from the bedroom and pulled the door closed.

In the living room, she counted the empty bottles of wine. One on the coffee table. One on the kitchen counter. One on the floor, tipped on its side. She and Thad had finished three bottles of wine? No wonder her head hurt.

She grabbed her phone. Did she dare to look at what the news was reporting?

The temptation was strong, and she opened the TV station's app.

The app had created a separate tab. *GGPD: A Department Embroiled in Scandal.* She touched the link with her thumb.

Yesterday's article was pinned at the top.

Below were comments about the police.

She scrolled through them all in seconds.

Then she stopped. Someone had posted a video from the press conference. Chastity turned down the volume on her phone and pressed Play.

She watched the chief of police give her statement. As the woman spoke, Chastity's pulse raced. What did the cops know? Did they suspect that someone had taken the gun? Correction: not just someone. Thad and Chastity.

The video began to scan the crowd. The grim-faced protesters who held signs. The police inside, the interior of the building so dark that they were only shadows. Except one man, who stood near a window. He was tall. Dark-haired. Chastity would've found him attractive if she didn't love Thad so much.

The video ended, and she closed the app. Slipping

her phone back into her pocket, she decided on a simple fact. The police were no closer to finding Thad and Chastity, the gun or even the truth.

A black hoodie lay over the arm of the sofa. She worked into the jacket and left the apartment without a backward glance.

On the street, the air was cool and bracing. She inhaled deeply, and the throbbing in her head lessened. After slipping on a pair of sunglasses, she pulled up the hood. It wasn't a great disguise but, she wasn't going to be outside for long.

Grave Gulch Coffee and Treats, her favorite coffee shop in the neighborhood, sat on the corner. Half a dozen tables filled the sidewalk. They were all empty, save for one guy sitting alone and twirling an old-school flip phone through his fingers. Pushing the door open with her shoulder, she entered the shop. The dark and nutty aroma of coffee brewing greeted her. Immediately, Chastity's headache disappeared. She'd been right to come out this morning.

"THAT'S HIM," SAID CAMDEN. A man sat at an outside table at Grave Gulch Coffee and Treats. He had short dark hair. Despite the fact that Baldwin was in a chair, Camden could tell that he was tall. He wore a T-shirt and jeans and had the look of a guy who knew how to throw a punch and take one. Troy was sitting opposite.

"That's Baldwin Bowe with your cousin," said Camden.

"I recognize him from the photos," said Bryce. They'd driven to the rendezvous. Turning off the car's ignition, he continued, "Let's go."

Baldwin looked up as Camden and Bryce exited

the car. His expression gave away nothing. Without a word, the two men crossed the street and slid into seats on either side of Baldwin.

Camden nodded a greeting to Troy.

Bryce spoke first. "You're a hard man to find."

"Correction," said Baldwin. "I'm impossible to find. Unless I want to be found, that is."

The hairs on Camden's arm stood on end. "I'm sure you heard that your brother wants to talk to you."

"What if I don't want to talk to him?"

Camden said, "You know that your brother let some serious criminals go free."

"I'm not my brother," Baldwin growled.

"Who are you?" Troy asked.

"I'm just a guy who's trying to do the right thing."

"So where have you been?" Camden asked.

Baldwin held a small burner cell phone—the kind that made and received calls and did little else. He tapped the plastic casing on the table. "Around," he said, in answer to Camden's question.

"What about your brother? Has he been around with you, too?" Bryce asked.

"Randall?" Baldwin snorted. "I have no love for my brother. I definitely wouldn't hide him from the police."

Camden was an only child, yet he imagined that siblings should act like the Colton family: loving, supportive, encouraging. For a split second, his memories were flooded with a dozen images of Grace. Her smile. Her laugh. The way her brows came together when she was thinking. Shifting in the small seat, he turned away from the recollections. "Why no love for your brother?"

"Randall's a sneaky piece of garbage. He always has been. In fact, I don't blame his wife for cheating."

Troy redirected him. "He's got some kind of score to settle with you. You know that, right?" He removed a slip of paper from his pocket and slid it across the table. "This is the number Randall gave to Chief Colton. He wants you to call."

"I assume you tried to trace it." Without looking at the number, Baldwin tucked it into his shirt pocket.

"Of course," Bryce replied. "It's registered to a burner phone, purchased with cash, at a convenience store outside of Grave Gulch. The phone hasn't been turned on, so there's no way to track it."

"That may change when you make a call," said Camden. The back of his neck itched, as if someone was watching him from behind. He glanced over his shoulder.

No one was there.

He looked back as Baldwin spoke. "If I call my brother, I need your word that you'll find him. Arrest him. He needs to be put away before more people get hurt."

"You have our word," said Bryce.

"Where can we find you?" Camden asked.

"If there's anything to report, I'll find you."

Obviously, Baldwin Bowe was being purposely evasive. He might've had his reasons. It's just that Camden wasn't willing to leave it alone. "Why don't you cut the crap?" he asked, being uncustomarily abrasive.

Baldwin sat back. "Excuse me?"

"You heard what I said. If you really want your brother caught and put away, you're going to have to cooperate with us." He flicked his thumb toward Bryce and Troy. "That means we need to find *you*."

"My job isn't one where I show up to an office or work regular hours," Baldwin began. He sighed. Maybe he really was ready to help find his brother. Or maybe he was just tired of hiding. He continued. "I've been working as a bounty hunter for years. But my typical client isn't a guy who's quit paying child support. Or someone who skipped their court date. The people who I find are really well hidden."

Camden nodded slowly. He was starting to get a picture of what Baldwin Bowe did for a living. More than that, he was coming to understand what kind of man he was.

"Ghost bounty hunter?" said Troy, putting a name to Baldwin's job.

"Of sorts." Leaning back in the seat, he folded his arms. "I work hard to operate under the radar, and that's where I plan to stay."

"Understood," said Bryce with a nod.

Again, Camden's neck itched. He glanced over his shoulder once more. This time, the door to the coffee shop swung shut as a young woman walked down the street, coffee cup in hand.

Camden only caught a glimpse of her reflection in the glass door. She looked familiar. But from where? Then it hit him. Gripping the edge of the table, he leaned forward. "That's her," he hissed.

"Her who?" Bryce asked, brows drawn together.

"The witness." Camden rose to his feet and stopped. In the split second that he'd turned away, the woman was gone. "Where in the hell did she go?"

"Witness? Go?" Bryce was on his feet, as well. "What're you talking about?"

"I swear that woman who just walked out of the shop looked exactly like the female witness to the shooting." Energy pent up in Camden's core made him feel like a compressed spring. He just didn't know which way to explode.

Troy scanned the street. "Where'd she go?"

"You looking for the girl in the hoodie?" Baldwin asked. "She went around the corner." Baldwin pointed to the right. "That way."

"I'll go after her," said Camden. And then to Bryce, "You come around the block. Troy, you stay here in case she comes back."

He didn't wait to see if the agent or the detective had anything else to say. Sprinting down the sidewalk. Camden skidded to a stop. Rows of brownstones, renovated into apartment buildings, lined both sides of the street. Cars were parked at the curb.

Yet the woman was gone.

Bryce sprinted up the street and skidded to a stop. Sweat dampened his brow, and his breaths came in sharp gasps. "Where'd she go?"

Turning in a slow circle, Camden shook his head. Hundreds of windows looked down on the street. The woman could be in any one of the dwellings. Or none at all. She might've gotten in a car and driven away before Camden even realized what he'd seen. Bryce's question still hung in the air. *Where'd she go?*

"I don't know where she is, man."

"Let's get back to Baldwin and from there call Shea. He can increase patrols in this neighborhood and put them on the lookout for the witness."

Camden nodded while he felt his cheeks sting with the failure. "Sure thing."

Camden and Bryce returned to the coffee shop. Troy and Baldwin Bowe were on their feet.

"No luck in finding her," said Bowe.

Camden shook his head. "None."

Lifting the slip of paper with Randall's number, Baldwin said, "Unless you need anything else, I'm outta here."

"You know," said Troy, "there's a lot of questions I have."

"I've got no answers for you," Baldwin said, walking backward. "We'll be in touch."

He rounded the corner. On his seat lay the burner phone.

Bryce cursed. "I guess our man has slipped back into the shadows. Who knows when we'll find him next?"

Picking up the phone, Camden said, "I don't think we'll find him. But as soon as he talks to his brother, he'll find us."

Chapter Twelve

Chastity crouched by the door. A paper cup was clutched to her chest. Her heartbeat hammered, and her stomach threatened to revolt. Why had she gone out?

Of course, the police were still looking for her and Thad.

When she walked into Grave Gulch Coffee and Treats, there had been one guy at the table. Then, when she came out, there were three more. Even worse, she'd recognized the dark-haired man. He was the same one in the video at the police press conference.

It had taken every bit of willpower to walk slowly by the men. But the second she rounded the corner, Chastity sprinted to her apartment. It was only luck that she was less than half a block away.

Two panes of a grimy window filled the top third of the door. Rising to her knees, Chastity peeked outside. Nobody stood on the sidewalk. No cop car drove slowly down the street. Had she imagined it all?

There had been a table with four guys. That was a fact.

She tried to recall each detail. They all looked tough and, at the same time, professional. Had they been cops? Or had it been her imagination—a combo of runaway nerves, isolation and her hangover?

She stood. Her legs were wobbly. Her hands shook. Coffee sloshed out of the lid and onto her hoodie. "Damn," Chastity cursed.

"There you are." Thad's voice boomed from the top of the stairwell. He stood on the landing, looking down. Bare-chested, with abs and pecs that were well defined and covered in a fine sprinkling of hair. His sweats hung low at his hips, accentuating that sexy V-thing at his waist. God, he looked good—better than someone like Chastity deserved. One day soon she'd lose the extra weight that Thad kept mentioning. "Where the hell did you go?"

"The coffee shop." At least she got her coffee. Climbing the stairs, she continued. "I picked up a latte."

The door to the apartment stood open. "My head's killing me. Coffee sounds good." As Chastity brushed past him, he snagged the cup from her hand. "Thanks."

She opened her mouth to protest. Whatever she was about to say was forgotten as Thad placed his lips on hers. He tasted of stale wine and vape juice. "You do take care of me." Brushing his thumb over her breast, he added, "I like that."

Like a thousand butterflies had been let loose in her stomach, a fluttering filled her middle.

"Maybe we should go back to bed." With a smile, he lifted the cup to his lips. Immediately, he gagged. Choking with each step, he moved to the adjacent kitchen.

Chastity followed. "Oh my god, Thad. What's the matter?"

He spit into the sink. "What the hell, Chas? That

tastes like garbage. I hate soy milk." Flipping the lid off the cup, he dumped the drink down the drain. "You know that. I'm going back to bed."

Her throat was tight. Still, he would make love to her, and everything would be better, right?

"Okay, we can go to bed."

"We? I don't think so. I said that I'm going back." Without a backward glance, he wandered into the bedroom, leaving Chastity standing in the living room—alone and lonely. It was the same as it had been when she was a kid and her parents fought. Both of them so wrapped up in the argument they forgot she even existed.

Her eyes burned, and she moved to the kitchen. Opening a cabinet, she pulled out the instant coffee and a mug. After wiping at her eyes with her sleeve, she set the kettle on the stove to boil. As she measured a scoop of coffee powder into her cup, Chastity swore that her future would be different from her past.

All she needed was a new direction—and the courage to take the first step.

As a freshman in college, Grace had taken a psychology class. She remembered very little from that course, except that singing increased endorphins, a chemical in the brain that makes people happy.

At the time, it had been nothing more than a fact to be memorized and then repeated for a test. Yet, as Grace sat in the passenger seat of Madison's red sedan with a song blasting through the speakers, she knew that singing really had lifted her mood. For two hours, the entire trip to Kendall, the cousins had listened to

Grace's playlist. They sang every word, even if they were never quite on key.

Don Henley's "The Boys of Summer" filled the car. Leaning together, they belted out the lyrics.

Even as she sang, her thoughts returned to last night. Had she really had sex with Camden on the patio, hidden only by the shadows? That was a stupid question to ask, even if in her own mind.

Obviously, they'd done the deed.

What now?

Or maybe she should be asking another question. What would happen if the truth came out? Grace shuddered at the possible headlines.

She couldn't change what happened. What's more, a small part of her didn't want to. Having sex with Camden had been the most natural thing in the world.

Maybe her mood was lighter because of him than the singing.

Did she have the right to be happy? Was it okay, just for now? But what about her future? Would she ever be the one to look for a wedding dress? "Thanks for inviting me to come with you."

"I wouldn't want to pick out my wedding dress with anyone else." They rolled past a sign that read *Welcome to Kendall*. "How're you doing, by the way?"

"Glad to be out of Grave Gulch."

Looking out the window, Grace studied the shopping district of Kendall as they drove past. The street was lined on both sides with boutiques and cafés. A used bookstore sat next to a jewelry store. Across from the bookshop was a store that specialized in crystals and herbs. A sandwich board sat on the sidewalk: *Madame Q's Tarot Card Readings. Today 12–5 p.m.*

"How's the investigation?" Madison asked.

Grace stared out the window. "There's not much to tell. There's still no evidence that proves my side of the story." She lifted one shoulder and let it drop. "I want my job back. I don't know if I'll get what I want, though."

After pulling into a parking spot across the street from the bridal salon, Madison turned to Grace. "You can't be out of options."

"There were two witnesses—a guy and girl. They saw everything. In fact, they approached the man who'd been shot. But now?" Grace shook her head. "They've disappeared."

"Disappeared? How can two people disappear?" Madison echoed. "Are they magicians?" she said jokingly.

Grace gave a quiet chuckle. "Maybe they are. But I've been asking myself the same question. How can two people just fade into the mist?"

"Have you come up with an answer?" Madison turned off the ignition. The car went still and silent.

"Maybe they were from out of town. Maybe they've left Grave Gulch and don't even know that we're looking for them."

"Or?"

"They know what they saw." Grace pushed the sunglasses to the top of her head and looked at her cousin. "In fact, I keep thinking that they might've even taken the gun. Because of that, they don't want to be found."

"What else can you do?"

It was a good question and one that Grace had asked herself more than once. "I'm going to start by forgetting about the witnesses. Today is about you. Let's go look at that dress. You ready?"

Pressing her lips together, Madison stared out the windshield.

Yet again, Grace was filled with disquiet. Why the hesitancy? Did Madison love her fiancé? Did she even want to get married?

Honestly, Grace liked Alec. Still, she couldn't help but wonder if Madison simply had a plan for her life. College. Job. Marriage. Kids. And since marriage was next on her list, Alec was her best option for a husband.

She should say something. But what if Grace ruined her cousin's happiness?

Finally, the corners of Madison's mouth turned upward. A small smile played on her lips. "Actually, I am ready."

Grace opened the door and stepped from the car. It was late morning. The sun was shining, and the air was warm. In short, it was a perfect day. "All right, then. Let's go."

Madison exited her car. After using the fob to lock the doors, she held out her hand to Grace. "Let's go," she echoed.

As they crossed the street, Grace's mood was lighter than it had been in days.

Grace scanned the dresses displayed in the window. The gowns ranged from snowy white to cream to ivory to champagne and blush. Despite the various colors, the dresses had one thing in common. They all represented a dream come true. Someone had found their forever partner, and they were willing to devote their life to that person.

Madison had.

Melissa, Annalise and Desirée, too. Even Palmer had found someone he wanted to marry.

What about Grace? Would she ever find *the one*?

Her mind filled with images of Camden Kingsley. His hand on her elbow as they ran through the rain. His chest pressed into hers as they huddled in the doorway. And finally, her thoughts returned to the kiss. His touch. The moment he slid inside her. She sucked in a breath at the memory.

"You okay?" Madison asked. "You look a little…" Her words trailed off and she gazed just over Grace's shoulder.

Was now the time for Grace to confess all? "Something happened last night," she began. But Madison wasn't listening. Instead, she dug through her bag and pulled out her phone. Without a word, she snapped a picture of the street. Her hands shook.

It was Grace's turn to ask, "You okay?"

"Did you see him?" Madison asked, her voice shaking. Her skin was pale and sweat dotted her upper lip.

Grace turned. A guy, walking down the street, turned the corner. "Who's he?"

"I dunno, but he looked exactly like my brother Bryce, except with blond hair. Maybe dyed." She drew in a deep breath. "He looked exactly like my dad would look." Sighing, she shook her head. "I don't know where he went."

Whoever, or whatever, Madison saw was obviously gone. "C'mon." Hand on elbow, she steered Madison toward the boutique's door. "Let's go inside."

Madison dug her heels into the sidewalk, refusing to budge. "I got a picture." She held up the phone. "It's a little blurry, but do you see what I mean?"

Grace leaned in close. "Wow," she whispered. For a moment, she was weightless with disbelief. "He definitely looks like Bryce. I'll give you that. What d'you think?"

Madison's dad had died in combat when all of the kids were young. Aunt Verity had never got over losing the love of her life.

Madison shook her head. "Honestly, I don't know." She paused.

"You want a cup of coffee?" Grace asked, pointing to a café half a block away. They still had time before the appointment at the bridal salon.

"Do I ever."

In silence, they walked to the restaurant. Several tables were scattered on the sidewalk. "You sit," said Madison. "I'll get the coffee and be right back."

"I can come in with you. Help with the cups."

"I'm not fragile," said Madison. "Seeing that guy, well, it freaked me out a bit. But I'm perfectly fine now."

"You sure?"

"Positive." Madison pushed the door open with her shoulder and disappeared inside.

Madison returned moments later, two white mugs in hand. "Here you go," she said, setting one of the cups in front of Grace. "Sugar, no milk."

"Aww. You remembered." She took a sip.

"That's because I love you. You're more than a cousin. You're my friend."

Grace shared those feelings. That fact cemented what she needed to do—and say. "Are you sure you want to get married? I'm worried that your moment of hesitation was more about Alec than your father."

"I saw something," she insisted. "Some*one*."

Grace recalled the picture Madison captured on her phone. "The guy who you saw definitely resembles your brother." Another thought occurred to Grace. "What're you going to say to Aunt Verity?" she asked.

Madison shook her head. "I don't know. Nothing. I mean, it's not my dad, right? It's just some man. There's no reason to make my mom sad about some random guy."

Grace took a sip of coffee for courage. She was a cop and went into lots of difficult situations every day. But this was different. If she said the wrong thing, her words could wound Madison. "Besides, you didn't answer my question. Do you really want to marry Alec?"

While stirring her coffee, Madison sighed. "I'm not sure what I want." She added quickly, "He's a great guy."

Grace nodded. "He is."

"Our life would be perfect. Both of us are teachers. We share a passion for instructing our students."

"That's true," Grace agreed. "But do you share a passion for each other?"

"The sex is good, if that's what you're asking."

"I've found that even bad sex can still be pretty good." After pausing a beat, she added, "I'm joking."

"Mostly," said Madison, smiling. With a sigh, she went on. "I care for Alec. I respect him. Maybe I'm not head over heels in love, but maybe I don't need to be. I just want a nice life with a nice man."

"If what you want is a nice life with a nice man, then I won't ever talk you out of your happiness. It's just that I've been wondering." She sipped her coffee again, not sure if she really wanted to continue the conversation. Actually, she didn't.

Madison coaxed her. "You've been wondering what?"

Grace had decided not to say anything, yet she couldn't help herself. "What's going on?"

"I always thought that once I found the dress, everything would feel different. I'd be ready to plan the wedding."

"And you aren't?"

Madison said nothing. The silence was an answer in itself.

Grace tried again. "Why aren't you sure about the wedding?"

"I don't know," said Madison, dropping her gaze to the table.

"Is it Alec?"

With a shake of her head, Madison said, "No. He's great."

"There's a difference between great and wanting to spend the rest of your life with someone." Again, Camden's face came to mind.

"I want to marry Alec. It's just… I know either one of my uncles will fill in, but my dad won't be there to walk me down the aisle."

"Oh, honey." She reached for Madison's hand. Grace was lucky to have both of her parents, and she could only imagine the hole that must take up a big part of Madison's heart. "Wherever your dad is, he's looking down on you right now and smiling."

"You think?" A single tear snaked down Madison's cheek.

"I know." She riffled through her bag for a pack of

tissues. Holding them out to Madison, she said, "I just wonder if all the reluctance about picking a dress has more to do with wanting more than safety than it does with finding the perfect dress."

Madison shrugged. "I'll think about what you said."

"I just want you to be happy, so that's all."

Madison smiled. "I want the same for me—and you, too."

The conversation hit a snag. For a long moment, the two women just sat, sipping their coffees. She wanted to tell Madison about what happened with Camden last night. Did she dare?

"So, what's the verdict on the dress?" Grace finally asked.

"Since I don't have a verdict on the wedding yet, I guess I shouldn't be worried about the dress."

Grace drank the last swallow of her coffee. There had been a definite tone to her cousin's voice. What had it been? Disappointment? Resignation? Then she knew: it had been relief.

"You ready?" Madison asked, getting to her feet.

"If you are." Grace stood, as well. They walked past the bridal boutique. The large window was filled with dresses. Pausing, Grace looked inside and saw her reflection superimposed on a wedding gown. As she stood there, she had but two thoughts. What would it feel like to be getting married? And what was Camden Kingsley doing at that exact moment?

SITTING ON HIS sofa after meeting Baldwin Bowe and losing the female witness, Camden knew his job to be objective about all investigations. However, this time was different. This time, he'd become personally involved with the subject, Grace Colton.

Actually, he was more than personally involved. He'd taken her as his lover. He needed to get off the case now before things got more complicated.

Picking up the phone from the coffee table, he placed the call without another thought.

Arielle answered on the third ring. "Camden?" The DA's voice was overly loud. In the background he could hear a cheering crowd. "Are you there?"

"I'm here," he yelled back.

"Give me a second."

"Sorry to interrupt," Camden began. It was noon on a Saturday. He should've guessed that she'd be busy. Maybe he shouldn't have called at all. "I have news."

"Good or bad?"

"A little of both. We made contact with Baldwin Bowe." Camden spent a few minutes telling the story of the meeting at the coffee shop. He included the details of Baldwin's job as a ghost bounty hunter and his acrimonious relationship with his brother. Camden continued, "He took the number for Randall and left his own burner behind."

"That's better than good news. That's actually great news," said Arielle. Her voice was so bright that Camden's phone practically glowed. "Anything else?"

"I saw someone who resembled the female witness from the shooting."

"Really? What did she say?"

"I never got a chance to speak to her. She seemed to…" Camden paused and rubbed the back of his neck. "She seemed to disappear."

"That is bad news," said Arielle.

"There's more." Camden inhaled. "I'm taking a leave of absence."

"You're doing what? The phone must have lousy reception at the park. It sounded like you said you're taking leave."

"I am, Arielle. I need…" What should he say next? *I need a break. Time off. Time to evaluate my career.* No, he owed her honesty at the very least. "Grace Colton's case has become more than a job for me."

The other line was filled with silence. Had the call dropped?

"You there?" he asked.

"I'm still here," she said, her words clipped. "Now I know what you've been trying to tell me and why." She didn't wait for him to reply. "You have feelings for Grace Colton, don't you?"

There was no denying the truth. Yet how had she guessed? "It's not something I planned."

"I'll give you today to think things through. Because if you take a leave now, I'll do everything in my power to make sure there's no job for you later." With that, Arielle ended the call.

The DA's words were like a knife to his chest, with the last little bit of a twist—just to be certain that it hurt like hell. She'd get him fired from a job? *Him?* Seriously?

Did it matter if he had to turn his back on the truth? Did he really want to keep his job if it meant staying away from Grace?

Maybe he should be asking another question. What did Grace want from him?

Well, as far as he was concerned, there was only one way to find out.

Chapter Thirteen

The drive back to Grave Gulch from Kendall was bleak and overcast. A bank of dark clouds hung low in the sky, and rain fell. The wipers moved back and forth. Grace stared at the trail on the windshield. The continual *swish*, *swish*, *swish* lulled her into a trance.

She kept asking herself a single question. What was she supposed to do about Camden Kingsley?

What would Melissa do?

Well, that question was easy to answer. Melissa would never allow herself to get into a such a mess.

Grace had to put Camden out of her mind, her life and her heart. It's just that sometimes doing the right thing was so damned hard.

"I have to say," Madison said, glancing at Grace, "you look miserable."

"Then, I look better than I feel." Grace gave a feeble laugh.

"You want to start your playlist?"

She looked out the side window. The dark and dreary weather matched her mood perfectly. "Not really."

"What's going on? Are you worried about the Internal Affairs investigation?"

"Among other things?"

"What *other things*?"

Grace silently cursed. She hadn't meant to drag Madison into what had happened with Camden last night. If she didn't want to talk to her cousin, she never should've given such an evasive answer. "I screwed up."

"What happened?"

"You know the IA investigator? Camden?"

"The sexy guy you brought to Palmer's party last night?"

"He's the one," she confirmed.

"And?"

"And last night we kissed." There, she'd said it. In truth, it had been so much more than just a kiss.

"Really?" Madison gaped at Grace.

"Hey, eyes back on the road," Grace said, using her best cop voice.

"Yes, Officer Colton. But what happened? I mean, aside from you kissing that dreamy guy." Madison took the exit that led to downtown Grave Gulch. Pulling up to a stoplight, she turned. "You have to tell me. What happened?"

"Well," Grace began, "we went out to the patio and… I don't know. His lips were on mine. Mine were on his. Hands were touching lots of interesting places." There was no way that she was going to admit to having had sex with Camden. Okay, she'd thought about sharing with Madison a little bit earlier, but there was no way she was going to drag her cousin into her mess. "But that's not the point of the story."

"It seems like a pretty solid story to me. Do you like him?"

"What's there to not like?" Her insides felt as if

they'd been filled with mud. It was disappointment. "He's handsome."

"I noticed," said Madison, with a smile. "Trust me."

"He's smart. He's dedicated. Honest. He has integrity. My middle fills with butterflies every time he's around. And if he smiles?" She shook her head. "Forget about it. I can't even." Grace sighed and leaned her head on the window. They were in Grace's neighborhood. Soon, she'd be home. Then, she'd hide in her apartment, shutting away her worries along with the rest of the world. "Basically, he's perfect."

"Okay, so why are you miserable?"

"He's with IA." She paused before adding the most damning part of all. "And he's investigating me."

"Oh," Madison slumped in her seat, a birthday balloon losing air. "I didn't think about it that way. I can see how the kissing and the touching could be a problem, then."

"Beyond being unprofessional, what if he thinks that I'm trying to influence the investigation? What if he thinks that I let this happen to distract him? What if he thinks Robert Grimaldi didn't have a gun and my whole story is BS?" Once she started to worry, it was impossible to turn it off. "What if he hates me?"

"I might not be the best person to give you advice on your love life. Still, I don't blame you for being upset. There could definitely be consequences."

It was a nice way of saying that if the situation ever became public, the GGPD would have to fire Grace—and Camden would lose his job, too. "I know."

"But you like him?" Madison asked, her voice soothing.

"I do like him a lot."

"That's a problem, then." Madison exhaled, as the car stopped once again at a traffic signal. "What are you going to do?"

"There's only one way out of this mess. I can't see Camden anymore." Grace shook her head.

"That's probably wise," said Madison. She turned onto Grace's street.

"What do I say to him?"

"I'm not sure what you should say." Madison pulled into a parking place in front of Grace's building. "Whatever it is, you have to figure it out now."

Before she got the chance to ask what Madison meant, Grace's eyes were drawn to the steps leading to her building. Leaning on the rail, there stood Camden Kingsley.

CAMDEN WATCHED AS a car pulled up next to the curb. It was Grace. If someone had asked him how he knew, he wasn't sure that he could put it into words. It was just something he sensed—not with his mind but his heart and his soul.

The passenger door opened, and she stepped from the car. His pulse raced.

"Hey. I didn't expect to see you here."

"I hope you don't mind," he began. Camden felt a pull—like iron to a magnet—drawing him to her. "I think we should talk."

"About the case?"

"About us," he said.

"First, I need to say goodbye." She glanced over her shoulder. With a wave, the woman behind the wheel drove off. "That was my cousin," Grace added. "I guess she had to go."

"I guess so." Was it his imagination or was Grace distant?

He asked, "Is there someplace we can talk?"

"What about here?"

No. It wasn't his imagination. There was something different about Grace. Well, he didn't need to waste time skirting the facts. "I quit my job."

"Your job? You quit?" she echoed. Grace would never give up being a police officer for anything—even an affair. "How can you walk away from your job? I thought you were devoted to your career."

"I am."

"Then, why?"

"You."

"Me?" She held up her palms. He'd quit? That was something Grace would never do. "You have to think this through."

"I have," he began.

"I know what happened last night was completely unprofessional. It was a mistake. If we just avoid each other, then nobody has to quit anything."

Camden's cheeks stung, as if he'd been slapped. To be honest, he didn't know what kind of reaction he had expected. Still, this wasn't it. *A mistake? He was a mistake?*

Or maybe *mistake* was the perfect word. He'd been mistaken about Grace and their connection. True, he didn't get serious about most of the women he dated. But he'd always been a good judge of character. How had he been so wrong this time?

Then the idea hit him, and he went cold. "Was last night an act? Was everything between us a ruse?"

"No, Camden. That's not it."

She reached for him. Her fingertips brushed the back of his hand. He shook off the touch.

"What is it, then?" he asked, filled with fury.

"I wish the circumstances were different. I wish I could be with you—that we could be together. I can't. We can't. It'd ruin both of our careers."

"Correction. It'll only ruin *your* job." Even he heard the venom in his tone. He didn't care. "I already quit."

"I didn't ask you to leave the DA's office. If you'd come to me first, maybe we could've figured this out."

Then he knew why it hurt so bad. Camden was willing to sacrifice everything for Grace. And she wasn't able to do the same for him. His anger vanished, leaving the landscape of his soul as nothing but a charred wasteland. He swallowed. What else was there to say?

His phone began to trill. The ringing was loud on the quiet street. Camden checked the caller ID. Bryce Colton. What'd Bryce have to say? Had Baldwin Bowe called back? If he wasn't working with the DA, then Randall Bowe wasn't his concern anymore, either.

"Go ahead," said Grace with a flick of her wrist. "I can tell that you want to answer it."

He swiped the call open. "What d'you have for me, man?"

"I was able to run Robert Grimaldi's name through the firearm registry for several states. Not all of them have a database, but he didn't turn up in the ones that do."

"So, he's never registered a gun?" Camden asked, his heart slammed into his chest. Was this another dead end to his attempts to prove that Grace's story was true?

"Like I said, several states don't monitor gun ownership. He could've crossed into Pennsylvania and bought a gun. It'd be a legal purchase, and he'd never show up because they don't keep records." Bryce paused. "Or the gun might be stolen. Bought illegally. There's lots of other ways that Grimaldi might've gotten his hands on a firearm. But if you're hoping to pressure him because he made a false statement to you, owning a gun won't work."

"Thanks for checking. I owe you a favor."

"I'll call it in someday. Gotta go."

The call ended. The line was dead. Still, Camden held the phone to his ear. The echo of his pulse resonated in the base of his skull. Only a moment ago, he'd been wounded. What else was he supposed to call it? He wanted Grace, but she clearly didn't want him in return.

Now, though, Camden had a different set of questions. Had he been duped? Was everything he'd been told—or heard from the police—meant to protect Grace Colton?

He placed his phone in his pocket.

"I'll ask you this for the last time." He drew in a deep breath and looked at Grace. "Are you positive that Robert Grimaldi had a gun?"

"Positive."

"Is there any way, at all, that you might've been mistaken?"

"None."

"Are you sure?"

Instead of answering the question, she turned to him. "Who was on the phone?"

Had Camden been a fool from the beginning? Certainly, he'd been a fool last night when he'd had sex with her on the patio. Finally, he saw how recklessly he'd acted. But had he been so enamored with Grace that he never thought the unthinkable? *Could* she have shot an unarmed civilian? "Why won't you answer the question?"

"Why won't you tell me who was on the phone? The call obviously changed your mood."

Fair enough. He shrugged. "It was your cousin, Bryce. He ran Robert Grimaldi's name through every firearm registry in the country."

"And?"

"And Grimaldi's name didn't come up."

"Oh."

Oh? Was that all she had to say? "You don't seem surprised."

"There are lots of states without databases. You said so yourself."

So he had. Still, Camden wasn't in the mood to be patronized. As if quitting his job over Grace Colton wasn't bad enough, Camden had compromised his character for nothing. Hell, he'd thrown away his dad's legacy. The fact that he'd been blind left him ill and filled with self-loathing. "Is there any way you could be mistaken about what you saw?"

Grace lifted her chin. "I know that Grimaldi had a gun. What's more, I don't think I like what you're implying."

"And what's that?"

She drew in a deep breath. "I've been lying to you all along."

Implying, hell. Camden was starting to think that might be the truth. He said nothing.

"In fact," she continued, "why don't you just go?"

HAD GRACE JUST told to Camden to leave? She had. Well, he didn't need to be told twice.

Stewing in the juices of his own anger, he'd gone directly from Grace's apartment to the DA's office. Having found some empty boxes in recycling, he stood in his office. One box was only halfway filled—yet it contained all of his personal belongings. There were two commendations. A picture of Camden with his state-police-academy class at graduation. A photograph of his father in uniform. He had a picture with his mom—also from the day he graduated from the state-police academy. A couple of coffee cups. A house plant, which needed water.

In a second box, he had all of the equipment belonging to the IA. His ID. His gun. His laptop. All the gear used for surveillance: a camera, a microphone, a wireless transmitter and receiver.

How many hours had he spent in this very room? Yet it took him only minutes to clear away any evidence that he'd ever been here at all. Wasn't that how he lived, too?

Never making connections.

Never having relationships.

Never really caring about anyone—and only searching for the truth.

That was, until he met Grace.

Regret sat heavy on his shoulders. Maybe it was better to be alone. He'd forgotten how much caring about another person could hurt.

"I didn't expect to see you here." Arielle stood at his door.

"I figured I'd take some time to get packed up. Save myself from coming in on Monday morning."

Arielle leaned on the doorjamb. "We have to talk, but I definitely don't want you to quit."

"I thought that you swore to get me fired."

She sighed. "I take that back."

Camden's pencil holder was an old tea tin that his grandmother had given him when he was in high school. Dumping the pens and pencils into a desk drawer, he placed the tin in the box. "I was wrong about everything with Grace Colton."

"Are you saying that Grimaldi didn't have a gun?"

"Not exactly."

"Are you saying that Grace lied to you? Or that she gave a false statement?"

"I'm not saying that, either."

"What are you saying, then?"

Now, that was a good question. "There's no way to prove Grace's version of events. Furthermore, I've been focused on proving that she was innocent, not on finding the facts."

"I won't argue with you there."

"I've lost your confidence. I should go."

"Obviously I can't force you to stay with Internal Affairs. Just know that everyone screws up," she said, "especially where the heart is concerned."

"Not me," said Camden. He picked up the box of his belongings.

"Why, because you don't have a heart? I know

you're with Internal Affairs, but I always thought the heartless thing was a joke."

"I have a heart," said Camden, ignoring the fact that Arielle's joke was a little funny. In fact, he knew that he had a heart, because right now his was breaking.

"I understand that love and attraction and passion make us all do crazy things."

"You do?"

"You don't have to sound surprised. I might be fifty-two years old, but I'm not dead. Besides, I have kids. You know where they come from."

Camden held the box in one hand and lifted the other palm in surrender. "I don't need the biology lesson, but thanks. I do have to ask, what're you getting at?"

"You tried to tell me about Grace from the beginning. I respect that, and I'm sorry that I didn't listen. Stay or go—the choice is yours."

GRACE STAYED ON the sidewalk long after Camden had driven away. Her low back was tight from time in shoes that were much more cute than comfortable. Pulling her phone from her bag, she placed a call.

Madison answered. "How'd it go?"

"Horrible," she said, her throat raw. Since she'd joined the force, being a good police officer had been her only priority. Even after having sex with Camden, she'd never intended for her focus to change.

Maybe that had been her first mistake.

"How are you?" Madison asked.

"Horrible," Grace said again. "Overwhelmed."

"Are you still at home?"

Technically, she was standing in front of her building. "I am."

"Hold on one second. I'll be right over."

Grace's legs felt like they'd been dipped in concrete. Slowly, she walked up the short flight of steps to the front door. Just as she slid the key into the lock, Madison parked at the curb.

"That was fast," said Grace, as her cousin stepped from her car.

"I didn't go far."

"I'm glad." She opened the door.

"Let's get to your apartment, and you can tell me everything."

Within minutes, they were sitting on Grace's sofa. Madison made both of them cups of tea. Grace held the steaming mug in her hands.

Tucking her feet beneath her, Madison asked, "What went so horribly?"

"He quit his job for me."

"He what?" Madison asked, her jaw slack.

"Yeah, he wanted to help me prove my innocence, and he quit."

"I can see why you'd be horrified. A great guy wants to make sure that you're treated fairly." She shivered with the willies. "Awful stuff."

"Can you be serious? Please?"

"I'm sorry for teasing, but I don't understand why you're upset. You met a lovely guy. He cares about you. You care about him. On top of it all, he's willing to sacrifice everything for you."

Grace wasn't sure that she understood, either. It was sort of like all the advice and warnings she'd been given after the shooting. True, her family meant well, but did they really think she couldn't make the right choices? "Maybe I don't want to be taken care of. I might be the Colton baby, but I'm not actually a child."

"In a perfect world, what would you have wanted from Camden?"

It was a good question and one which Grace didn't have a ready answer for. She sipped her tea. "I wish he had talked to me first. Told me what he planned to do."

"Then what would you have done?"

"I don't know. I mean, we only met a few days ago. It seems a little hasty to change our lives for one another." She knew what her cousin was trying to do: make Grace see that her situation wasn't as awful as she originally thought. She wasn't ready to calm down or to forgive Camden, though. "He accused me of lying about the gun. He asked me if I was mistaken."

"Are you? Lying or mistaken?"

"Of course not."

"But you're offended that he asked?"

"Damn straight."

"Can I tell you what I see?" Madison stretched out her final word, and Grace knew she wouldn't like the picture her cousin wanted to present. "You're in a tough situation. But it's not impossible. If you care for Camden, you might have to make some sacrifices, but you two can be together. Look at Troy and Evangeline. But they talked to each other and worked it out." Madison's words hung in the air. "If you want to be with Camden, you can. If you don't, you never have to see him again. The choice is up to you, Grace. The question is, what do you want?"

CAMDEN STOOD IN his office. On the desk sat the two boxes. He needed to take one with him. But which should he choose?

True, he'd overreacted to Grace's rejection.

He could've handled the whole situation a little bit—okay, make that a whole lot—better.

Even without the romance in question, he still had a choice to make.

If he'd been wrong about Grace, then his personal and professional judgment was fried. There was no need for him to stay at Internal Affairs. Camden would never again trust himself.

It was just that he was so damn sure that Grimaldi had a gun—forget that there wasn't a single fact to prove that theory.

Was it him? Was he wrong?

No gun had been found at the scene.

Nobody had called the police with the witnesses' identities.

In fact, nobody had seen them at all since the night of the shooting.

Correction: Camden had seen the female witness. He was certain that she'd run from him.

It brought up an interesting question. How had she known he was working with the cops? He wasn't exactly in the public eye.

Then again...

He took his phone from his pocket and opened the app for the TV station out of Kendall.

A story about the press conference at GGPD appeared first. It was accompanied by dozens of comments and a video. He pressed the play arrow. The camera focused on Melissa as the briefing began. Then with Melissa's voice still in the background, the aspect moved and panned the crowd.

"Well, I have a second announcement to make. I can see that the citizens of Grave Gulch have lost confidence in the GGPD and in our ability to keep peace in the city. But it's my responsibility to maintain a trust between the town and the police department. I haven't. Therefore, I'll be stepping down as chief of police."

Behind the podium, a group of police officers were gathered inside. Most of the people were little more than shadowy figures, yet a single face was recognizable.

It was Camden's.

Picking up a box from his desk, he walked out the door.

Chapter Fourteen

Grace's career was in tatters. Her love life was a wreck. Sitting on the sofa, she didn't know which was worse—or how she could make either one right. The indecision ate at her.

Her phone rang. It was Camden. She sucked in a breath. What was she supposed to say? Did she want to apologize? Ignore the call? Tell him to leave her alone?

"I didn't know if you'd call me again," she said, answering the phone.

"I think there's a lot for us to talk about, but there's something I need to show you. Can you let me in?"

"In?"

"Look outside."

Grace moved to her window. Pulling aside the curtain, she looked onto the street. Camden stood on the sidewalk, cardboard box in hand. He saw her and waved. That same old fluttering erupted in her belly, traveling down her arms and legs until her toes tingled.

"Give me a second," she said into the phone.

On the street, he gave her a *thumbs-up*.

Within seconds, she was standing at the front door. Camden was at her side.

"I'm not sure where to begin," she said.

He held up the box. "There's something I want to show you, first."

"Come up to my place," she said.

They said nothing as they walked up to her apartment. Inside, Camden put the box on her kitchen table. It settled with a thunk.

"What's in there?"

He opened the lid and lifted out a picture of a man who looked an awful lot like Camden. "This is my dad," he said, handing her the photo.

"He looks nice. Detroit beat cop, right?"

"My dad was charged with unauthorized use of force, too. IA was called." He paused. "The investigation didn't go well for him. It was easier to blame my dad than have the public indict the entire department."

Grace stepped closer to him. She wanted to touch him again. Did she dare? "I'm sorry."

"It's why…" he began.

"It's why you do what you do. Why you're always fair. And why you're always looking for the truth."

"There's more, though."

"Oh?"

"It's what happened with him afterward." Camden paused. "He, well, he took his own life because of it. I was fifteen years old."

"Oh, Camden, I am so, so sorry." Her chest ached as it opened to a bottomless well of grief. She needed to console him. But how? She touched his arm. "Sincerely."

"I never talk about, but it's always with me."

"What happened to your mom?"

"She still lives in Detroit. I don't see her a lot, even though I should."

"Family is a good thing to have."

"After being around the Coltons for the past two days, I'm starting to think that they are. A good family, I mean."

Grace traced the side of his face with her finger. He leaned in to her touch. "You're a good man, Camden Kingsley."

"Am I?" He reached for her hand. She wound her fingers through his, and he pulled her close. He caressed the inside of her wrist with his thumb.

"You are."

He shook his head. "If I was a good guy, I never would have made love to you last night. I never would've taken advantage."

"You act like I didn't have a say-so in what happened. You aren't to blame. For anything."

"There's more, though." He unloaded the box. There was a wireless microphone. A camera with a long-range lens. A remote receiver for the mic.

"What's all of this for?" she asked.

"This is what we're going to use to prove that Robert Grimaldi had a gun."

Camden's plan was simple, direct and all the more difficult in its simplicity.

He started by telling Grace, "I saw the female witness this morning."

"You what?" Grace's tone was incredulous. "How'd you see her? What happened?"

"I was with your cousin Bryce this morning."

"What were you doing with him?"

Grace had about a million questions. He told the story about meeting Bryce at the FBI office. The call from her brother, Troy. Camden going with Bryce to meet with Randall's brother because of his involvement in the case. The woman who came out of the coffee shop and then vanished. He ended with, "I didn't get a great look at the woman, but I swear it was her."

"What d'you think? Where'd she go?"

"At first, I assumed it was all just a string of coincidences. Maybe the lady I saw looked like the witness, but was it her?" He shrugged. "Then, as far as the disappearance, Bryce and I figured it was a car parked nearby. I mean, even if it was the witness, she'd have no reason to run from me. Then I saw this." He played the press-conference video on his phone.

Grace chewed on her bottom lip. "I saw it yesterday. There's footage of you in the film."

"Exactly." He stopped the video at the moment his face was visible.

"So what're you thinking?"

"I think that this woman lives near Grave Gulch Coffee and Treats. I think she knows that the police want to talk to her, and that's why she ran."

"It also means she has something to hide."

"She has something to hide," he repeated. "But we know more about her."

"Which is?"

This was the part that he loved—when all the pieces fell into place, and the puzzle became a picture. "She keeps track of what's posted about the story. Although, no surprise there. Most criminals do. But I think she's a fan of this reporter—Harper Sullivan."

"I don't disagree with anything you're saying, but how does that help us at all?"

Camden's eyes were bright with hope and anticipation. "If we could get a specific kind of story on the news—one that reaches out to the witness—I think she might react. But this was the place where my plan falls apart. To make that happen, we have to get the reporter to work with us."

Grace lifted a brow. Her cousin Stanton had connections to the media, through his love, reporter Dominique. "I think I know someone who might help…"

IT TOOK ONLY a few texts to get a number for Harper Sullivan. After a short call, she agreed to meet at Grace's apartment. On the phone Grace had given few details, but as she settled on a chair, Camden knew that to get the reporter's cooperation, they had to be more than honest: they had to be compelling.

Grace sat on one end of the sofa; Camden was on the other side. Harper sat in a chair and faced them both. Camden glanced at his watch—two thirty—as Grace started the conversation.

"We have reason to believe that the witnesses to Thursday night's shooting live near Grave Gulch Coffee and Treats. We also think she follows your reporting online. I'd like to use the TV station's platform to reach out."

Harper stared at Grace. Several seconds passed. "You what?"

"My gut tells me that this witness might feel guilty for hiding. I think reaching out personally could help her find the courage to contact the authorities."

"I'd like to help you, Grace. Trust me, nobody wants to find the truth more than I do. But I'll be honest. This isn't how our station typically works."

"Think of it this way. The TV station will get an exclusive interview with Grace," said Camden. Harper lifted a brow. From the look, he could tell she wasn't convinced. After pausing, he added, "We can give you a heads-up if the interview leads to an arrest."

Harper's eyes widened as she drew in a short breath. Both gestures were subtle, gone as quickly as they came. Yet he was trained to look for the almost imperceptible and, moreover, discern what it meant. Right now, Sullivan was hooked. But was she interested enough for Camden to reel her in?

"Arrest for what?"

"Tampering with evidence," said Grace.

"The missing gun?" Harper asked.

Camden had been right. The reporter was smart.

With a quick nod, Grace echoed, "The missing gun."

Harper wrote in her notebook. "What else can you tell me? Something I haven't already heard."

"They're in Grave Gulch." Camden leaned forward. "Hiding from the police. They might have a firearm, along with a willingness to break the law. We need to reach them—the woman, in particular. You say you want to keep the community safe, but are you really ready to help?"

Tapping her pen on the paper, Harper sighed. "I'll do it. Tell me what you need."

4:11 p.m.

CHASTITY HAD DONE little all day...beyond refreshing the TV station's app, that is. Nothing had been posted to the site or app since the release of this morning's stories.

Maybe she'd gotten it all wrong. Maybe the guy she saw was, well, just a guy and not the same one from the press-conference video. Maybe him being at the coffee shop had nothing to do with Chastity, and the problem really was in her imagination.

Rolling her shoulders, she smirked.

Yeah, it was all just imagination.

What would it hurt to refresh the app one last time?

A new article appeared at the top of the list. The headline read: *Witness Sought in Police Shooting. Cop Asks for Community Help.*

There, next to an embedded video, was the sketch of Chastity. She studied the image. The nose on the drawing was too big. Still, it was a decent likeness. If she and Thad had bothered to make any friends in Grave Gulch, certainly someone would've recognized her already.

An entire month in one place and not a single friend—except Thad.

She glanced at the open bedroom door. The curtains were still drawn, leaving the room gloomy. Yet his form, draped over the bed, was unmistakable—as were the snores and the stench of stale booze and BO.

Chastity glanced back to the phone in her hand. A triangle-shaped Play button was superimposed on the video. Drawing in a deep breath, she pressed it.

The fuzzy image cleared, and the face of a blonde woman filled the screen. Chastity swallowed. It was the cop she'd seen on the street. Funny, at the time she hadn't realized that the officer was young—for a cop, anyway. In fact, she wasn't much older than Chastity.

A caption read: *Officer Grace Colton, accused of shooting an unarmed civilian, has been put on administrative leave pending the results of an investigation.*

"Officer Colton" came an off-camera voice. Was

that a reporter? Chastity assumed so. "What do you want our viewers to know about the witnesses you saw at the scene of the shooting?"

Grace looked directly into the camera. Chastity shivered, though she certainly wasn't cold. Was it excitement? Trepidation?

The video continued to play. "First, I know that they're still in the area. The female witness was seen this morning. She knows that the police want to speak to her, but she's hiding."

"What if she doesn't want to be found? What will you do then?" the reporter's voice asked.

"I'd like to make a direct plea." Sitting taller, Grace continued. "We both know what you saw, and I can only guess why you haven't come forward. Maybe you don't like the police much. Or maybe you're worried about getting into trouble because you ran. If you're hiding, then you know what really happened. If you care about the community—you need to tell the truth. I want you to know you can come to me." Grace paused. The seconds passed like an eternity, and a breath was trapped in Chastity's chest. "I can help. If you let me, I can be your friend."

Friend. The word echoed through the silent room, louder than cannon fire.

Could Chastity and Grace really be friends? Grace had been right. Chastity did need help. Could she trust the cop, though? Hadn't she tried that before? That time, her trust had been completely misplaced.

Yet her gaze was drawn to Thad's computer system. Multiple monitors, keyboards and a server all sat on a folding table.

She'd met Thad in the first week of college, both

of them majoring in IT. The professor paired them to work together on a project. Chastity still recalled the feeling of her stomach being tied in knots as the teams were announced.

Thad was in his last year of school and the best-looking guy in a room filled with men. He had an easy smile that Chastity, barely out of high school, had felt in her toes. The first time he smiled *at her*—well, she felt it in an entirely different part of her body.

Did it matter that once they'd become a couple, she dropped out of school and worked at a fast-food restaurant to help pay for Thad's degree? Honestly, it made sense that one of them work while the other went to school. Right? Besides, Thad was closer to graduating than she had been.

She might not have a degree yet. Still, she knew her way around the internet better than most. Taking a deep breath, Chastity rose from the sofa and walked quietly across the room. She closed the bedroom door. After taking a seat at the workstation, she booted up Thad's computer. It wouldn't take her long to find a number for Grace Colton—no matter how well she protected her account.

Once she got the number, then what? Well, Chastity would have to make some tough choices.

4:26 p.m.

THE INTERVIEW HAD gone live only moments earlier. Sitting on her sofa, Grace couldn't slow the racing drumbeat of her pulse. Nor could she stop from asking a single question. What if the plan didn't work?

Leaning back into the cushion, she sighed.

Camden sat beside her. She glanced his way. His dark hair was tousled. Stubble covered his cheeks and chin. He was exquisite, and her stomach tightened.

Her phone pinged with an incoming text. Grace glanced at the screen. The message came from a blocked number. Her pulse picked up speed.

I saw your interview on the TV station's site.

She held up the phone for Camden to see.

"That was fast," he said. "You think it's the witness?"

That's exactly what she thought—or hoped, at least. She tapped out her reply.

You did? Who's this?

Three dots danced in the reply field as the other person responded. The seconds stretched out.

"Come on," Camden urged. "Come on."

Ping.

Grace read the message out loud. "*A friend.*" She paused. "A friend?"

"It's the witness." Camden gave her wrist a squeeze. "They're repeating the last lines in your interview, you remember?"

"*I can help,*" she repeated her earlier words. "*If you let me, I can be your friend.*"

"She wants your help," said Camden. "My guess, she feels trapped and needs a way out."

Grace exhaled. Did she dare to hope this nightmare was finally ending? "What do I do? What do I say?"

"You want to try and meet with her," said Camden. "That's the end game." He paused. "Ask her if she saw something."

"*I need all the friends I can get.*" Grace spoke while typing the message. "*Did you see something?*" She sent the text.

The dots flashed in the text field again.

"She's thinking about what to say," said Camden.

Grace tried to swallow. Her mouth was too dry.

The phone pinged with another message.

I know what happened…

Grace texted back.

How?

The reply:

I heard something at a party.

Camden said, "It's the witness, for sure."

"How do you know?"

"The text is a lie. The witnesses haven't been out. They haven't spoken to anyone. Nobody around here has heard anything."

Grace:

Do you know who saw the shooting?

Unknown number:

I've heard some names mentioned.

Grace replied.

Who???

Grace watched the text field. She waited a minute. Then a minute more. Five minutes passed. It was then she asked another question aloud. "What if this is a random prankster?"

Camden shifted where he sat. His shoulder grazed hers. Grace wanted to lean in to him and ask him to hold her once more. She sat up taller.

"That's a fair question. You need to get her to interact with you more."

"So, what do I do? You're the expert in getting people to tell the truth."

"Be honest with her. Tell her you're worried that she's a scam. Then suggest a meeting."

"What good will a meeting do? What if I talk to her and she still doesn't want to come forward?" She lifted her phone, letting the dropped thread prove her point. "I don't see this person being overly eager to chat with the police."

"That's why you're lucky I'm here. I brought all my surveillance equipment. Camera. Microphone and receiver. You wear the wire. I'll park at the end of the block. If you get this person to talk to you, I can record every word spoken."

"Is this legal? Will this be admissible at a trial?" She knew the answer to the first question. Michigan was a "one-party" state. Simply put, one party in a conversation could legally record what was being said without notifying the other. Truly, she didn't know if the recording would stand up in a trial, or not.

Camden said, "Right now, let's see what we get. If we can prove your story, then this case may never go to court."

On a certain level, the whole setup felt sneaky to Grace. True, she wasn't pretending to be someone—or something—she wasn't. If the witness was willing to meet. If the witness had anything important to share. *If. If. If.*

Grace typed a message before holding up the phone for Camden to read.

"Looks good," he said.

She pressed the Send button. "It's done," she said. "Now all we can do is hope that she replies…"

CHASTITY'S CHEST WAS TIGHT; her breastbone hurt. Contacting Grace Colton had been a mistake. The police weren't to be trusted. They'd failed her before. All those years ago, they'd failed her mother, as well.

Yet, she reread the text.

If you saw something, we need to talk. There's a coffee shop near the park. Grave Gulch Coffee and Treats. Meet me there in 20 mins?

It was almost five o'clock in the evening. Thad was still in bed. She knew the weekend routine. Drink too much and stay up late on Friday. Sleep all day Saturday. Up again at 9:00 p.m., ready for another round of bingeing on booze.

Okay, she was only nineteen years old. But was this the life she wanted?

Now was the time that Chastity needed to decide about her loyalty. Was it to Thad? Or the truth?

She felt the gun's presence, tucked into the drawer and hidden under a stack of papers. In her mind's eye she saw it, dangerous and deadly. Having it in her house wasn't actually making the world a better place. In fact, it was the opposite.

It was true that nobody actually liked the cops. Unless they needed help.

On top of that, Grace Colton had already seen Chastity—and Thad, too. If Chastity showed up at the meeting, the police officer would know that Chastity hadn't heard rumors or stories at a party. She'd been the one who'd caused all the trouble by grabbing the weapon and refusing to come forward. Was she really willing to take that kind of heat? What if leaving the scene was a crime? Certainly, taking the gun would be illegal.

After tapping in her message, she hit Send. Leaning back into the sofa, she sighed and looked at the screen one last time.

I'll be there, the message read.

She'd told Grace Colton that she'd meet with her. But there was something else she had to decide. Was Chastity really willing to tell the cop everything she knew?

Chapter Fifteen

Grace sat near the window of Grave Gulch Coffee and Treats. For what actually might be the hundredth time, she checked her phone.

The time was five thirty.

She hadn't missed a single message.

The witness was almost twenty minutes late.

Moreover, she hadn't bothered to text with an excuse. Nor had she suggested a new meeting time.

A lot of police work was waiting around for something to happen. Grace knew better. It was time to face facts. The woman wasn't going to show.

A lump stuck in her throat. She set the phone down and reached for a cup of coffee, now lukewarm, and gagged down a sip.

Her phone vibrated. She scooped it up and opened the call. Heart racing, Grace was breathless. "Hello?"

"Hey." It was Camden. At this very moment, he sat in his car that was parked at the end of the street. He also had his camera, equipped with a lens powerful enough to get clear photos of anyone entering the coffee shop, even from a block away. Beyond the camera, Grace wore a small microphone, the size of a pen cap. It was taped between her breasts and hidden by her bra.

The microphone recorded every noise within twenty feet and transmitted it to a broadcaster in Camden's car.

"You see anything?" she asked.

"Nothing on the street."

The invisible kernel in Grace's throat hardened as it filled with disappointment. Without the witness, she had no other way to clear her name or save her career.

"Anything in the coffee shop?"

"Nope," she said, her voice cracking.

"Tell me what you see."

Grace scanned the shop. Ten small tables filled the room; less than half were occupied. Nearest to Grace was a mother staring at her cell phone, while her two children fought with swizzle sticks. At the table next to the door sat a guy with a beard and a laptop who muttered at the screen as he typed. An elderly couple was huddled in the corner, bent over two cups of coffee and a single blueberry scone. Their happiness was almost palpable, and Grace wondered if she'd ever find the kind of love that could last a lifetime.

"There's nothing to see."

"Hold on," he interrupted. "I have another call."

"Go ahead," she said, dark humor starting to take over. "I've got nowhere else to be and nothing else to do."

Camden was gone for less than a minute before he was back on the line. "That was your cousin Bryce."

Bryce? When had the two men become so chummy? "What's he want?"

"Someone called. They think they saw Len Davison at a local campground. Right now, Bryce needs backup."

"From you?"

"From me, but I don't need to leave if you need me."

"There's no way I'm going to stop you from searching for Davison." She dropped her voice to keep the conversation from being overheard by her fellow patrons. "Go," she said. "I'll be fine."

"Really, I can't leave you alone. You aren't even an active cop."

His words stung, like a slap to the face. "Excuse me?" Even Grace heard the steely tone of her voice.

"I didn't mean it that way…"

She didn't have the energy to argue with him. "I'm hanging up now. You go." She ended the call. A moment later a sleek silver car passed the window, and she knew that Camden had driven away. Her eyes were dry and gritty. She screwed them shut.

Inhale. Exhale. Just breathe.

Well, there was nothing more for Grace to do—other than finish her coffee and maybe order one of the blueberry scones.

Opening her eyes, she lifted the cup to her lips and took a small sip. The door opened. A person stepped into the coffee shop wearing a hoodie and a large pair of sunglasses. Even with the features hidden, Grace recognized her at once.

It was the female witness.

CAMDEN DROPPED HIS foot onto the accelerator, and his car shot down the road. The rendezvous point, located at a secluded state park outside of town, was still several miles away. At this speed, he'd be there soon.

As he drove, he cataloged his lengthy list of problems. First was the most obvious. Without being able to prove her innocence, Grace would be considered guilty.

Even if Camden could show that Robert Grimaldi owned a gun, even if Arielle Parks didn't file criminal charges, Grace would lose her job.

Certainly, there was more that could be done. But what? Right now, he was fresh out of ideas.

Another looming problem was much more immediate. Technically, he'd taken leave from his work. It enabled him to help Grace without the implication of favoritism—and yeah, he did favor Grace Colton a lot.

Nevertheless, facts were facts. Only a few hours before, he'd stepped away from his job. It meant that he shouldn't even be racing down the tree-lined road to help Bryce Colton. In reality, his presence could muck up any subsequent prosecutions.

Camden gripped the steering wheel as his imagination took over for a single moment. Sitting on the witness stand, Camden would be faced with a sly defense attorney.

Mr. Kingsley, can you explain why you assisted Special Agent Colton in the apprehension of Len Davison? Make sure you include the details about why you were there, especially since you weren't technically working for Internal Affairs.

Camden turned off the main road. With less than a mile to the rendezvous, he didn't have a plausible reason for helping the Fed.

It meant only one thing.

Camden had to tell Bryce everything.

The shores of Lake Michigan were filled with recreational areas. There were several near Grave Gulch. A sign pointed to the park's entrance. A narrow drive was lined on both sides with a thick forest. In the distance, sun glinted off the gunmetal-gray water of the lake.

During the summer, this was a popular destination. At any time from Memorial Day to Labor Day, the park would be busy with picnickers, swimmers and boaters. But the season had ended weeks before. Now, a single car was parked near the entrance. Bryce Colton sat on the trunk. He stood as Camden pulled to a stop.

"Thanks for coming on such short notice," said Bryce as Camden opened the door. "Looks like I'm calling in that favor you owe pretty quickly."

"Before we get started, I need to come clean."

"Come clean?" Bryce echoed. "About what?"

"Technically, I'm on leave."

Bryce gaped. "This is news to me, man. Why?"

Camden knew he was wasting time by not being forthright. "It's Grace."

"My cousin?" Bryce drew his brows together. "What happened to her?"

"I've become…" Camden searched for the right word. "Attached."

"Like, how attached?"

"Attached enough." He exhaled. "Listen, I'm willing to step away from my job for her. I have to help Grace prove that she's innocent." Camden searched for the right words. He continued, "You gotta know that I could mess up your investigation. Or bring any arrests into question at trial."

"As far as I'm concerned, following this lead is more important. If it makes you feel better, I'll deputize you as a task force officer. Because what I need now is someone I can count on. And you just told me everything I need to know."

"Which is what?"

"If you're the kind of guy who's willing to give up

everything for the truth, then you're the kind of guy who I can count on."

It might not have been the perfect answer. Still, it was enough for Camden. "You have a lead?"

"Sure do. This afternoon, there was a woman walking her dog. She saw someone and swears it was Len Davison."

A road, barely big enough for two cars to pass side by side, led to the water's edge. Was this how the Len Davison investigation ended? Him spotted by a woman who was walking her dog?

"Swears?" Camden echoed Bryce's earlier choice of word. "That's sounds pretty certain."

Bryce grunted. "It is, and yet..."

Camden picked up the thread of conversation that Bryce had let unravel. "What else did the woman say?"

"She went on a bit about keeping close tabs on the press coverage about Davison. She also mentioned her name several times, in case I need to pass it on to any reporters."

"Sounds a little dubious," said Camden.

"I was thinking the same thing. She said that the guy was camping. But all the campgrounds are closed for the season."

"Living rough follows Davison's MO."

Bryce nodded. "Right again. Besides, we have to follow up on every lead. Just because someone wants a little publicity doesn't mean they're lying."

"What's the plan?" Camden asked. "Where's everyone else? Air support? State police? Canine units?"

A search for the serial killer should involve more than two people.

"For the moment, it's just us. We'll search the area

where the man was seen. If there's reason to suspect it was Len, we call in the rest of the troops."

So the mission was just reconnaissance.

"Give me a second." He reached into the car's glove box.

On a day-to-day basis, Camden had little use for his weapon. He kept the Glock 9 mm in his glove box, which was kept locked. The pistol was stored in a holster, and Camden removed them both. Sliding back the sight, he chambered a round. After he secured the gun back in the holster, he threaded both onto his belt. Taking a moment to adjust the entire rig on his hip, he untucked his shirt and let the tail hide the firearm.

"You ready?" asked Bryce, sliding a gun into the shoulder holster he wore. He donned a jacket, and the sidearm was no longer visible.

Bryce's question hung in the air. Was Camden ready? He nodded once. "Let's roll."

They didn't stay on the road, which ran directly to the lake's shore. Instead, the duo took a path that led through the woods. The sun now hung on the western horizon. Still, there would be hours of twilight before it became fully dark. The half-light leached the forest of its colors, turning everything murky and muted.

Then Camden caught a glimpse of bright red through the trees. Was it a person? Pulse spiking, he dropped his hand to his Glock.

A moment later Bryce tapped him on the shoulder, a silent command to stop. "I think this is it. We've found what the woman saw."

Camden nodded.

Less than fifty yards away, a campsite was hidden at the base of a large tree. The tent was little more than two plastic tarps held up by a frame. A firepit, just a divot in the earth, was surrounded with stones. A banked fire smoldered. Several cans of food were stacked next to a pot that was propped up on a nearby rock. A cord, stretched between two branches, held several articles of tattered and frayed clothing.

A red jacket hung limply and swayed slightly with the breeze. It was that coat which Camden had seen first. Keeping his hand close to his gun, he whispered back. "We've definitely found a campsite. The question is, who's been staying here?"

As if on cue, a person emerged from the tent. Narrowing his eyes, Camden peered through the woods. It was a man—that much was obvious from the build and the thick brown mustache and beard. His dark hair was lanky, dirty and tangled.

He'd seen pictures of the serial killer and imagined that he'd recognize him on sight. But with the distance, the trees and the waning light, Camden couldn't be certain.

He wore a sweatshirt with frayed cuffs and a pair of ripped and stained jeans. Camden didn't see a weapon—a gun or even a knife. From this distance, what he saw meant next to nothing.

The man went down on one knee next to the pile of cans. After lifting one from the stack, he scanned the label.

Without question, the guy had been living out of doors for a while. Moreover, he had the hungry look that came with desperation.

But there was one question that was yet to be answered.

Was this man Len Davison, the serial killer wanted by the GGPD?

Bryce took a step. Underfoot, a twig snapped. In the quiet woods, the sound ricocheted off the trees.

"Damn it," Bryce mouthed.

Camden's gut clenched as the guy slowly glanced over his shoulder. At fifty yards, Camden could clearly see the man, even through the trees.

It meant that the guy could see them, but only if he knew where to look. For the span of a heartbeat, he scanned the woods. His eyes were narrowed, and his brows drawn together. If Camden had to guess, he'd say that the guy hadn't seen them—yet.

Then his gaze stopped. He looked directly at Camden. The two men made eye contact. There was no use in trying to hide now. Resting one hand near the gun at his hip, Camden raised his other. "Hey," he said. "I'm with Internal Affairs. This is Special Agent Colton with the FBI. Do you have a minute to chat with us?"

The man slowly rose to his feet. For an instant, Camden was certain that he would cooperate. Without a word, the man turned and sprinted farther into the woods.

THE WOMAN TOOK off her sunglasses and slid into the seat across from Grace. She was young—under twenty years old, by Grace's estimation. She stared at her hands, and Grace shifted in her place.

The small microphone that was taped to her chest shuddered with each beat of her heart. Even though she'd seen Camden drive away, she glanced at the window, hoping beyond hope that he'd come back. His car wasn't on the street. Of course: he was gone. All the same, without him to capture the images, there would be no evidence that the woman had been here at all.

Would the meeting even matter?

"You alone?" the woman asked, her eyes trained on the table.

Nodding, Grace said, "I am."

"Anybody on the street?" The woman looked toward the large window.

"Nobody."

The witness sat in silence. Grace knew it was up to her to start a dialogue. She was new on the police force, but she'd been taught that the best way to connect with a suspect was to build a rapport.

"I'm glad you're here," she said. "I'd started to think that you wouldn't come at all."

"To be honest, I'm still not sure that I should've."

"But you did come," said Grace quickly, before the woman could talk herself out of confessing what she knew. Or, worse, leave. "It means you're ready to do the right thing."

She gave a snort-laugh. "If you say so."

"You are here," Grace said again, putting more force in her words. "And you were there on Thursday night, too. I saw you."

"If you say so." She paused before adding, "*Cop*."

There was enough venom in the single word that it sounded like a curse.

Grace's temperature rose, along with her temper. After everything she'd been through, this woman—and her attitude—was the last thing she wanted to deal with. Sitting back in her seat, Grace folded her arms across her chest. "Okay, then, why did you show up? It's certainly not to help. Or to do the right thing." She flicked her wrist toward the door. "Go back to hiding. Go back to not showing your face in public."

The woman looked up. Her eyes were wide. "That's not…" Her voice trailed off, thick with emotion.

Grace tried to muster some sympathy. Despite all the trouble this person and her friend had caused by running off—and possibly taking the gun—she could imagine how meeting with Grace would be personally difficult. She decided to try another tactic. "The guy you were with…"

"What about him?"

"He doesn't know that you're here, does he?"

"Thad?" She shook her head and gave a chuckle. "He's clueless that I've even left the apartment."

It just seemed like chitchat. In reality, the woman had shared a good bit of important information. Grace cataloged what she now knew: the witness lived in a nearby apartment with a guy named Thad, who also happened to be the other witness.

"Clueless?" Grace echoed, matching the woman's laugh with one of her own. "How?"

"He's still asleep."

"Really?" Grace glanced outside. The sun had set, turning the sky orange and pink. "He's been asleep all day? Does he work nights?"

"Hungover is more like it. But yeah, he's been out most of the day."

"That must be hard on you."

The woman shrugged. "Sometimes."

"I'm Grace, by the way."

"Yeah, I know. I saw your video."

Grace nodded and then waited a beat. "You are?"

"Chastity."

Yes! I have names for both witnesses. "Chastity what?"

"Just Chastity."

"Okay." She paused a beat. "You want a coffee or something?"

Chastity shook her head. "I'm okay for now."

Just like in the textbook, Grace had followed all the rules for building a bond with a subject. Yet, she had one more question. Now what?

She was still mad at Camden for his "not an active cop" comment. All the same, he was a hell of an investigator and had given her decent advice. What had he said? Oh, yeah. *Be honest.*

And honestly, Grace was anxious to find out what Chastity knew—and what else she might say. "Do you mind telling me what you saw on Thursday night?"

Scratching the side of her face, Chastity sighed. "It was really dark."

Was this another dead end? "You seemed upset that night. You had to have seen something."

"I know that you fired a gun. I could see the flash of flames coming out of the end part."

"The muzzle?"

"I guess that's what you call it."

"Thad approached the man who was shot. Do you know what was said?"

Dropping her gaze to the table, Chastity traced a whorl in the wood with her fingernail. "I'm starting to think that coming was a bad idea. Maybe I should go."

Damn. Grace had been too direct. She'd pushed Chastity too hard. Now she'd scared off the one person who could help clear her name. It also confirmed Grace's suspicion: Chastity definitely had something to hide.

"Don't go," she said quickly. "I mean, you just got here. You want a coffee?"

"You've already asked me about that, and I've already told you I'm not interested." Pushing back from the table, she stood. "Besides, you lied in your video. You don't want to help me. You just need me. That's it." With a roll of her eyes, she added, "I hope that they hang you for what you've done, cop."

Grace had been taught how to deal with members of the public who were difficult or hostile. But she'd never been told how to deal with someone who was as mercurial as Chastity. It left her with one thing to do—rely on her instincts. The question was, would it be enough?

Camden had said that Chastity was looking for a friend. Could Grace be that friend and find out the truth at the same time?

"You're right," Grace said with an exhale. "I want to clear my name. But you're wrong when you say that I don't want to help. I do. Right now, you're caught in a trap that you set. You can't go anywhere in Grave Gulch without being turned in to the police. But if you talk to me, I can help clear your name, as well."

"Or I can stay in my apartment. Face it, all of this will eventually blow over…" Her words trailed off as her decisive tone weakened.

"Is that what Thad told you?"

Chastity dropped back into her seat. "Maybe that's what I told him."

Thad was the one who made all the decisions. Why break the law, though? Did Chastity's love for Thad leave her blind? Or was there something else?

Grace asked, "You don't like the police much, do you?"

"Let's just say that the police haven't always been on the job when it comes to protecting and serving."

Grace would bet good money there was a lot more to Chastity's story. "So what happened?"

"Nothing," said Chastity. It was clearly a lie.

"Most everyone in my family works for the Grave Gulch Police Department—except for a few people. Like my cousin Bryce."

"What's he do?"

"He's a special agent with the FBI." The mention of her cousin brought back Camden's abrupt exit. She couldn't help but wonder if they'd actually found the serial killer—and if everyone was safe.

"Sounds like he's a cop, too."

"I guess," said Grace. "Just with a fancier badge."

Her small joke earned a smirk from Chastity. "Must be nice to have such a close family."

"Most of the time, it is. We all gravitated to law enforcement for a specific reason." Grace continued, launching into the story she hadn't planned to share. "My dad was married years ago to another woman. Amanda's the mom of Troy and Desiree, my half siblings. Anyway, when Troy and Desiree were little, Amanda was murdered. To this day, the killer's never been found."

"Why go into law enforcement? The police failed you like they fail everyone else. It's not a reason to be a cop."

"That's just the thing. The pain my family felt is something we want to keep others from feeling, too. We want to do our job."

Leaning back in her chair, Chastity folded her arms tight across her chest. Grace didn't need any police training to understand the body language.

Chastity was trying to protect herself. But why?

Was the younger woman trying to keep Grace out?

Or was she trying to put up an emotional wall before Grace had a chance to get in?

"Hey," Grace said, her voice low and soft. "We all have past hurts. I think you have one that involves the police. I'm sorry for whatever happened."

A fat tear snaked down the side of Chastity's cheek. She wiped it away with her sleeve. "It wasn't me. It was my mom. My dad." Exhaling, she shook her head. "He liked to drink and fight. Sometimes, well, he hit my mom."

"That must've been a hard way to grow up."

"The thing is, at first you don't know better. Then you realize that your family isn't like everyone else's. When that day comes, well, it sucks. From then on, all you want is to look normal. But one day…" She wiped away another tear and turned to look out the window.

It was then that Grace realized she'd been holding her breath. "But one day…" she coaxed.

"One day I couldn't stand it anymore. I called 9-1-1. A police officer showed up. My dad spoke to him outside. I watched from my bedroom window. I couldn't hear what they were saying, but it didn't matter. I could tell. They started off all serious, heads bowed together. Then my dad must've said something funny because the cop laughed. A minute or two later, they were slapping each other on the back. It was just like they'd been friends since forever. The cop left, and my dad came back into the house."

Grace was afraid of the answer, yet she had to ask. "What happened then?"

"My dad *told* me." She hooked air quotes around the word. Grace assumed that the telling was closer to yelling. "He explained to the cop that I was just a bratty teenager, bent on getting my dad in trouble. He lied. But what's worse, the cop never checked it out. He never talked to my mom, who had a black eye. He never asked to see me. The cop just talked to my dad, who gave him some BS answer, and left."

Chastity's voice had risen. The elderly couple glanced over. Chastity slouched in her seat.

"I can't speak for that police officer, but you have every right to be mad at him." Grace knew what she had to do now—much as she hated the sacrifice. Shoving back from the table, she stood. "We both know that Robert Grimaldi had a gun. I saw it, and you did, too. I'm not going to ask you to come forward. I'll handle whatever happens to me. Well, thanks for showing up."

"Wait." Chastity was on her feet. "What will happen?"

Grace was already across the room. Without a word, she opened the door and stepped into the cool evening air.

Chastity followed. They both stood on the empty sidewalk. "What will happen?" she asked again.

"To be honest, I don't know."

"I mean, there's some other way to prove that guy had a gun, right?"

Grace shook her head. "That's the thing. There isn't."

"What'll happen to you? Let me guess. You'll get a few weeks off with pay. It'll be like a vacation."

"I know for a fact that I'll lose my job. With an unauthorized use of force on my résumé, I'll never work in law enforcement again. Hell, it'll be hard to get hired anywhere. Who wants to hire an unstable cop? Then, there's the worst-case scenario."

"What's worse than losing your job? Or not getting another one?"

"I'll end up in jail."

"They can't do that." Chastity's voice had risen again. "You didn't do anything wrong."

"Without video or a witness or even the gun, I have no proof. It's my word against Grimaldi's." After the last few days, Grace was exhausted. She only wanted to go home and sleep. When she woke, what then? Well, then she'd have to figure out the rest of her life.

"You're wrong," said Chastity. "You do have a witness. You have me."

"Are you willing to speak to the authorities now?"

Chastity gave a quick nod. "I figure there have to be at least some good cops out there. It seems like you're one of them. You should keep your job. Right?"

Grace's shoulders relaxed, letting go of tension she didn't realize that she'd been holding. "Right," she echoed.

"And that's not all. I know something about the gun."

"What about the gun?" Grace asked, her voice a whisper.

"I know where it is."

"You do? Where?"

Chastity looked up and down the street. "I have it. It's in my apartment. We've wiped off all the prints, so you won't be able to tie me or Thad to the gun."

Did Chastity really have the gun? There was no reason for her lie. She knew it really didn't matter. It'd be foolish for Grace to go into an apartment where a desperate and dangerous man had a weapon—especially since she didn't have a sidearm of her own—or backup. Just thinking the single word hit her like a slap to the face. Her cheeks burned and her eyes stung.

Camden had said many things and all of them had turned out to be true.

Right now, she wasn't officially on duty. That meant she couldn't call in the help she needed.

Which meant her next move should be what? They definitely never covered this scenario at the police academy. In an instant, she knew that sending Camden away had been wrong, because without him she was truly on her own.

Chapter Sixteen

Camden sprinted through the woods. He jumped over a felled tree at the same moment a branch lashed his arm. Ignoring the sting of broken flesh, he focused on his quarry. The man from the campsite ran ahead. The sun had slipped below the horizon, and the fugitive was little more than a shadow. What was worse, if he wasn't captured quickly, then night would fall. In the darkness, he'd be impossible to find.

Next to Camden, matching him stride for stride, was Bryce. Then the special agent pulled ahead, although the extra speed wasn't enough.

Catching the suspect was going to take not just stamina but a strategy, as well.

The man turned, veering to the right. It was then that Camden understood his plan. The suspect need not outrun the police. He only needed to get to the lake first and a rowboat that sat on the sand. There, he could get away in the water.

Peeling away from the direct pursuit, Camden cut a path toward the shore. If his guess was right, he'd be able to intercept the man as he ran for the water. If he was wrong? Well, then he'd just left Bryce on his own.

Skidding to a stop at the tree line, Camden wiped

sweat from his brow. There was a rustling in the trees an instant before the man burst onto the shoreline. He was less than a dozen yards from where Camden waited.

Launching forward, Camden sprinted across the sandy beach. Just as the man waded into the water, Camden dove. He grabbed the man by the middle, pushing them both down with a splash.

Bryce was right behind. Grabbing the man by the back of his shirt, the special agent hauled the suspect to his feet.

"Let me go," the man growled. He threw a punch. The man's fist missed Camden's chin by inches.

"You know I'm not going to do that," said Bryce, his breath labored. "We can do this the easy way, where you calm down. Or my friend and I can wrestle you into cuffs. Your choice, but you aren't going anywhere."

"This is total crap. Police harassment." Yet, the man placed his hands behind his back, intertwining his fingers. To Camden, it looked like the guy might have been arrested more than once. Bryce produced a set of cuffs from his jacket pocket and slipped them onto the man's wrists.

The pause gave Camden time to think. Would Len Davison instinctively know how to respond to an arrest? That brought up another question worth asking. Would the serial killer give up without much of a fight?

"What d'you want?" the man asked, his voice hoarse.

"We need to talk." Bryce led the man to the shore.

"Is it about the campsite? I know it's past the season, that's why I came here. My old lady kicked me out last week. I got out of jail in July and haven't been able to get back on my feet. I just need a few days more to straighten some things out. To begin with, her loser brother owes me money."

In his time with IA, Camden had investigated more than one high-functioning sociopath: charming, calculating, with an inclination toward violence if things didn't go their way. In his estimation, this guy didn't come across as suffering from an antisocial personality disorder.

Most sociopaths had a high IQ. The guy they'd just apprehended seemed a little dimmer than most—likely not a sociopath, then.

"What's your name?" Camden asked, while patting down the guy for anything that might be used as a weapon. In his back pocket was a wallet.

"Hank Ford." Camden opened the wallet.

There was still enough light to read the license. Hank Ford was a resident of Grave Gulch. Beyond that, the picture on the license matched that of the man in their custody—who only had a passing resemblance in age, race and build to Len Davison.

Still, Camden quizzed Hank on his date of birth, address and social security number.

He knew all the right information.

What Camden didn't know was what to do with the guy now.

He moved several feet away from Hank Ford. Lowering his voice, he asked Bryce, "What d'you think? Is this Davison?"

"My gut tells me it's not."

"Mine, too. But after everything he's done, it's not a big deal to steal a wallet and pose as someone else."

"We need to compare fingerprints or DNA."

Camden agreed. "Both will be on file if Mr. Ford was incarcerated." He paused. "I hate to turn him back to the system."

"Maybe there's a little more that we can do," said Bryce. Stepping closer to Hank, the special agent said, "You can't be camping out here."

"Where am I supposed to go?" Hank asked. "What can I do?"

Bryce said, "There's a shelter in town run by a church. They can give you a bed, a shower and a hot meal. More than that, they've helped plenty of people find a job and a permanent residence. How's that sound to you?"

Hank nodded eagerly. "Sounds good. I haven't really had any decent food in a week."

Since Camden was technically on leave, a patrol officer was called to process Mr. Ford. Assuming that his story checked out, Ford, along with his scant belongings, would be taken to the shelter. It took only minutes for the man to be secured in the back seat of the police cruiser for the ride back to Grave Gulch.

As the taillights faded to nothing, Camden admitted that he'd done some good with his day. Then, just as quickly, his thoughts went to Grace. Where was she now, and what was she doing?

CHASTITY'S APARTMENT BUILDING was around the corner from Grave Gulch Coffee and Treats. Grace stood on the sidewalk and waited.

While working the key into the door, Chastity spoke. "I have one favor to ask. You can't implicate me or Thad in any of this. I mean, I'll talk to the police and tell them what I saw. But you can't tell them who gave you the gun."

Honestly, Grace wasn't sure that was a promise she could make. "I swear that I'll do what I can."

She unlatched the lock. "I guess that's enough."

The door opened to a dingy square of vinyl tile that hadn't seen a broom in months. A side wall was filled with a bank of mailboxes. It looked like there were four apartments on each floor, two in the front of the building and two in the back. A set of stairs led upward.

"We're on the third floor." Chastity began to climb the steps.

Without comment, Grace followed.

They stopped on the landing. Chastity moved to the unit at the front right corner. "Wait here," she said, producing a second key from the ring. After working it into the door's lock, she continued. "I'll get the gun and then be right back." Opening the door, she slid inside.

Grace leaned against the wall and closed her eyes. She wanted to pray that this was all about to end. She knew enough not to hope—not yet, at least.

THE SCENT OF old wine and stale body odor filled the apartment. Closing the door, Chastity pressed her back to the wall. The curtains were open, letting in the last light of day. She glanced into the bedroom. A pile of blankets was draped over the mattress edge, but she couldn't see Thad in the gloom.

Still, the metallic taste of panic coated her tongue. Her heartbeat raced. Thad would be pissed at Chastity for turning over the gun. But when they were able to leave the apartment, he'd thank her. Right?

Walking quietly to the end of the sofa, she knelt in

front of the small table and pulled on the handle. The drawer didn't move. She tugged again, harder this time. The wood creaked as the drawer opened an inch.

Damn.

Chastity froze and held her breath. The room was silent. Holding the corners, she walked the drawer forward. A stack of bills sat atop a loose-leaf textbook. She moved it all aside and sucked in a quick breath. The drawer was empty. Chastity rifled through the drawer once more, despite the fact that the gun was undoubtedly missing.

Straining, she listened for Thad's quiet snores as he slept. There was nothing.

Moving on tiptoe, she crossed the living room and peeked through the open door. The bed was empty. Thad wasn't here.

LEANING AGAINST THE WALL, Grace exhaled. A spark of excitement warmed her chest. Was the nightmare really about to end?

If it did, what did that mean for her and Camden?

A relationship between them would raise more than a few eyebrows. An IA investigator involved with a cop?

He was worth a couple of sideways glances.

The apartment door opened slowly, and Grace pushed off the wall. She stopped, her heart thundering. Chastity stood in the apartment. Her eyes were moist and rimmed in red. "He's gone," she said.

Grace could guess the answer. Still, she asked, "Who's gone?"

"Thad," said Chastity as the first fat tear rolled

down her cheek. "And what's more, he's taken the gun with him."

Grace went cold. Thad had taken the single piece of evidence that could prove her innocence. Yet there was more. Thad was armed, on the loose, and there was no telling what he might do. Or who he might hurt.

DRIVING BACK TO Grave Gulch, Camden broke more than one speed limit.

Did he and Grace have a future together?

There was only one way to find out. Using the controls on his steering wheel, he placed a call. The phone rang four times before being answered by voice mail.

"This is Grace." Her tone was so cheerful that he smiled. "You know what to do at the beep."

The phone started recording. "Hey, it's me. Camden. I'd really like to see you soon." He paused. What else was there to say? "Call me back." He ended the call.

Without a plan, he drove to her place. The apartment was dark—not even the flicker of light from the TV or computer screen.

Obviously, she wasn't home.

But where would she have gone?

With all her Colton kin, Grace could be almost anywhere.

Settling back into the seat, he shook his head. Right now, he had no choice but to wait for her to call him. Too bad that waiting was the last thing he wanted to do.

He pictured her, sitting at the table, glancing his way as he drove by. Her shoulders were rounded. Her slouched posture made it look as if she were exhausted. But he knew better. She was more than tired: she was defeated. The witness was the key to proving her version of the shooting.

And they'd been a no-show.

Or had they?

Camden called Grace a second time. Once again, the phone went straight to voice mail. He hung up without leaving a message.

Could it be that Grace was still at the coffee shop?

Had the witness shown up after all?

Camden drove to Grave Gulch Coffee and Treats. His car idled as he counted over a dozen patrons. None of them were Grace.

But he'd seen something out of the corner of his eye. A glint of light and color. What had it been?

He glanced to the console between the seats. There, wedged between two cup holders, sat the black plastic audio receiver. It was the same one that was attached to the microphone Grace wore. A set of red lights flashed. It meant one thing: voices were being picked up.

He reached for the volume control. His fingertips brushed the dial, and he stopped. Should he be listening to Grace?

If she were having a private conversation, she'd know enough to remove the wire. Right?

Without another thought, he turned up the volume.

"Who's gone?" she asked. Her voice was a breathless whisper.

"Thad," said a female. "And what's more, he's taken the gun with him."

And what's more, he's taken the gun with him.

The woman's words echoed in Camden's mind—leaving no room for thought.

Camden was a creature of the rational and logical.

He pushed all emotion aside. If he was picking up the broadcast, it meant that Grace was close. He drove, turning right at the next corner. It was the same path he'd taken that morning when following the witness.

The street was narrow, quiet and dark. Late-model cars were parked at both curbs. Brick buildings rose up on either side, three and four stories tall. They were all filled with apartments.

Just as he had stood on the street this morning, looking for where the witness had gone, Camden now stared at each and every window. Grace was close. He knew that for a fact.

But where?

GRACE ASSESSED HER SITUATION. In a word, it was bad. She smothered a curse with her hand and wondered, what next?

"I think," said Chastity, wiping her face with her sleeve. "I can find him."

Grace lifted her brow. "How?"

A folding table with several monitors and a hard drive sat in the corner. Chastity moved to one of the keyboards and began to type. "I should be able to find his phone," she began. "Damn it."

"Damn it?" Grace echoed. "*Damn it* doesn't sound good. What's wrong?"

"Nothing's good. And a lot is wrong." A loud *ping* came from the bedroom. "Thad left his phone. He must've known what I was doing and wanted to get rid of the gun before I could give it to you."

Grace pushed open the bedroom door. The stink of body odor, stale wine and tropical-scented vape smoke filled the small room. The cell sat in the middle of the mattress. She picked it up and silenced the alarm.

Yet, she couldn't help but ask herself a single question. "How'd he know you were meeting with me?" Grace handed Chastity the phone. "Was it a guess?"

Chastity gave a slow shake of her head. "I don't know," she began. "Or maybe I do..."

She typed onto the keyboard. The screen filled with a text exchange. Grace read the first few messages.

It began with:

I saw your interview on the TV station's site.

Followed by:

You did? Who's this?

And then:

I know what happened...

"These are our texts," said Grace. "Was he able to hack into your phone?"

"He was able to access my account," said Chastity. "Not exactly a hack and not exactly hard, either. If you know what you're doing."

"That brings up an important question, Chastity. Do you know what you're doing on a computer?"

She sat up taller. "Of course. I'm better than Thad."

"Good." Grace's pulse began to race as she formed a plan. "Because if he can search through your account, can you search through his?"

Chapter Seventeen

Chastity had a decision to make. Sure, she'd contacted the police about the gun. Was she willing to lead them to Thad? Especially since it was obvious that he was trying to destroy or hide evidence?

She already knew. She was going to do the right thing. It was people like her dad, or the cop from all those years ago or even Thad, who thought that rules weren't meant for them. Those were the people who had to be stopped.

Exhaling, she picked up his cell. "We have to assume that he left his phone so he couldn't be tracked," she said.

"That's smart of him," said Grace. "Where do you think he went? Do you have a car?"

Chastity shook her head. "No car."

"Could he have gotten a ride from someone? A friend?"

Chastity wasn't about to admit they had no friends. Still, she opened his text messages.

Nothing.

"Do we assume he's close?" Grace asked. "What would he do with the gun?"

It was a good question. Thad designed games. He

always inserted a way to escape in every situation. Real life would be no different. Yet Grace's question still hung in the air.

"What would he do with the gun?" Chastity repeated. Then she recalled. He did have a plan. They were supposed to lay low for weeks, then... "He's going to throw the gun into Lake Michigan."

"How would he get there without a car? Ride share?" Grace answered her own query. "That wouldn't make sense. Whoever drove Thad would be one more witness."

"Let's see what he looked up on his phone." She scrolled through his internet history. "There's nothing."

"But if he left his phone so you couldn't track him, then I doubt he left any clues on it, either."

Grace was right and Chastity's jaw tightened with frustration. As she leaned back in the chair, her eye was drawn to Thad's computer system. She entered some keystrokes.

An internet history appeared. "It looks like he deleted some of his searches, but I can work around that." It took only a few seconds and Chastity had recovered everything.

Grace read from over her shoulder. "Grave Gulch Car Sharing. He rented a car?"

Chastity continued to type. A map, along with a flashing red dot, appeared on the screen. Chastity pointed to the dot. "There he is." Her mouth was dry. "That's the car Thad rented."

GRACE BOUNDED DOWN the stairs from the apartment to the street level. Chastity had transferred all of the data from Thad's car share to her phone and was at her side.

They knew where Thad was at this moment, but where was he going? How would they catch him?

Grace opened the door to the sidewalk as a set of headlights cut through the gathering darkness and she glanced down the street. It was a sleek, silver sedan. Her heart skipped a beat.

"Camden?" She whispered his name.

Chastity followed her gaze. Eyes narrowed, she asked, "Who's that?"

The car pulled to the curb and the passenger-side window rolled down without a sound. Camden leaned across the seat. He lifted his chin. "Hey."

Grace exhaled. "Hey."

"Who's he?" Chastity asked, her voice brittle.

"He's the guy who'll help us get that gun."

"The gun?" Camden echoed. "You mean to tell me that you've found Robert Grimaldi's gun?"

Chastity bit the cuticle of her thumb. The nailbed filled with blood. "I know you. I saw you on the video. You were at the press conference yesterday."

He gave a quick nod. "That's me."

Grace would never know why Camden appearing in the online video made him someone that Chastity could trust. Or maybe the younger woman was just tired of hiding, and running, and lying. In the end, it really didn't matter.

"I know where he is," she said, holding up her phone. The GPS hadn't updated in several minutes, leaving the pinpoint for his car on the outskirts of Grave Gulch. "I'm not sure where he's going."

Camden put the gearshift into Park and the doors automatically unlocked. "I know where he's headed. Get in."

Grace slipped into the passenger seat as Chastity got into the back.

"You know where he's going?" Grace pulled the door shut and put on her seat belt. "How?"

"That road leads to a state park on the shores of Lake Michigan. I was just there."

Was that where Camden and her cousin had been searching for the serial killer? Grace glanced over her shoulder. Certainly, they shouldn't talk about an open investigation in front of Chastity.

Camden must have guessed at her hesitation to continue the conversation. He added, "It wasn't him."

"Lake Michigan?" Chastity echoed from the back seat. "It's what he planned to do with the gun from the beginning."

"So, this guy is who? Your boyfriend?" He glanced at Chastity through the rearview mirror.

For half a second, Grace wondered how Camden knew about the relationship between Chastity and Thad. Or for that matter, how he had found her in the first place. Then she saw the receiver that was tucked between the seats. For the first time in nearly an hour, she felt the tiny microphone taped to her chest.

Had Camden been listening to her? She had to assume so. In the end, there was only one thing that mattered. He was here. Could Grace finally let go of the dread and despair of the last two days? Was everything going to finally turn out okay?

"I think I should tell you," said Chastity, her voice barely rising above the revving engine and the road noise, "Thad won't let you arrest him. He's hell-bent on winning."

Grace turned in her seat, so she could see the other woman. "This isn't a game."

"It is to him," she said. "Winning or losing, that's all there is."

"If the police find him, he'll go to jail. There is no other choice," Camden said.

"There is one more choice." The car suddenly felt cold. Goose flesh covered Grace's arms and she quelled a shiver. Before she could ask what Thad planned, Chastity spoke. "He'll die before he loses. That, or he'll kill someone else."

CAMDEN TIGHTENED HIS grip on the steering wheel and dropped his foot onto the accelerator. There was no way he was letting another criminal go free. "I'm calling backup." Using the controls on the steering wheel, he contacted Bryce Colton. Since he was heading back to the park they'd just left, Camden might get lucky. The Fed might still be nearby.

"This is Agent Colton."

"Bryce, I'm heading back to the park in pursuit of the male who witnessed the shooting. He has the gun and is driving a..."

From the back seat, Chastity said, "Blue, hybrid hatchback."

"Blue, hybrid hatchback," he repeated. "Any chance you're around?"

"Sorry, man. I'm no help at all. I'm headed in the opposite direction. Someone called in another sighting of Len Davison."

Is that all the Fed did with his day? "I'll call Troy."

"And Brett," Bryce suggested. He paused. "You do

good work. Not many guys like us left who only focus on the job."

Camden placed the two calls, gave the information and got the response he hoped to hear from both. "On the way."

Yet, as he spoke and planned, his mind worked through a completely different set of problems. Camden wondered if what Bryce said was true. Was Camden only focused on the job?

That used to be the case.

Was it still true, or had Grace changed everything?

The park entrance was dark. In the distance, the water of Lake Michigan reflected the night sky.

"Where is he?" Grace whispered, even though the area seemed to be empty.

Chastity looked at the phone. The screen illuminated her from beneath. Grace recalled all those sleepovers as a kid when her siblings and cousins took turns telling scary stories and used a flashlight to cast ghoulish shadows on their faces. But this was no childhood party.

"The app still won't update," said Chastity. She sucked in a breath. "Unless..."

"Unless what?" Camden turned off the engine and the lights.

"Unless," Chastity said, "he disabled it from his end."

Camden cursed.

Grace's stomach dropped to her shoes. "Think about it," she said. "He's still on the way here, even if he thought to disable the app."

In the dark, Camden's profile was a shadow. Grace's

fingers itched with the need to touch him. But now wasn't the time. "You might be right, Grace," he said, his words seeming to come out from nowhere and everywhere all at once. "We should pull off the main road and wait to see if he shows up."

Without turning on the lights, he drove toward the lake. A narrow dirt path ran into the woods. Camden maneuvered the car into the space so that the nose faced out and the road was visible, yet their auto was hidden by the shadows.

"We should tell Brett and Troy where we are right now," she said. "They should be here soon."

Grace placed two brief calls. Both men less than five minutes away. Then there was nothing to do besides wait—and hope that Thad was really coming to the park. There was so much she wanted to say to Camden. To ask him. Did they have a future together? Is that what she wanted?

Yet, she sat without speaking. She couldn't have the conversation with Chastity in the back seat.

A blue car sped past.

"It's him," said Chastity.

"Coming up on foot is the best plan," said Camden. He retrieved a gun from the glove box of his car. He slipped the firearm into the waistband of his jeans at his back.

Grace unclipped her seat belt. "Let's go."

"Go?" Camden echoed. "You can't go anywhere."

"Don't bring up the bull about me not being a cop. I might be on administrative leave, but I'm as dedicated to upholding justice as anyone on the force."

Camden let out a long exhale. "Is there anything I can say to convince you to stay?"

"You heard what Troy and Brett said. They're still five minutes out. This is going to be over before they get here." She saw the flash in his eyes and knew that she'd hit on a nerve. Since his father's death, he'd been trying to save the world all on his own. Reaching for his arm, she continued, "Camden, you cannot do this alone. We're better together."

"You win." He exhaled. "But you have to do as I say."

Grace smiled. "Yes, sir."

"Chastity," he continued, "you have to stay in the car."

"I won't go anywhere," the young woman said.

Grace and Camden exited the car. Keeping to the tree line, they walked quietly and quickly to the water's edge and the blue car.

"Where is he?" Camden asked at the same moment Grace noticed that the car was empty.

She swallowed down a wave of despair that rose from her middle. Were they too late? Had Thad already thrown the gun into the water? Would Grace ever truly clear her name?

Then she heard a metallic click. Soft, but unmistakable, it was the sound of a safety being released from a gun.

CAMDEN HEARD THE NOISE. The hair at the nape of his neck stood straight. Someone was standing behind them and that was bad enough. What was worse—the person had a gun, and they were ready to use it.

His own firearm was tucked into the small of his back, hidden by his jacket. Could he draw, turn and fire before the assailant got off a shot? He thought not.

Holding up his hands in mock surrender, Camden asked, "What d'you want?"

"I'm not going to jail."

Camden glanced over his shoulder. A guy, brown hair covered by a beanie, held the gun in both hands. With his feet planted on the ground, he looked like he'd learned to shoot by playing laser tag.

"You Thad?" Camden asked, turning slowly. He had one objective—to disarm the suspect.

"How'd you know my name? You a cop?"

"I'm with Internal Affairs, so I'm worse. I'm a cop's cop."

"Listen," said Grace as she turned to face Thad, as well. "I think we can work our way out of this mess. All of us. You hand over the gun and let us go. We don't have to say anything about how it was found…"

"Chastity might be a moron." Thad aimed the gun at Grace. "But I'm not. I don't believe you for a minute. I'm not going to jail, now or ever. But you do bring up an interesting point. I don't know how this all ends, especially since all of you cops are corrupt." He cursed quietly and narrowed his eyes. "Besides, she's definitely guilty. Which is good for me, because I can't have any witnesses."

Camden's blood went cold. No witnesses?

Before Camden could speak, Thad rolled back his shoulders. "Say your prayers now, both of you. It's time for you to die."

IN HER SHORT time on the force, Grace had faced more than one dangerous individual. Yet, Thad had two things that made him different. He had a gun and enough desperation to use it.

"Walk towards the water," he snarled.

Before that moment, Grace had wondered how the simple threat of violence had the ability to make people compliant—even to the point of putting themselves in greater danger. At that instant, she understood.

It was all about survival. If you cooperated, you might live.

Hands up and palms out, she walked toward the lake.

Thad had a gun. He was all emotion and no lucid thought.

Could she get him to think?

"You can't do it, you know."

A sheen of sweat covered Thad's brow. "What d'you mean?"

Grace needed something—anything—to use as a weapon. There was a boat several yards away. Was there an oar inside? She had no way of knowing.

"What d'you mean?" he asked again. "I can't do what?"

Camden said, "Kill us and get away with it."

"Oh, yeah?" Thad laughed at the statement. "You don't think I can pull this trigger and end your life?"

"You can shoot us, if you want." Grace veered toward the boat. "But murder is messy business. There'll be blood everywhere. I don't care what you do with the gun. Our DNA will be all over this beach. There are other cops on the way right now and that brings up another important question. Do you really think you can get rid of two corpses before they show? I don't."

"Stop walking. Shut up and let me think," Thad growled. Was there a slight tremor in his voice?

"Thad, just let us go." Camden glanced at Grace.

Was he willing her to move forward? Or warning her to stay put?

She took another step to the side, another step closer to the boat. He continued, "You're already in deep trouble. Don't make it worse."

Grace's chest was tight. Her focus was razor-sharp but also divided.

There was Thad, anxious and ill, along with his gun.

Could she make him see how killing her—a police officer—would make his situation go from bad to beyond terrible?

There was also the boat. It was her only means of attack, escape and survival.

She knew one thing: unless she did something, she would die on this beach. Shifting her weight to the left, she scooted her foot a fraction of an inch. Thad seemed not to notice. She moved again—and then, once more.

"What're you doing, cop?" he snarled.

Grace froze.

"Stop fidgeting. It's giving me a headache. Hell, I already have a headache."

Camden said, "You don't want to break the law."

"Couldn't you have just left me alone?" Thad drew in a ragged breath. "Because of you, now I'm a criminal? And it's the cops who are corrupt. It doesn't matter that the guy on the street pulled his gun first. She—" he hitched his chin toward Grace "—deserves to die."

Grace understood the truth, and it chilled her soul. Thad was more than frantic. He was unhinged. She'd never be able to reason with him. Which meant she had to act.

Without another thought, she sprinted toward the boat.

At that moment, all hell broke loose.

CAMDEN WATCHED AS Thad turned toward Grace and hooked his thumb onto the hammer. He pulled it back with a *click* that Camden felt in his teeth. A round was in the chamber.

Yet Thad's attention was on Grace and that was all Camden needed to draw and aim his own weapon. "Move another inch, and I'll paint the beach with your brains," Camden said.

Thad didn't bother to turn around.

"You think I care what happens now? I'd rather die than go to jail."

Only moments before, time had been slow, yet now it raced. Thad lifted the gun, aiming at his own head.

"No!" Camden launched himself at the other man, while slipping his gun back into the waistband of his jeans. As he approached, Thad whirled around and slammed the weapon into the side of Camden's head. For a moment, his vision went black.

He grabbed Thad's arm. They both fell to the sand. Holding Thad's wrist, he pulled back. Thad screamed in pain. Thad's gun fired. Where had the shot gone? Where was Grace?

"You…" Thad held tight to the gun. Snarling, he slammed his skull into the bridge of Camden's nose.

Camden's skull ached, yet he refused to let go. Shifting his body weight, he flipped over, pinning Thad's arm behind his back. Camden pried one finger loose and then another. As he heard the crunch of tires on gravel, three sets of headlights swept over the beach. Finally, the backup.

Guns drawn, Brett Shea, Daniel Coleman, Troy Colton and two others ran toward the water's edge. The fight seemed to leave Thad. Brett dragged Thad to his feet. "You're coming with us," he growled, cuffing the witness's hands behind his back.

Camden rose to his feet. A round had been fired, but where had the bullet gone? Where was Grace? Was she okay? The sand shifted and he listed to the side. "My car." He pointed to where he'd parked. "The female witness is in my car."

One of the uniformed officers said, "I'll get her."

"What happened?" Grace ran over to Camden and wrapped her arms around his middle. God, it felt so good to hold her that his head buzzed. "The gun went off."

"I don't know where the bullet went." A halo surrounded the headlights. A pain drove through his brow and his thoughts seemed lost in a mist.

"Camden? Camden!" Grace's voice echoed, as if she were yelling at him from beneath the waves. "Are you okay?"

He tried to nod, but his head wouldn't move.

Grace called out, "Brett. Daniel. Someone! I need an ambulance."

Brett slipped his arm under Camden's shoulder and lowered him back to the beach. "Looks like you got hit in the head. An ambulance is on the way. You need to sit until it shows up."

"I've got this." Grace knelt at his side. "Brett, you secure the scene."

The wail of a far-off siren grew louder, the noise drove into his brain.

"Sounds like the ambulance," said Grace.

Camden's eyes were heavy. Blackness surrounded him on all sides, like he was in a tunnel. He was tired, so tired. It would be so easy to rest, just for a minute.

"Stay awake, Camden. You'll be okay." She choked on her words. "For me, you have to be okay."

"I'll do anything for you," he said, his hand on hers.

Then he stopped fighting and stepped into the darkness.

A PAIR OF EMTs rushed toward the shore at the same moment that Camden lost consciousness.

"We have this," one of them told Grace.

She still held Camden and didn't want to let go of him.

"Grace," said Troy. His hand was on her arm. "Let the EMTs do their work."

Her brother was right. She stood. Her hands shook. Her legs trembled. Her eyes burned, and her throat was raw. Despite everything she'd been taught about being a police officer, nothing had prepared her for this moment. "Will he be okay?" she asked Troy.

"I hope so."

"Officer Coleman, call the hospital," one EMT said. Camden was strapped to a gurney. An oxygen mask covered his nose and mouth. An IV was attached to his arm. "This guy has a head injury. We need a scan to determine if there's a brain bleed."

"I'm on it," said Daniel. He used his mic to connect with Dispatch.

"Camden's getting the best treatment." Troy still had hold of her arm. "Let's get out of their way so they can get their job done."

Grace didn't want to leave Camden's side, but she let him lead her to the waiting police cruisers. Hands secured behind her back with flex-cuffs, Chastity sat in the back of a black-and-white police car. A patrol officer read her the Miranda rights. "You have the right to remain silent." *Blah, blah, blah.*

Grace glanced at the other woman. Rage boiled up from her gut, leaving her hot and sweating. She clenched her fists and looked away.

"Grace, wait," Chastity called out. "I want to talk to you."

That was the last thing Grace wanted. In fact, what she wanted more than anything was to be furious. "If you hadn't interfered the other night, then none of this would've happened."

"I'm sorry for everything."

Grace wasn't in the mood to be forgiving. But she said, "If you're actually sorry, you have to tell the truth."

"I know. I will. I just wanted to apologize."

Would Chastity really take responsibility? Would she be honest about what she'd done? Would she really be able to start over?

After all, she had helped find Thad, so maybe she would change.

She gave a small nod.

"Let me take you home," said Troy. "Or, better yet, I'll drop you off at Dad and Leanne's house."

"I'm not going to lie. I want my mom right now."

"No shame in that." He opened the passenger door to his police car, a blue SUV. "Let's go."

Grace shook her head. "There's someplace else I need to be."

"Where's that?"

A pair of EMTs walked toward the waiting ambulance. One held the top of a stretcher, the other carried the foot. Camden was under a sheet and secured with straps.

"Take me to the hospital. I need to be with Camden."

GRACE SAT IN the waiting room at Grave Gulch Hospital. On a Saturday evening, the room was deserted—except for her. Grace held an unopened pack of graham crackers and stared at a muted TV that hung on the wall.

"Troy said I'd find you here."

Grace looked up as Melissa stepped into the room. "Hey."

"You know I never wanted any of this to happen, right? I might've said some harsh things about Camden, but it was because I was worried about you." She paused. "Turns out I was wasting my time being concerned. He's a great guy."

"I'm not mad at you, I promise. I'm just worried."

"What'd they say about Camden's condition?"

"He's getting a scan. I was told that the concussion was severe, but there might be other problems." Grace glanced at the clock on the wall. It was half-past ten. "He's already been gone for more than an hour. Not sure how much longer it'll take." She paused. "What's going on with the case?"

"Brett talked to Chastity Shoals, the female witness. She's confessed to hiding the gun and confirms that it was taken from Robert Grimaldi. She also told Brett that Grimaldi pulled his gun on you. The serial number matches a gun that was reported stolen from Grimaldi's mother. In short, your name's been cleared. On Monday, you'll be reinstated to the force."

Obviously, that was good news. Still, she couldn't help but wonder. "Was all of this worth it?"

"Sometimes finding justice is messy business. Aside from you being exonerated, there's more good news. Some of the protesters are meeting with the mayor, Arielle and Brett on Monday. It seems that this episode has opened up a dialogue."

Okay, that was more good news. "Why's Brett going to the meeting and not you?"

"Because he's the police chief."

"If my name gets cleared, then your name will be cleared, too. Aren't you going back to work?"

"It's like I said at Palmer's party. Antonio and I are thinking about the future. I won't be coming back to the GGPD."

"You what? Why?"

"Well, I got some pretty surprising news this morning." Melissa rested her hand on her abdomen.

The gesture was a not-too-subtle hint. "A baby? Are you kidding? Congrats!" Grace opened her arms for an embrace.

Melissa laughed. "The Colton family just keeps growing and growing."

"Family is nice," she said. Yet, her mind was drawn to the picture of Camden's father—a man whose death had shaped his son's life. Certainly, Camden deserved all the happiness a family could bring.

A dark-haired woman in scrubs, lab coat and surgical cap entered the waiting room.

"Are you Grace Colton?" the doctor asked. A badge hung on a lanyard around her neck. It read: *Dr. Shah.*

"I am." Grace was on her feet, though she didn't remember standing. "How's Camden?"

"I can't say much since you aren't a family member, but we're done with all the tests."

"Can I see him?"

"We sedated him in case there was any swelling in the brain. Now that I've seen the scan, we'll take him off the meds. He should be up for a visit in a few hours."

"Thanks for the update," said Grace.

The doctor said, "You're welcome" and then left.

"Why don't I give you a ride home?" Melissa offered.

"You know," said Grace, "I think I'm going to stay here and wait for Camden to wake up."

"Are you kidding? You heard what the doctor said. It could be hours."

How long would it take to get from Detroit to Grave Gulch? A few hours seemed about right. "Don't worry about me. Besides, I have to make a call."

Camden stood at the end of a long tunnel. It looked familiar. Yet how did he know? There were no features, it was simply dark. A light shone in the distance, but to him it looked like it was miles away.

He wanted to stay in the darkness, where it was quiet and warm.

Then he heard a woman's voice. "Camden? Can you hear me?"

He knew the woman's face. She had blue eyes and hair that shone like gold in the sunshine.

"Camden?"

The light was brighter now. He was almost at the end of the tunnel. Would the woman be waiting for him?

"Camden. It's me, Grace."

Grace. Grace. Grace. His heartbeat resonated with her name.

He burst from the tunnel and opened his eyes. He squinted against the glare and the throbbing pain in his head.

"Where am I?" he croaked. It felt like he'd swallowed glass. What the hell?

"You're in the hospital with a concussion."

Just his head? The localized pain had spread, and now his whole body hurt. His eyes were dry, yet he peeled them open. Grace looked down on him. He touched her face. She was warm and soft and real. "You're here."

"Of course I'm here. Where else would I be?"

Camden couldn't focus on much, but he did remember her rather large and tight-knit clan. "At another family party," he said.

She laughed, although he hadn't meant it as a joke. Well, maybe it was a little funny. "No parties on a Sunday morning."

Sunday morning? The last thing Camden remembered was that it had been Saturday evening. The fog surrounding his thoughts cleared, and he recalled the park. The witnesses. The gun.

He tried to sit up. His head swam, and his stomach churned. "What now?"

"There's someone who wants to see you."

Grace stepped aside, and for the first time, Camden realized that someone else was in the room. He screwed his eyes shut. Maybe he was seeing things. Opening his eyes again, he said, "Mom?"

His mother stood near the door, clasping her hands. "I got a call from your girlfriend about what happened. I came. I hope you don't mind."

Camden's eyes watered. "It's good to see you." He paused, yet there was so much he wanted to say.

"I'll let the doctor know that you're awake," said Grace. He saw through her ploy. She just wanted to give Camden and his mom a moment alone.

His mother waited until Grace had left the room before moving closer to his bed. "I know we don't talk much. But I like that girl. She's a keeper."

At one time, the Kingsleys had been a happy family. Then his dad had fallen victim to his shame and disgrace, taking not only his own life but the joy from those he left behind. Could Camden and his mother, well, maybe not rebuild that old relationship, but could they create something new? And if they did, he'd have Grace to thank.

"You know, Mom, I think that you're right."

Epilogue

Grace stood at the foot of the hospital bed a few days later. Camden sat on the edge of the mattress. Dr. Murielle Shah held a stack of papers. "These are all the discharge orders. I expect you to follow all protocols." She tapped him on the knee with the pages. "Got it?"

"Got it."

She turned her gaze to Grace.

"Got it," Grace echoed. She'd read through the pages already and knew what needed to be done.

Grace had been Camden's constant companion since the he took a blow to the head two and a half days prior. She'd gone home for short periods, to change and shower. But otherwise, they'd been together. At the beginning of the following week, he'd be returning to his job with Internal Affairs. Until then, he needed to rest but he wasn't going home. To allow him more time to heal, it was decided that he'd stay with Grace. After Camden went back to work, she'd be returning to the GGPD. She'd seen the counselor, the shooting had been ruled as justified, and in a few more days she'd be back at work, like she'd wanted from the beginning.

Having Camden at her place wasn't a sacrifice. She

liked his company. For the past few days, they'd talked. Laughed. Watched reruns on TV and laughed some more.

An orderly with a wheelchair came into the room as the doctor left. "Ready to go home?" he asked Camden.

Camden looked at Grace and smiled.

Wow, he did know how to release those butterflies in her belly.

He said, "Sure am."

The orderly wheeled Camden through the hospital and out the front door. He stopped the wheelchair in front of Grace's car.

"What's that?" Camden asked.

Her car was old. And okay, maybe there was some rust and a few dents, but it had been hers since high school. "Hey, it still runs." Grace got behind the steering wheel as the orderly helped Camden into the passenger seat. She started the engine, and the car whined.

"Still runs?" Camden echoed.

Grace ignored the comment and put the gearshift into Drive. It lurched forward.

"Maybe I should get you a new car."

"Are we that serious?"

"I'm not sure, but this one…" He shook his head. "I just can't put it into words."

"First, I walk everywhere. Second, it still runs. Third, everyone in my family learned to drive in this car. It's like an heirloom or something. Finally, I've had this car since I was sixteen."

"Sixteen, huh? Why am I not surprised?" he teased. And then, "If you like the car, I like it for you. You could get a nicer car… Something that an adult would drive."

She'd gone through a lot in the past week. Melissa

was no longer at the GGPD, leaving Grace without her mentor and champion. For the first time, she was on her own. She'd been Camden's advocate at the hospital, and now he was her responsibility.

Maybe she was a bona fide grown-up, after all.

"I'll think about a new car," she said, parking in front of her building.

It took only a few minutes to get Camden up to her apartment. She led him to her room. "You should get some rest," she said, helping him onto the bed.

"I haven't done much besides rest the last few days." He kicked off his shoes and lay back. "You could stay with me."

His voice was dark and seductive. Was he suggesting what she thought he was? A thrill danced along her skin until her toes tingled. "You just got out of the hospital."

Twining his fingers through hers, Camden pulled her to him. Grace didn't resist. "Don't you think I should celebrate being alive?"

"You have a point." The thing was, she wanted him, too. "I don't want to hurt you."

"The only way you'll hurt me is if you don't kiss me now."

Leaning in to him, Grace brushed her lips on his. She sighed, and Camden slipped his tongue into her mouth. His hand slid under her shirt. Under her bra. He teased her nipple, rolling it between finger and thumb, until it was hard.

"Oh, Camden."

"Take off your shirt," he ordered. "Your bra."

She did as she was told, slipping the fabric over her head.

"Take off your pants. Your panties."

She did as he bid. He stared at her, his eyes filled with desire, and Grace felt beautiful. "Come here," he whispered, his voice intoxicating. "And kiss me."

Camden reached for her, his hand tracing her body. His touch like a moving prayer. She kissed him, hungrily, as she unbuttoned his shirt. The muscles of his pecs were firm. She moved her kiss lower, running her tongue over his well-defined abs—just to taste the salt of his skin.

He was hard and pressed against the fly of his jeans. Grace traced him with her fingertip. Camden hissed. "You're driving me crazy."

"I am?" she teased, flicking her tongue over his flat nipple.

"I want to touch you." He reached between her thighs and slid a finger inside her. "You're so hot. So tight. So wet."

She unbuttoned the fly of his jeans. Grace spit on her palm before reaching inside his shorts. She ran her hand up and down Camden's length. His fingers were inside her. She matched her strokes to his thrusts. His breath came harder and faster. She felt herself swirling upward, to the place where she would break into pieces of ecstasy, desire and longing.

"You need to stop." Camden reached for her wrist. "Or I'm going to come undone."

"Maybe that's what I want. To drive you wild."

"You do drive me wild." He placed his mouth on hers, separated the seam between her lips with his tongue and deepened the kiss. "But I want to be inside you."

Grace wanted to explore every inch of Camden, yet the desire to have him inside her was stronger.

There was a box of condoms in the drawer of her nightstand. Sadly, they'd been there for a while. Still, they hadn't expired. She reached for the handle and opened the drawer.

She held up the foil packet. "Can I help you with this?"

"I was hoping you'd offer."

He stripped out of his jeans and shorts. God, Camden was perfection. And he was about to be hers. Grace rolled the condom down his length and straddled him. She lowered herself onto him in one slow stroke. Camden gripped her ass as Grace rode his sex. Having him inside her was a beautiful torture. He touched the top of her sex. Every nerve ending tingled. She was caught in the pleasure; it pulled her from her body, drawing her higher and higher. At the moment Grace thought she could go no further, she cried out.

Settling back in her body, Grace leaned forward and placed her lips on Camden's.

He stroked the side of her breast. She licked the side of his neck, tasting the salt of his skin. He growled with desire.

So, this is what he likes? She nipped his flesh and ran her tongue over the lobe of his ear.

Breathing hard, he held her hips. She ground down on his pelvis as he cried out.

"That was magnificent." Panting, he placed a kiss on her lips. "You are magnificent."

Grace felt pretty damn magnificent. For the first time in, well, forever she felt a complete connection with another person. Was she in love? Honestly, she couldn't wait to find out.

"I have to admit it." She rolled off Camden. "I feel pretty damn magnificent right now."

Camden stood. "Bathroom?"

"Down the hall. You'll see it. The apartment's small."

"Be right back. Have to take care of the condom."

Grace slid under the blankets and Camden was back in less than a minute.

"Hey." Grace saw one of those smiles that landed with a tingle in her belly.

"Hey yourself," she said.

"Can I join you?" he asked, kneeling on the edge of the bed.

"Sure."

She lifted the comforter. He slipped between the covers and lay on his back. Grace rested her head on his shoulder. Camden's heartbeat was strong and steady. Grace could feel the pull of sleep dragging her under. She knew she should wonder what the future would hold for her and Camden. Soon, he'd go back to Internal Affairs. She'd still be a cop.

However, this moment was perfect. Did she really want to ruin it with worry? Rolling to her belly, she met his gaze. "I was just thinking."

"Oh, yeah?" he asked. "About what?"

"I'm not sure how our story will end, Camden. But for now, you're the only one I want."

"Grace." He kissed her softly. "I couldn't have said it better myself."

* * * * *

LET'S TALK
Romance

For exclusive extracts, competitions
and special offers, find us online:

- **f** facebook.com/millsandboon
- **🐦** @MillsandBoon
- **📷** @MillsandBoonUK

Get in touch on 01413 063232

For all the latest titles coming soon, visit
millsandboon.co.uk/nextmonth

JOIN US ON SOCIAL MEDIA!

Stay up to date with our latest releases, author news and gossip, special offers and discounts, and all the behind-the-scenes action from Mills & Boon...

 millsandboon

 millsandboonuk

 millsandboon

't might just be true love...

MILLS & BOON

Desire

Indulge in secrets and scandal, intense drama and plenty of sizzling hot action with powerful and passionate heroes who have it all: wealth, status, good looks…everything but the right woman.

MILLS & BOON
MODERN
Power and Passion

Prepare to be swept off your feet by sophisticated, sexy and seductive heroes, in some of the world's most glamourous and romantic locations, where power and passion collide.

MILLS & BOON
MEDICAL
Pulse-Racing Passion

Set your pulse racing with dedicated, delectable doctors in the high-pressure world of medicine, where emotions run high and passion, comfort and love are the best medicine.